Learning to Trust

J. Y. Morgan

Yellow Rose Books

Nederland, Texas

Copyright © 2006 by J. Y. Morgan

ISBN 978-1-932300-59-8

First Printing 2006

9 8 7 6 5 4 3 2 1

Cover design by Valerie Hayken

Published by:

Regal Crest Enterprises, LLC
4700 Highway 365, Suite A, PMB 210
Port Arthur, Texas 77642

Find us on the World Wide Web at
http://www.regalcrest.biz

Printed in the United States of America

Acknowledgements:

I have always loved reading ever since I could hold a book. However, it wasn't until I discovered a special show and an endless amount of online fiction that I found a home...and the love of my life. For this, I have to thank the MerwolfPack and MerwolfVoices for being my playground for the past 6 years. Special thanks go to the Academy of Bards and Midget for hosting my stories, giving them a home and endless amounts of encouragement to many first time writers.

My thanks go to Reagan and Kelly for your initial Beta reading; and other supporters on the Jules Matthews group who encouraged me to write a sequel to Download and helped bring Learning to Trust alive.

Huge thanks go to Jennifer Knight, my editor with Regal Crest, whose time, patience and skill found a love story within the depths of my endless ramblings. Thanks to Valerie Hayken for her artistic design in producing the front cover of Learning to Trust. Also, many thanks to Lori Lake and Cathy LeNoir for answering my many questions and all their support with publishing the story. My gratitude goes to the rest of the Regal Crest team who helped publish the story and continue to supply their readers with high quality alternative fiction.

I'd like to thank my friends in England for supporting me; encouraging me to follow my dreams and heart; and always being there despite the miles. For my American friends — you have helped make America a home for me. You are my true family.

Finally, to Lester Mary — you are the one I love with all my heart — home is wherever you are...your Boo xx

Dedicated to my granddad... I miss you so much.

Chapter
One

JACE XANTHOS GLANCED down the table at her new graduate assistant and rifled the recesses of her mind for the young woman's name. Taryn Murphy. Normally, she could depend on her well trained memory to deliver such information. As Director of the Academic Support Services for an institution with approximately five thousand students, she'd long ago developed a knack for associating names with faces.

Waterbridge was a small state college nestled in the rural outskirts on the South Shore of Massachusetts. The college had always had a good reputation for turning out well trained teachers. However, over the past five years they'd been attempting to increase the retention and grades in other academic departments. Jace spent a good deal of her time securing the grants and finances that enabled the Center to provide extra support to students who needed it. Thanks to her efforts, the college was making leaps and bounds in its approach to developmental education. She had every reason to feel satisfied with herself, and most of the time she did.

She focused more intently on Taryn, committing her face to memory. The student was blonde, her hair cut in a short spiky fashion. She was compactly built and appeared to be in her early twenties but that couldn't be true. According to Anne Weston, the assistant director of the Achievement Center, Taryn had taught for a few years and was halfway through her Master's degree. So, she had to be around twenty-eight. Jace turned her attention to Anne, but continued to observe Taryn out of the corner of her eye. The young woman walked to the edge of the room, cell phone to her ear.

"Think you two will get along?" Anne asked, following the direction of her boss's gaze.

"Shouldn't be a problem. Hopefully, once we set up the developmental programs, she'll only be with me for an hour or so each week."

Anne sighed. In the four years they'd worked together, she'd tried constantly to convince Jace to cut back her nightmare work schedule so she could have a life. "The idea of this is to take the strain off you," she said, carefully concealing her frustration. "Taryn Murphy seems very bright and eager. The Education Department folks are sorry to see her go."

Jace frowned. She hated when Anne read her like a book. But Anne didn't have to figure out how to run the Center when they now had more students but less classes, thanks to a recent budget cut. Her job involved day-to-day administration, including advising on and hiring of staff. Jace knew Anne thought she drove herself too hard, but if she wanted a job that didn't challenge her, she'd be working as a cashier, or on some factory assembly line.

"It's time you found other interests, outside of work," her colleague pressed on. "Having some help will let you do that."

Anne hated sounding like a nag but when she went home to the loving arms of her husband, her boss stayed working long into the night and lately Jace had looked older than her thirty-five years. She met the blue hollow eyes of her boss and friend, willing her to at least consider the option.

"I'll think about it." Jace said, getting to her feet.

Anne touched her arm. "Where are you going? We still have another fifteen minutes before we have to be in the library."

"I thought I'd go and introduce myself to Taryn, since we're going to be stuck with each other for a while." With a sweet smile, Jace headed towards the blonde woman.

TARYN STARED AT the wall as she waited for the phone to connect to her girlfriend's voicemail. She was pissed. The weather was bright and sunny when she'd arrived at the parking lot opposite the college. It was supposed to soar into the 90s by the afternoon and she would be stuck here instead of enjoying herself at the beach. It was the beginning of June, and the Massachusetts summer was just starting to hit the high numbers.

In her previous year at the college, Taryn had never ventured into the Achievement Center. She knew vaguely where it was and that she had to report to a J. Xanthos. Beyond that she really had no idea what her new graduate assistant position entailed. She supposed she should be thankful that her aunt had arranged the job for her, even more so since they'd barely seen one another for several years. Any additional money was a welcome bonus to her savings account.

"Hey, Marti. It's me," she spoke to the machine. "I just wanted to check on our plans for tonight. I think I can blow this joint by three unless the old dragon I've been assigned to keeps me longer than necessary. Catch you later, babe."

She switched off the phone and turned straight into a body standing very close to hers. "Hey, back up a bit. There is such a thing as invading someone's personal spa..." Her torrent of words dried up as she found herself caught in the blast of an ice cold stare. She could almost feel her blood freezing and tried to look away, but the stare was hypnotic. She wanted to shrink into the wall and disappear, but instead she gave a meek smile.

Jace took a deep breath, "I didn't mean to interrupt your phone call. I just wanted to say how much I am looking forward to working with you, Taryn." She held out her hand and forced a smile onto her face. Inside she was seething. *Dragon, she thinks I'm a dragon. And an old one to boot.*

Taryn swallowed a gulp. "Hi. No worries. I'd finished anyway." She shook the hand offered. *Fuck. Why me!* "I'm looking forward to working with you, too."

Sure you are. Jace squeezed the hand in hers a little harder than necessary. "I was just heading back to the office. Anne is going to run the next section of the training. Maybe we'll catch up later."

Taryn nodded and tried not to wince from the handshake. "I'd like that."

As her new boss disappeared down the corridor, Taryn leaned against the wall and wished she could go back in time and rethink her decision to leave the Education Department.

Sure, she'd been content to work there during the past academic year, but it had been mindless photocopying and collating work and she'd yearned for a challenge. Her girlfriend, Marti, had suggested she take a teaching job near their home, but the thought of all the correcting and grading combined with her studies had made her reject that option. Now, she wondered if she'd been too hasty.

She'd already had one minor altercation with her new boss when she'd been caught daydreaming during the introductory talk. J. Xanthos had sent her a look that could have killed her in one shot had those chilly blue eyes fired darts. Now, she felt sure her new boss had heard her derogatory comment. She wished she could begin the day again.

She caught her Aunt Anne's eye and realized she must look sorry for herself because Anne immediately walked toward her, wearing a sympathetic smile.

"Auntie Anne, you could have warned me," Taryn said through gritted teeth.

"If you remember, this was your idea," Anne said briskly.

"You're the one who didn't want anyone to know we're related, so you'd be treated like any other new assistant."

Taryn nodded. "I know, but I think I just ruined my new career before it began."

"I don't think so, and cut the 'auntie' crap. There's barely ten years between us." Anne cast an eye over her niece. She hadn't seen her in several years. Taryn had a more defined figure made obvious by the curves that clung to the soft cotton material of her shirt. Her facial features had also become more angular and distinct. Gone were any traces of the puppy fat that had once softened her cheeks and jaw bone. "You look good."

"You look good, too. Thank you for this. I was so bored last year." Taryn stepped away from the wall. "Want to walk?"

"Sure, we have a few minutes. How have you been?"

Taryn breathed in the warm, muggy air. "I'm holding my own. I'm sorry for not visiting last year. I kept meaning to come across campus, but I never got the chance."

Anne knew it was a poor excuse, but she didn't push Taryn. "Well, I'm looking forward to having you around. Your mom would have liked it, too, Ryn."

Taryn could feel the emotions rising when she heard her childhood name. She closed her eyes and tried to push back the memories. "So, how are the kids? I heard through the grapevine there was a third one."

"Yes, you have another cousin. Thomas Jace Weston."

Taryn coughed. "You named him after your boss?"

"No, I named him after my friend." Smiling, Anne checked her watch. "We need to get back. How about coming over for dinner tonight?" She saw a shadow of doubt cross Taryn's path. "The coast is clear."

Taryn shook her head. "I have plans, but I promise I will come over soon. I've missed the kids."

"And they've missed you." Anne said.

STANDING AT THE back of the large study hall room, Jace was surprised to see her assistant director and grad student walk in together. She noticed that Taryn didn't even try to mask her displeasure about being there. Anne gave the introductory speech and set up the activities, leaving the Orientation Leaders, or O.L.s as they were more commonly referenced, to handle the icebreakers, then she cut through the room to Jace's side.

They watched in silence for a few minutes as the graduate students mingled with each other, then Anne said, "I think they'll do well this year."

Jace kept her eyes on the crowd. "You may need to do some switching around."

"Why, what's wrong?"

"I don't think Taryn and I are going to get along. She seems to have an attitude problem." Jace shifted position, crossing one foot over the other and leaning squarely against the wall.

Anne could not help feeling dwarfed in her presence. Jace had the longest legs she'd ever seen on a woman. She lifted her eyes upwards and over Jace's torso. Her shoulders were broad, but made much broader with the matching suit jacket. Flowing like a river down the middle of her back was her ebony, curled hair. When she walked, it bounced slightly as her head moved from side to side. She reminded Anne of a panther. Her eyes were always searching, and her movements unhurried, nevertheless there was a hidden strength.

"Jace, you've barely met the girl," she said. "Give her a chance. Anyway, since when have you been concerned about whether you like someone or not."

Jace chewed absently on her lip. "She hates me."

Anne turned her attention to Taryn. Her niece was laughing with the other grads. Her brown eyes sparkled. Anne couldn't remember the last time she'd seen such life in her eyes. *Not since Penny's illness.*

"You've spoken to her once today, for about a minute, and on the strength of that one conversation you've decided she hates you. You sound like Josie and Ricky! At least they have an excuse—they're kids. What did she say exactly?"

"She called me a dragon!" Jace winced when she saw the grin on Anne's face.

"She didn't!"

"Yes, she did, and an old one."

Jace's expression was so close to a pout, Anne almost burst out laughing. It had always amazed her that her boss, invariably assertive in her professional interactions, sometimes faltered on a personal level. She'd lost count of the times she'd told Jace to ignore stupid things she heard about herself on the grapevine; no one in her occupation could afford to be overly sensitive. Anne flicked another glance at her niece. She knew Taryn had a temper, but she couldn't imagine her being that rude.

"She said that to your face?"

Jace consulted her watch. "Time to move onto the individual sessions."

Anne put her hand on Jace's arm. "Did she say it to your face?"

"Not exactly. I heard her on the phone."

"Well that will teach you to listen in on private phone calls. She's young. They think it's mandatory to call their boss names. Anyway, you should hear the things I say about you!"

"No way! I thought you loved me?"

Anne nudged her. "Look, I know you don't want anybody interfering with your work, but you do need help and I think she could learn a good deal about leadership from you. You're a natural leader and the best supervisor I've ever worked for. Try it out for a month at least and if you don't like Taryn I'll switch her for one of the other grads."

Something about Anne's determined brown eyes gave Jace a sense of déjà vu, but she couldn't put her finger on its roots. She'd looked into her friend's eyes countless times and had never noticed the feeling before.

Slightly unnerved, she said, "Okay. You win. I'll give her a chance."

ANNE HAD JUST paid for a pizza when she saw Taryn pull onto the drive. She walked down the path to welcome her, trying not to overreact to the fear on her face. She was just glad Taryn had decided to take this first step and come to her childhood home. She hadn't visited the place in years. Anne knew that the continued presence of Patrick and Bill in the house was what kept Taryn away. Her trepidation was natural. She had hurtful memories and no reason to believe things would be any different now.

Anne knew the time was approaching when they would all have to address the past. But for now, she could delay the inevitable.

"It's just the two of us," she said, knowing this was what Taryn needed to hear. "Come on, I have pizza."

Taryn followed Anne into the house she knew all too well as a child. "You've done it up nice. Gram would be pleased if she could see it."

Anne pulled Taryn to her. "She'll be more than pleased that you're home. I promise you, Taryn, things are changing. Slowly, but surely, they are."

Taryn followed her aunt into the kitchen. She had promised herself not to think about the past. She wanted a future and she wanted to know her cousins. She sat down at the table and inhaled the mouth-watering aroma of pepperoni pizza as Anne served slices. "So, how do you think today went?"

Anne smiled. "You and Jace are just the same."

"What do you mean?" Taryn took her first bite.

"Always changing the subject when things get too personal."

"It's probably the only thing we have in common. She's a bit cold for my liking."

"She has a certain persona around the students but with everyone else she's kind of relaxed." Anne tried to be diplomatic. She knew her boss had a reputation for being hard to work with, but she was respected, and Anne loved her.

"Well, she definitely considers me a student. She's been cold as ice to me from the get go." Taryn took another piece of pizza and picked at the pepperoni.

Anne laughed. "Well, my darling, Ryn. If you will insist on describing your boss as an 'old dragon', what can you expect?"

Taryn blushed. "Oh! She told you. I didn't say it to her face. It was nothing personal."

Anne studied her niece. Her skin was lightly tanned and her hair cut short. If her eyes weren't brown, she'd pass for a Meg Ryan look-alike. "I know. Just give her time to see what a good person you are."

"I won't hold my breath."

Anne sighed. "So how's life in general? Are you dating somebody?"

Taryn pushed the crust of her pizza around the plate. She knew she couldn't avoid these questions forever. "Yeah."

"Is she nice?" Anne didn't want to push her niece for too much information in case she crossed the line that Taryn appeared to have built in regards to her personal life.

"Yeah. I think so." Taryn knew she was being difficult, but opening up wasn't easy for her. She'd made that mistake too many times in the past, putting her trust in someone only to have them let her down when it really mattered.

Anne took a deep breath but couldn't hold her curiosity any longer. "For crying out loud, Ryn. This is me you're talking to. Remember me? I'm the person you called up when you lost your virginity. I'm the person you talked to when you went through your insecurities about being gay. I'm the one you came crying to when you got your heart broken for the first time. Is it so hard to tell me a little bit about your life now?"

Taryn suppressed a biting comment. She wanted to go on the defensive, but that would help nothing and probably make things doubly difficult at work.

Anne wiped the tears from her eyes. "I'm sorry, I promised myself I wouldn't break down in front of you, but I've just missed you so much. I know things have been difficult between us, but you're still special to me. I promised your mom I'd take care of you and I feel like I failed her...and failed us. You were more like a sister to me than a niece."

Taryn took a deep breath, closed her eyes and whispered, "I've missed you, too. Hey, don't cry. Please, Anne." She got out of her chair and went to stand behind her aunt, hugging her from behind. "I'm sorry, I'm such a jerk at times. But I'm here now and you'll get to see me nearly everyday. I'm okay. I have a nice girlfriend, Marti, who is dying to meet you." Taryn knew she was rambling, but she didn't know how else to stop her aunt from crying. "I never meant to shut you out. I just had to get over my past, over myself, and find out who I was. You know why I left. It hurt too much to stay." She kept rocking her aunt until the sobs quieted down.

Anne held onto Taryn's arms. "So you have a girlfriend?" She sniffed back the tears. "Is it serious?"

"I suppose so. We live together."

Anne couldn't help but laugh out loud. "You're living together and you think it might be serious. I see you're still looking after that heart of yours." She had watched Taryn grow up battling more demons than an average child should have to. Her niece had once promised never to give her heart away again.

"Marti's nice. She's an accountant. We've been dating for a year now. She's very supportive."

Taryn felt a small pang of guilt. Marti *had* been really supportive, particularly about college. But Taryn was aware that she tried her lover's patience at times. She found it hard to open up even though she knew Marti was hurt about being shut out. They'd met at a bar not long after Taryn decided to leave her teaching job in Ireland and return to the US. She'd been raw with emotions following her mother's death, and Marti had been a calming influence on her. A few dates later, they'd moved in together and for the moment, Taryn was content.

"I'm happy for you," Anne touched Taryn's cheek. "You and Jace have another thing in common." She realized what she had said, "I'm sorry, I know you're not crazy about her, and I'm not sure why I keep comparing the two of you. It's just you're both very guarded about your personal life."

"Perhaps we both have good reason." Taryn had a feeling Jace probably left out a lot when she talked to Anne, no matter how friendly they were. She turned to the plates on the counter and began to clear up.

Anne wanted to say more, but she could tell Taryn wasn't ready to talk about Patrick and Bill. Keeping her impatience in check, she said, "Taryn, I wanted to ask a favor."

"Sure. I'll try with Jace, Auntie Anne, I promise."

"This has nothing to do with Jace but thanks, sweetie. I appreciate the thought and I may take you up on that promise."

Taryn laughed. "Okay, now I'm curious. What do you want?"

"I was hoping that maybe you'd tutor Ricky. He's having difficulties at school and refuses to do any homework. It's turning into a battle field."

"What's the problem? Is something going on at school?"

"Not that I know of. He just hates reading and writing, and I thought a new person might ignite something in him. I know you taught older students in Ireland, but I was hoping you'd give it a shot. He still remembers you."

Taryn frowned slightly. "Where would I tutor him?"

Anne knew what she was hinting at. "Bill and Patrick go to the local sports bar on Mondays. They never come home before eleven."

"I'll think about it and let you know," Taryn said. "When would you want me to start?"

"As soon as possible. I don't want Ricky going through the summer without a tutor. I'll pay you, of course."

Taryn glared at her aunt. "You will not. If, and I mean if, I decide to do this, I'll do it for family not for money."

"Whatever you want, Taryn." Anne kept her tone low key, revealing nothing of her delight. She had expected Taryn to turn her down flat. This was progress.

"We'll make a deal." Taryn seemed to be thinking out loud. "We'll do pizza and a movie when the kids are in bed. I'll talk to Marti about it. I'm taking classes two nights a week, and I don't know how she'd feel if I was out another night." She glanced at her watch. "I'd better be going. I have an early start in the morning. I work for these real slave drivers and they have scheduled a meeting at seven thirty! Thanks for the pizza."

Anne walked with her to the door and they stood in silence for a moment staring out into the night.

"I'm so glad you came over," Anne said. Her throat felt sore with emotion.

To her surprise Taryn reached out for her and they hugged one another tightly.

"I missed you so much," Taryn murmured. Dropping a kiss on Anne's cheek, she strolled off down the path.

Chapter
Two

JACE YAWNED, STRETCHING her arms over the back of her chair. It was 7 a.m. She had been unable to sleep, so after a quick run in the early morning sun, she had showered and driven into the Center. She opened her eyes and visibly jumped as she met the gaze of Taryn, who was leaning on her office door.

Taryn sensed she had unnerved the woman. That hadn't been her plan. She had meant to announce herself, but when she'd seen Jace stretch out and caught sight of the firm breasts straining against the soft material of the silk blouse, she'd lost all focus. She was now caught in the same icy glare that seemed to constantly emanate her way. *Aunt Anne you so owe me. Here goes nothing.*

"Hi...err...I thought you might like some coffee." She was babbling; a sudden nervousness had enveloped her. "I didn't mean to creep up on you." She placed the extra cup of coffee on the desk, and offered the bag of donuts towards the frigid looking woman. *Relax. You can do this. Talk about the weather. Talk about the drive in. Just don't give in.* Taking a deep breath, she continued, "The weather's supposed to be very hot today. Some say it's going to hit the high 90s. I just hope they crank up the air conditioning."

Jace was trying hard not to smile. The young woman in front of her was obviously trying to make peace between them. *Well she's a stronger person than I am. I'm not sure I would have offered the white flag first.* She listened a little longer, and then decided to put Taryn out of her misery.

"Thanks." She took the coffee cup. "You must have read my mind. I was just trying to work out where I could get my caffeine boost from."

Taryn blushed. She wasn't used to praise from the intimidating woman in front of her and this was definitely the first time in a long week that Jace's smile had actually reached her eyes. "No worries. I was up early this morning and decided I couldn't wait for the meeting to have breakfast. I...err...I noticed you come in early, so I thought I'd share the drugs around."

Jace laughed. "Yep caffeine is definitely my chosen drug of the day. So, what's in the bag?" She was warming to Taryn. She couldn't keep the smile off her face.

"Donuts. Plain ones. I wasn't sure what kind you like. So I got the bare basics." Taryn was babbling again. Her hands were shaking. She'd thought long and hard about the things Anne had said concerning Jace, and had decided she really was the one who needed to make the first move. In all honesty, she didn't think Jace would ever hold out the olive branch toward her.

"I can do plain. I really like all donuts. I think it's the sugar rush. Thank you, Taryn." She watched as a light blush lit up her assistant's skin. "Take a seat. We may as well eat together." She indicated to the chair in front of her desk.

Taryn sat down and tried to keep her food inside her stomach. The woman in front of her had an air of cockiness she found disturbing. She also wanted to knock the smirk off her face. *Breathe. In. Out. You are the bigger person. Remember you're doing this for Anne. You're doing this so you have a good year. You're doing this so you don't end up back at the Ed. Department, photocopying and avoiding the groping hands of Dr. Bacon.* At a loss for words, a first for her, she forced a smile and decided to eat.

Jace was enjoying herself. She could see that Taryn was trying, and that it was killing her. *Oh, Anne, you'd love to see this one. I'm trying to play nice.* "So, Taryn, how do you like the Center?"

"It's good. The atmosphere in here is very relaxed. I like that, and the other grads seem very friendly. I missed mixing with other students last year."

Jace chewed on her donut. *Okay, short and sweet.* Small talk was not one of her own favorite past times either. She wracked her brain, trying to think of a topic that would get the conversation going. "How did classes go last semester?"

Taryn shrugged. "Okay. Some of them were really interesting. Others didn't really teach me anything I didn't already know. It was interesting to learn more about the US educational system, from an administrative point of view. When you're in the classroom you think all the roadblocks are just someone's idea of a joke. Then you put on an administrator's hat and you realize you're playing with a different hand of cards."

Jace nodded in agreement. "I hear you. It's the same over here. You have all the professors wanting different things from their students. They don't understand that we only have a set amount of money or resources." Jace sensed she had found a subject that Taryn seemed interested in. "Anne tells me you were a teacher before this. Which school system did you work in?"

Uncertain how much Anne had told Jace about her background, Taryn said, "The Irish system. I lived over there for a few years after graduation."

"I thought I heard a slight lilt to the accent. Do you have family over there?"

"Yeah, I used to." *Please change the subject, please change the subject.* Her thoughts were interrupted by a knock at the door.

"Good morning, is this a private party or can anyone join in?" Anne entered the room, looking pleased to see them together.

"Taryn surprised me with an early breakfast. You can't beat Dunkin Donuts coffee." Jace stood and immediately felt like she was towering above Taryn.

Anne smiled. "Yes, the catering coffee just doesn't meet the grade."

Sandwiched between her boss and her aunt, Taryn felt uncomfortable and decided she'd outstayed her welcome. "Is it that time already? I have some stuff to do before the meeting so I'll see you both later."

She brushed past Anne, catching a very quiet "Thank you" as she went by.

Anne settled into the chair her niece had vacated. "Yesterday, you two could barely stand to be in the same room and this morning you're doing breakfast together." She placed her hand on Jace's arm. "Thanks for making the effort. I know you didn't have to."

Jace shrugged. "Taryn made the first move." As she sat down she noticed dark rings under Anne's eyes. "Tough night?"

Anne unconsciously touched her face. "Bill and I had an argument."

Jace did her best not to show her astonishment. Anne and Bill had a perfect marriage, or so she thought. "You two are my heroes. Please don't tell me there's trouble in paradise."

"We're fine. It was just a difference of opinion." Anne didn't feel like conducting a post-mortem. She wished she could tell Jace that the argument had started because Taryn had agreed to tutor Ricky and this had increased the tension in the house. Especially, as Patrick had found out that his daughter was back in their lives. "Are we really your heroes?"

"Absolutely. You just seem so good together. So in love. I guess I would want what you have, if I ever found someone."

Anne was struck by the wistful expression on Jace's face.

This was the first time her colleague had ever mentioned wanting a partner.

Jace looked at her quizzically, "What?"

"Huh?" Anne knew she'd been caught staring.

"You have that expression again. That *why is she still single?* look on your face."

"I can't help it," Anne said. "I look at you sometimes and I know that underneath the bravado there's a warm hearted, lovable woman. Who, I might add, is drop dead gorgeous."

"Oh, please." Jace shuffled some papers, her discomfort apparent.

It was always the same when Anne raised the topic of her lack of a love life, or to put it bluntly, lack of life in general. She'd never known Jace to have a relationship, or do anything outside of work except run, read, or hang out with Anne's clan.

Predictably, Jace steered the subject back to Anne. "Well, I'm glad the perfect marriage is still intact," she said lightly.

Anne shrugged. "Don't believe all you see."

Jace registered the edge of bitterness in Anne's voice with puzzlement. She wanted to dig a little deeper but she sensed things could easily go down a path neither woman had time for, so she stood and said, "Come on. Let's go and face the troops."

Chapter
Three

JACE ENTERED THE West Key on Revere Street and immediately spotted Anne standing with a group of students and colleagues. Jace made her way over, wondering what had possessed her to agree to this rare social outing. It was the end of June, and the last student had been advised and sent on their way. Anne had insisted that with orientation over, everyone deserved some fun, Jace included. As usual, she found her colleague's pleas difficult to resist.

As she reached Anne's side, she looked around the small bar. Beyond a group of pool tables doors led out the back to decking and an additional bar.

"They have sand on the floor, so you feel like you're at a clambake," Anne said. "Bill brought me here a few weeks ago. I thought it would appeal to the young and old. What would you like?"

"A beer, thanks." Jace glanced around again. For some reason she felt distracted. Maybe she shouldn't have come. There was work she needed to do. Admittedly none of it was urgent, but the fact was, her professional life was following the plan she had set for herself many years earlier, and that made it satisfying. Her personal life was another story. Being at a place like this only brought that fact home.

"No Taryn tonight?" she asked for the sake of making conversation.

"No, she said she was going to the movies. It's a shame, as I hoped we'd all get to know each other better." Anne noticed Jace scanning the room. "What do you think? Anyone interesting?"

"You're interesting enough company," Jace said dryly. Anne never gave up. A compulsive matchmaker, she didn't seem to understand that Jace had no plans to engage in panic-stricken dating like some singles her age.

They moved out onto the deck. There was still plenty of light and warmth, and the beers and chatter flowed. Everyone ordered the bar special of clambake with lobster tails. As the waitress left, Jace looked up and saw a now familiar blonde head. She smiled when she saw her grad assistant walking towards them.

"Taryn! You made it!" Anne jumped up from her seat. "Come over here and sit by me."

Jace was a little disappointed that Taryn took the seat on the other side of Anne. Surprised by the feeling, she moved her chair slightly to make more room and attempted to look nonchalant. *Who are you kidding, in work she has to be nice, but out of it she doesn't have any allegiance to you.* She tried to listen in on Anne's conversation with her assistant.

"What happened?" Anne seemed very concerned.

"Nothing, just a change of plans," Taryn said. "Have you ordered?"

"Yes, but only a few minutes ago. We all ordered the specials. If you go to the bar you should be able to add your order to ours."

Great. She'll probably run into some other friends and that will be the last we'll see of her. Jace covertly watched her walk away, drawn by the snug fit of the jeans over a pert ass.

Upon her return, Taryn said hello to several friends She couldn't help noticing Jace, sitting on the other side of Anne, looking intently at her knife. "You were right when you said she didn't get out much," she whispered to her aunt.

"Behave," Anne responded in a muted tone. "I said no such thing. Anyway, I'm pleased you came. You look awesome."

Taryn blushed. She had decided to dress in her black jeans and a tight white shirt. Her black sweater was slung over her shoulder in case it got colder later. She knew her tan stood out against the white of her top.

Jace hadn't missed the look of pleasure in Anne's eye as she appraised Taryn. There was a familiarity about the pair that made her feel jealous. She wasn't sure if it was Anne's attention to Taryn or lack of attention to her. She thought back over the past few weeks. Contrary to her earlier misgivings, she'd enjoyed Taryn's presence in the Center. Her workload had decreased and Taryn had turned out to be a valuable asset over the orientation process. Her assistant's quick mind and attention to detail had allowed Jace more time to focus more clearly on the next semester. She had to admit that she wasn't looking forward to the rest of the summer by herself. She would miss their morning coffee, the half hour when Taryn filled her in on the comings and goings of the Center. And she would miss getting an edited account of her email rather than having to trawl through the masses herself.

Her thoughts were interrupted by the prompt arrival of their food. The aroma of freshly baked bread and garlic butter always made her mouth water. All the same, she found it hard to concentrate on her meal. Her mind and eyes continually wandered to Taryn. She hoped nobody else noticed her sideways glances, but there was something about her assistant she found compelling tonight.

She looked different, Jace decided. Her clothes were a little dressier than usual and showed off her sensational shape. Jace wasn't dead from the waist down. Taryn was an attractive young woman. It was okay for her to notice that.

After dinner, Anne and several others abandoned the group for the dance floor. Patty had taken her leave, as she hadn't been able to get her baby sitter to stay too late. Jace retreated to the bar and ordered a seltzer, relieved to be alone with her wayward thoughts. The respite didn't last long.

"Having fun?" A familiar female voice enquired from slightly behind her and to her surprise, and just a little dismay, Taryn occupied the barstool next to hers.

"Put it this way. I'm full to bursting and today I had to nearly sell my soul to the devil, but I feel fine."

Taryn grinned. "Ah, this afternoon's meeting?"

"It took negotiating skills I didn't think I possessed, but I now have two months of grace to try and put some plans into action."

"That's great. So you're celebrating?"

"I guess I am." Jace surveyed the women dancing. "I don't know how they can jig around without their food coming back up." She heard a giggle from Taryn and asked, "Can I buy you a beer?"

"Sure. A Guinness, please."

"A true Irish girl, huh?" Jace teased.

"Guinness, forever. Although I have yet to find a bar in America that can pour one as good as the Irish." Taryn relaxed against the bar and watched the barwoman pour the black liquid into a glass. She'd made the right decision to come here tonight. "They make the shape of a shamrock on top of a pint in Ireland. That's how thick the head can be. Do you like it?"

"I can't say I've tasted it before."

"Go ahead." Taryn lifted the glass toward her.

Jace was surprised by the gesture but before she could react she felt the glass against her lips. Tentatively, she took a short sip of the creamy liquid and swallowed. The liquid was bitter. "Ummm... wonderful." She grimaced.

Taryn shook her head, "You're such a liar." She blushed when she remembered who she was talking to. "I'm sorry."

Jace could feel the atmosphere shift between them. She saw Taryn's eyes widen slightly and noticed her cheeks redden. "No worries. I know you were teasing. I started it. Look, at work I am your boss and colleague. But out of work, well maybe we could try and be friends."

Taryn was astonished. She hadn't expected those words to ever leave Jace's lips. "Okay, sounds good to me."

Jace smiled, unsure where to go with the conversation. She didn't even know why she'd offered her friendship to Taryn. Something about the young woman reminded her of someone else. She opted for a safe conversation starter. "So tell me a little about yourself."

Taryn froze as she heard the words. She hated when conversations centered on her. "Uh...well..."

"I'm not asking for a whole blow by blow account, just a little. Anne is always telling me it's what friends do. They exchange information."

Taryn grinned. She had heard little tidbits from her aunt over the past few Monday nights about her boss. Nothing too deep but when Anne wasn't thinking, her frustrations about her boss's reclusive nature sometimes caused her to vent.

"My name is Taryn Meghan Murphy—a true Irish name. My mother was born in Ireland and moved to America when her parents came here searching for fortune. They moved back about ten years later but my mother stayed. She got pregnant with me and decided I'd have more of a life in America than in the little village in Ireland. I did my undergraduate in education, and began teaching. Unfortunately, my mother became very ill and decided to move back to Ireland. I followed as she needed more help than she'd ever admit to me." Taryn took a gulp of her beer. *Why am I telling her this? I could have just stuck to the basic half-truths. God it hurts to remember.*

"I took a teaching job at the local town and nursed her. She died a few years later. I stayed on for a while, and then moved back over here to do my Master's. That's it. My life history in two hundred words."

"I'm sorry," Jace said. Heart-to-hearts weren't her strong point and she longed for Anne to come over and take control of the situation. Putting her hand on Taryn's knee, she added, "I didn't mean to upset you."

"You did nothing wrong." Taryn smiled meekly. "It just never seems to get better."

"It does in time. Trust me." She withdrew her hand,

suddenly embarrassed about her impulse. She didn't normally touch the legs of attractive young women who worked for her.

Taryn noticed the withdrawal of Jace's hand almost more than she'd noticed its presence; the touch had been so gentle. The gesture had surprised her, but looking into Jace's eyes, she saw a pain that mirrored her own and something else, an odd connection. Trying not to read anything into it, she said, "Anyway, just after I got back here, I met Marti."

Jace felt that stab of jealousy again. "True love, huh?"

Taryn shrugged. "Who knows. So what about you? Fair's fair. Remember, friends share information." She caught her aunt staring at them and waved to her.

"Well as you can tell from the name, my family isn't native to America either. I was born in Greece, thirty-five years ago. My mama and papa stayed in Greece, but I wanted more. My mother's sister had moved to America after the Second World War, and as my cousins grew and flew the nest, she offered to take me in. She gave me a chance at an education. I did my undergraduate degree in California and then applied to Boston University for my Master's, I stayed on and did my Doctorate there, too. Occasionally I went back to Greece. My mama was happy that I had made something of myself." Jace took a deep breath. "She died a few years ago, too. Cancer. I didn't get home in time to see her."

Jace felt a hand on her leg. She smiled. It was the same show of comfort she had offered Taryn. "My family was in denial about how ill she was. When I did find out, I booked a ticket but it was too late." She paused for a few seconds letting the past dwell in the corner of her mind. *Always too late.* "So, I think we have a few things in common. Taryn, if you ever want to talk more about your mother, I'll always listen."

"Thanks." Taryn felt uncomfortable with the direction of the conversation so she decided a change of subject was needed. "Any husband? Or significant other?" she asked.

"No." Jace looked at her watch and stood. "It's time I made tracks. Think of me slaving away while you get to enjoy the whole summer off."

"Yeah, sun, sea and plenty of time to get bored." Taryn realized she was not looking forward to vacation time. She'd become accustomed to working at the Center, and with the exception of the first week, she had to admit she'd been content working there. She and Jace had called a truce and settled into a comfortable comradeship. Every now and again Taryn even offered more about herself to Jace, but her boss had not been so forthcoming until a few moments ago.

"Bored? During the vacation?" Jace looked amazed.

"I hate being left to my own devices," Taryn confessed. "I think I have a short attention span."

Jace seemed lost in thought for a moment, then she said, "So how would you feel about working the rest of the summer?"

"At the Center?"

Jace nodded. "We need a few people to help set up some pilot programs. We have another grad student coming in, Cory Williams. In fact, you two may have a lot in common as she's coming from across the ocean, too. It's not great money, but it'll keep you honest."

The idea was tempting, but Taryn needed to check with Marti. "How long do I have to think about it?"

"You could call me over the weekend or e-mail me." Jace wrote her number down on a piece of paper. "I know Jessie is interested but it would be a good opportunity for you to get some experience in developing support programs."

"Let me talk to my partner and I'll call you." Taryn took the number and their eyes met.

Jace's eyes were so blue. Even in the light of the bar, Taryn could feel her penetrating gaze. She thought about the offer. Her instinct was to turn it down, but something about the evening made her reconsider. She had seen a small glimpse into a side of Jace that she hadn't been privy to before, a side her aunt obviously knew. Taryn wanted to know more, and two months away from work was not going to do a thing for their fledgling friendship. For some reason she cared about that. Impulsively, she held out her hand. "Second thought, you have a deal. I'd be delighted to slave the summer away with you!" *I'll deal with Marti later. Hopefully, she'll forgive me.*

Jace didn't even realize she was holding her breath as she thanked Taryn and said goodbye. As her assistant walked away, she found herself repeating the word "partner" and trying not to feel that same uneasy sense of disappointment she'd felt when Taryn first arrived and sat next to Anne.

She sent a silent prayer upward toward the heavens to whichever gods were looking down on her. *Please let her like me more. Please don't let me drive her away.* She hoped they were listening.

ANNE RETURNED FROM putting the kids to bed. "Ricky really is enjoying spending time with you, Ryn." She was just as excited about Ricky's A as he had been.

"He's a good kid," Taryn said, toying with her spaghetti.

"Has he been for academic testing? I think he may have receptive and expressive processing deficits."

Anne shook her head. "Not yet. At first, his teachers thought he was just attention seeking in the classroom because his behavior coincided with Tom's birth."

"What did you think?"

"That year was a mess. He's been a little better this year, but seems to be missing the foundations. I think his lack of concentration in that crucial first year affected him."

"Maybe the tutoring will help make him feel like he is getting more attention." Taryn said.

"That's one of the reasons I wanted you to do it. He gets really excited when he knows you're coming, and I appreciate the extra time you give him."

Taryn blushed. "He's my cousin, and I love him. The kids shouldn't have to miss out because I was an asshole."

Anne banged the counter top making Taryn jump. "You are not the asshole, Taryn! I'm sorry you felt you had to stay away but I don't blame you. I keep hoping Patrick will change, but maybe I'm being unrealistic."

"How has my return affected the atmosphere here? Does he know I'm back?"

Anne rubbed her hand over her face. She was tired of all the arguing, tired of all the remarks. "Bill told him. We didn't want the children to have to lie and we knew we'd be living on a time bomb if we kept it quiet."

"How'd he take it?" Taryn didn't know why she asked. She really shouldn't care anymore.

"Went out and got trashed. Bad mouthed us all. Told me I had no loyalty to family and dictated when you could visit. Besides that, it's been a blast." Anne was about to continue, but the slamming of the front door interrupted her. Fear gripped her and she saw the same fear reflected in Taryn's eyes.

"Shh. Go...into the dining room." Anne jumped up from the stool and went into the hallway. She breathed a sigh of relief when she saw the tall figure of her boss, a tray of sodas in her hands. "God, you scared me!"

"Sorry, I tried to knock but the sodas were slipping." Jace noted the ashen face of her friend. "Am I interrupting something? Are you okay? You look pale."

Anne took a tray from Jace and walked back to the kitchen. "I wasn't expecting company."

Jace glanced at the two dishes on the counter. "I'm sorry. I can leave you to it."

"No. It's fine. We just finished." Anne had no idea how to

explain Taryn's presence in her house. Indicating the two plates of food, she said, "Ricky's tutor is here."

Jace looked puzzled. "A tutor?"

Anne saw Taryn in the hall, approaching with Ricky's reading book "You wanted to see this, didn't you, Anne?" She took her stool and greeted Jace with a casual smile.

"I was just telling Jace about you tutoring Ricky." Anne said.

Jace felt uncomfortable. Seeing Taryn and Anne together so informally made the hairs on the back of her neck prickle. "I didn't mean to intrude. I just saw the sodas on special at BJ's and decided to bring them over. I'll go."

"You don't have to go. There's plenty of pasta left." Anne hastily filled another bowl with pasta and stuck it in front of Jace before she could say no. She was relieved when she heard her son call out. "Let me just go and see what my baby wants."

The silence in the room was deafening. Taryn tried to work out what to say to Jace. She felt bad for her aunt. Anne had never wanted the cloak and dagger scenario. Normally, she supposed, her aunt would have mentioned having a tutor for Ricky. Both women seemed to let out a sigh of relief when Anne appeared with her grumpy son in her arms.

"I have no idea what's wrong with him. I think he senses his Auntie Jace is around." She grinned as Tom leaned towards the tall brunette.

Jace put down her fork and opened her arms. "How's my boy?" She cuddled Tom to her.

"Hurts Dantie Dace." Tom pointed to the gums of his mouth.

"The back molars are coming through," Anne said. "His are a little later than the others were. Here, I have some teething gel in the fridge." She moved to the other side of the room. "Here you go, Jace. This should settle him."

Jace took the tube and placed a small amount on her finger. She placed the finger inside Tom's mouth. As he settled into her arms she caught the gaze of both the other women at the table. "What?" she asked.

Anne laughed, "Nothing. You're so good with him. No one would ever guess that in the day time you're this mean and nasty warrior, and by night you turn into Mary Poppins."

Taryn couldn't help but laugh. "You read my mind Au...Anne." She sent an apologetic look Anne's way.

"Hey, I'm his godmother. I should be allowed to turn to mush when he's in my vicinity." Jace kissed the boy's head as he snuggled into her body. It felt so right holding him. She caught

Taryn's eye and smiled.

Taryn's stomach fluttered. The contentment and relaxation on Jace's face made her look so beautiful. Taryn had admired that beauty before, but it had been fleeting. She'd never given Jace a second thought, though she had to admit her boss was stunning. Desire began to replace the fluttering inside. *Hello, Earth to Taryn! What are you thinking? She's your boss! She's your aunt's boss and friend! Reality check! Reality check!*

Taryn shook her head to rid the images of Jace from her mind. She was holding Tom so tenderly, it also made Taryn realize that she had missed out on knowing her little cousin. She had missed being the person he wanted when he was hurting. Tears came to her eyes. She looked up when she felt Anne's hand on her arm.

"Are you okay?" Anne asked.

Jace let her eyes rest on the two women. She'd noticed Anne's habit of touching Taryn. Her mind replayed the past month over and she realized she had caught them together a few times. They always appeared to be either talking heatedly, on the verge of tears or had guilty expressions on their faces. Now there was an unmistakable tenderness in Anne's eyes as she asked Taryn the question. It looked like love. *Shit. Anne's in love with Taryn. No! What about Bill? The kids?*

Jace pulled Tom closer to her and saw he had fallen asleep. She needed to get out of the room and think. She stood hurriedly. "Umm...I'll take the little guy upstairs."

Anne nodded absently at Jace. Her mind was fixed on her niece. Something had happened in those last few moments that had driven the sparkle from Taryn's beautiful, soulful eyes.

"Are you okay?" Anne asked her once more.

"Yeah. I'm sorry. I was just thinking...you're my only family and I've missed out on a lot." She looked into her aunt's eyes. "I think I should leave before I make a scene. I think we just blew our secret though."

"What?" Anne asked.

"Jace knows something is up. Look where your hand is! I think it's time to tell her before she finds out from the kids. I'd stay, but I think she'd rather hear it from you."

"You're comfortable with that?"

Taryn thought for a second. "There's no need to give her all the sordid details. Just tell her what you think she needs to know."

"Okay, honey. Drive safely. I love you."

"Love you, too."

They hugged and just as Taryn kissed her on the cheek,

Anne looked past her to the hall and met an icy blue gaze.

Stunned, Jace ducked out of the doorway as Taryn turned to leave. Sliding along the wall, she waited for the sound of the front door closing. *She loves her. They love each other.*

"Did he stay asleep?" Anne asked when Jace finally stalked into the kitchen.

"Yes." *Oh god, what's Bill going to do when he finds out? His wife is a lesbian! My best friend is gay!*

Watching the myriad of expressions cross Jace's face, Anne groaned inwardly. There was no way she could leave things unsaid. "Jace, come and sit down," she said. "There's something I need to tell you."

Jace's temper was simmering close to boiling point. She tried counting to ten but it didn't seem to be working. "What the hell is going on?" she demanded. "You love her? What about Bill? What about the kids? Not to mention the fact that she's a student and an employee."

"Will you calm down and quit shouting," Anne said, keeping her voice calm. "You'll wake the children."

Jace shook her head in disbelief. Was Anne trying to pretend nothing had happened? "What are you thinking? It's clear you're not thinking. You love her?" She paced back and forth across the room. "I can't believe you'd be so reckless. Shit, I can't believe I didn't notice what was happening right in front of my eyes. Shit! You love her?"

"Yes, I love her. But it's not what you think. If you sit down and stop asking questions I'll tell you." Anne followed Jace across the room, and for an instant she thought the taller woman was going to bolt. "Please."

The imploring tone pulled Jace out of her fury. "I'll listen but this better be good."

The terseness of Jace's voice made Anne shiver. She had never had Jace's anger aimed toward her. She realized in that moment why Jace was such an effective leader. No one dared cross this woman.

"Taryn's my niece." That simple statement seemed to pull Jace closer to her.

"Your niece? Hold on a minute. I've been to all your family parties for the past few years and I've never heard any mention of her name. Why would Bill's mother not have mentioned her granddaughter to me at Christmas or Thanksgiving? I'm a little lost here?"

Anne rubbed Jace's shoulder. "Taryn's not related to Bill's family. She's part of mine."

"I don't understand. You're not old enough to be her aunt.

She's your niece?" She looked into Anne's hurt eyes. Such deep brown soulful looking eyes and then it hit her. *The eyes.* She could see Taryn's eyes in Anne. The same eyes that had haunted her since the night in the bar were right in front of her.

"Now I see it. I knew there was something familiar about her when we met. I just couldn't put my finger on it. She has your eyes." Jace knew she had to stop talking if she ever wanted to find out why her friend had intentionally concealed Taryn's identity. It was so unlike Anne, there had to be a good reason.

"If you must know, I've barely slept this past month," Anne said wearily. "I wanted to tell you, but each day something would come up, and Taryn wanted to gain recognition for her work, not because she was related to me. I'm sorry I kept it from you, and I'll understand if you want me to hand in my resignation. I let you down." Anne wiped a tear from her cheek.

"Don't be ridiculous." Jace replayed all that Anne had told her about Taryn and tried to remember what Taryn had said at the bar. She still didn't get the whole picture.

"You had a right to know," Anne insisted. "I guess my personal need to see Taryn overrode my professional judgment."

"I did and I'm hurt by this. I value your trust and honesty." Jace saw Anne physically wince as she said the words. "So I know you must have a genuine reason for this deception. I mean, you just talked about your personal need to see Taryn. Couldn't you just have her around the house?"

Anne's shoulders shook and she began to cry in earnest. "God, I wish I could. We were such good friends. I let her down and now I've let you down." She dropped her head into her hands. "I feel like I've been crying for a whole month. When will it stop?"

Jace got up from the counter and went for the Kleenex box beside the sink. "Here, blow your nose and take a deep breath." Tenderly she dried Anne's eyes and wiped her face, dropping a kiss on her forehead. "You haven't let me down. As for Taryn, I think you went out on a limb for her. There is a certain amount of protocol involved when employing a member of family, but we'll cross that bridge when we get to it. At the moment, I'm more concerned about my best friend. How about I grab us two bottles of beer, and we go and sit out on the deck? The stars are out and the moon is bright, just the right atmosphere for a heart to heart."

She collected the alcohol from the fridge and ushered Anne out the door. Anne sat in the rocker and looked up as Jace passed her the beer. She chuckled.

"What's so funny, Weston." Jace asked.

"I've just realized what you were thinking when you saw Taryn and I together. You thought I was in love with her physically!" Anne laughed out loud.

Jace pouted. "Hey, fair's fair. Look at it from my point of view. I was a little shocked at the thought of you betraying Bill."

Anne mulled over Jace's comment. They'd never discussed sexuality before and she was pleased that Jace was more shocked with the idea of her betraying Bill than the fact it would have been with a woman.

"I'd never cheat on Bill. I love him. He's been very supportive over the years. It's a long story, Jace, and I don't think it's my place to air all Taryn's secrets without her being here. But I can give you the edited version."

Jace placed her arm around Anne's shoulder and gave it a squeeze. "Just tell me what you're comfortable with."

"Well, remember I once told you my mom and dad inherited this home from Dad's parents. The written rule is that it's a Clary household, meaning any Clary who needs shelter has the rights to live here and make it a home. Luckily we're a small family."

"Sounds like one of those altruistic dreams that are fine in theory and not so easy in practice," Jace remarked, thinking about some of the comments Anne had let slip occasionally about having her older brother at the house.

"Yes, it can be quite a challenge," Anne said dryly. "I was brought up here and Mom was 42 when I was born. To cut a long story short, they had Patrick ten years before me and he was one of twins, but his brother, Sean died from SIDS. Mom was very depressed for years afterward, and I think Patrick felt she blamed him. They never considered having any more children so they were very surprised when I appeared. I think I was my mother's hysterectomy!"

The humor seemed to lighten the atmosphere and Jace reaffirmed she was listening by squeezing Anne's shoulder again.

"Patrick was a wild child and grew into a bitter teenager. He resented my birth, I'm sure of it. He used to bring girlfriends home all the time, then, one day he brought Penny. He was twenty two and she was eighteen." Silent tears tracked down Anne's face. "Mom and Dad weren't happy, but because of the trust they couldn't force him to leave. Penny's parents were Irish and had moved back there, but she didn't want to go."

"Difficult situation," Jace said.

"I don't think my great-grandparents thought it through fully when they set up the trust."

"Family values were stronger then," Jace said. "And wasn't

your Grandfather an only child? They probably thought they were doing him a favor, making sure there would always be younger generations in the house to care for their elders."

"I guess so, and they were right. The family has always looked after its oldest members." Anne paused and sipped her drink. Taryn had said she could tell Jace the story, but now that she was getting to the point, she wasn't sure how deep to go.

"Anyway, one day I came home from school and found Penny had been beaten. She vanished not long after that and showed up months later with a baby. I was thirteen then." Anne paused, treading carefully." Patrick swore blind that Taryn wasn't his. He still refuses to acknowledge her. Mom and Dad believed Penny. They were the ones who made her come back. They wanted to know their only grandchild."

"What did Patrick do?"

"Got himself a job on a building crew and went with them out of state. He was gone for quite a while but things didn't work out for him and he came back when Taryn was seven. By then Penny and I had become very good friends. She was my confidante and felt like my older sister, and I became Taryn's. Sometimes it seemed like I was trapped between the two of them, with my loyalties torn."

"Sounds like a real life soap opera." Jace was shocked. How could Patrick deny Taryn was his? She'd spent many occasions talking to him and he had even flirted with her every now and again. He didn't seem like a complete idiot. "I don't get it," she said. "You just have to look at Taryn to know she's Patrick's."

"I think that's what pissed him off the most," Anne replied. "The older she got, the more obvious it was. So it made him look like an idiot for denying her. In the end, Dad got fed up with his attitude and decided to get legal proof so Taryn would always have a home. He made Patrick do a paternity test." She laughed bitterly. "The problem was, having the proof only seemed to make Patrick angrier and he made her life hell. Now she can barely tolerate stepping across the threshold."

Jace continued to support Anne, gently stroking her neck and passing her tissues when the tears flowed freely. "At least your parents were supportive."

Anne nodded. "They love Taryn very much and she gets on great with them. We did our best to make it work once Patrick moved back, but his drinking increased, and so did his verbal abuse. Penny couldn't take it and he finally drove them out on Taryn's tenth birthday. I feel like I let them both down."

"What could you have done?" Jace could only imagine how Anne felt. She was such a responsible woman when it came to her family.

"I don't know. I was in college at the time and it wasn't practical to commute. In the end, Mom and Dad helped Penny pay rent on an apartment until Taryn reached eighteen. Then they helped Taryn through college."

"It's a shame they're so far away," Jace said, aware that Anne's parents had moved to Florida for health reasons some time ago.

"They'd still be up here if it wasn't for Patrick," Anne said, with a flare of anger. "I think his bitterness and drinking just wore them down."

"I guess you really never know what goes on behind closed doors." Jace said sadly, memories of her own childhood and estrangement from her family running through her head. "What happened to Penny? Taryn told me she'd died, but she didn't go into detail."

"Penny had Lupus. So when Bill and I married and made the decision to move back into the house, I insisted that she move in. When Taryn found out how ill she was, she moved back in to help care for her and that's when the shit really hit the fan."

"I'd have thought things would have gotten better," Jace said. "Taryn doesn't seem the type to let anyone beat her down. Did she ever stand up to Patrick?"

Anne nodded. "Yes, but his rejection still hurt her. Kids wonder if they're somehow to blame when a parent does that. Then she fell in love."

"I bet that helped the situation. She had a boyfriend to defend her." Jace felt like punching Patrick out.

"No. Taryn was always different. She fell in love with a woman called Colette." Anne tried to gauge Jace's reaction but her expression gave little away. "I feel bad that I'm telling you this. She doesn't hide her sexuality, but you're her employer. I hope this won't affect the way you view her."

Jace was shocked. She'd never outwardly discussed sexuality with Anne. She'd never had the need as conversations had never arisen. But she was appalled that Anne would think she was homophobic. "Give me some credit! I wouldn't judge anybody because of their choice of partners. I hope I've never given you that impression."

"I'm sorry, Jace. I never meant to imply anything, but you'd be surprised how many people can change their opinion of someone when they find out. Even people you think you know well." Sadness etched Anne's voice. "Anyway, Taryn came out to the family. Patrick's a huge homophobe, no surprise there. But what hurt was Bill's reaction. He took Patrick's side, all of a sudden, and went out of his way to be hurtful. He even told her she wasn't welcome around the kids."

"That's insane. What did you do?"

"I didn't know what to do. I kept thinking he would see sense, but Penny's illness got worse and before I could deal with Bill, they moved to Ireland. I went to the funeral, when she died, but Taryn didn't really talk to me much. I think she felt betrayed that I had chosen to stay with Bill, rather than following them to Ireland."

"It's not that easy when you have kids," Jace said. She could imagine how Anne beat herself up over this. She must have felt completely torn.

"Taryn didn't seem to think that was any excuse," Anne said bitterly. "When she came back here, she wouldn't see me, only her grandparents. It was Mom who convinced her to take me up on the offer of the assistantship."

Jace was stunned. Anne hadn't said anything at the time. "I feel bad that I didn't know. I should have helped you."

"Don't feel bad. It was at a time when we were changing from colleagues to friends. I didn't want you to judge me. I had let my best friends walk out of my life without a fight. I was very lonely when I got back from Ireland, so it meant a lot to me that you were becoming a friend." Anne's tears came streaming down.

"I can't believe Bill would be so cruel," Jace commented. "That must have been awful for you."

"It was. I suppose I made excuses for him at first. His mother brought him up as a staunch Catholic and he has a black and white view of the world. But I blamed him for Taryn and Penny leaving and it hurt our marriage."

Jace felt singularly unobservant. How could she not have noticed the strain Anne was under? She'd glimpsed it at times, but always assumed the stress of juggling work with motherhood was the culprit. "I would never have guessed. You two always seemed so solid. How did you work it out?"

"Well, when I got back from the funeral in Ireland, I moved out of the bedroom and refused to be with someone who couldn't love people because they were different."

"Oh, my God. I guess that got his attention."

Anne laughed, partly from the sheer relief of being able to tell the truth about her life. She'd taken such pains to hide what was happening, it had been impossible to get support. "It sure did. We ended up in marriage counseling and joined a support group for families of gay children. Over time, he starting rethinking his attitude and these days he's pretty embarrassed about his past behavior."

"So, Tom was..."

"Exactly." Anne chuckled. "Born nine months after our marriage got back on track."

"I can't believe this was going on right under my nose and I had no clue. What kind of friend am I? I'm sorry."

They hugged one another and Anne said, "Don't beat yourself up. It's not your fault I wanted to pretend life was perfect for the Weston family. Anyway, I think you kept me sane. If it wasn't for work, I'd have had no escape from my problems!"

As they hugged again, the back screen door opened and Patrick staggered through it.

"Fucking queers. Bill, I warned you!" He leaned against the wall a beer in his hand.

Jace leapt to her feet, her fists clenched. She could feel Anne's grip on her arm.

"He's drunk, Jace. Ignore him."

Bill followed his brother-in-law outdoors, looking annoyed. "What are you yelling about, Pat? You'll wake the kids." Catching sight of Jace, he said, "Hi, Jace. I didn't know you were visiting tonight."

"She's doing my sister!" Patrick fumed. "I told you this would happen if we let that...thing back in the house." He spat on the deck as if to get a bad taste from his mouth.

Anne couldn't hold back any longer. "Bill, get him out of my sight before I do or say something I'll regret." She stormed down the wooden steps and into the garden.

Jace hesitated for a moment, wondering if she should help Bill get Patrick indoors. But she doubted she'd be able to keep her hands off his neck. How Anne and that jerk could have sprung from the same gene pool was beyond her. Disgusted, she went after Anne, and found her leaning against the old oak tree.

"Are you okay?" she asked, knowing it was a really lame question.

"Still think I live in paradise?" Anne was embarrassed. She hadn't realized it had gotten so late. She knew she should have sent Jace home before Patrick returned.

"You're still my hero," Jace said. "Even more so now that I know what you've put up with over the years. Is he always like this?"

"No," a male voice answered, and Bill walked the last few steps up the garden path to take his wife in his arms. "He's always liked his alcohol but he's been hitting the bottle more recently."

"Since Taryn returned?" Jace asked.

"You told her?" he asked Anne, holding her close and rubbing her back.

"It was time," she said. "How about we go inside and make some hot chocolate?"

Jace felt it was her cue to leave. "I had better be going. Anne, if you don't feel up to it, please take a personal day tomorrow. We're going to be very quiet this week. I know you have a lot of things to do before Wednesday."

"Thanks. I'll see how it goes." Anne drew away from her husband, "What's going to happen about Taryn?"

"Nothing. It makes no difference to me that she's a relative of yours. Work is work. Her performance is up to her."

"You won't say anything about tonight?"

"Of course not. Now go back inside and rest. I'll see you on Wednesday."

Jace gave Anne a brief hug, smiled a farewell to Bill and escaped to her car. She felt shell shocked. *So much for family life.*

Chapter
Four

THE SUMMER HEAT was unbearable and just seemed to intensify Taryn's bad mood. She had barely slept. She'd woken up crabby and had purposefully goaded Marti into a fight. A stupid, futile fight. All Marti had done was ask what was on her mind because she'd tossed and turned all night, which according to Marti was a clear sign that she was stressed. Instead of giving a simple answer, Taryn had snapped at her to mind her own business and leave her alone. This had ignited Marti's temper and she'd yelled at Taryn about how tired she was of being shut out of her life. As she left for work she'd threatened to sleep at her parents' if Taryn wasn't in a better mood when she arrived home.

Guiltily aware of the upset and hurt she was causing, Taryn went to work earlier than necessary, stopping on the way to buy some coffee at the now familiar Dunkin Donuts. She paused when she reached the Center's doors. *Just go inside. What's the worst that can happen? She tells you to find an assistantship elsewhere. Shit happens. Suck it up and get in there.*

Jace looked up and smiled as she saw Taryn in her doorway dangling coffee before her. "I think you read my mind some mornings."

"It's your caffeine buzz. It can be heard through the state of Massachusetts." Taryn was pleased to see that her employer seemed relaxed enough to joke with her. She decided she'd wait until Jace brought up the subject of the previous night before she said anything.

Jace sipped the hot liquid. "Ummm...that hit the spot. I'm glad you're in so early. I have to go to several meetings, and wasn't sure we'd cross paths today. She handed Taryn a sheet of paper. "I've written down what I need you to do today. Any problems e-mail me. I'll be up in the President's office for most of the day."

Taryn stared down at the strong bold strokes written on the

page while Jace grabbed various folders from the shelf.

"I'm going now," she said as she walked through the doorway.

Taryn wasn't listening to Jace. She was transfixed by the last line on the sheet of instructions. '*By the way, you still work for me!*'

Grinning, she ran out into the corridor and shouted after Jace, "Thanks."

TARYN WAS OUT of the office by 2pm. Having decided that she owed Marti an apology, she had bought some steak and a bottle of wine. Although steak was bound to be offered at the fourth of July barbecue the next day, she thought a cookout on the deck would help appease Marti. She'd even bought a bunch of flowers.

Marti would be home any minute, so Taryn hurried to heat the grill as soon as she got home. She placed the large steaks on the metal rack and covered them with the lid. The table was set and the flowers made a pretty centerpiece. She poured herself a glass of wine and settled into the soft deck chair.

Their home was a small two-bedroom country ranch house off a main road. It was surrounded on three sides by tall trees, but the neighbors' houses could still be seen on either side. Taryn liked the feeling of privacy the trees gave her. She looked up as she heard Marti's car pull into their small driveway.

"I'm out back, Marti," she yelled as soon as the car door slammed.

Her girlfriend came round the corner, her tawny copper hair radiant in the late afternoon, a smile gracing her fair complexion. "This is a nice surprise. I expected you to be late. You've been putting in some long hours." She kissed Taryn on the lips. "I see your mood has improved. Do you want to talk about it?"

Marti knew the answer before she even asked, but in her own masochistic way, she had to try. Getting Taryn to talk voluntarily was like pulling teeth: slow and painful.

Taryn wrapped her arms around Marti's slim waist. "PMS, babe."

"Yeah, and I'm the tooth fairy. You had your period last week. Don't worry, your secrets are your own. This looks nice. Are the flowers for me?" Marti was pleasantly surprised that Taryn had gone to so much trouble. It wasn't her nature to be so romantic.

"The flowers are my way of saying sorry. I know I've been a bitch to live with." Taryn let go of Marti and turned to the grill to flip the steaks.

"You're forgiven." Marti came up behind her and nibbled on Taryn's ear.

"Nooo... Marti that tickles." Marti continued to suckle the sweet tasting skin. "Cut it out or I'll end up setting the deck on fire."

Marti laughed sexily into Taryn's ear. "I know something else that's on fire!"

Taryn squirmed 'round and kissed her girlfriend soundly. "Well, maybe that will keep you stoked, because we're eating first. I'm starving. Make yourself useful and go and get the potatoes out of the oven."

She tapped Marti's ass and got a hundred watt smile for a reply. *Life is good. Who'd have thought I'd be this settled? Maybe it is time to introduce Marti to the family. Who am I kidding? Bill would never let Anne visit here with the kids.*

"Hey watch it, Emeril, the steaks are burning!" Marti placed the potatoes on the table and went back inside for the salad.

Taryn grabbed a plate and put the steaks on it. She carried them, and the corn she had been cooking, over to the table. After they were both seated, she poured the wine and toasted, "Here's to a good Fourth of July."

They clinked glasses and Marti cut up her steak, happy that Taryn looked relaxed. Her lover was so complex in many ways and rarely gave herself time to wind down. But it seemed like she'd been thinking about her unreasonable behavior.

Reading this as a sign that Taryn might be ready to move forward, Marti said, "Taryn, I was thinking about tomorrow."

Taryn chewed on her steak. She had a feeling Marti was going to try and get her to visit the family. When the Weston invitation had arrived addressed to the both of them, Marti had opened it and asked if they were going to go. Taryn had refused then and she hadn't changed her mind since.

Wishing Marti had just left it alone, she said, "I told you...we're not going to Anne's. We're going to your mom's. End of story."

"Oh, I see." Marti swept a hand toward the flowers and the wine. "All of this is just for show." She couldn't contain her frustration any longer. "Well, don't do me any favors. I'm not a student in one of your classrooms. *I'm* not the one who's acting like child. I'm sick of your attitude. You need to fucking grow up."

"Look who's talking," Taryn threw back. "I ask you to respect my privacy. I beg you to leave my family out of discussions for reasons I don't want to go into. So why don't *you* try acting like an adult and accept that we're not all from the Brady fucking Bunch. I'm sorry if it hurts you when I don't share but this is who I am. Take it or leave it."

The rest of the meal was eaten in sullen silence.

JACE SWAM ACROSS the pool to Anne, avoiding the errant splashes of water that came her way. "Good turnout," she said.

"Yes, I think there are more Weston's this year than last." Anne glanced past Jace to her son, who was being cradled poolside by his grandmother. "Doesn't Tom just look so cute in his swimming trunks?"

"They're very sweet at that age," Jace said.

"I wish they stayed that way." Anne couldn't help but notice Ricky was still playing with his GameBoy under the big willow tree. Her middle child tended to withdraw when he was angry or thinking about something.

"He doesn't seem to mix with his cousins very well." Jace could tell Anne was distracted and she sympathized. Ricky knew how to make his point.

"He's sulking," Anne responded. "He wanted Taryn to come, then Patrick shouted at him and he hasn't spoken to any of us since."

"I wish I could help." Jace swallowed some impatience. Ever since she'd learned the truth about Patrick, she had struggled to mind her own business and refrain from telling Anne to stand up to him. It was ridiculous that her family had to be affected by that jerk. "For what it's worth, I appreciate you having me here. If it weren't for you, I'd be spending every holiday alone."

"I think I prevent you having a sex life!" Anne ducked under the water and swam as fast as she could. Five strokes later, she was struggling for air. She could feel Jace's strong fingers wrapped around her leg. As she turned to swim upwards, Jace's arms were on her waist and she was lifted up for air.

"Explain yourself!" Her friend swam toward the edge of the pool, dragging Anne with her. "I could have a sex life if I wanted one."

Anne coughed the remnants of water out of her mouth. "Maybe. Don't take what I'm about to say the wrong way. I just think if you were on your own at these times of year, you'd get lonely and that would force you out into the world of dating." When Jace frowned, she added, "Have I overstepped the mark?"

Jace ran her fingers through her wet curls. "No. Maybe you're right. Although I really do enjoy spending time with the children."

"You're good with them," Anne said.

"It's funny. I get a sense of belonging with your kids that I don't have with my own nieces and nephews." She sensed Anne was waiting for more, but today was about making Anne feel better, not dragging her own past over the coals. Changing the topic, she said, "Enough of the sensitive chats. I'm going to go talk to the second man in my life!"

She jumped out of the pool and lifted her towel from the deck chair and strolled toward Ricky, an idea forming in her mind.

SEVERAL HOURS LATER, back home in her apartment, Jace paced back and forth across her living room floor staring at her cell phone. She had tried calling Taryn a few times, but it had gone directly to voicemail. *Quit pacing. It's past eleven. Obviously she's not going to call now. You've certainly gotten yourself into a mess. Just go to bed!*

What on earth made her promise Ricky an outing with Taryn, one that Taryn knew nothing about? They were going to Chuck E. Cheeses on Friday night. The problem was, she'd announced this thrilling plan before checking if Taryn was available and willing. It had seemed like the perfect way to pull Ricky out of his withdrawn mood, and had worked like magic. Then she told Anne, who said Taryn might be going away with Marti. Jace had been trying to get hold of Taryn ever since.

Frustrated by her lack of success, she turned off the lights and climbed the stairs. She hoped that her impulsive decision wouldn't backfire on her. She didn't need to add to Anne's problems. Jace sighed. She wasn't going to get anywhere worrying about it. It was out of her hands until she could speak with Taryn, and it was way too late for that to happen now.

TARYN CARESSED MARTI'S skin. "That was great. You were giving me the eye all day! It drove me crazy." She kissed Marti's lips. "And if you think I didn't notice the way you rubbed past me in the pool, you're wrong. If your mother hadn't been watching, I'd have taken you then and there."

Marti just flashed a bright smile and winked. Taryn swallowed. "I think you've drained all the liquid out of my body. I'll be back in a minute." Taryn climbed over the naked body, tweaking a nipple as she departed. "Paybacks are a bitch!"

She strolled down the hallway into the kitchen and got two bottles of water from the fridge. As she walked back toward the bedroom, the blinking red light illuminating in the dark caught her attention. *Probably Gram and Gramps. I'll check it in the morning.* She turned in to the master bedroom.

"What took you so long?" Marti whispered as she snaked her arm round Taryn's waist.

"I'm running on empty!" Taryn lay on the bed staring at the ceiling fans going round and round. The message on the answering machine was making her curious. "It's no use."

"What's wrong now?" Marti grumbled.

"There's a message on the machine. I think it's Gram, but if I don't check it out, I won't sleep all night. I'll be right back."

She padded back down the hallway collecting the discarded clothes as she went. She pressed play. *"You have one message. Wednesday, 2.44pm. Taryn, this is Jace. I'm sorry for calling you outside of work hours. I need to talk to you urgently. Call me back on 508-555-1214 as soon as possible"*

Taryn's heart began to beat faster.

"Who was that?" Marti asked from the bedroom.

"Jace." Taryn replied still in shock. The last voice she'd expected to hear on the machine was her boss. She walked back into the bedroom.

"What did she want?" Marti propped a pillow behind her head.

"She said it was urgent."

Marti took Taryn's hand. "Didn't you say she was spending the day with Anne?"

"Yeah. Oh my god, what if something happened to Anne or the kids? What if Anne was hurt and couldn't phone?" Memories of her father's anger burned in her mind. *He wouldn't hurt the kids.* Tears blinded her eyes, as she fumbled for the bedroom phone and hit the redial button.

Come on. Pick up.

"Hello?"

Taryn recognized the croaky voice of her boss. "Are they okay? What happened?" She was frantic. Taryn rubbed her cheek, plagued by memories of Patrick's hand hitting her face over and over again.

"Taryn?" Jace was trying to rid the fog of sleep from her head. "What time is it?"

"After twelve. Where are they? You said it was urgent."

Realization dawned on Jace. "They're fine, Taryn. I promise." *Stupid! Couldn't have worried the girl anymore if you'd tried.* "I'm sorry, I needed to ask you something as soon as possible. I should have explained myself better." She rubbed the sleep out of her eyes and yawned.

Taryn sat on the end of the bed. She was shivering and could feel Marti come up behind her.

"I'm here, babe. What's wrong?" Marti held Taryn close to her.

Taryn shook her head and held a finger to her lips to silence Marti. "I'm sorry, Jace, I'm a little discombobulated."

"That's a big word for this time of night." Jace tried to lighten the mood. She could hear the sound of a woman in the background, and an ache she'd never felt before began in the pit of her stomach. "I'm sorry about the message. Ricky was really upset because you weren't at the party, and good old Uncle Patrick yelled at him. I was just trying to make him feel better."

"Patrick didn't hurt him, did he?" Taryn knew exactly what the man was capable of.

"No. Ricky kept saying you didn't come because he was stupid. So I lied to him."

Taryn could feel the tears welling up in her eyes. She broke the hold that Marti had on her body and walked out into the hallway. "What did you say?" She sniffed and wiped the tears away.

Jace could hear the sniffles at the other end of the line. "I told him you had promised to take him out Friday night."

"You did?" Taryn hadn't expected any of this.

"I'm sorry, I had no right to plan your evening, but I just couldn't watch him beat himself up anymore. It hurt too much." The last words were whispered as memories from her childhood returned. "Anne said you might go on vacation and I panicked, hence the urgent message. I didn't mean to worry you."

"Aunt Anne was right. I was planning to go away, but Marti has to work Friday." Taryn replied.

"Oh... Good."

She must be uncomfortable about me mentioning Marti. I wonder what Anne told her. Taryn could sense Jace's discomfort. "So where am I going on my date?" She asked, trying to change the subject.

"How do you feel about Chuck E. Cheese's?"

Taryn groaned. "I hear it's a madhouse! What time should I pick him up?"

"You'll come?" Jace mouthed a silent thank you to the gods.

Taryn leaned against the wall. "It's a date. I'd do anything for those kids. I know what living with Patrick can be like to one's self esteem." Jace heard the bitterness creep into Taryn's voice. "Should I call Anne to make arrangements?"

"No. She said we should all meet outside the one at Brockton around five. If you couldn't make it, she said I was to

grovel and offer you a promotion!" Jace relaxed back into the
pillows on her bed.

Taryn laughed. "I guess I should have held out a bit longer.
I think it would be fun to see you beg! Did I hear you say you
were going as well?"

Jace groaned. "Yes. Your aunt said it wasn't fair to send you
to that place without other adult company so we're triple dating.
Your aunt is taking Josie. I'm escorting Tom, and you have
Ricky."

"Good, I lucked out!" Taryn laughed as she tried to picture
her cool, calm boss changing a diaper.

"How so?" Jace was enjoying the friendly banter between
the two. Conversation with Taryn often led to the two of them
teasing each other.

"My date's potty trained." Taryn yawned. "I should go back
to bed before Marti sends out a search party. Thanks, Jace."

Jace felt the twinge in her stomach again when Taryn
mentioned her partner. "Thanks for what? You're digging me
out of a hole. Sleep well."

"You, too. Goodnight Jace." Taryn heard the click of the
phone and smiled at the receiver. She turned, banging straight
into Marti who was leaning on the doorframe to their room.

"What's going on, Taryn? One minute you're screaming and
crying, the next you're laughing like you haven't got a care in
the world. I heard you say the word 'date' and I got worried."

Taryn knew there was no way out of the conversation, so she
relayed the story minus the bit about Patrick.

Marti frowned. "I thought *we* had a date Friday night?"

"You cancelled on me last week for your family. Besides, I'm
not canceling our date, I'm just changing the venue."

She knew she'd said the right thing when she saw Marti's
face light up. Marti was always asking to meet Anne, especially
after Taryn took the new job. But Taryn had been putting it off.
Even though her aunt said things were changing, Taryn needed
to see that her father and uncle were different before she would
ever risk bringing Marti into an abusive environment. She still
wasn't certain if she even wanted to reconnect more
meaningfully with anyone except her young cousins. It had hurt
too much when she'd left before, and she still couldn't forgive
her aunt's choices.

"Are you saying I'm invited?"

Taryn nodded. "You keep asking when you'll meet the
family. Friday seems ideal. The attention will be on the kids so
we shouldn't get the third degree from Auntie Anne. You'll get
to meet the boss, too."

Chapter
Five

"I TOLD HIM this would happen." Anne said.

Jace had a feeling she knew what was going on, but she wasn't a mind reader, so she asked, "Told him what would happen?" She watched Bill as he struggled to hold both Ricky and Tom in his arms.

"I told him that it might be awkward with Taryn if he came to pick us up. But he said he wants to clear the air. I didn't tell Taryn earlier because I didn't want to spoil the evening."

Jace smiled as the six-foot man approached their section of seating inside Chuck E Cheese's.

Bill lowered his two sons to the ground. "I see you're still alive, Jace?"

"Just about." She ruffled Ricky's hair.

"Daddy, come and see Ryn. She's my date for the evening." The young boy dragged his father over to where Taryn and Marti were putting their coats on. "Ryn, where are you going?" Ricky let go of his father's hand and ran to Taryn.

Taryn looked from the young boy and up to the larger carbon copy, and then back down to Ricky. "I'm sorry, Ricky. Marti and I have to go. It's getting late."

Ricky looked at his watch, "But it's only..." He carefully counted the digits. "It's only seven twenty three."

Taryn couldn't keep the grin off her face when she saw the earnest look on his face. "I'm impressed, Ricky. I didn't know you could tell the time so accurately."

He beamed proudly. "Mrs. Lopez says I'm one of the best students when we do time."

Bill put his hand on Ricky's shoulder, "I need to talk to Taryn for a moment. Would you keep her friend company for me?"

"My name is Marti." Marti glared.

"Bill Weston, I'm pleased to meet you, Marti."

Marti accepted his hand and shook it firmly. "Likewise."

Taryn wasn't sure what to do. In her heart she wanted to run. Just looking at her uncle reminded her of all the times he'd said spiteful things. Her aunt had promised he'd changed, but how could she know for sure. She looked beseechingly at Jace, asking a silent question. *Should I talk to him?*

Jace looked at the frightened face. She felt like she could see right into Taryn's soul. She knew Bill only wanted to apologize, so she answered the silent question by nodding her head.

Taryn turned back to her uncle. "Okay, but I need a few moments with Marti."

She guided Marti away from the crowd. "I'm going to talk to him but I don't want you with me."

Marti gasped a protest. "I don't think it's a good idea to do this by yourself. I'm coming with you."

"No." Taryn took her hand and gave it a reassuring squeeze. She knew it was a lot to ask of Marti, but she had to do this her way. "Please, I need you to trust me on this. You're right. Uncle Bill and I haven't always gotten along. So I'm going to ask Jace to come outside with us. She knows him well, and I think he'll be more reasonable with her there. Besides," she tried to lighten things up, "I feel safe knowing she stands a good two inches above him."

With a forced smile, Marti relinquished her hand and said, "Okay. If that's what you want."

THE COOL EVENING air out in the parking lot felt good against Jace's skin and she ran her fingers through her hair. She was unsure what she should do. She had no idea if she should stay by Taryn, or give the pair some privacy. Her thoughts were answered when Taryn spoke.

"Thank you. I don't trust my temper if I'm on my own, and I didn't want Marti to hear any of his insults. I'm used to them from family, but she's not."

Jace squeezed Taryn's arm reassuringly. "You're welcome, Taryn, but I think your uncle may surprise you. Anne says he's changed."

"You believe her?"

Bill answered the question, approaching the women from one side. "Anne is telling the truth. I'm not the bigoted man I used to be, Taryn. I nearly lost my family because of my warped thinking."

"What do you mean?" Taryn slipped her hand into Jace's.

"Your aunt and I almost split up. I guess she never told you that. She had her bags packed and a ticket booked for Ireland. I begged her to stay and she did, but on her terms. She demanded I get help." Jace liked the feeling of Taryn's hand, it was soft and small just like its owner, but there was strength there. Jace could feel it pulsing through her as Bill talked about going to counseling and joining the support group. "The sessions made me think about what I would do if one of the kids told me they were gay," he said awkwardly. "I'd still love them. What I'm trying to say, Taryn — and making a mess of it — is I am so sorry. Can you forgive me?"

"It still hurts." Taryn whispered. "But I'm willing to try."

Bill gave a sigh of relief. "Listen, you're welcome to the house any time, I want you to know that. I was a fool to try and prevent you seeing the kids."

"Uncle Bill, you know the main reason why I stay away. While that bastard is in the house, I will never visit."

"But, Taryn, by staying away you give Patrick power. He revels in it. Over the years I've seen him for what he really is. A fake. He'll never admit he's wrong and it's about time we all stood up against him. He'll be one against an army, and we'll be the army. Think about it. We're hosting a Labor Day barbecue and I'd be honored if you would attend with Marti." He took a step toward her and opened his arms. "Forgive me?"

Taryn felt like a child again. Unsure of what to do, she reluctantly released Jace's hand and walked toward her uncle. Unable to stop herself, she wrapped her arms around the big man. "I'll try. No promises."

"That's all I ask." Sounding choked up, Bill backed away from her and said, "I'd better be going. It's time the kids got home." As he passed Jace, he hugged her and said, "Thank you, Jace, for all you do."

Momentarily knocked off balance, she could not mutter a reply and she wasn't sure whether to follow Bill or stay with Taryn. When the silence made her even more nervous, she started walking after him.

Taryn immediately moved alongside her, one hand coming to rest on her arm. "Wait. Please. Can we talk for a moment?"

Jace tried not to show her surprise. So far, it had been quite a night. "Sure."

"I guess I'm a little taken aback." Taryn sounded dazed. "You live your life hating people for their actions, and then suddenly they change and you get blown away. It's as if you're meant to forget the pain and shut out the hurt. But, I don't know how. It's been too long."

Jace placed a hand on Taryn's shoulder. "It takes time. You never forget the hurt, but you use it to make you a stronger

person. You don't have to be like them. You're better than that."
She drew Taryn closer. "I'm here for you if you need to talk
about it."

Unable to help herself, Taryn melted into the tall body,
allowing Jace's strong arms to wrap around her. She rested her
head on Jace's chest and inhaled a mixture of vanilla and soap
powder. She needed this, she thought, drawing on Jace's
strength. In fact, she would have been perfectly content to
remain in her arms for hours, had a cough not reminded them
that they were not alone.

Jace turned her head and immediately dropped her arms
from Taryn's body. "It's Marti," she mouthed, then said for
Marti's benefit. "Feeling better now?"

"Yes. Thanks, Jace." Taryn took an unhurried step back, not
wanting to seem uncomfortable or guilty. "I needed someone
who would be subjective. You knew Anne's side of the story and
I felt safe knowing you'd give me an honest opinion."

"You're welcome," Jace said. She could feel the all too
familiar distance between them once more. Gone was Taryn's
need to be close, to be held. Jace was back to being the boss and
Taryn her subordinate. Jace had always enjoyed the distance that
power afforded her. Now, watching Taryn walk toward Marti,
who stood impatiently tapping her foot, she wished her life were
different. She wished Taryn saw her as something else.

Kissing Marti lightly on the cheek, Taryn said, "Let me just
go and say goodbye and then I'm all yours."

If Marti could shoot daggers from her eyes, Jace was sure
she would be dead. As nonchalantly as she could, she walked
over to Marti and said, "It was nice meeting you. I hope to see
you again."

"Same here." Marti shook her hand. "I'm sure we will."

Jace told herself she was only imagining that she saw anger
in Marti's eyes and that Marti knew her secret. But, when she
glanced back to smile a goodbye, her suspicions were confirmed
as Marti's green eyes sent a very clear message: *I know how you
feel about Taryn.*

But how? Jace had only just worked it out it herself in the
same moment! Confused, she walked briskly to her car so she
wouldn't get caught up in any protracted goodbyes. She needed
space and lots of it.

THE SILENCE IN the car was deafening. Taryn steadied the
wheel with one hand and used the other to turn the radio on, just
to break the monotony. She had looked Marti's way a few times

but her girlfriend's jaw was set and her eyes fixed ahead. *I knew she was going to be pissed, but I didn't think she'd go for the full silent treatment.* Taryn began to tap out the beat of the music. She knew it would bug Marti even more, but any reaction was better than the silence. Her actions were paid off when Marti turned her head.

"Do you have to do that?"

"No. Are you going to tell me what's wrong?"

"What makes you think something is wrong?"

"Well, the silence for a starter, then there's the grinding of your teeth. If you clamp your jaw any tighter your fillings will fall out. I think you've stared a hole in the windshield, and you have that pissy look."

Marti turned to face Taryn. "What do you mean 'pissy' look?"

"Honey, we've lived together for over a year. I know your pissy look." Taryn checked behind her and changed lane. "Okay, so what did I do wrong?"

Marti was silent for a few more seconds. "I'm jealous."

Taryn spluttered. "You're jealous? Why?"

"I think you fancy Jace." Marti fiddled with her cell phone.

Taryn shook her head. "Why would you think that?"

"She's gorgeous. You never told me how good looking she is. I pictured an older, plain looking woman, especially after your comment about her being an old dragon. What you forgot to mention were the striking blue eyes, hair most woman would die for, a stunning body, a smile to kill for, and a tan that most people spend a whole summer trying to achieve. Did I miss anything?"

Taryn laughed. "Not that you were looking or anything. Honey, if I didn't know better, I'd say *you* have a crush on my boss!"

"I'm being serious." Marti whined.

Taryn lightly strummed the steering wheel. She had noticed Jace's good looks. Anyone would; the woman was gorgeous. But Taryn had never looked beyond an initial admiration. The woman was her boss, friend, and straight. Jace had never given her any reason to think otherwise, and Taryn's gaydar hadn't registered anything on the 'pingometer'.

"Marti, it's not an issue. What's brought this on?"

"It hurt me when you asked Jace to go outside with you," Marti said in a small voice. "I should be the person you choose to support you. Why didn't you pick me? I'm supposed to be your girlfriend."

"You are my girlfriend. I think I made that very clear when I told my nine year old niece who you were."

Marti sighed and Taryn tried again.

"I wasn't sure if Bill was being serious. Your family has always been supportive of your sexuality so you have no idea what it can be like when things turn nasty. I just wanted to protect you."

Taryn fell silent, aware that she seemed to be trying to convince herself as much as she wanted to reassure Marti. An uneasy silence surrounded the two.

"She likes you." Marti whispered.

"What?"

"I said she likes you. I can tell."

"Of course she likes me, we're friends."

"No," Marti insisted. "She really likes you. She couldn't stop watching you over dinner. And when I came outside—it was obvious. I could see the longing in her face. I swear."

Taryn mentally replayed the hug she'd shared with Jace. She couldn't deny Jace had held her possessively, but Taryn had returned the hug just as fiercely. There had been a connection between them, a feeling she couldn't put words to but had definitely experienced.

"Marti, I think you're seeing things. But let's just say you're right. There are three reasons why the relationship would go no further." She paused waiting for Marti to stop gazing at passing traffic and look at her. "Number one, she's my boss. Number two, I am a student and she is a member of staff. Number three, and probably the most important to us, I'm not interested in Jace that way. I have you, and I'm very happy."

As Taryn pulled into their driveway, Marti leaned over and kissed her on the cheek. "I'm sorry. You just seemed so relaxed around her."

"Marti, I have to play nice if I want to survive the next two semesters. You told me that! Do you want her writing 'sulks like a baby' on my references?" Feeling Marti thaw, she said, "Come on, there's still time to watch a movie. Want to have some fun, maybe?"

Chapter
Six

TARYN STARED IN horror at the tender skin at the base of her throat. "I can't believe you weren't careful! Remember the rule, bite below the collarbone, not above."

"Toothpaste. I heard once that toothpaste takes the redness out." Marti offered the tube to her. "Hey, it's worth a try."

"I can't believe I'm doing this." Taryn rubbed a generous amount of paste over the red mark. "You couldn't have lost control last week when no one was in the office. No, you have to wait until everyone is back from their vacation. God, that new girl Cory is starting, too. She's going to think I'm a hussy."

"I doubt it. She'll probably be jealous as hell that you're getting some!" Marti replied, pleased that Jace would see her warning mark.

"I don't think the paste is working. We'd better shower or we'll both be late for work. Fuck! I have no summer clothes that go that high."

Taryn was still mumbling beneath her breath when she arrived at work. She plastered extra concealer over the hickey just before she got out of the car. Maybe she could pass it off as a regular bruise. She was still trying to come up with a credible explanation for how she could have sustained a minor neck injury as she walked through the Center's doors, and her heart dropped when she saw Brenda Eldredge standing in the entrance hall talking to another blonde woman.

Brenda, a robust, gray-haired, middle-aged woman was the chief administrator of the Center. She was also a vital lynchpin in the smooth running of the front desk; the hub of the Achievement Center. She was the first person most students turned to when they had an issue and many employees loved her motherly approach to life. She was also fiercely protective of her colleagues and could be trusted beyond reproach. However, she had a tendency to notice everything and difficulty keeping quiet about it. Taryn had hoped to sneak into the building and hide until Jace or Anne came looking for her. She should have known she would never make it past Brenda.

The eager administrator waved her over and said, "Taryn, come and meet Cory."

Taryn raised the collar on her polo shirt and walked over to the two women. Shaking the newcomer's hand, she said, "Hey, it's good to finally meet you."

"Nice to meet you, too." Cory's voice was enthusiastic and upbeat and her British accent was cute.

"Taryn, why don't you give Cory a tour of the place while you wait for Anne and Jace," Brenda suggested, then her eyes dropped and she gasped, "Oh my god! You have a growth on your neck! Let me look, maybe it's a rash!"

Taryn turned a bright shade of red. No matter how hard she'd tried, her polo collar only covered half of the mark. Marti had suggested a silk scarf, but Taryn never wore scarves. She might as well stick a sign on her forehead and announce the bite. "Leave it alone, Brenda," she said, doubly embarrassed that this was going on in front of the new staffer. "Come on, Cory. I'll give you the nickel tour. We're not all juvenile, I promise."

Giggling, Brenda called after them, "You should get down to the Health Center. That could be catching!"

As she gave Cory the tour, Taryn described what she'd been doing all summer and explained the plans Jace had for the two of them. Most of July had turned out to be a boring month. Anne had decided she needed a vacation away from the monotony of the Center, she and Bill took the boys for a two-week trip to Florida. Instead of finding herself working virtually alone with Jace, Taryn was dismayed when her boss decided to take her own vacation time a few days after Anne.

She supposed she shouldn't have been surprised. Ever since the night at Chuck E. Cheese's, Jace seemed to have gone out of her way to put distance between them. It was as if she were letting Taryn know that somehow she'd overstepped, and just because they'd connected on a personal level, it didn't mean anything would change at work. She was never unprofessional or unfriendly. But she'd kept her distance, and that, coupled with her aunt's absence made Taryn feel strangely excluded. Eventually she'd received a postcard with a photo of her grandparent's hometown depicted on the front and the classic 'Welcome to Naples'. She'd thrown it in the trash.

"If you keep rubbing it, you'll break the skin."

Cory's voice arrested Taryn's hand. She hadn't even realized she was worrying the spot and now it felt like the tender skin was indeed broken in places.

"Great," she muttered. "I'm so embarrassed. This wasn't how I'd planned to start my morning."

"It could be worse," Cory said. "Students could be here and then you'd never live it down."

Taryn smiled. "You're right. So when did you arrive in America? Why did you pick this college out of all the colleges in the world?" She led her companion to the tiny graduate assistant offices and they sat down.

Cory studied Taryn carefully. She'd been extremely nervous about starting work so soon after arriving in America, but so far everyone had been very nice to her, and now, unless her instincts were affected by jetlag, she was certain the woman in front of her was a lesbian.

Taking the chance, she said, "I landed on Friday. My girlfriend and I spent the weekend getting reacquainted with each other." She blushed. After talking with her girlfriend, Dylan, she'd decided to be open about their relationship, as open as she could be, but she had thought she'd wait until she knew people before announcing her sexuality.

To her relief, Taryn immediately confirmed her suspicions. "Well, at least your girlfriend knows how to keep control!" She indicated the bruise on her neck. "Mine doesn't! So she came over here with you?"

Cory shook her head. "No. Dylan's American. We met online and have spent the best part of the year communicating by phone and e-mail."

"No way! Wow, you hear about it, but I never thought e-mail relationships lasted! She must be pleased to have you here." This day could just be getting better, Taryn decided. *At least I don't have to think before I speak around Cory, she's family.*

"We both had things to sort out, but it was easier for me to move than for her—my teaching career allowed me more flexibility. I was working at a small junior school and the head teacher offered me a two year unpaid sabbatical."

"So you have a job to go back to, if you want? That's lucky. I guess it's really hard for most people in your situation." Taryn was amazed that someone was willing to give up everything they knew for love. She verbalized this thought out loud. "You gave up everything for her!"

"We both made sacrifices," Cory said. "Dylan sold her house and is going to have to support me through these two years, and there's always a risk that things won't work out once we see each other everyday. But we're prepared to do whatever it takes to be together. So, how about you? Who's the woman that didn't get fed last night?"

"Huh?" Taryn didn't get the joke, and then it dawned on her and she rubbed her neck again. "Her name is Marti."

"Serious relationship?" Cory liked the blonde in front of her. She seemed very friendly.

Taryn thought about the question. She wasn't in the habit of analyzing her relationship with Marti. "We live together. My aunt says that means we're serious! We do okay. Maybe, once you've settled in we could double date?"

Taryn's question never got answered as a tanned Anne arrived at her cubicle. "Hello, stranger." She stood with her arms opened wide for a hug.

Taryn got up and hugged Anne to her. "You look great. I can't believe how brown you are." Kissing her on the cheek, she drew back and said, "Anne, this is Cory."

Anne greeted Cory with a handshake. "Welcome to America. I'm Anne Weston. It's nice to finally meet you, Cory. Has Taryn given you a tour?"

"Yes. She showed me around and filled me in on what's been happening. I'm very excited."

"Good. How about you follow me to my office and we'll go over some of the paperwork and look at your contract." Her eyes strayed to Taryn's neck and she said, "Taryn, I think you might like to reread the employee's handbook again!" Winking as she walked by, she whispered, "I see you weren't lonely while we were gone, but I'd keep out of Jace's way with that er ... blemish. She's been a bear to live with the past two weeks."

Taryn stared at her aunt's retreating back. *Jace went on vacation with Anne? How? When? Why hadn't she been invited?*

JACE TOOK A deep breath as she stood outside the door of the Achievement Center. *Just walk in, you, wuss. This feeling will pass, whatever it is. You are in control. You always have been, and you always will be.* She straightened her shoulders and pushed through the doors, greeting Brenda in her usual pleasant professional manner.

"Hey, Jace," Brenda smiled. "Good to have you back. I'll let you get to your office before I begin to bombard you with letters and questions."

"Thank you. Is everyone else in?" Jace knew Anne and Taryn were in, she'd seen their cars in the parking lot.

"Anne and Taryn are out back, and Cory has arrived. She seems nice. Patty will be in a little later, as she had car trouble. I've cleared your schedule for this morning. Taryn's been pretty good at replying to your non-urgent e-mail. There are a few meetings that need to be set up. I've sent you an e-mail of the main questions and things that need to be done before pre-college week." Brenda grinned. "Welcome back!"

"Now I know why I don't usually take time off." Jace walked down the corridor to her office and dropped her briefcase onto her chair. She could hear Anne's voice coming from the next room and what was clearly a British accent replying. Jace quickly checked her organizer, automatically planning her time. She knew she should stick her head around the door and introduce herself to the new student, but her mind was already straying to Taryn Murphy. She couldn't avoid seeing her. Maybe it was just a phase. Maybe the break will have had the desired effect. *You'll look at her and there will be no feelings.*

Jace strolled down the hallway to Taryn's door and peeped in. Taryn was staring at her computer, lost in thought. *You are a chicken shit, just knock!* Jace tapped lightly on the doorframe. "Hey there." Taryn turned to her. Jace's heart fluttered. *So much for that theory!* "How are you?"

Taryn tried not to grin at the sight of Jace. She realized how much she'd missed her company. "I'm okay. How are you?" Her heart lurched when she saw Jace's eyes fix on her neck. Her face hardened instantly. Embarrassed, she put her hand over the bite and tried to continue speaking as if everything was normal. "How was the vacation?"

Jace couldn't tear her eyes away from Taryn's neck, from the ugly mark that reminded her that Taryn was involved with someone else. *Breathe. She's an adult. She's a student and your employee. Suck it up. Smile and make nice. Then you can go and crawl into your hole, and maybe hibernate for the rest of the year.* She forced a smile but she knew her voice sounded tight and cold. "It was good. I need you to brief Cory about what's been happening since orientation."

Taryn hadn't expected the icy response. *I feel like I'm back in the first week. What happened to our friendship?* "I did that this morning before Anne came in."

Jace focused on the wall behind Taryn's head. "Good. Well now that she's here, you two can pool your ideas and come up with some support programs to match the criteria we've identified." She started to leave, then decided against it, and turned back. "Taryn, as your supervisor I need to say something. What you do in your own time is none of my business, but if it affects your job, or makes the Center appear less than professional, then it becomes my concern."

"It won't happen again," Taryn said, feeling her cheeks flame.

"It shouldn't have happened at all," Jace continued lecturing her as if she couldn't be trusted to know what was appropriate and what wasn't. "To be honest I have never had to deal with this issue, most graduates and staff members have matured beyond teenage displays of affection."

Taryn stifled the defensive retort that trembled on her lips. "I understand." She could hear her voice shaking and wanted desperately for the conversation to be over. Unable to stop herself, she blurted, "Look, if you want to sack me because I have sex, just do it. Okay?"

Jace's stomach clenched. "I do not want to sack you, Taryn. I am just as unhappy having this conversation as you are, trust me. But I have no choice. A love bite, hickey, or whatever you want to call it, is not okay to flaunt at work. But there are no students in at the moment, so I'm willing to let it pass this time."

She paused. *This is the reason you do not become friends with the subordinates! It makes doing your job harder than it should be!* Hating what she was about to say, she stared straight into Taryn's soulful blue eyes. "But if you come to work with a mark on your neck like that again, I'll have to send you home with a written warning."

Taryn flinched at the disdain in Jace's expression. She could hardly believe the woman talking now was the same one who'd been so gentle and supportive the night she'd spoken to her uncle in the parking lot at Chuck E Cheese's. Not wanting to believe their budding friendship meant so little to her boss, she felt herself tuning out as Jace kept talking,

"As a potential education leader, you need to understand that employees will look to you to make the rules and keep them. A good manager leads by example."

Taryn could only stare after Jace as she stalked from the office. She supposed she'd deserved the telling off, but Jace's reaction seemed over the top. Taryn banged her head on her desk. *Why me? Marti, you have so much to answer for later!* Taryn wanted to run into Jace's office and vent her temper, but it was Marti she needed to shout at, not Jace. This thought didn't make her feel any better.

"Are you okay?" Cory asked as she watched Taryn bang her head one more time on the desk. "You could lose valuable brain cells doing that!"

"The boss just chewed me a new asshole but I'll recover. Did you meet her?" Taryn indicated the spare chair and Cory sat down.

"Yes. I had a strange déjà vu when I did. She looks so much like Dylan it's spooky! Do you have a warehouse in

Massachusetts that churns out tall, dark, and gorgeous women?"

Taryn laughed. Some humor was just what she needed to help alleviate her down mood. "Too funny! I wish! So you think the boss is gorgeous, huh? You don't waste any time!"

Cory blushed, "What can I say? She looks so much like Dylan that I have to go with the gorgeous comment, but I'm a one-woman lady!"

Taryn grinned. She liked Cory's straight forwardness and humor. "She definitely catches the eye. Marti made similar comments to me. I must be immune to tall, black haired, blue eyed women, because she's just the boss to me."

"Keep telling yourself that, mate!" Cory chuckled. "So your girlfriend has met her? No wonder you have a bite mark. She's marking her property."

"What?"

Cory hesitated, as she saw Taryn's face change instantaneously. "I'm kidding. Dylan says I have to learn when to stop the humor."

"I'm not mad," Taryn smiled at Cory but her mind was racing.

Marti had known Jace was returning and she'd made comments now and again about Jace liking Taryn. *She wouldn't have bitten me on purpose? She wouldn't be that mean, would she?* Taryn made a mental note to talk to her about it as soon as she got home.

TARYN HEARD THE screen door open, but she kept her eyes on the yard and took a slow sip of her beer. It was still early, and the August sky was bright, beautiful, and clear, but the lovely evening did nothing for her. She had no desire to talk to anyone. The events of the day replayed over and over in her mind. She was mad at the world and her mood darkened. Memories of Patrick filled her head. She had his temper. She could feel it boiling inside her. Stirring inside her soul; swirling and swelling.

Taryn clenched her teeth, and counted to ten. She didn't want to be like him. She didn't want to hurt people. She flexed her hand, clenching it into a fist. *You're not him! Control your anger. Breathe, Taryn. Focus.* Taryn tried to center on a calming thought.

"Taryn, you're home early!" Marti approached Taryn to kiss her hello, then halted when there was no sign that Taryn had heard her. She'd seen her girlfriend in moods but her face had never looked like this. Nervously, Marti spoke again. "You're scaring me. I asked if you were okay." Still there was no answer. Marti could see the tension in Taryn's shoulders. "Taryn? What's happened? Talk to me. Did you have a bad day? How was work?"

Taryn turned, a fire burning in her eyes. "How the fuck do you think work went? I have a bite the size of a fist on my neck!" Taryn held up her clenched fist to emphasize her words. There was no affection in her expression. "I was the butt of every joke."

"I'm sorry, honey. I lost control and you had a crappy day." Marti touched Taryn's shoulder and that seemed to bring Taryn present a little. As her expression softened, Marti asked, "What else happened? You're home earlier than usual."

Taryn shrugged. The anger had disappeared just like the wind from a ship's sail. She'd battled with her inner demon and won. "Work sucked. Shitty students that don't know I'm trying to save their ass gave me grief on the phone. I'm home early because I was just over it."

"All because of the bite?"

"Well, Jace ripped me a new asshole for that one. She gave me a dressing down and made me feel like a five year old." Taryn saw a fleeting smirk appear on Marti's face, and Cory's words came back to her. *No, Marti wouldn't have done it on purpose. She just wouldn't have!*

"So, Jace isn't talking to you?" Marti asked.

Taryn hesitated. Watching Marti carefully, she lied, "Nothing like that." *Two can play games, Marti.* "She had to give me the usual talk because I broke staff policy, but then she was fine. We even laughed about it, later." She could tell this news disturbed Marti. Unconsciously, her girlfriend's face twitched and her lips scrunched up.

"Good. I was worried," Marti said without conviction. "How was the new girl?"

"Great. I think we're going to get on wonderfully. I think I really lucked out. She's gay *and* cute."

Taryn seemed rather too enthusiastic for Marti's liking. "Have you eaten?"

Marti's sudden change of topic made Taryn smile, the first smile of the evening. "No. I'll grab something later. I just want to be on my own, right now. I have some issues that I need to sort out."

Marti was disappointed. She hated it when Taryn pushed her away. Tentatively, she offered, "Can I help?"

"No."

That one word sent Marti back into the house. Tears of

rejection ran down her cheeks. This wasn't how it was supposed to be. Taryn was supposed to love her and open up to her, not push her away and make her feel discarded. She slammed the screen door and turned to watch Taryn. Her lover never flinched, never even turned back.

Chapter
Seven

JACE'S CLOTHES STUCK to her. The short walk from the car to the building was disgusting. The humidity was making her perspire profusely and she could feel a small bead trickle down the dip in her back. She looked at the flagpole, not a breeze in sight. She had arrived the normal time for work but had been called to a meeting at the administration block. The walk across campus was normally nice but Jace had chosen to take her car, it had one thing she desperately needed: air conditioning.

Jace entered the building and sniffed. She could smell burning. The smell seemed to get stronger as she passed the elevators and she increased her speed. When she reached the front desk, she asked, "Hey, Brenda. Can you smell anything?"

Brenda sniffed the air. "Something fishy?"

Jace nodded. "Burning?"

Before either of them could confer and investigate further, Anne entered the lobby and announced, "We're being evacuated."

"What?" Jace leaned her tall frame against the doorframe.

"The air conditioning is broken," Anne said. "The maintenance guy's giving everyone thirty minutes and then he's locking the doors because there's some problem with air quality. The parts won't be in until later so we get to go home early."

"That's great." Brenda promptly dropped the file she was holding and reached for her bag. "I'm off to Filenes. They're having a one day sale. You know me, never one to miss a bargain. I'm leaving before maintenance change their mind!"

Jace looked at her watch. It was nearly lunchtime. Bad enough she was starting the day so late without losing hours of work. "I have too much to do," she told Anne. "I'm going to stay and start clearing the backlog from vacation."

"But they're locking up."

"I can stay in the computer lab. It has its own air supply."

Jace saw the usual stubborn expression cross Anne's face.

"Well, if you're staying, then so will I."

"No," Jace insisted. "Go home, Anne. Spend some time with the kids."

"The kids are with their grandparents. Is your work urgent?" Anne saw the lines of concentration on Jace's face and knew she was mentally going through her 'to-do' list.

Jace shook her head. "Not urgent, just time consuming. Taryn and Cory have cut some of it down. They seem to work well together. It's hard to believe they only met yesterday." Jace instantly felt the gnawing sensation she'd come to associate with Taryn.

Impulsively, Anne grabbed her pocket book. "I have an idea. Let's go out somewhere. Make a day of it. I need to talk to someone, and I feel like letting my hair down."

Jace grinned. "That sounds dangerous, Weston. Problems on the home front?"

"When isn't there, lately? So will you come out with me? It's a beautiful day. Maybe, we could drive to Sakonnet."

"What's out there?" Jace was interested. She had a lot on her mind, too. Maybe it was time to talk to Anne about some things.

"A vineyard. They do wine testing and have a pretty view. Please, I've been meaning to go back and get a few bottles of wine. Humor an old lady."

"Okay. I'll meet you up at the front in five minutes. Will you tell Taryn and Cory they can go home?"

"Sure. I'll see you at the elevators."

With a resigned half-smile, Jace went to her office to collect a few folders and email addresses. She could work from home, later.

THE FOUR WOMEN walked to the parking lot together. Jace noticed a distance between Taryn and Anne. *Unusual. They're generally chatting about something.* She concluded that something must have happened in their delicate family dynamic, something less than ideal for working relationships. Wondering whether she should intervene or leave well alone, she glanced sideways at Anne and caught a hurt expression in her eyes that made her mind up. *You are going to owe me big time, Weston.*

"So," Jace asked innocently. "What do you guys have planned for the rest of the day?"

Taryn shrugged. "Not much. What about you?" On the inside, Taryn was happy that Jace had begun the conversation. The silence leaving the building had been awkward.

"Anne is leading me astray!"

Surprised by the light-hearted response, Taryn gazed for a moment too long at Jace's twinkling blue eyes. The mischievous grin that Jace usually hid so well had surfaced and Taryn was reminded of the carefree woman she'd started forming a friendship with before things got so complicated. She'd missed this side of Jace.

Playing along, she said, "Astray, huh? Well I don't see you kicking and screaming. Where are you going?"

"Wine tasting!" Jace smirked. "The perfect way to spend a working day."

Taryn could just picture her straight-laced aunt and her 'needs-to-get-out-more' boss drunk. "Are you sure it's safe to let you two loose on your own?"

"I've never been wine tasting," Cory said. "But I've seen it on the television. Most of the time the people end up spitting the wine into a bucket."

"Where's the fun in that?" Taryn asked.

"Why don't you both join us?" Jace invited. "We could kill two birds with one stone. We'll choose a designated driver and Cory can attend her first wine testing. We'll show the British how the Americans do a wine tasting. What do you think, Anne?"

Anne was a little flustered. The last thing she'd expected from her reserved boss was this. She cast a quick glance at Taryn and when her niece didn't look away, Anne took this as a good sign. "Sure. The more the merrier, if the girls want to come?"

"Sounds like a brilliant plan." Cory enthused, turning her head to Taryn and shielding her sea-green eyes from the glare of the sun. The rays emphasizing the natural blonde highlights in her hair.

Taryn grinned. "That sounded so British. Okay, who's driving?"

All four stood silently in the parking lot. "I'd offer," Cory said. "But it would be a drive of a lifetime for the rest of you! I'm not quite oriented to driving on the right side, yet."

"Mine wouldn't be comfortable for four people." Taryn added.

"We could take the Jeep," Jace glanced across at her vehicle.

"I'll drive." Anne said. "The RAV has more space. And it was my idea."

Jace frowned, clearly trying to think through all the practical logistics. "Maybe we should take two vehicles. What if Cory and Taryn want to leave sooner and —"

"If we keep this up they'll be harvesting the grapes by the

time we get there," Anne said. "We're taking the RAV. Get in, everybody."

"IT'S BEAUTIFUL!" CORY commented as she viewed the landscape in front of her.

Sakonnet Vineyard was situated outside of Newport, Rhode Island in the tiny village of Little Compton. The small winery was nestled on beautifully manicured grounds. As they drove slowly down the winding gravel driveway, Cory regarded the breathtaking views of rolling fields filled with carefully tended vines and the occasional cow. She had to stifle a gasp when the magnificent view of the glittering reservoir came into view. They pulled into a parking space in front of a red wooden barn style building.

"This way." Anne led the way to the reception area.

The rustic wine store was deceptively large. The walls were lined with shelves stacked with racks and racks of wine bottles. In the center of the room, a square wooden wine tasting bar was manned by two servers. Within this building the old world met the new with modern day utensils lying side by side with the ancient tools of the trade. Only a few customers perused the contents of the shop and the foursome had little trouble being tended to.

An hour later, they had tried various selections and agreed on a Sauvignon Blanc and a Merlot to take out into the garden. Anne ordered two bottles, some baguettes, and three flavors of goat's cheese and they strolled out the French doors and found a table.

The garden area was large. There were walkways and benches scattered amongst the brightly, colored flowers. Once settled at a table, Anne played hostess and poured wine for everyone. She made sure her glass held only half of what everyone else's held. She knew her limit when it came to wine.

They chatted for a while, but although they were all quite relaxed, Anne detected a distance in Taryn every time their eyes met. Eventually, weary of her niece's moodiness, she stood up and said, "I think I'll stretch my legs."

"Would you like company?" Jace also stood. She had seen a few of the glances Anne and Taryn exchanged and was baffled by the tension between them. To Cory and Taryn, she said, "You two won't mind if we leave you here with the wine all to yourselves, will you?"

"Not at all," Cory said cheerfully. "I can pick Taryn's brain about work."

As Anne and Jace walk away into the flower-lined pathway,

Cory tried making small talk with Taryn. When the answers she got were monosyllabic, she sighed aloud. "Should I leave you alone?"

"No. I'm sorry." Taryn gave her an apologetic half-smile. "I'm really not making a good impression with you, am I? Be honest!"

Cory took a sip of wine and said, "I would have to say if I was trying to date you, I'd be out of the door by now. But as I'm hoping we're going to be friends, I'm offering a friendly ear." Cory's green eyes showed a path straight to her soul, and what Taryn saw there was compassion and honesty.

"It's complicated."

Cory laughed. "Taryn, I know complicated very well. You could call it my second cousin. How about I tell you my story? Then you can see whether I'll understand." Taryn seemed interested in the suggestion. "To cut a long story very short. I told you Dylan and I met online. What I didn't say was that we were both in long term steady relationships."

Surprise widened Taryn's eyes. "Really?"

"Yes. It gets juicier. I was married."

"Married? No way, you're so..."

"Dykish? Gay?"

Taryn blushed. "I'm sorry. Not dykish. You're just so out. I mean my gaydar pinged the moment you walked in, and I wasn't surprised when you told me you had a girlfriend. I mean you're pretty in a cute way, and your clothing is just boyish. I know, I'm babbling. Carry on."

"I had dated a woman in college, but that didn't go anywhere. When I left college, I was celibate for two years, then I met Sam and we fell in love. Things were never quite right between us and I didn't have the heart to admit it. Anyway to cut a long story short I met Dylan online she was in a similar stale relationship and a friendship grew, very quickly. We just seemed connected. It's hard to explain. Even with the physical distance between us, I knew what she was thinking and feeling. I ended things with Sam, and Dylan split up with her girlfriend. I came out here for a visit at Easter, applied for college, and got accepted as a quick admit. It's been a difficult few months."

"Wow. It must have been hell," Taryn empathized.

"It wasn't exactly a picnic but I'm with Dylan, so it's been worth it." Cory took a large gulp of wine. "I needed that! So now that you know some of my secrets, what's your story? You seem like a really nice person, so what's up with you and Anne? In fact, all three of you."

"What do you mean?"

Cory realized she was going to have to pull the information out of Taryn. "Yesterday, Anne and you were acting like best mates. Today you can barely talk to each other. Anne's been fine around me, so it isn't just Anne in a bad mood. I think I've worked it out though."

Taryn was curious. "You have?"

Cory nodded as she sipped her wine. "I may be totally wrong but I think you're jealous of Jace."

Taryn spat her wine out. "What? I'm sorry I didn't mean to cover you. You took me by surprise. Jace?"

"I knew I was right. You're jealous that Jace and Anne are together. I saw your face when they were talking about their vacation. Do you fancy Anne or something?"

Taryn tried to swallow her wine before laughing but ended up choking instead. She spluttered and coughed. Cory tried to help her out. She gently patted Taryn's back.

"Too funny!" Taryn gasped. "Wait until Anne and I are talking again! She'll have a blast over this one!" Catching Cory's puzzled expression, she explained, "Anne's my aunt."

"Is that it? I'm disappointed. I expected deep, dark secrets and a lot of passion." Cory's teasing stopped when she saw the glare in Taryn's eyes. "Sorry. Did I put my foot in my mouth."

Taryn waved a hand. "No, I'm the one who should be sorry. I guess I'm over-sensitive. You're right. I think I am jealous. There's nothing going on between Jace and Anne. They're just close friends. But my aunt and I used to be like sisters. I lived with her, growing up, then I went to Ireland, and when I came back things had changed. I miss the closeness, I suppose."

Cory looked embarrassed. "Looks like I misread everything. Is Jace even gay?"

"No." When Taryn saw the doubtful look on Cory's face, she added. "I don't think she is. Why?"

"The way she looks at you."

Again, Taryn spluttered her drink across the table. "You're going to have to warn me next time. I'm wasting precious wine! Marti's been telling me the same thing. We went out a few weeks ago with Anne and her kids, and Jace. It was Marti's first time meeting everyone, and she decided there was something going on with me and Jace."

Taryn shook her head, trying to think it over objectively. Jace had barely spoken to her in weeks. Marti was just being jealous and Cory probably read too many romances. They were both reading far too much into Jace's manner.

"What do you think of her?" Cory asked.

"She's okay."

"That's an understatement. You're not attracted to her?"

Taryn shrugged her shoulders. "She's my boss and I'm a student. Plus I'm living with someone else."

Cory sipped her wine. "It never stopped anyone before."

"Touché."

They slipped into silence, sipping their wine and gazing into the gardens. Taryn's mind kept replaying the conversation. Was it possible Jace was interested in her? Taryn couldn't see it at all. Who knew if she was even a lesbian? She thought about Marti and felt a pang of guilt. She was probably jealous of Jace because she felt insecure in their relationship. It couldn't help that Taryn kept shutting her out. Why was it so difficult for them? *Do I love her?*

She put her wineglass down , and asked Cory, "How did you know Dylan was the one for you?"

Cory's eyes roamed the rolling vineyards for a few seconds, then she said, "She just completed me. It's hard to explain. I understood her, and she me. There's nothing we can't talk about. You hear the songs about giving it all up for love. I did just that. Not just material things. That's easy. I broke down all my walls, I swallowed my fears, opened my heart, and let her in. Every day it gets stronger. That's how I know what we have is love."

"That simple, huh?" Taryn nudged her and they both laughed. "Thanks, Cory. Here's to friendship." Taryn lifted her glass to Cory's.

"I GUESS WE should go back." Anne pulled her hands through her hair. The air was cooler now. The wind had picked up slightly, making the hot day bearable. She and Jace were sitting on one of the benches that sporadically lined the path.

"No let's stay a little longer," Jace said. "It's kind of hard to relax when the atmosphere between Taryn and you is so hostile today. What happened? Was it Patrick?"

"Indirectly, yes. My mouth ran away with me."

"Want to talk about it?"

"I'm not sure if there's any point. I'm just worn-out from stepping lightly around Patrick and Taryn. Ricky is going through a rough time at school. He's not like Josie. He's very sensitive and naïve. The kids tease him and when he comes home, Patrick does the same. We've tried to stop him, and last night Ricky must have said something to Taryn because she ripped into me. She thinks I'm being unfair to the kids by keeping them in the same house as Patrick. I feel like we go around in circles. Always the same arguments..." Anne paused. "I hate myself for thinking this, but at times I wish she'd stayed away."

"Why? It was your idea to hire her," Jace asked.

"I know. I thought things would be different. I guess I was living in a dream world. I thought she would come back stronger and finally stand up to Patrick. She is stronger but it's not a positive energy. She keeps things locked inside, like you..." Anne sighed. "It's not healthy. Patrick will never change. He's bitter and resentful. But I fear that Taryn is becoming like him. She's so stubborn. I know she thinks talking about her fears is a sign of weakness..."

"But she has someone. She must talk to Marti."

"No. That night we went out together...Marti was asking all kinds of questions. About Taryn's mother and Taryn's childhood. She doesn't know anything. She didn't even know about Patrick. It worries me. Taryn's going to miss out on so much love because she's afraid to open her heart."

"Maybe, she's happy," Jace said. "Not everyone needs to be in love."

"Bullshit! I'm sorry, but everyone needs to be wanted and to feel love. Taryn desperately wanted her father's love. I'm sure it hurts everyday. She displays typical abandonment issues. She's distant, controlling, won't let anyone in..."Anne hesitated. She knew from past experience that Jace's past was a closed subject, but she wanted her friend to know they could talk about it any time she was ready. "You know, don't you?"

"Know what?"

"What Taryn feels like inside. I can see it in your eyes."

Jace turned her head away. "It's Taryn's life, Anne. She's a big girl."

"I know I just want my family to be happy." Anne touched Jace's arm and said pointedly, "I want *all* my family to be happy."

"I *am* happy."

"And I'm the President of the United States. Jace, you know I love you?"

"I love you, too, Anne. Should we head back?"

"Not so fast. Jace Xanthos, you're impossible. I spill my heart out to you on a regular basis and you're always there for me. It's been obvious since Florida that you have something on your mind, but here we are, talking about my family dramas."

Jace shook her head. *Tell her. Swallow your pride and open up. She's your best friend.* With difficulty, she said, "Okay, since you're going to wring it out of me. I've been having feelings for someone. "

"Oh my god...you're in love?"

"Shush...I don't think they heard you in Massachusetts. I didn't say I was in love."

Anne tried to calm down. Jace had never willingly discussed relationships with her. "You've met someone?"

Jace felt like a teenager. "I don't know."

Anne was confused. "You don't know. You've either met someone or you haven't?"

"There is someone. But I'm not sure about the feelings."

"Compare it to previous relationships. Is this person special?" Anne was trying to be patient.

Jace wriggled in her seat. "Umm...that's the problem...I haven't had a previous relationship."

"Okay, so you haven't had anything serious. But you must have been with people, guys... Does this feel more...intense?"

Jace couldn't hold Anne's eye contact anymore. She dropped her head into her hands and whispered. "Anne. I'm telling you there's never been anyone."

"Oh... Shit... Wow..." Anne was lost for what to say. "But...you're thirty five."

Jace remained bent over, studying the ground. Her secret was finally out. She could hear Anne stuttering above her.

"You're a virgin? I'm sorry, I know I'm being an idiot. No one has ever shocked me this much. I mean...I'm just surprised...you're so sexual."

Jace laughed and the atmosphere between them relaxed. "I'm what?"

"Sexual. I don't know, you just ooze sexuality. You're beautiful, you have a body to die for, you're intelligent, and have a great sense of humor. Everything your average everyday guy is looking for. Have you dated?"

Jace shook her head. "I was raised by strict Orthodox Greeks and I was different to the other kids. Kinda makes it hard to fit in. I was so busy trying to make sure I could make something of myself, I never had time to date. I just seemed to bypass all that and then I got really involved in my career."

Jace swallowed. She wouldn't cry. It wasn't in her nature. She tried not to think about the unexplored parts of life and self. The truth was, most of the time she never felt anything was lacking. It was only recently that she'd become aware of a hollow feeling every time she saw people in happy pairs. She hadn't even thought of having a relationship until now.

"I don't know why I'm suddenly feeling like this," she told Anne. "Early mid-life crisis, maybe."

Anne rubbed Jace's back. She felt completely thrown, and not sure whether to end the conversation or press Jace for a little more. She had finally broken through Jace's barriers, and she didn't want her to build them back up. Finally her curiosity won out and she asked, "Who is it?"

Jace wouldn't look at her.

"Jace, talk to me, please."

Jace took a deep breath. "It's Taryn."

That one word silenced any questions Anne had wanted to ask. She let go of Jace's hand. Her head spun. The thought had never crossed her mind. She had pictured various male colleagues, but never Taryn. Seeing the torment in Jace's eyes, she tried to get over her shock, asking,. "You love, Taryn?"

"I'm not even close to thinking it's love. I don't know. She makes me feel things I haven't felt before."

"So, you've never felt like this for another woman?"

"I've never felt like this period."

"Are you gay?"

Jace shrugged. "I think I'm asexual." She saw Anne smile. "I don't know. I've never thought about it. I think I've always noticed women more than men, but I've never classified my feelings. I might be. My feelings may even be displaced."

"What do you mean?"

"This is embarrassing."

"Just tell me." Anne stroked Jace's back. "I'm not going anywhere. Talk to me."

"She has your eyes."

Anne nodded her encouragement. "Go on."

"That night at Chuck E. Cheese's, I held her and it just felt so right. For the first time in my life I wanted to kiss someone. So I'm wondering if maybe I like her because she's so much like you. I could just be transferring my feelings for you to Taryn."

Anne was briefly lost for words. She thought she understood what Jace was saying. She and Jace were very close, so perhaps there could even be some truth in what she was suggesting. "You've really analyzed this, haven't you?"

"I've had a lot of down time," Jace said dryly. "Marti made me nervous that night. I think she saw the way I looked at Taryn. I was jealous of their relationship, and I didn't hide it well enough. That's why I came down to Florida. I couldn't handle Taryn finding out."

"Now I understand why you went off about that lovebite," Anne mused aloud.

"It certainly reminded me that she's taken," Jace conceded with irony. "I think it's just a teenage crush. I'm obviously going through my adolescent years now. Call me a late bloomer!"

"What if it's not? Let me play devil's advocate for a moment. What if it's not a crush? What if you do like her? You can't have her, Jace."

Jace's shoulders slumped even further down. "I know. She's my employee, a student, and already with someone. I've tried to stay away, Anne, but it hurts, here." Jace pointed to her heart.

"You've definitely been hit by Cupid's arrow, my friend." Carefully, Anne asked, "Could you just be Taryn's friend?"

"I think so."

Anne was silent for a few seconds trying to think of how to word her thoughts. "Jace, Taryn has a lot of baggage. Even if circumstances were different, I think it would be unhealthy for you two to be in a relationship. You both need to open up more. Trust people. Learn to love. But I think you could have a great friendship. She needs someone to talk to, Jace. Be that friend. Get to know her better, then you'll get your answers."

Jace nodded. "You're not angry with me?"

"I love you. I love Taryn. You two are my best friends. If circumstances were different I'd be over the moon to see you together." She glanced at her watch. "We should walk back before the girls drink all the wine."

Jace stood up and linked arms with her. "Anne...what I just told you...it's a secret, right?"

"Of course."

"Even from Bill?"

"Definitely from Bill. I wouldn't want to ruin his image of you!" Anne sniggered.

"What image?" Jace laughed nervously.

"He has two images of you. His frequent fantasy is that you have hordes of men chasing you. In the second fantasy he thinks you're hopelessly in love...with me." Anne blushed.

"No way!" Jace blathered. "I mean 'no way' to his dreams of men chasing me, not to my being in love with you. I mean I am in love with you. I..."

"Jace, you love me. You are not *in* love with me. There's a difference." She could see the blonde heads of Taryn and Cory in the distance. "This conversation is not over, Jace. We'll continue at a later date, I promise. But I will take your little secret to the grave, my friend."

"Thank you, Anne. I feel much better. Let's go and have some fun!"

Chapter
Eight

THE DRIVE BACK to Waterbridge was relaxed. They hadn't even pulled onto the highway before Cory started to fall asleep. Taryn had too many things going through her head to sleep. She closed her eyes to cut out the image of Jace. She had been analyzing her feelings for her boss since Cory's observations. She liked Jace. The tall woman was definitely good looking in an androgynous way. It was Jace's personality that confused her. Some days she blew hot and others cold. Taryn had an undeniable attraction toward the older woman, but she didn't think it went too deep. She had Marti to think about.

She opened her eyes and caught bright, blue eyes staring back at her.

Look away! Smile! Do something you idiot! Stop staring! Jace's inner voice was screaming at her. She had pulled the visor down to shield her eyes from the bright, evening sun, and the mirror reflected Taryn's image. Like a moth to a flame, Jace was drawn to that image deep, brown eyes held hers. Neither woman blinked. Jace could feel a fuzzy feeling in her tummy. It tingled its way down towards the core of her body.

She's beautiful. Jace was relieved when Taryn closed her eyes. She used this time to reflect on her conversation with Anne. *Can I be her friend? Or do I want more?* She didn't think she could ever just be a friend to Taryn. Even now she wanted to be closer to Taryn. The urge to reach out and touch the mirror — touch the image of Taryn — was becoming irresistible and she hastily flipped the visor up removing the temptation.

The comfortable silence in the car allowed her to think about her past. About her life before America. She reminisced about the small island, of her birth. Agistri, a two-hour boat ride from Athens. She thought how her early childhood mirrored Taryn's in many respects. Her father had always wanted a large family of boys who would carry on the family business of fishing. Having a daughter and only two sons had upset him immensely, and his disdain for Jace increased as she grew, especially as there was little family resemblance.

By the time she was ten, he refused to accept her as his own, and had become violent toward her mother, constantly asking what man she had slept with while he was away working. He never believed she hadn't been unfaithful. Jace's maternal grandparents had died, and her mother's sister had left the island to live in America. When Jace was eleven her mother had sent her away, afraid she would be hurt by her father if she remained.

Jace could feel the anger stirring inside: anger and resentment of a different life and lack of understanding. She turned her head to stare at the monotony of the passing towns and countryside. Wanting to remember the past but not feel the pain. An impossible task.

He should have just listened to my mother and taken her love, trust, and truth as her word. Is this why I never got close to people?

Jace closed her eyes, and summoned up a picture of her mother. *You were so beautiful, Mitera,* she silently whispered to her mother's angel. Jace swallowed the lump in her throat. She desperately wanted to cry and be held, just like her mother would do for her.

WHEN THEY ARRIVED back at the College, Anne knew, without asking, that Taryn would not accept a lift from her. So she offered Cory a lift and casually suggested Jace take Taryn.

Taryn shuffled her feet and wrapped her arms round her chilled body. She wanted to give her aunt a hug, but she had the impression Anne was out of patience with her today. "I'm fine. I don't need a ride." Taryn headed toward her car.

"Taryn, wait." Jace struggled to sound normal. "I'd feel better if you would let me take you home. I only had two small glasses of wine. Please."

Taryn was surprised by the offer. "Are you sure you're not going out of your way?"

"Your street is on my way. I could pick you up tomorrow morning. I know you're not drunk but alcohol can still have an effect on the body." Jace pointed toward the Jeep.

Taryn told herself not to read anything into this. Jace was just being a responsible adult. Thanking her politely, she walked to the Jeep and climbed into the passenger seat.

The short drive home was pleasant, with the conversation focused on the trip down to Sakonnet.

When Jace pulled up to Taryn's house, she realized she didn't want the young woman to leave. She also wanted to help Anne out. "Nice house," she remarked, buying some time.

"It's Marti's house." Taryn paused trying to think of things to say to prolong the conversation. "Thanks for the ride. What time in the morning?"

Jace thought about it. She usually ran in the morning. "I could pick you up at seven-thirty, unless you want to go in later?"

"Sounds good to me." As Taryn grabbed the car handle, Jace placed her hand on Taryn's other arm.

"Taryn, this is none of my business. Well, it is in a way. Talk to Anne."

Taryn turned to Jace, a curious expression on her face. "What did she say?"

Jace shrugged, "Not a lot. Just that you'd argued and she upset you."

Taryn remained motionless. "That's right! She upset me. She should talk to me."

Jace tentatively rubbed Taryn's arm. She needed contact with the young woman. "Taryn, take it from an experienced sulker, she's waiting for you to make the first move. She's worried she'll make it worse. You and I, we're very much alike. And I know your aunt very well. Please...for me?"

Taryn sighed. She knew Jace was right. "No promises, but I'll try."

"SO THAT'S YOUR uncle's mother?" Marti asked inquisitively as she drank from her soda can.

"Yes. There aren't as many cousins here this year. They all have partners and they tend to switch venues." Taryn answered, scanning the family members around her. She couldn't believe that the summer vacation was nearly over. August had been a hectic, but fun month. The weather was still gorgeous and Taryn was enjoying soaking up the last few rays of summer sun. Fall was just around the corner.

She had been reluctant to attend the Weston's Labor Day cookout, but Anne had sent a formal invitation, which Marti had promptly replied to. Taryn had sulked for a few days until she'd seen the joy on Anne's face when her aunt had mentioned the subject. Taryn hadn't quite managed to clear the air between Anne and herself. At work they were always polite to each other. When she tutored Ricky, Taryn would leave as soon as she was finished, telling her aunt she had barbecues or outings with Marti.

Overall, Taryn had been extremely relieved when Anne told her that Patrick would be spending Labor Day weekend visiting her grandparents in Florida.

"You seem miles away!" Marti commented. "Do you want a drink? I'll grab the sunscreen as well. You're burning a little."

Taryn looked at her shoulders as she dangled her legs over the edge of the pool. She adjusted the straps of her two-piece swimsuit, looking for telltale signs of red, and finding none. "Marti, not everyone is as susceptible to the sun as you are. I guess the build in tan is the only thing I can thank my father for. He and Anne both got that instead of red hair and freckles." As soon as the words were out of her mouth, she realized that Marti would pick up on the slip.

Marti frowned, her eyes flicking around the pool area. Anne and Jace were in the shallow end playing with the children. Bill was cooking at the grill, no doubt discussing with his father, the baseball season and the bad luck the Red Sox were having. "Am I missing something?" she asked. "Are you saying Anne is related to your father?"

Taryn knew Marti would find out from someone. The kids all knew Patrick was Taryn's father. She quietly answered the question. "My father is Anne's brother."

Frustrated, Marti threw her hands into the air. "Well, I'm always the last to know. Why all the secrecy? Is he here?" She looked round furtively, trying to remember names and faces. "Is he coming..." She stopped mid-sentence, and her voice turned softer when she realized there could be another reason why he wasn't there. "I'm sorry, he isn't dead, is he?"

No such luck. Taryn raised her sunglasses and glared at Marti. "No. Unfortunately, he's very much alive. Patrick is spending time in Florida with my grandparents. We don't get on. End of story! Weren't you getting a drink?"

Marti registered the hate in Taryn's eyes. and the anger emanating from her. It scared her. "Yeah...I'm just going. Do you want something?" She tried to halt the tears but she could feel them welling.

Taryn was lost in her own world. She didn't reply to Marti, or see her retreat hastily to the house. Memories of Labor Day's long gone were replaying over and over in her mind. She was jolted out of her nightmares by a gentle hand on her leg. She looked down at the very tanned hand and wet dark hairs that lined the toned arm. Her eyes traveled up the appendage until she met concerned crystal, blue eyes.

"Enjoying yourself?" Jace asked, as she placed a hand on the side of the pool to steady herself. Although she'd been playing with Tom, her eyes had rarely left Taryn. After seeing Marti run into the house, she'd excused herself from the fun and games.

"Not really." Taryn replied honestly.

"I didn't think so. Is Marti okay? I saw her leave pretty hastily."

Taryn looked in the direction of the house. "She's fine. She just has a jerk for a girlfriend, that's all." When she felt Jace squeeze her leg a little, Taryn continued. "She knows I hate family occasions and she purposely replied to the invite without checking with me."

"Oh. That explains it. Anne was amazed since it seems you still haven't forgiven her over the quarrel about Patrick." Jace paused. She could sense Taryn's dark mood, but she couldn't resist asking, "I thought you were going to talk to her?"

Taryn thought back to the conversation the two had had in the car all those weeks ago. "I haven't had the time or opportunity." She knew it was a weak argument.

" Yes, it must be really hard to find time when you only see her for eight hours a day." Jace hadn't meant the comment to sound as sarcastic as it had.

"That's not fair," Taryn protested vehemently. "You were the one who didn't want our personal relationship to interfere with our working relationship." She stopped to think things over. Quietly she added, "It hasn't, has it?"

Jace ran her fingers through her curly wet hair and slid her sunglasses back on. "No. I can't fault your work, Taryn. But there is still an atmosphere between you and Anne. She tells me you haven't been around the house much." Jace realized her hand was still resting on Taryn's thigh. Reluctantly she moved it away, and levered herself out of the water to sit in the same spot Marti had just vacated.

Taryn watched Jace's body as she slid out of the pool. Drips of water cascaded off the woman's tanned back and torso. The one-piece suit hid nothing. Taryn could see the slight curve of Jace's small breasts and the tiny paunch that appeared as the woman sat next to her. Jace's legs seemed to go on forever, not surprising for a woman over six feet tall. She averted her eyes and returned to the conversation, pleased to see that Jace hadn't noticed her appraisal. "I go to the house. I tutor Ricky just like I said I would."

"And you leave straight after. Anne's not stupid, Taryn, and she is too scared of losing you to say anything." Jace tried not to sound as irritated as she felt. Taryn's self-centered attitude was getting on her nerves.

"I'm here, aren't I?" Taryn smugly held Jace's gaze.

"Only because your girlfriend sent the RSVP back!"

Taryn sighed. Not for the first time she wished she had just told Marti to come by herself if she was so keen. She stared down at Jace's thighs, momentarily distracted by her proximity. She really was beautiful. Jace was talking, but she was only half-listening. She tuned in again just in time to be lectured.

"You're so wrapped up in yourself you don't know what she's been through with Patrick this month."

"What?" Taryn felt vaguely ashamed that her boss seemed to know more about the Weston family dramas than she did, herself. "What's he done now?"

"Other than verbally abusing Anne every time she asks him to be nice to Ricky and to you?"

Taryn winced and lowered her eyes.

"To cut a long story short, he was drunk on a job the other week and the foreman gave him a warning," Jace said with an edge of impatience that made it clear she thought Taryn was behaving badly. "Anne thinks he's gambling, as well. He didn't have any money to pay his part of the household bills. He gave an excuse about a late paycheck, but Anne didn't buy it. That's why she bought him a ticket to Florida and gave him some money to stay down there for a week. She's hoping your grandparents can help him."

"The bastard can't even pay for his own ticket!" Taryn spat out the words.

Jace took Taryn's hand and stroked the delicate fingers. "Anne would kill me if she thought I was telling you. But it's time you put yourself in her shoes for a minute. What would you do in her place?"

Taryn watched Anne playing with the kids at the other end of the pool. She looked more relaxed and happy than she had in ages. Huskily Taryn said, "Thanks for telling me, Jace. I promise I'll make things better."

Jace patted Taryn's hand. "I know you will..."

Taryn turned her head when she heard the back door slam and saw Marti sit on the deck steps.

Jace followed Taryn's eyes. She could sense Marti's anger. "Trouble?"

"Maybe," Taryn mumbled.

Jace squeezed Taryn's hand one more time and released it. "Talk to Anne. In that department, she's wiser than me!"

Taryn watched Jace dive smoothly back into the pool. Her body cut gracefully through the water and she surfaced behind Anne, who looked like she got a fright. Taryn wanted to follow. She felt safe around Jace but she knew she had to go and make peace with Marti. It had become a regular thing over the month. Any mention of Jace or Cory sent Marti into a jealous rage, and the two of them would argue. Taryn stood up, wrapped her towel around her waist, and adjusted her sunglasses. Smiling at a few of Bill's siblings that she passed along the way, she crossed the yard and sat down next to Marti.

"Hey," she said. When there was no response, she lowered her head to look into Marti's red-rimmed eyes, and put her arm around her. "Come here."

Marti turned into Taryn's embrace. "I don't understand what's going wrong. We never used to argue. I don't know why you don't talk to me. I'd listen, Taryn... I don't understand how you can talk to others and not me. Why don't you talk to me?" Marti swallowed the sob that she could feel climbing up her throat. The last thing she wanted to do was make a spectacle of herself in front of Taryn's family.

"I don't know." Taryn squeezed her lover. She had no real answer to the question. "Maybe, it's a butch thing?" She was pleased to hear a giggle come out of Marti.

"She was holding your hand." Marti said matter-of-factly.

"Who was?" Taryn continued to rub Marti's shoulder. She really didn't want a scene and could sense eyes facing their way.

"Jace."

"Marti, we've talked about this." Taryn didn't speak angrily. She took Marti's hand and gave her the same comfort Jace had just given her. "It meant nothing. I swear. She's only trying to help."

"She hardly says a word to me."

"I think the silence is mutual." Taryn looked over to the pool, even though Jace and Anne were wearing sunglasses, Taryn had a feeling all eyes were on them.

Marti laughed softly at the teasing remark and wiped her eyes. "I'm sorry. I'm being silly."

A tiny voice in the back of Taryn's mind disagreed, but she didn't want to think about that. Instead, she stood up and pulled Marti to her feet. "Come and play with the kids, and I promise I'll try harder. But you have to promise to stop being pushy, and leave out the jealous comments. I'm *your* girlfriend."

ANNE WAS RELIEVED to see Taryn holding Marti's hand as they crossed to the pool. "How are you doing with the friendship idea?" she asked Jace.

Jace wasn't shocked at the question. She'd expected Anne to bring the subject up sometime since the trip to Sakonnet. She shrugged. "I'm okay."

"You're good for her, Jace, and she looks up to you. So...do you still like her?"

"I guess so."

"You guess so?" Anne nearly choked on the drink she was sipping between times. She set the glass back on the tray at the side of the pool. "Is that it? After thirty five years you find someone who turns your head, and you *guess* you still like her?" Anne was beginning to see why the beautiful woman in front of her hadn't ever had a date. Sometimes she seemed so detached, and void of emotion.

"Well, either I have to like her or have nothing to do with her," Jace said. "Most of the time, it's fine I can keep the feelings at a distance. But occasionally, I just want to touch her...I can't help it. It's like I'm a magnet and she's metal, I get drawn towards her and I have to fight it. When that happens, I usually just leave the building or office, and it passes." Jace smiled sheepishly at Anne. "Stupid? Huh?"

"No. It's not stupid. It's very sensible." Anne seemed lost in thought, then she said, "I think you need some action. Maybe you should try dating?"

"I'm fine. My needs get met." She wiggled her eyebrows.

Anne blushed. "Oh...err...do you want something to eat?"

"Gotcha!" Jace grinned, a full wattage smile that made Anne splash some water at her. "That will teach you, Weston. Food sounds great!"

Chapter
Nine

TARYN STRETCHED OUT on the sofa. She was tired, and it was only Monday evening. The first week of work with students involved had gone well, except that she'd barely seen her supervisor since school had begun. Jace's office was nearly always empty, and she left notes on Taryn's desk, or sent her emails, letting her know what was required of her. On the odd occasion she glimpsed Jace, it was always in passing. Jace was either going to a meeting or coming back. She never seemed to have time to talk.

Taryn returned her attention to the show on the television. "Who's that character she's kissing? I'm confused. Wasn't she married to his father? Isn't that a little incestuous?"

Marti slapped her on the leg. "Stop being facetious. It's a soap opera. If you're not going to be quiet, I can watch this alone."

"I just don't understand what you see in it? Real life doesn't happen like that."

"That's why it's so entertaining. It takes you away from real life. Speaking of real life, my mother called and asked us to dinner tomorrow night. I accepted. You're not in class, are you?"

Taryn stopped moving her fingers. She was planning to meet up with Cory but after Marti's recent insecurities, she hadn't mentioned Cory or Jace at all, and the atmosphere at home had been more settled. She knew it was no way to live, but she hated conflict. "I can't make it. I have a group meeting," she lied.

"So soon? Classes have just begun."

"I'm in a group of over-achievers. We want to make sure our chapter presentation goes well. If I'd known earlier I could have changed it."

"You can meet me there. Your group meetings never last more than an hour."

Taryn pushed Marti's head gently off her lap. "The meeting is later. One person has a class, and we're hooking up afterward."

Marti sat upright and looked questioningly at Taryn. "Well, that's okay. We can meet here after work, go over to my mother's, and then I can drop you off at your meeting. I'll bring a book and wait for you."

Taryn fidgeted on the sofa. Now she knew why people didn't lie, it always came back to bite them on the ass. "I wasn't coming back. I was going to do some research. You know, make sure I had all the information, so I could contribute to the discussions." *You make a lousy liar! Since when have you been the star student? Suck it up and tell her! Ugh...and face her wrath! She'll jump to way too many conclusions! Stick with the story.*

Marti raised her eyebrows. It wasn't like Taryn to be so conscientious. But maybe she was trying to excel this semester. She seemed more settled and they hadn't been fighting so much. Marti felt a pang of guilt for pushing her. "It's okay," she said. "I'll call Mom. We can go another night."

"Good idea." Taryn rose from the couch. The whole subject was making her uneasy. Why did she feel like she was having some sordid affair? "I'm going to get another beer. Do you want one?"

Marti sensed the conversation was finished but something didn't feel right. Taryn could barely look at her. "No. I'm going to watch the rest of this in bed. Are you joining me?"

Taryn was at the door. She turned around, but couldn't look at Marti. When had things begun to go wrong? She shouldn't be lying to her girlfriend. "Not just yet. I thought I'd sit on the deck and check out the stars. I'll be in before you fall asleep." She knew she wouldn't. They hadn't gone to bed at the same time since Labor Day.

A FEW WEEKS later, Anne knocked lightly on Taryn's door. "Happy birthday!" She walked in and kissed her niece on the cheek. "I can't believe you're thirty-one! It seems like only yesterday when your mom had you. I remember how excited I was to have a baby in the house."

Taryn gave Anne a solemn smile. "I thought I'd be able to get through the day without people knowing it was my birthday! What did you do—put an ad on the notice board?"

It was Anne's turn to blush. "I may have mentioned it to one, two...or maybe a dozen people."

"I'm surprised you came in today. How did Tom make out at the doctor's?"

Anne sat in the chair opposite. "Better than expected. The doctor said he just has a cold. Bill and I were worried for a minute that he could have something more serious. The little guy has been up these past few nights crying."

"Poor baby. So, are you still coming tonight? I'll understand if you have to stay home with Tom."

"Wild horses couldn't keep me away. I've missed your last few birthdays." Anne looked at the bunch of roses sitting on Taryn's desk. "Nice flowers. I wish Bill was as romantic as Marti."

Taryn blushed. "They're not from Marti. Jace gave them to me. She said it was an office tradition. Everyone gets them on their birthday."

Anne coughed in surprise. "Oh...of course. Yes. Jace gives everyone flowers on their birthday." Taryn seemed oblivious to Anne's bumbling. *Nice one, Jace. A little warning would be in order!* Anne couldn't wait to see Jace's face when she confronted her. She took a small box from her pocket. "Here's a gift from Bill, me and the kids. I hope you like it."

Taryn unwrapped the gift and gasped in surprise. Small diamond studs glittered back at her. "They're beautiful! You shouldn't have, but I'm glad you did!" She hugged Anne and took the card that her aunt handed to her.

"Ricky picked the card. I promised him we'd have cake on Monday when you come over." Anne stood up. "I have to talk to Jace about some students, so, if I don't see you before you leave, nine tonight at the club?"

"Are you sure it's not too late?" Taryn was having dinner with Marti beforehand.

"Don't worry, I have a date for dinner first."

Taryn didn't get a chance to ask who it was; Anne left too quickly.

JACE WAS SURPRISED to hear someone knocking. It was just Anne. She quickly closed the book she'd been flipping through and signaled for her friend to come in.

"Hey, what's up?" Anne smiled. Jace glanced down the at the book her arm all but covered, and Anne was surprised to see beads of sweat forming on her brow. "Good book?"

Jace looked into her friend's brown eyes and said, "I just grabbed the first thing in the diversity section of the library." She lifted her arm, exposing the cover.

Anne's eyes widened as she read the title aloud, "How to be a Happy Lesbian. A Coming Out Guide. Is it useful?"

"I don't know. But I've never been to a gay bar before, so I thought I should read up before tonight."

"I shouldn't imagine it's that different from a straight one," Anne said. "Are you worried?"

"I don't know. Maybe. I'm not sure what to do."

"When?"

"If I get asked to dance, if someone takes an interest in me..."

"You can say yes or no. Jace, stop analyzing everything." Anne could see the worry lines across Jace's forehead. "Would it make you feel better if I masqueraded as your girlfriend?"

"It might be simpler. I just want to go there and see how I feel. Regardless of my feelings for anyone, I need to feel comfortable with who I am. I think my sexuality question has been answered. I've been noticing that women seem to catch my eye more and more."

"You'll be fine."

Jace rolled her shoulders to try and release some of the tension. "I'm not sure how I'll feel seeing Taryn with Marti. They might be...smoochy."

"Smoochy! Now there's an adult expression." She looked at the hurt in Jace's eyes. "I'm sorry. Sometimes I forget you're a novice at this. I shouldn't have asked you to go. I never looked at it from your point of view."

"No. I want to be there. I want to celebrate with her. I just don't know how to handle these feelings that keep running through my body. Thank you for not teasing me about the book." Jace's eyes returned their usual blue hue.

Anne grinned mischievously, "You're welcome. But you're not off the hook yet, Xanthos. I hear there's a new tradition in the Center."

"Tradition?"

"Yes, and an expensive one at that." She saw realization in Jace's eyes, and quickly added, "Don't worry. I covered for you."

"I wanted to get her a gift, and I thought flowers would be simple. When I gave them to her she seemed embarrassed, so I told her that I gave everyone a bunch for their birthday."

"Jace, a word of advice. A simple bunch of flowers would be carnations, or some other nice generic garden variety. A dozen red roses...well they're more your lover's flowers."

Jace blushed. "It was a spur of the moment thing, and the florist recommended them." She felt flustered. *Red roses. Not very subtle.* Her mind had been on making Taryn happy and giving her a gift, not on the innuendos her gift might inspire.

"It's okay. She didn't make anything of it," Anne assured her.

Jace wasn't sure how she felt about that. Weirdly

disappointed on some level. She shook herself mentally and tried to seem genuinely amused as Anne teased her.

"Just remember, young lady, when my birthday comes 'round I expect the same treatment!" Anne chuckled. "Now, I need to check my email and get out of here. I have a date with a tall, mysterious, and fantastically good-looking woman tonight. If only I wasn't married."

Jace rolled her eyes. "In your dreams, Weston!"

MARTI CLUNG TIGHTLY to Taryn's hand as they approached the Twist & Turn in downtown Boston. "Do you think your friends will like me?"

Taryn opened the door for Marti. "Just be yourself, what's not to like?"

"Do I look okay?"

"Marti, will you give it a rest." Taryn signed the entry book, flashed her ID card, paid the cover charge, and moved through to the initial bar area. She waited for Marti to follow. "What does it matter what people think of you? You look wonderful. Your hair looks nice. Your make-up is perfect."

"I'm being a pain, aren't I?"

Taryn nodded. "I think we're meeting up in the main bar, but I feel like I should wait for Anne out here. It might be weird for her. And I'm not sure how Uncle Bill will feel being here."

Taryn glanced around at the other early clubbers. There were a wide variety of looks, ages, and cultures.

"What do you want to drink?" Marti asked as she also perused the crowd.

"I'll have a beer. Remember, you promised to be the designated driver." Taryn quietly reminded Marti.

"I know. Oh...is that Jace?"

Taryn swung around in the direction Marti was looking. She smiled when she saw her aunt holding hands with her supervisor.

"I thought you said she was bringing Bill?" Marti sounded unenthusiastic.

"I just assumed. Hold on, don't go to the bar yet." Taryn called Anne's name and was met with a beaming smile.

"Taryn, you look great! Marti, it's nice to see you again. So, what do you think of my date?" Anne pulled Jace forward by her hand as if she was a prize stud.

Taryn found it hard to breath. Jace looked stunning. The curls in her hair were accentuated with either gel or wax and the additional shine emphasized the deep ebony color. Black Levis rose up her legs, a vest clung to the lithe body, and a white shirt hung loosely from her shoulders. Her tan was intensified by the whiteness of her shirt.

"Hey there. I didn't know you were coming," Taryn said.

Jace flashed a bright white smile at Taryn. Anne had been right. Taryn looked great. Loose fitting jeans, sneakers, and a polo shirt made her look tomboyish, in a cute and very adorable way. The short-cropped blonde hair was slightly disheveled. Small diamond earrings were her only visible jewelry. Jace could feel her pulse racing, and she clung to Anne's hand.

"I hope you don't mind. Anne asked if I'd be her date. I think I lucked out and got one of the prettiest women in the room."

Taryn grinned. "Well, I'll take that as a compliment. The looks run in the family." She noticed the slight blush that rose up Jace's cheeks. At the same time, she felt Marti's arm slide around her waist.

"Come here, birthday girl, and give your aunt a hug."

Taryn could feel Marti's reluctance to surrender her hold. Subtly, Taryn removed the hand from her waist and pulled her aunt into a hug.

"The earrings look great, honey," Anne said. "I'm glad you like them."

"I love them. Thanks again." Taryn kissed Anne on the cheek. "Jace is right, you look wonderful."

Impulsively, Taryn held her arms out. "It's my birthday and I'm allowed hugs off everybody." She pulled a surprised Jace into her arms.

Jace was breathless. She could smell the delicate scent that she associated with Taryn. Her heart fluttered and she quickly hugged Taryn and backed away a step or two.

Taryn didn't look at Jace as they parted. She had felt something, being in Jace's arms. It was something very different than the last time. "We were just about to order drinks." She stammered. "What would you like?"

After taking everyone's order, Marti made her way to the bar. Her evening had taken a dramatic turn for the worse when Jace showed up. All she needed now was to find out that Cory was gorgeous and her night would be complete. She waited impatiently as the barwoman served the drinks, glancing back at Taryn every few seconds. The women just seemed to be talking and laughing and when Marti made it back with the drinks, Taryn kissed her on the cheek and took the bottles.

"I think the others may be in the main bar." She hooked a finger in the loop of Marti's jeans and set off across the room.

"Cory wasn't sure what time they'd be arriving."

Jace followed Taryn, leading Anne by the hand through the mass of bodies. She felt excitement stir in her body when she glanced at a couple absorbed in a very public display of affection. Holding Anne's hand even tighter, she averted her eyes and was relieved when Taryn stopped at an empty table.

"We may as well make camp here." Taryn pulled a chair out for Anne, then followed suit with Marti. "It'll get really packed later on and we're not as young as we used to be. A seat will be very welcome."

Anne spoke quietly to Jace. "I think you can let go of my hand now."

"Are you sure?" Jace whispered back.

"Please. I think the circulation will return this time next year." When she saw the uncertainty on Jace's face, she added, "I'm kidding. Relax. You'll give yourself a coronary otherwise. How are you holding up?"

Jace looked over at Taryn and Marti to see if they were listening, luckily they seemed to be involved in their own discussion and she relaxed a little more. "I'm doing okay."

"Have you put your eyes back in?" Anne teased.

Jace blushed. "I feel like a kid in a candy shop. There are so many women. Where are all the guys?"

Anne looked around surreptitiously, "I don't know. Hey, Ryn, where are all the guys?"

Taryn chuckled at her aunt. "Geez, you straight women. Five minutes in a lesbian bar and you're asking where the men are!"

Anne blushed. "I meant gay guys, you tease. You said this was a gay bar."

Taryn leaned forward so Jace and Anne could hear her over the music. "It is, but the guys tend to hang downstairs. Some of them will come in here later if the music's better. A few transvestites come in occasionally. I think it's less threatening up here than downstairs. I'll give you a tour later." Taryn's head shot up when she heard her name being screamed. She waved back at Cory.

Jace looked over and did a double take. "Whoa."

Anne followed Jace's gaze. "Oh my Lord, you never said you had a sister."

"I don't." Jace said bluntly.

Taryn looked from Dylan to Jace, then to Cory. "Definitely separated at birth I'd say."

Jace stood up and held out her hand. "Hello, I'm Jace Xanthos."

"Hi, Dylan Matthews. Cory's told me a lot about you."

Cory introduced two other women. "These are our friends, Helen and Jo."

Taryn shook their hands. "Nice to meet you. Thanks for coming. Helen, I think you know Anne and this is my girlfriend, Marti." Everyone shook hands and Taryn returned her attention to Dylan and Jace. The two women side-by-side looked formidable. They just oozed sex and danger. She could feel the stares coming from other tables.

Laughing, she remarked, "I think we're going to have to protect you two from the madding crowds."

Dylan grinned. "We sure could have fun tonight!" She ruffled Cory's hair. "I'm just kidding. My heart belongs to you, pumpkin."

An hour later, Dylan yelled over the table, "Okay, It's my turn at the bar. Get your orders in."

The Twist & Turn was just as packed as Taryn had predicted. The lines to the bar were at least three people deep at some points. Clientele were clamoring for attention and a few rambunctious, impatient patrons were jostling others for a prime position in front of one of the three bar staff. The dance floor was heaving; packed bodies swayed in unison to the fast beat. A mixture of heat, sweat, cologne and various body sprays mingled to form an invisible cloud that enveloped the scene.

"I'll help you." Jace stood up and followed Dylan to the crowded bar. She felt oddly drawn to her. *I wish I could appear as relaxed and natural as Dylan seems to be. She's just settled right in with everyone. Not bad looking either. Is that how people view me?* "It's not often I have to look up to another woman."

Dylan commented. "Sometimes it sucks being so tall."

"Tell me about it. I got sick of being called 'stretch' through high school." Jace leaned against the bar securing the space for them. "So how did you and Cory meet?"

"The Internet." At Jace's raised eyebrow, she said, "It's not as bad as it sounds. Just call us modern day pen pals."

Jace had no idea what to say. She couldn't imagine getting a date with a woman in her own country, let alone Internet dating. She moved to the side as a woman pushed her way up to Dylan.

"Hey. Long time no see."

Dylan finished ordering the drinks and turned around. She looked less than thrilled. "Sarah...how are you?"

"Calm down, Dylan, I'm not about to make trouble. I just wanted to say hello. Who's your friend?" Sarah looked Jace up and down.

Dylan paid the bartender, and passed some drinks back to Jace. "Sarah, this is Jace, Cory's boss. Jace, this is my ex-girlfriend, Sarah."

Jace said hello and took the cold drinks out of Dylan's hands. "I'll come back for the rest."

She escaped quickly and wove her way through the throng of women, pleasantly aware of bodies brushing hers.

"Where's Dylan?" Taryn asked when Jace finally made it to the table. "You didn't leave her to the hordes of women. I knew it was a bad idea to let you two loose."

"She met a friend. I said I'd go back for the rest of the drinks." Jace gazed in Dylan's direction but all she could see was the top of her head. She cast a quick look at Cory, but the young woman was deep in conversation with Marti, both of them apparently oblivious. Next to them Anne was chatting with the other couple.

"Need some help?" Taryn offered.

"Please." Jace was thankful for the offer. When they were clear of the table, she put a hand on Taryn's shoulder. "Dylan's ex-girlfriend is at the bar. I wasn't sure what to do. Dylan looked aggravated. What's the deal?"

"I'm not sure. Cory's told me a bit. Sarah was mad for a while, but I think Dylan and her settled things when they sold the house. Can you handle the drinks while I warn Cory?"

"Sure." Jace replied and she began to push her way through the crowd.

Taryn edged past her aunt and tapped Cory on the shoulder. There was no subtle way of asking, so Taryn just came out with a question, "How do you get on with Dylan's ex?"

Cory paled. "Why? Oh... Is Sarah here?".

"Yeah. According to Jace, she's talking to Dylan at the bar. I just wanted to give you the heads up."

Helen stood up. "Cory stay here. I'll go and help Jace with the drinks, and check out the scene."

Taryn sat in the chair next to Cory's. She could feel her friend shaking. She placed an arm around Cory's shoulder and massaged the growing tension. "It'll be fine."

"I hope so. Dylan said Sarah's seeing someone new and all is forgiven But hearing it and seeing it are two different things. I just hope Sarah doesn't make a scene. I don't want to ruin your birthday night."

Taryn listened to Cory's version of events while she watched the scene at the bar. "I think Dylan was right. I don't see any fists flying."

When Dylan returned, she hugged Cory and spoke to her quietly. Feeling like she was intruding in a private moment, Taryn asked Marti if she wanted to dance.

Anne took her cue and grabbed Jace by the arm. They followed her niece to the dance floor.

Jace felt the music move through her. She felt exhilarated and for the first time in the evening, she truly relaxed. Songs merged into each other, and Jace wasn't sure how long they'd been out there. She was always conscious of Taryn's presence but at the same time she was constantly reminded that Taryn had a girlfriend.

As the music slowed, Anne pulled her near and asked, "Are you having fun?"

"A blast. I can't believe I've missed out on all this. I love dancing."

"Are you okay with this? Us, dancing like this, I mean."

"Dancing with you isn't a problem. You're my best friend. I'm not sure how I'd feel if it was someone else."

"You should try it." Anne was thankful when the song came to an end. Her feet were beginning to ache. "I'm going to sit this one out."

Jace tickled the edge of Anne's ribs. "I keep telling you to join the gym."

"I hear you."

Anne waved to Taryn as she exited the dance floor and her niece grinned and waved back. She was happy that Taryn seemed to have put their disagreement behind them and was acting normal around her. Over the past few weeks, the issues that they had argued over drifted into the distance and the usual camaraderie between them had slowly returned. Taryn appeared in her element out on the dance floor. Her body moved in synchronization to her partner and the smile that seemed to be a permanent fixture that night was a welcome sight.

THEY'D RETURNED TO the table for their drinks and Taryn was enjoying the eclectic conversations that passed among the group. However, all she wanted was a few minutes to circulate and chat with people, but Marti hadn't made any effort to socialize. As hard as she had tried all evening, she couldn't get her girlfriend to relax. Taryn was relieved when Marti released her hold on her hand and went to the bathroom. The beat on the dance floor changed and Taryn caught Cory's excited energy.

"You like the Vengaboys?"

Cory jumped up. "Yes! You've heard of them?"

"They played them all the time at school discos in Ireland."

Taryn held onto Cory's arm and wove a pathway to the dance floor, which had cleared significantly. The beat was strong and soon both women were jumping and bouncing, paying no mind to the stares they were getting from around the room.

Watching from the table, Dylan shook her head. "Look at them. I can't believe my girl found someone who dances just the same as she does. The first time she started leaping and bouncing around the dance floor, I thought she was having a fit." Everyone giggled and watched the antics. "Gotta love 'em."

Jace watched Taryn leap and twist on the floor. Every now and then, Taryn would grab Cory's hands and they'd choreograph their steps. Jace wished she could lose all control and go out on the dance floor. She wanted to desperately. The song changed and she felt a prickle of envy as Taryn and Cory wrapped an arm around each other's waist and tried to do a little Latino dancing.

To Jace's dismay, she saw a familiar figure move onto the dance floor and head straight toward Cory. She bent across and whispered into Dylan's ear. "I think you should be on the dance floor."

Dylan got to her feet. "Want to lend a hand?"

Jace nodded and before she had time to question what she was thinking, she was striding after Dylan toward what could be trouble.

CORY BELLY LAUGHED. "We're making idiots of ourselves. I can't dance to this music. My hips don't move like that."

Taryn lost her rhythm as she tried to keep her friend from falling over. "Just follow my lead." Over Cory's shoulder she met a pair of questioning eyes.

"May I cut in?" Sarah asked politely.

Taryn glanced back at Cory. Her facial features that had been relaxed and happy a few moments earlier were tense. Taryn saw the slight nod of Cory's head and released her hold.

"Thank you." Sarah said and took Cory in her arms.

Taryn backed away until she felt a solid body behind her. She turned, meeting friendly, blue eyes. "Hey."

Jace swallowed. "Sarah promised Dylan she wanted to make peace. I'm just here for additional support."

Taryn observed Cory dancing. "She seems okay." The dance floor was filling up pushing Taryn further into Jace's body.

Jace automatically wrapped a protective arm around Taryn's waist. "It's a little crushed over here." She was thankful she was leaning against the ceiling support because her body was trembling. Having Taryn in her arms was tantalizing. She could feel the damp material of Taryn's shirt under the palm she'd rested on Taryn's stomach. She knew she should remove her arm but it felt so right, and it kept Taryn away from the energetic dancers.

Jace used her other hand to tap Dylan on the shoulder. "She seems okay."

"Yeah. I'm all set here if you two want to go back to the table."

"We'll stay a little longer. Just in case..." Jace was reluctant to give up holding Taryn until she had to. Taryn heard Jace speak to Dylan and took the opportunity to study her boss more closely. Her features were softer than Dylan's. Long, dark eyelashes fluttered over her eyes, and her mouth curved into a wide smile when she laughed at the joke Dylan told her. Taryn wanted to run her fingers through the loose curls that hung over Jace's shoulder. She imagined they were soft like silk. Her eyes returned to Jace's and locked with dark orbs, sparkling in the dim lighting.

"Would you like to dance?" Taryn asked, a little embarrassed that Jace had caught her staring.

Jace desperately wanted to say yes, but her mouth refused to move. The few minutes they'd been standing had seemed like a lifetime. It took all the strength she possessed to look away from Taryn. She tried hard to focus somewhere else in the room, but the ripple of Taryn's stomach when she moved sent a small shock wave through Jace's arm.

"I'm not sure I could dance to this rhythm," she said lamely.

"Just follow my lead." Taryn gently pulled Jace the few steps to the dance floor and placed her hand on Jace's waist holding their joined hands to the side. "Put your other hand on my shoulder. Okay, now loosen these hips." She gently tapped Jace's hipbone. "More. That's it. Now feel the rhythm of the music and follow my lead."

Jace was struggling to calm down. The more Taryn told her to relax, the more rigid she became. Every step brought Taryn closer and Jace could feel the heat move down to her core.

Taryn could feel the body in her arms tense. She gently rubbed Jace's back. "Relax. Give control to me."

Jace shut her eyes. *Breathe. How long can one song last. Ignore it. Think of your budget. Do something, Xanthos, before you lose it all.* Thankfully, her prayers were answered when she felt a tap on her shoulder. She opened her eyes, turned her head and saw Anne standing behind her.

"My turn." Anne took Taryn's hand from her friend's.

Jace blew out a relieved sigh, "No problem. Taryn was

trying to teach me to dance. I don't think I have the rhythm."

"She was doing fine," Taryn responded. "Maybe I'll have to give you private lessons in your office." She winked at Jace and turned fully into her aunt's arms.

The image of dancing with Taryn in the office was too much for Jace. She needed some fresh air.

AFTER A LONG stint on the dance floor, Taryn made her way back to the lone figure sitting at the table. "Where'd everybody go?"

Fierce green eyes bore into her. Marti forced a smile on her face. "Dylan took Anne and Jace downstairs. Helen and Jo are over there playing pool, and Cory was dancing with you."

Taryn shrugged. "Why didn't you come out and join us?"

"You seemed to be having fun without me."

The comment stung Taryn, more because she knew it to be true. While on the dance floor, she hadn't given much thought to where Marti was. "Does it bother you that I'm having fun on my birthday?"

Marti didn't answer her. She glanced at her watch. "It's late. I want to go home."

Taryn's fist hit the table. "Why do you always do this? Every time we go out it's on your terms. You decide where we go, whom we go with, and how long we stay. For once, on my goddamn birthday, I want to be in charge. What is your problem?"

"You are! I've been sitting here while you've danced with practically every woman in the place. You never once looked over here."

Taryn could feel her temper simmering. "Marti, you have a pair of legs, you could have joined us."

"What...and you would have fitted me in between your two Amazon protectors, your new little buddy, and your aunt."

Taryn stood up. "I'm going to get some fresh air. If you decide to be reasonable about this, I'll be outside. Otherwise, I'll see you at home."

ANNE STOPPED JACE from following Taryn. They had just turned the corner of the bar and watched as Taryn had stormed away from the table.

"Let her cool off first." Anne advised. It didn't take a genius to work out Marti and Taryn had been fighting.

"Should we go and sit with Marti?"

Anne shook her head. "Let's just pretend we saw nothing and

hang out over here. We'll give them five minutes. If she doesn't move, then I'll go and talk to her and you can tackle Taryn."

Jace leaned against the wall. "Why do I get to go outside?"

"No offence, Jace, but I think you'd make the situation worse if you talked to Marti." Anne sipped her water. "Are you having fun?"

Jace scanned the crowd. She could see that Dylan had joined Cory on the dance floor. "I've really enjoyed the evening. Although, dancing with Taryn was incredible and scary..."

"I noticed." Anne replied quietly. "I hope you didn't mind me interrupting, but you looked like you were either going to faint or kiss her."

Jace laughed. "Your timing was perfect."

Anne checked her watch. "Our five minutes are almost up."

JACE BUTTONED UP her shirt. The autumn wind felt cool against her sweat soaked vest. She glanced around the parking lot and saw Taryn leaning against a tree. She walked toward her, still unsure of what to say. *Just listen. Be her friend.*

"Do you come here often?" She gave Taryn a quirky grin.

Taryn smiled back. "I think you need to practice those chat up lines, or you'll be going home alone."

"You'll have to give me lessons. Want to talk?"

Taryn shrugged. "I'm just cooling down my body and my temper. Women...I'll never understand them. No wonder you and Anne stick to men."

Jace wanted to admit to Taryn she was gay, but it wouldn't help. "I don't think the gender matters. Relationships are difficult either way."

"Tell me about it!"

Jace waited silently. She had learned from the few months of knowing Taryn that she would open up if she wasn't coerced.

Taryn kicked some loose pebbles into the hedge area. "I'm beginning to realize Marti's not the person I thought she was." Taryn didn't look at Jace, but she sensed the woman was willing to just listen. "She gets wicked jealous if I'm not with her. I never noticed it before but since July she's constantly been on my back about people I spend time with and what I do. I feel like I'm constantly being interrogated."

"Is she jealous of the family? I thought she was excited to meet the kids and Anne?"

Taryn continued to kick at the pebbles. "She was at first. But she doesn't like it when I go alone. She thinks I'm seeing someone."

"Are you?" Jace asked reflexively.

"No! Credit me with some morals. But Marti thinks I am." Taryn faced away from Jace. She wanted to be truthful, but she was embarrassed at the same time. "She thinks I'm seeing someone at my aunt's...she thinks I like...you."

Jace was shocked. Her heart was pounding. She hadn't expected that answer. "Whoa. I thought you were going to say Cory's name."

Taryn shook her head and grimaced at Jace. "She thinks that, too. Don't take offence, but any person that is female comes under scrutiny. It's driving me crazy!"

"Are you talking to each other?" Jace edged a little closer to Taryn.

"We're in a vicious circle. She accuses me, I get defensive, we shout, I run off, we make up, we end up in bed, and then we're fine until the next time she accuses me. It's happening so often. The only time we make love now is when we're both hurting...and I don't enjoy it."

"How come?" Jace wished she could self-edit. She didn't want to hear about Taryn making love with another woman, but her morbid curiosity got the better of her.

"She's rougher..." Taryn saw only compassion on Jace's face and she opened up more. "She bites me...and becomes very...demanding."

Jace reached out and touched Taryn's cheek tenderly. "Taryn, that's not right or healthy. Some people may get off on that but it has to be reciprocated, otherwise it's abuse."

"I know." Taryn lowered her head dejectedly.

"Come here, birthday girl." Jace enveloped Taryn in her arms. She just wanted to hold her and give her comfort. She increased the pressure slightly and relaxed when she felt Taryn do the same. After a minute, Jace stepped away from Taryn. "How about we go back inside and see if your aunt has managed to talk some sense into Marti?"

"Sounds like a plan. Thanks for the chat. You never judge me or offer me advice. You just listen. I feel bad that I always use you as a sounding board."

Jace shrugged. "I don't think it would be fair to offer advice when I've never been in your situation." *I wish I had. I wish I was the one who got to be with you every night! Marti better not come near me the rest of the evening.*

"A love 'em and leave 'em kind of woman, huh?"

Jace winked at Taryn. "I've learned from my many years on this planet..."

"'Cause you're so ancient," Taryn interjected jokingly.

Jace conceded the point with a tiny smile, and continued, "I've learned that it's easy to give advice, but in the end it's the person living the problem who has to decide what to do. You'll make your own choices, but I'm here to listen if you need someone."

Chapter
Ten

JACE SAT DOWN in the armchair that was located inside Anne's office. "Are they sick?"

"No. Cory is helping Taryn move out while Marti is at work."

Jace was shocked. "What happened?"

"All I know is in here." Anne opened up her email. "Apparently, Marti didn't like the amount of time Taryn has been spending with Cory. Last night she accused Taryn of sleeping with her. To cut a long story short, she asked Taryn to quit working at the Center and return to the Education Department or they were over. Taryn wouldn't be emotionally blackmailed and packed a bag. She stayed at Cory's last night. Dylan has offered their spare room indefinitely, and Taryn's accepted."

"Wow, all that happened last night?" Jace was not sure how she felt about the news. *Taryn's single. Oh shit, she must be going through hell and all I can think about is the fact that she no longer has a partner. Some friend I am!*

"So what do you think?" Anne had been observing Jace's face as she'd reacted to the news.

"About what?"

"Taryn's new situation."

"Anne, what am I supposed to say? It doesn't change anything. I feel concerned for her and I want to support her." *Keep telling yourself that, Champ, and you might just believe it.* "The bottom line is I promised her a friendship and I keep my promises."

Anne didn't say anymore on the topic. She'd seen a little glimmer of hope flicker in Jace's eyes. *Those who protest the loudest have the furthest to fall and you, my friend, have fallen hard!*

ANNE HELPED TARYN put the last few books onto the shelves. "It's beginning to look lived in." Taryn didn't answer her, so Anne pushed a little more. "If things get too much, you know you're welcome at the house. Just think about it."

Taryn sank down onto the bed. "We both know I'm not welcome by everyone. I feel lousy that I couldn't work things out with Marti. I feel like shit that I'm invading Cory and Dylan's lives. And I feel like I've let you down by not coming home with you. But this wasn't a rash decision. It's been building up for a while." She could see the disappointment on Anne's face. "It's not a forever thing. I'm just not very strong emotionally at the moment, and I don't think I could bear Patrick's taunting. I've just had six months of mental torture from Marti."

Anne sat next to her and took her hand. "I'm sorry, I don't mean to add to your troubles."

"Let's see what happens next week. If things go well, then I'll reconsider my options. It's nice here, and Cory and Dylan are my first real friends since Ireland. I think staying here for a while will be good for me."

"They're a lovely couple," Anne agreed. "I just hope their togetherness doesn't get to you. It's hard getting over someone, and it's even harder when you see other people being happy."

"I know. I'm trying to be positive. This was my choice. I'm going to meet Marti on Saturday. I feel I owe her that. There are still some things we need to sort out. What are you doing on Saturday night?"

Anne shook her head. "Bill is taking me out for a meal and a movie. The kids are staying at their grandparents." Anne wiggled her eyebrows. "I have a busy night planned for him."

Taryn blushed when she imagined Anne and Bill together, "Too much information! The poor guy has no idea what you're planning. I think I should warn him."

"Don't you dare!"

"No worries, I was going to see if you wanted to watch Dylan play hockey, but there'll be other times. I really do appreciate you helping me out this afternoon." Taryn leaned over as she spoke and gave her aunt a kiss on the cheek.

After her aunt had left, Taryn unpacked some more and took a shower. As she dressed, she surveyed her new bedroom. She'd slept in the bed the night before and it was going to take a little time to get used to. The room itself was small, but luckily she hadn't accumulated much over the years. Her clothes were already hung in the oak wardrobe Dylan had picked up earlier. A few boxes remained scattered around the room. Taryn knew she had done the right thing moving out, but it still hurt.

Taryn opened her door and heard Dylan muttering obscenities in another room. She wandered along the hallway to see what was causing her new roommate problems. Dylan had taken all the computer equipment from the spare bedroom and was trying to squeeze her tall frame behind the computer desk she had just rebuilt in the corner of the dining room. "Need some help?"

"No. If I can just reach the outlet, I'll be all set." Dylan stretched her arm up the narrow space, cursed a couple more times, then sighed, "Okay. Got it."

"I can certainly tell you work with computers." Taryn eyed the desktop computer and two printers that were scattered on the rug. "This is impressive."

Dylan moved into the kitchen and took two sodas out of the fridge. Handing one to Taryn, she cracked open her own and settled on the office chair in front of the computer. Taryn rested her back against the nearest chair and allowed her eyes to travel slowly around the room. She liked the small apartment. Cory had definitely stamped her character on it.

She pointed at the huge Union Jack flag that hung on the wall. "Very patriotic!"

Dylan snickered. "Hopefully, having another American around the house will rub off on her and we can take it down..." The door buzzer interrupted her sentence, and Dylan pressed the release to let the visitors in. "Shit! I forgot to tell you Anne called. You were in the shower."

"No worries. I had a feeling she'd be back over."

Taryn got up and went to the front door. She expected to see her aunt again, but was surprised when her gaze encountered sky blue eyes. "Hey."

"Hello." Jace handed Taryn a small bottle of champagne. "Anne and I wanted to make sure you were settled and doing okay."

Taryn hugged Jace and waved her and Anne into the apartment. "As you can see, we're still a little disorganized. Dylan has graciously given up her computer room so I have a place to sleep."

At the sound of her name, Dylan poked her head around the corner of the dining room wall. "I keep telling her it's no big deal, but she doesn't believe me. Can I get you guys a drink? We have Pepsi, Sprite, or beer."

"Sprite for me." Jace said, staring at the dark circles that stood out against the Taryn's pale skin.

"I'll have the same. Is Cory still in class?" Anne asked.

"She'll be home soon." Taryn replied.

"Why don't you give Jace a tour." Anne said. "I had one earlier."

Taryn led Jace into the living room where Dylan was placing glasses of soda on coasters. "I'm just showing Jace around. Do you mind if I show your room?"

"Be my guest! Any incriminating evidence or kinky stuff belongs to Cory!" Dylan winked, and Taryn was surprised to see Jace blush.

"Cory says the Center is really busy." Dylan made friendly conversation. "You must look forward to the weekends?"

"Yes, although I sometimes wonder what to do with myself when I'm not dealing with the usual chaos. "

"I hear you. The User Support desk gets so many calls that by Friday I shudder when the phone rings. I get my stress relief playing hockey on the weekends. Do you play?"

"No. I run, but that's about all." Jace examined Taryn's new roommate. Dylan was tall and had an athletic build. "I do like watching sports on the TV, especially hockey."

"We're playing this Saturday if you'd like to come along. Nothing fancy. Just a Cape Cod women's league. Helen is on the team and Cory, Taryn and Jo will be there. We usually have a meal and a few beers afterwards."

Jace hesitated. She wasn't sure whether hanging out with Dylan and Cory was a good idea.

"Just think about it," Dylan said. "We're trying to distract Taryn. Ending a relationship is hard." She fell silent when Taryn gave her a look and steered Jace away.

"You don't have to come," Taryn said.

Jace smiled. "I know."

TARYN TUCKED HER hands further under her armpits; the Falmouth rink air was frigid. The crowd was sparse and she was huddled with Jace, Cory and Jo on the bleacher opposite Dylan and Helen's team. Her attention wasn't fully on the game. Her thoughts and her eyes kept drifting to Jace, who was leaning against the wall, sipping coffee from her cup. Taryn envied her apparent knack for keeping warm. Jace had on blue jeans, a gray hooded sweatshirt, and a black leather jacket. She wasn't wearing gloves but her hands still looked their usual healthy color.

Every now and then a small smile would grace Jace's face, linger, and then disappear into a frown as her eyes darted back and forth across the ice following the puck.

The woman was a complete mystery. On the car ride down

she'd seemed sullen most of the way, then out-of-the-blue had said, "Let's try and establish some ground rules for future engagements. Nothing too serious. I just want you to consider me your friend as well as supervisor. So when we're out of work, let's try and be equals. I don't want you always thinking I've come around or phoned because I have bad news about Jane or the kids."

"Okay," Taryn had said, wondering why Jace was suddenly talking to her like a real person.

"I like you," Jace had surprised her by saying. "And I'm beginning to realize how important friends are."

Taryn felt a shiver travel up her spine, and stamped her feet to ward off the cold. She wondered how serious Jace was about being friends. Maybe she was just trying to be supportive to help Taryn through her break-up. All her friends seemed to be conspiring to make it as easy on her as possible. Taryn felt almost guilty that she was not having a breakdown. She caught Jace's eye and could not do more than give a pained smile, her teeth were chattering so badly.

"Cold?" Jace asked.

Taryn just nodded. To speak would require her to open her mouth and let out valuable warm air.

Jace was concerned. The air in the rink was damp and extremely cold. She looked up toward the balcony seating. Things were probably warmer away from the ice, so she asked, "Want to move up there?"

Taryn opened blue lips and blew out a breath. "Sure. It can't be any colder." She turned to Cory and Jo, "Are you guys coming?"

Cory shook her head. "No, we're used to this cold."

"When your girlfriend is a rink rat, it's second nature to freeze your butt off in the name of love." Jo agreed. "Here, take the blanket."

Jace didn't need any more encouragement. She picked up the blanket, grabbed Taryn's hand, and led her down the corridor and up the stairs. There was no one else up on the balcony and Jace chose some middle seats and spread the blanket out. Quickly, they sat on it, pulling the edges around their bodies.

"Come closer," Jace said. "You look frozen."

Taryn shuffled toward her. She really wanted to snuggle as close to the warm woman as possible, however, her sense of decorum held her back.

Jace lifted her arm and placed it behind Taryn, coaxing her all the way across the gap between them . "Come on. I promise not to bite." She revealed her white teeth and flashed her eyes at Taryn.

Taryn moved against Jace and felt a sudden warmth flow through her as their bodies connected through the layers of clothing. With a sigh, she relaxed. Feeling the tension leave Taryn's body, Jace drew her close. It felt so good to hold her. A wave of guilt washed over her and she tensed up. *She's cold! She just wants warmth. Don't make more of it! A friendly hug, that's all.*

The more she tried to block out the thoughts, the warmer her body became. When she felt Taryn nestle even closer, she shuddered: a very different kind of shudder.

Taryn responded by reaching for Jace's hand beneath the blanket and rubbing it to help with circulation. Jace tried to focus on the game, anything to take her mind off the feelings soaring through her body.

"They're pretty fast for an over thirties team," she said.

Taryn was only half-watching the game, content that her body was beginning to warm up. It also felt good to have Jace's hand in hers. By unspoken agreement they took turns stroking and warming each other's chilly fingers. Taryn thought she could probably put up with the cold for quite a lot longer if it meant enjoying Jace's warmth and her gentle ministrations.

"Dylan used to play semi-professionally in Germany," she said. "Helen looks good, too. They just switched to this team so Dylan could spend more time with Cory. It's kind of cute."

Jace looked blankly at her. "What is?"

"The way they are with each other. I mean, for a couple that met online and have only lived together for about four months. They're very settled. They seem very comfortable around each other, and so open. I'm a little jealous."

"Really?"

"I half wish Marti and I could have had that."

"Do you think you were like them at the beginning?" Jace was interested in what Taryn perceived as a good relationship.

"No. We were companions and sleeping partners, I never allowed the relationship to go any further." Taryn chuckled to herself.

"What's so funny?" Jace asked, confused at how Taryn could laugh at such an admission.

Taryn looked bemused. "Nothing. I'm just constantly amazed at how easy it is to talk to you and it just surprises me how you can manipulate a conversation away from yourself and onto me."

Jace bit back a caustic comment. The word "manipulate" had hurt. She mentally chastised herself for being so sensitive. "I'm sorry, I didn't realize I was doing that."

"It wasn't a criticism, Jace. It's just... I'm the one who usually clams up. I'm beginning to understand what it must have been like for Marti, or even Anne, to have a conversation with me. I just thought it was ironic as I had planned to use this time to...to get to know who you are."

Jace sighed. She knew the time had come where she needed to try and be open with Taryn. If she wanted Taryn to see who the real Jace Xanthos was, then she needed to let her in, a little. "You could just ask."

"I don't know how." Taryn watched the players as they skated back onto the ice. "You're my boss and I respect you, but tonight you said you wanted us to try and be friends and equals. Well, I tend to want to know about my friend's lives."

Jace tried not to drown in the chocolate colored eyes that seemed so open and honest. "Taryn, I know how deeply you need your own privacy, and because of this I know you will respect mine. You have your aunt's integrity."

Taryn giggled, nervously relieved that Jace wasn't mad at her for being curious. A blush warmed her cold cheeks. "I've asked her about you, but she never gives anything away."

Jace pondered that admission. She was thankful for Anne's discretion, but also felt a twinge of sadness, as there really wasn't much that Anne could have said anyway. She made a decision then and there that she would rectify that fact, beginning right now.

"Let's make our second deal of the evening. Let's say we can ask each other anything, and we'll try to give an honest answer."

"What if one of us doesn't want to answer the question?"

"We respect the decision and leave it alone. I'm willing to try being more open if you are?"

Taryn scrutinized Jace's face. "You're serious, aren't you?"

"What have we got to lose?"

Taryn thought about that. "Not a whole lot, in my case. I'll try."

Jace gave her shoulders a squeeze. Once Taryn had recovered from the shock of their agreement, she would soon be asking awkward questions. Jace just needed to decide which ones she would answer.

AFTER THE GAME they adjourned for beers and food at Circadia, an eclectic gay bar in Falmouth. The place was spacious and not as packed as the bar where they'd celebrated Taryn's birthday. Jace was pleased that there was less smoke and she relaxed back in her seat praying that Taryn wouldn't ask her to dance.

She glanced across at her dining partner. Taryn had a wistful expression on her face; a tiny furrow of lines ran across her forehead. Jace knew Taryn's expressions well. She'd spent the last few months studying her from afar. There were times when Jace found her concentration lacking. It was always when Taryn was in the vicinity. Rather than continue fruitlessly with her work, she would just watch the younger woman. At this very moment, she could tell Taryn was running something through her mind.

"How was the food?" Jace asked.

"It's fine. How are you coping with this place?"

"You mean because it's a gay bar?" Jace felt slightly defensive. "I don't have a problem. I went to a gay bar for your birthday, remember."

Taryn took a deep breath. *Here goes. Now we'll see how this friendship deal works.* "Yes, and I remember you barely left Anne's side all night. Whenever a woman so much as looked in your direction you grabbed Anne's hand. It...well, it was as if you were scared."

Jace felt her face blanch. She hadn't realized she had been so transparent. "I...I was okay. I was trying to make Anne feel comfortable."

Taryn could tell Jace was lying. Her normally bronzed skin was pale and a mild sheen covered her face. "Remember our pact. The deal was that we would answer honestly or not answer at all. Look, I know how I feel when I go into straight bars. I feel out of place and uncomfortable, and if I'm honest, I get scared that someone will ask me out and they won't like my response. If it's going to make you uneasy we can go to a generic place. I'm sure there's a Friendly's or a Chili's close by."

Jace shook her head. This was her first opportunity to be honest and open with Taryn and so far she'd flunked. "I promise you, Taryn. I have no problem going to a gay bar." *Dancing with you, I have an issue with. Watching other women kiss and getting so turned on, I have a problem with. Wanting to take you in my arms and hold you forever, I have a concern about...*

Taryn watched the emotions fleeting across Jace's face, and suspected she was leaving a lot unsaid. But her friends were watching them from the dance floor, identical quizzical looks on their faces. Taryn gave them a small wave then met Jace's dark cerulean eyes. "Okay, but this conversation is not over."

Jace took a sip of her beer and tried to settle her emotions. She could feel a subtle shift in mood between them. Taryn's expression had turned sober and she'd straightened in her seat. Jace sensed a serious conversation was looming on the horizon.

"Are you seeing anybody?" Taryn came right out and asked.

"No."

"How come?"

Jace shrugged, "Work, I guess."

"Has it been a long time since you dated?"

Jace thought about the question. "It seems like a lifetime." That was about as honest as she could get. Doing what she did best, she immediately moved the conversation away from her secrets. "What about you? How are you feeling?"

Taryn sensed that her open question session had just been closed, nevertheless she felt pleased that she knew a little more about Jace. "I'm doing okay. I'm feeling a little sad, but I'll survive. I'm just a little depressed. I thought I'd gotten past the whole dating scene." She surveyed the bar and shuddered. "One thing I do know is that I'm not ready to get back into it just yet."

Jace nodded in agreement. "Before Marti, did you date a lot?"

"It depends what you call dating. In Ireland I went a little crazy. I needed some relief from nursing my mom. When the opportunity arose I would drive to the city and visit one particular bar. Well...let's just say I didn't go there to make friends..." Seeing the shocked look on Jace's face, she added. "I'm not proud of myself."

Jace gulped. They were so different. She had held no pretense that Taryn was innocent, but finding out that Taryn was a very experienced lover made her nervous. They were way too different. "So you were an Irish Romeo?" She laughed nervously, "What about before Ireland? I mean, when did you know you were gay?"

Taryn relaxed when she didn't see repulsion or shock in Jace's eyes, although she sensed some discomfort. "Tough question. I'm someone who believes you're born with a defined sexuality. I always knew I was different from other girls. In school, I had the usual teenage crushes, except mine were on female friends or teachers. I didn't come out until college. However, when I did, my mom and Anne were very accepting. I hadn't planned on telling the family but then I met Colette."

Taryn took a large gulp of her beer. Talking about Colette always brought back painful memories. "Unfortunately, I was just another notch on her bedpost. It hurt like hell and I felt rejected again. Since then I've played it safe. I thought I'd found happiness with Marti, but over the past few months I began to question my motives for being with her. So there's my love life in a nutshell. How about your sexual awakening?"

Jace's analytical mind was replaying her own childhood and teenage years. She tried to remember a time when she'd been attracted to anyone. She couldn't. *I must be one hell of a slow learner.* She didn't want to admit to Taryn that she hadn't slept with anyone, but she'd promised honesty and she didn't want to put a damper on the rest of their conversation. Taking an enormous leap of faith, she said, "I haven't had as much experience as you."

"I'd swap all my previous experience to find a relationship like Dylan and Cory have."

Jace followed Taryn's stare. Dylan and Cory were kissing each other slowly, while Helen and Jo played a game of pool together. "Speaking of Cory and Dylan, I couldn't help but notice the photo on the table at your place. Was that Cory, dressed as a bride?"

Taryn nodded. She'd seen Jace's questioning look when she'd visited the house. Knowing Anne would have noticed the picture too, Taryn had asked Cory what she could say if people asked. Cory had given her permission to tell Jace or Anne that she had been married.

"Yes. Cory left her husband to be with Dylan, and Dylan left her long time partner. The man in the photo was Cory's grandfather."

"I never would have guessed. So, is Cory bisexual?"

"No. She knew all along she was a lesbian, but she was trying to please her family." She watched the two lovers as they comfortably displayed their affection. Taryn finished her bottle of beer. She didn't want the conversation to end. "Let's see, we've discussed my sexuality...and Cory's. You dodged my previous question, so I'll rephrase it. When did you realize you were straight?" She winked at Jace expecting to get a huge grin in return, but what she saw instead was fear.

Tell her. No lies. Just tell her the truth and move on. Jace's pulse raced and her heart fluttered. She'd been nervous telling Anne, but nothing like this. She stared down at her hands and swallowed. It was so ironic. Here she was in the middle of a predominantly lesbian bar, coming out to her gay friend, and she had a dreadful feeling that she wasn't going to be accepted.

"I'm not straight," she said.

Taryn was shocked at the admission. Even after all the hints from Marti, and the odd comment from Cory, she had never considered Jace could be a lesbian. Or maybe she just hadn't wanted to contemplate the possibility. "I'm sorry, I just assumed."

Jace began to reply, but unfortunately, Helen and Jo chose that moment to reappear at the table. Jace tried to look interested as Helen gave a running commentary on the pool game they'd played. She caught Taryn's eye a few times, wanting to somehow let her know that she wanted to talk more. She didn't want her coming out to be like a white elephant in the room, something that would always be there and hard to ignore. She was thankful that Taryn never looked away. In fact, Taryn looked as pissed about the interruption as she was.

Chapter
Eleven

JACE CARRIED THE Thanksgiving turkey into the dining room and set it down on the table. She had insisted on cooking this year, as her contribution to the family holiday. She wanted to show Anne how thankful she was for their friendship. Taryn was behind her with three bowls of potatoes balanced in her hands, and Cory brought in the cranberry sauce, gravy, and a bottle of white wine. Anne and Dylan followed with red wine and various vegetable dishes, and after all the food had been arranged, the adults helped seat the children.

"You cook up a great looking turkey, Jace. I'm salivating just looking at it." Bill said from head of the table. "Thank you for everything, ladies."

"Some ladies." Patrick mumbled. Forcing a smile onto his face, he took a seat at the bottom of the table.

Jace hadn't seen this side of him. Whenever she'd been around, Patrick had always been quite charming, except for the one drunken evening, but now she could see deep furrows on his forehead and he had yet to make eye contact with Taryn. Jace could feel the tension rising in the room and most of it was emanating from her right, where Taryn was seated. Jace subtly dropped her hand to Taryn's leg and gave it a quick squeeze.

Taryn summoned all her inner strength and politely introduced her guests. As she'd expected, Patrick made a point of coughing when she mentioned the word "partner" as she presented Cory and Dylan. For the first time since Patrick had walked into the room, Taryn made eye contact with him. The antagonistic glare she received curdled her blood.

Bill stood up at that point and said, "Let's hold hands and give thanks for this sumptuous meal."

Everyone managed to get through the main course without any comments from Patrick. Taryn felt his piercing stare constantly, but had refused to look his way. Jace noticed that Patrick steadfastly refused to talk to Dylan and Cory. Neither woman seemed concerned about this fact. Dylan had been quite content in talking to Anne about her new computer, and Cory seemed to have bonded well with Josie and Bill. Jace had spent most of the meal eating with one hand, and helping Tom with his. She couldn't help but notice that Patrick had been drinking the table wine like water.

When she heard a gleeful squeal next to her, Jace turned just in time to see Tom hurl his squash through the air. It splattered down the front of Patrick's white shirt and he lurched to his feet.

"You, little shit!"

"Don't swear at him like that," Taryn objected. "He's just a kid."

"Who gave you permission to tell me what to do? I don't take orders from perverts! I never have and I never will!"

Bill stood up. "Patrick, either shut up, or leave this table before I do something I'll regret."

Patrick looked incensed. "I'll do what the fuck I like in my own home. If you kept more control over your own wife and kids this wouldn't have happened."

Bill turned to his wife, "Anne, I think the kids can eat their dessert in the kitchen."

Unable to hold her tongue anymore, Anne stood and said, "I warned you not to use that kind of language around my children, Patrick. I'm sorry for what Tom did to you, but was your outburst really necessary?"

"Things were fine until she walked in the door," he retorted with a sneer in Taryn's direction. "I warned you not to let *her* back in this house. She's bad news...always has been and always will be! She should have stayed away like her whore of a mother."

Taryn shot out of her seat and raced toward Patrick with murder on her mind. "You, bastard. You can't leave my poor mother out of it even when she's dead!" She swung a fist at Patrick, but her arm was caught before she could connect with his jaw. She turned and saw Jace standing behind her. "Let me go, Jace! He's had this coming! All those fucking years he made my life and my mother's miserable! I just want to wipe that smug smile off his face."

"He's not worth it, Taryn."

"I know what you really are! She told me what you did to her!" Taryn took in a lungful of air, and then spat in Patrick's face. "You're an evil son-of-a-bitch..." The words were barely out, when she felt the fist connect to her cheek. She fell to the floor, a black fog swirling in front of her eyes.

"You bastard!" Jace yelled as she grabbed at Patrick. "She'd better be okay, otherwise I will come after you, and I swear I'll make you pay!"

Jace's blood was boiling, and she found it hard to control her rage. Sobs racked Anne's usually composed features and she knelt down beside her niece, urging her to wake up.

"Is she okay," Jace asked, horrified by the swelling on Taryn's cheek where Patrick's fist had connected with the soft skin. "We need to get some ice on that and I think we should call the paramedics."

"No..." Taryn's eyes fluttered open, then closed again.

"I think she's coming around." Anne said.

Jace forced herself to look at Bill, disgusted that even now he did nothing to deal with the man who had almost destroyed his family. "Bill, I suggest you kick this drunken excuse for a human being out of the house before Dylan and I do something we'll regret." The blue ice chips glinting in Dylan's eyes reflected her own feelings, and Jace was amazed at the confidence and strength radiating from the hockey player.

"I'm pretty sure the local police will be pissed to have their Thanksgiving dinner interrupted because you couldn't control your drinking or your temper," Dylan told Patrick. "You can either leave, or I will call 911. There are plenty of witnesses here who saw you hit her. As you said when you walked in the room, I'm no lady and I'm pretty sure I could wipe the floor with your drunken piss-ant body!"

For a split-second it appeared that Patrick was going to put up a fight, but fear clouded his eyes and he stalked out of the room, muttering curses beneath his breath. The tension in the room immediately evaporated and as Jace calmed down, she realized how scared she had been for Taryn, and how close she had come to violence herself.

Supporting Taryn's neck and back, she helped her into a sitting position and asked, "How's your head?"

"I think I banged the back of it on the floor. I can't believe I let that bastard hit me again!"

Jace repeated the words silently, sensing Taryn had just let a secret slip out, but this was not the time for twenty questions. She met Anne's uneasy gaze. "Where's Patrick?"

Anne looked up. "Bill's packing him a bag. He's not staying here tonight."

Feeling the body tense in her arms, Jace bent down and whispered reassurance in Taryn's ear. "Dylan's up there as well. I think she scared him, because she sure scared me."

Anne laughed. "You were pretty intimidating yourself. I tell you, Taryn, you had two tall, dark and deadly warriors in this room protecting you. How does your head feel now?"

Taryn carefully put her fingers to the back of her head and felt around, a little embarrassed when her hand brushed against the swell of Jace's breast. "I think I'll live. There's a bump the size of an egg on the back, but nothing I haven't had before."

Jace tried not to wriggle as she felt the innocent fingers against her body. Her breast tingled, waking the nipple and sending signals to every other tender zone. "I think we should get you into the living room and onto the sofa. Do you think you're up to walking?"

Taryn was oblivious to the effect her wandering hand had had on Jace. "I can manage."

Together Jace and Anne got her to her feet, and Taryn stood still, waiting for the dizziness to stop. She felt Jace come up behind her and slide her arms around her. As she leaned into her and they walked toward the living room, Taryn experienced a sense of safety she could not remember feeling in her life. She wished they could stay like this indefinitely just so she could soak it up.

A FEW HOURS after Taryn had been examined in the ER, they returned to Anne's house and settled Taryn in her childhood bedroom with a mug of hot chocolate. Jace had already planned to stay over and asked Taryn if she wanted to do the same. Patrick wasn't going to be allowed home until the weekend, and Taryn figured Dylan and Cory could do with the privacy, so she'd agreed. It felt strange being back. She half expected her mother to come through the connecting doors like she had so many times over the years.

"Why don't you sleep next door, Jace?" Taryn indicated the adjoining room. "I'm sure you'd be more comfortable."

Jace looked at the door. Anne had offered her the same room, however, Jace had declined in favor of sleeping in Josie's room. She knew she wouldn't sleep if she was only a door away from Taryn; the woman haunted her dreams as it was. Jace's mind hadn't stopped clattering since she'd entered the room. For some reason, she felt like a teenager sneaking around the house trying to spend some time with a date.

"Do you have any clothes here?" she asked Taryn in an attempt to sound normal.

Taryn indicated a tall dresser. "I'm sure there's an old t-shirt lying around in the drawers over there. I hadn't really thought about it. I guess I can't sleep in my jeans and sweater."

Jace rummaged around and pulled out a loose button-up

cotton shirt. "This will do."

"Thanks. Do you mind if I change?"

"No, be my guest. I'll just make myself comfortable and then we can talk. If you feel like it."

After changing, Taryn settled her pillows against the headboard in much the same manner as Jace had. She climbed under the covers to ward off the slight chill of the winter's night. Jace had dimmed the main bedroom light, and if the circumstances were different, Taryn would have described the room as romantic. She glanced to her side and caught the slight tremble as Jace's hands held the still warm mug of chocolate.

"This is a little surreal when you think about it?"

Jace smiled nervously, "How so?"

"Well, it's not everyday that a girl has her boss sitting on her bed wearing pajamas. In fact, the whole day seems like a scene from a bad film." Taryn had hoped her comment would relax her brooding companion, but it seemed to do the complete opposite. "Are you okay?"

Jace shook her head, "I'm just a little nervous."

"What's wrong?"

"Well, it's not everyday a boss gets to sit on an employee's bed!" She tried to laugh off her anxiety, but it didn't work. "I'm not used to telling people about me. I don't know what it is about you, Taryn, but I find myself wanting to tell you; maybe, even needing to tell you. This is a new thing for me."

"We can leave it 'till another time," Taryn said.

"Are you too tired?"

"No, I'm just letting you off the hook."

Her tone was so gentle and playful, Jace relaxed a little and said, "It's been quite a memorable day."

"No kidding." Taryn's face was suddenly flushed. "I'm so embarrassed that he's my fucking father. And I'm disgusted because I lost my temper and goaded him into hitting me. I knew what he was like and I still opened my mouth..." For the first time that day, Taryn cried. The tears flowed freely, and she wiped furiously at them, even more embarrassed that Jace was watching this breakdown.

"It wasn't your fault, Taryn. No one blames you...all your friends are still here. We all care for you too much to leave you alone." Jace spoke from her heart as she shifted across the bed to sit closer to the woman she adored. "Come on...cry it out. Anybody with a heart would have reacted when he called your mother that name. I know I would have."

Taryn listened to the soothing words, her mind paying more attention to them than her heart, which was still bleeding from years of paternal rejection. "You wouldn't have...you're always in control."

"I'm not always in such good control of my emotions..." *Especially when I'm around you,* she added internally. "Trust me when I say I would have done the same thing...in fact I have."

This simple declaration gained Taryn's full attention, but she had no real idea what Jace was hinting at. "When?"

Jace took a little breath and rearranged her body, so she was sitting slightly behind Taryn, supporting her. "Years ago, on my last visit to Agistri."

Taryn settled her back against Jace. "Was that when you went back for your mother's funeral?"

Jace nodded. "I hadn't been back to the island in years...I wasn't welcome by my father or brothers."

"How come?" Taryn asked, turning to look directly at Jace. "I just assumed you got on well with your brothers. You've mentioned Nikos with such love."

Jace shrugged nonchalantly, "Time changes things. But I do understand how you feel about Patrick, at least to a certain extent. I would bet my life that you feel rejection everyday of your life...and as much as you detest Patrick, it hurts when he doesn't admit he's your father."

Initially, Taryn had been desperate to tell Jace she was wrong, but the more she listened, the more she realized that Jace understood her plight, understood her demons. "Tell me about it." She implored in a desperate whisper.

"I'll try. I just don't like talking about times in my past when I've felt weak. I guess...that's why I come across maybe as a cold, controlling person when I'm at work. I don't want people to see I have an Achilles' heel that they can exploit. Does that make sense?"

"Totally. I got so used to being rejected as a child that I didn't want to tell people things that might cause them to reject me. It took me a long time to tell my family I was gay. I didn't want to be rejected by those I loved. Is that how you felt?"

Jace gulped. The conversation had been reflected back to her, and the one subject she knew she couldn't avoid anymore. "I never had to tell my family...it was never an issue. I haven't talked to anyone in my family for years...since my mother died. "

"Can I ask why?"

"Sure...it's why we're sitting here. I promised to tell you."

Taryn looked at Jace sympathetically, "You don't have to tell me because you promised me. I'd rather you talked to me because you want to tell me."

"I do...I'm just trying to work out how to start. Like I said, it's no big dirty secret, so don't get your hopes up that I'm going to dazzle you with a life of drugs and crime," she chuckled nervously. "Okay...what's the first thing you notice when you look at me?"

Taryn swallowed slightly. *What a question! What do I see? At the moment I see a gorgeous, fit body; pert breasts; a beautiful smile; amazing blue eyes...shit! I can't tell her that!* Taryn wiped those thoughts from her mind, and looked seriously at Jace, "Err...I'd say your eyes and height were what caught my attention the first time I saw you."

"I know...it's what everyone notices, especially my father. I think I told you I come from a very tiny island, in fact the smallest island in the Aegean Sea. Of course, with any small population, come small-minded people and traditions."

"I know. I met my fair share in my Irish village." Taryn interjected.

Jace smiled. "Anyway, my father was desperate for boys who would carry on the family business of fishing. When Mika was born, my mother said he was the apple of my father's eye. Mika is the spitting image of my father. My father was determined to have another boy but he fished away from home a lot. Sometimes he would only come back to the island at weekends. It took my mother a few years to conceive, but finally, she got pregnant with me. My father was overjoyed, and began to work more locally. I'm sure the fact that I was a girl upset him immensely. Soon after me, my mother got pregnant with Nikos. My father's dream of having more sons was becoming a reality."

"Did you and your father get along?"

Jace took a moment to reflect. She sipped her chocolate and tried to remember when the comments began. "He would say things to my mother. I think I was seven at the time. I was growing taller each day and I didn't look like anyone in my family. No one could understand where the blue eyes came from. My mother has brown, her parents had brown, and it was the same with my father's family. The older I got the more doubt my father placed on my paternity."

"Oh." Taryn had no other words to say, but wanted to let Jace know she was listening.

"It got worse. He became so paranoid that he demanded my mother never leave the house. By the time I was ten, he refused to accept me as his own, and became violent toward my mother. He would constantly ask her what man she had slept with while he was away working. He never believed her when she said she hadn't been unfaithful. By that time, my maternal grandparents had died, and her sister had left the island to live in America.

She had no one to turn to, and I think she was afraid my father would hurt me, so she sent me away..." Jace could feel the anger stirring inside: anger and resentment of a different life and lack of understanding.

"That's when you came to America?" Taryn queried.

Jace nodded slowly. "Yes. I was scared, and lonely. My mother tried to explain to me that it was for my own good. If I had stayed I would have ended up marrying one of the locals and tormented the rest of my life by my brothers. Mika was mean to me. He understood what my father called me; I had no idea. My aunt gave me a good life, and as I grew older she would tell me stories about her grandparents and their history. She thinks I just got hit with all the recessive genes of the family or just a kick back of nature."

Taryn looked at Jace, it seemed a feasible explanation. "Didn't your father understand?"

Jace shook her head again, "No, he had his two sons who were his image."

"But what about blood tests? I mean that's what my grandparents did to prove my paternity. Couldn't you prove this to your father?"

Jace moved her head so it was resting on the headboard, and stretched out her body. Her dark, brooding eyes searched the ceiling, trying to put into context how different her family's culture was to Taryn's. "Taryn, when I say a small island, I mean really small. There are three towns, and one road. Horses and carts work as taxis and there is now one bus. The way of life is simple. There isn't really a proper doctor's office, let alone blood testing opportunities. He should have just listened to my mother and taken her love, trust, and truth as her word."

Taryn was astonished, but not shocked at the demographics and simple way of life Jace had described. Her heart went out to Jace. They were so alike in many ways. She moved slightly, and took Jace's hand in her own. She wanted to hear more, but not at the risk of making Jace more upset. "Couldn't you bring your mom here?"

Jace closed her eyes, and summoned up a picture of her mother. *You were so beautiful, Mitera.* She silently whispered to her mother's angel. "When I grew older, I went back to visit. By then, I towered over my father. This added fuel to his hate campaign. He even managed to turn Nikos against me. To them I was just a freak of nature, and my mother was no more than a whore. I tried to get her to leave with me, but she believed she'd done something wrong as a wife and was being punished."

"I'm so sorry." Taryn said, feeling completely ineffectual.

Jace wiped a tear away from the edge of her eye. "When I heard Patrick call your mother a similar name today, I thought I was going to lose control." Jace's body shook, with the rage she had stored inside. "I miss her so...much. She deserved so much more, and I never got to say goodbye." It was with those words that the tears erupted.

Taryn immediately opened her arms but when Jace refused to move, Taryn crawled closer and physically pulled her into an embrace. "Let it out...Jace, you've supported me so many times over the past few months." Taryn rocked Jace gently in her arms. She had no words of comfort; there weren't any to give.

JACE WOKE UP disorientated. She knew she wasn't at home, but for a brief moment she had no idea where she was. Then she remembered Taryn's strong arms holding her, and the soft touch of Taryn's fingertips stroking her head. She didn't remember falling asleep. After rubbing her sore eyes, she looked around and saw Taryn tucked up on the small love seat. She was in two minds whether to stay where she was or go to Josie's room, but her bladder was pleading for relief, so she had little option but to get up. She walked quietly across the room and placed the warmer bed cover over Taryn. For a moment she stared down at her sleeping friend, then she brushed a wisp of hair away from Taryn's forehead and placed a feather light kiss of thanks where her fingers had been.

Chapter
Twelve

CONDENSATION MISTED THE windows of Taryn's bedroom. She glanced at her watch, it was past nine, and she had only woken up because she was in the direct glare of the morning sunlight. Her muscles ached after a whole night curled up on the couch, and the bruise on her cheek throbbed. After a quick search in the bureau, she found some old underwear and a clean sweatshirt that would suffice until she got back to the apartment. She dressed quickly, hoping that she could still catch Jace before she left.

Taryn suspected Jace might be feeling embarrassed. She didn't appear to be a person that cried very often, if at all, and maybe she wouldn't want to hang around to face the person who'd seen her at her most vulnerable. Taryn rushed down the stairs expecting to find the whole Weston clan, and maybe Jace, still eating breakfast, but was dismayed to see just Anne in the kitchen.

Anne looked up from the newspaper she was reading. "Hello, sleepyhead. Old habits are hard to break. You were never an early riser."

"Good morning. Where is everyone?" Taryn went over to the coffee pot and filled a mug.

"Bill took the kids to his parent's house. We hardly have any time for just the two of us, so he's planned a date for us! Can you believe that? There are pancakes warming in the oven, but don't steal them all, as Jace hasn't eaten yet." Anne stated matter-of-factly, a glint of trouble in her eyes. She studied Taryn's body and face looking for any answers to the questions she had running through her head.

Taryn looked over at her aunt, "Where is she?"

Anne had noted the slight concern in Taryn's question. The tone of her voice had more of an edge to it; there was more than just simple curiosity in the question. "Out running," she said, and then added, "She looked like crap this morning, and her mood left something to be desired."

"Oh. It must have been spending a night in such a small bed." *No need to tell Anne about Jace's meltdown.* Taryn finished putting a few pancakes on her plate, took a seat opposite her aunt, and began to devour the food.

After a few minutes, she could feel Anne's stare burning a hole through her. "What? Are my table manners still poor? I thought I'd improved on those." She smiled, but the smile soon disappeared when she saw the frown on her aunt's face. "I know the bruise looks bad. I'm hoping it fades by Monday." When Anne's expression didn't change, Taryn realized the condition of her face wasn't the problem. "What is wrong with you?"

Anne looked away from Taryn, unsure how to begin the conversation, and not even certain she was on the right track. "I went to the bathroom in the night, and out of habit I checked on the kids. Josie's spare bed was empty."

"Jace slept in my bed." Taryn answered matter-of-factly, not thinking anything more of the subject. She was about to fill her mouth with another forkful of pancakes, when Anne's fist banged the table, and she dropped the fork in surprise.

"How can you be so blasé about the fact? No wonder she's in such a bad mood." Anne's protectiveness of Jace surfaced, and she lashed out at Taryn. "She's not used to one night stands, Taryn. She's not one of your bar girls to use and abuse. Please don't hurt her."

Taryn spewed remnants of food out of her mouth. "Stop!" She jumped up from her seat, a little insulted by the accusations and assumptions Anne had jumped to. "I said she slept in my bed. I didn't say I had *slept* with her. Credit me with some sense, will you?"

What hurt more than the accusation was her aunt's knowledge of her previous dalliances. That news could only have come from one source...Jace.

"I'm sorry," Anne said. "I just put two and two together—"

"And came up with ten! For crying out loud, does anybody in this family have faith in me?"

"Calm down. I'm sorry. I get very protective about people hurting Jace. I wasn't thinking."

"Did I just miss something monumental?" Jace entered the room with slight trepidation. She had heard the raised voices when she'd come through the front door. "Remind me to hang around next time."

This flippant remark earned a cold, accusatory stare from Taryn, then she switched her glare from Jace back to her aunt. "You can explain. I'm sure Jace would love to hear this one."

Anne blushed. It had been hard enough questioning her niece about her sex life, let alone her best friend and boss. "I...err...I jumped to some conclusions."

"Jumped? Fucking leapt!" Taryn shot back.

"Whoa. Calm down." Jace switched her role from innocent bystander to leader. "Let's do this my way. I'll ask the questions, you'll do the answering." Before either woman could object, she asked Anne, "Okay, what conclusion did you jump to?"

Anne felt humiliated. She should have just kept quiet and waited for Jace to explain. All her years of counseling and at the first opportunity of divided loyalty, she had chosen sides, trying innocently to protect her naive friend. "I...accused Taryn of sleeping with you."

The truth deadpanned Jace for a second. "What?"

"That was my comment exactly!" Taryn retorted, pissed with both women for different reasons. Anne for believing she could do that to a friend and employer, and Jace because she obviously couldn't be trusted. The ice-cool stare radiating from Jace was the only thing that prevented her from slamming out of the room.

"Cut the attitude," Jace said. "I don't see what your problem is. You know the truth and I know the truth. Why didn't you just tell Anne the truth?"

When Taryn didn't reply, Anne came to her defense. "She didn't really get a chance. I made an inappropriate comment about her relationship history. I'm sorry, Taryn."

Taryn's temper ignited once more. "How could you tell her that stuff about me?" she hurled at Jace. "I trusted you and you broke that trust." Trying not to cry with fury and hurt, she grabbed her jacket and ran out of the house.

Jace looked at Anne. "What the hell just happened?"

"Me and my big mouth. I tell you, sometimes I think I only open my mouth to change feet when she's around. I'm at a loss to why she blamed you."

"Maybe I should go find her."

"I wouldn't bother. Let her calm down first."

Jace sat down at the table. "How could you think I'd sleep with her? She's only just split with Marti and I'm nowhere near ready to make my feelings known. I don't understand them myself."

Anne rubbed her face, blowing out a deep breath. "The two of you seemed different yesterday, it was as if you had a secret conversation going on between you. I just jumped to all the wrong conclusions."

"You were right about yesterday. We did get closer, but not

in a romantic manner. What happened to her reminded me a little of my childhood. I thought if I talked about how I'd grown up and why I left Greece, then maybe she'd open up about her own issues. I just wanted to get closer to her."

"She doesn't make it easy," Anne said dryly.

"She's important to me, but she doesn't realize that. I'm still a stranger in her eyes. Look at her behavior just now."

"Did it help you...talking to her?"

"Yes. I think for the first time I actually grieved for my mother. That's how I ended up staying in her room. I cried myself to sleep. I haven't done that since I came back from my last trip home. While I was out running, I realized I feel much better about myself. I should have talked with you about my past, and I will." She paused, pleased to see a slight smile appear on Anne's face. "But I need to understand why Taryn acted like I'd betrayed her somehow."

Anne hung her head. "When Penny was ill, Taryn really lost control of her ability to deal with issues and it seemed like her solution to the problems in her life was to have a different woman every other day. Penny told me about it in her letters. I didn't want her using you the same way and I more or less told her so."

"Well that explains a few things. She told me about her past on Saturday when we had our little sexual experience chat. I guess she thinks I told you. "Jace raised an eyebrow, "She really had a lot of women, huh?"

Anne reluctantly nodded. "Penny thought Taryn was treating women with the same disrespect that Patrick treated her. She didn't want Taryn ending up as cold and bitter as her father. Luckily, she seems to have pulled herself together."

Jace sighed. She felt more hurt by Taryn's explosive behavior and automatic mistrust of her than angry. Part of her wanted to chase after Taryn and explain, but the other more logical side of her told her to wait for Taryn to realize she'd made some pretty big assumptions herself and apologize. *When did life get so difficult?*

"I'm going to leave you guys to your day," she said, standing up.

Anne followed her into the hallway. "You don't have to leave, Jace."

"No. I need to go home and clear my head. I think I've bitten off more than I can chew with Taryn. I thought I could be her friend, but who was I trying to kid? I'm just going to concentrate on being a good supervisor from now on." She leaned over and gently kissed Anne's cheek. "Whatever happens between Taryn and me, you will always be my special friend...my first real friend. I'll see you on Monday."

"So, you're not going to visit her?" Anne wanted to fix things between the two women she dearly loved, but she had no idea where to start. She could see Jace was hurt, but she didn't want to pressure her. People just had to work some things out for themselves.

"I wouldn't know where to start. She accused me and disappeared without bothering to check the facts." Jace paused at the door. "I don't think I could handle being with someone like that even if she was interested. It's probably a good thing that I figured that out now before I got in too deep."

Forcing a smile, she walked out into the chill air. *You already are in way too deep! Admit it, who's running away now?*

Chapter
Thirteen

TARYN DRUMMED HER fingers on her desk reviewing the
past few weeks. After hearing Anne's message, Taryn had called
her aunt back and the two women had called a truce and agreed
to forget the fateful conversation.

Unfortunately, her attempts to make peace with Jace hadn't
been as easy. The taller woman had retreated back to just formal
conversation. The closeness they had developed was gone, and
Jace treated Taryn very much as she had those first few weeks.
Taryn knew she had no one to blame but herself; she had lost her
cool and ruined everything. Any attempt Taryn had made to get
time alone with Jace had been thwarted. When Taryn had
managed to talk, Jace had just listened to Taryn's apologies,
smiled, and said things were okay between them. But Taryn
knew they weren't. The woman she had spent holding that long
night was gone, and in her place was a stranger. They rarely
laughed like they used to, or talked longer than necessary.

Taryn reread her email from Jace. Her supervisor had taken
to sending her requests through email, rather than talking to her
face-to-face. On impulse, and through frustration, Taryn hit the
reply button and typed:

> On a personal note, I wish things could go back to
> the way they were. I miss your friendship, and know I
> screwed up. You keep saying things are fine between us,
> but they're not. How can I make it better?

She pressed the send button and returned to the pile of
surveys the students had filled out. After a few minutes, she
heard the beep of the email icon and clicked on it. Jace had
thanked her formally for her email and written:

> I am fine and we are fine. On a professional level, I
> feel we are still committed to doing the best for our

students. I value the input Cory and you have given the Center this semester and look forward to the same professionalism next semester. On the personal note, words were said, and unfortunately, those words cannot be taken back. I gave you my trust and you returned it to me. I find it hard to deal with someone on a personal level who does not trust me. Let's leave it at that.

Taryn banged her hand hard on the desk, and then threw the surveys across the room. *How fucking arrogant!* She wanted to be back in Jace's good graces. If Jace needed the numbers crunched by Wednesday, then Taryn was determined to work overtime, even if it was Friday. She got up and grabbed her coat. She needed a cup of coffee desperately.

Jace hammered her frustrations out on the keyboard. Taryn's persistence was remarkable, but annoying. She had spent the few weeks after the argument trying to get Taryn out of her head. Her work had not suffered through this ordeal; in fact, she'd managed to immerse herself into projects she had been avoiding. But she did miss Taryn and it hurt to see her melancholy face around the office.

She pulled up the email Taryn had sent her earlier. The plea at the bottom had ripped Jace's heart in two. She desperately wanted Taryn's friendship and so much more, but she was wary. No matter how much Anne reasoned with her, and even after she had told Anne about her own demons, she couldn't offer friendship to Taryn because if she rejected her again it would do more than hurt her. She checked her watch and noticed that it was way past quitting time for her grad assistant. She looked up when she heard the quiet, short knock on the door.

"Come in." Jace was temporarily surprised to see Taryn standing in her doorway, two polystyrene cups in her hand, and a bag of donuts.

Be brave! Ask her for help. Keep it professional, Taryn mentored her nervous stomach. She'd come up with various plans to get back on Jace's good side over the past few weeks, but couldn't think of anything except to show that she was trying to change.

She smiled meekly at Jace. "Am I disturbing you?"

Jace's face was almost expressionless. "A little. What can I do for you?"

Ouch! She really is a cold bitch when she wants to be. "I actually need some help with the SPSS program. It's very different from Excel." It was true. The database software was new to her, and she had no idea how to configure the variables to accept the data. She had decided to suck it up and ask Jace for help, and a little bribery never hurt.

Jace frowned. She didn't want to be around Taryn, just seeing the woman caused her skin to tingle and her heart to flutter. "I gave Cory the manual. Didn't she pass it on to you?"

"I've looked at it, but data handling isn't my strong point. I just need five minutes of your time, please? I brought your favorite donut...a Boston Kreme with sprinkles." Taryn held up the bag and the coffee. Jace couldn't suppress the smile that curled her lips. Taryn knew her weaknesses and didn't seem to mind exploiting them. *What harm can five minutes do?* "Okay, but let's make it quick. I need to get back to these projections. Leave the donut and go fetch the data. My office is bigger, we'll work here."

Fearing that if she dilly-dallied Jace would change her mind, Taryn raced to her office and hurried back. She sipped her coffee and watched as Jace scanned the surveys. Raven curls fell over her shoulder, and Taryn wanted desperately to run her fingers through the tresses. The distance between her and Jace was making her crazy. She hadn't realized until now how important Jace was to her. She had started to take their friendship for granted; it provided a sense of stability she hadn't even known she needed, and since her tantrum, she'd missed it terribly.

Taryn felt a longing in her soul as she watched Jace's nimble fingers stroke the keyboard. No matter what it took, she was going to win back Jace's trust and companionship. Jace spent a few minutes explaining the tasks Taryn was struggling with, and Taryn subtly moved closer as she spoke. When her arm brushed Jace's, the familiarity made her feel secure. She wanted to feel those arms around her, like she had so many times before. Finding it difficult to concentrate, she took a step back and said something vaguely related to the topic so it would seem like she was listening.

Feeling Taryn move away, Jace was torn between relief and regret. She now knew what an addict felt like, starved of her drugs. Taryn's scent was overwhelming and Jace forced herself to sober up. *How easily you get sidetracked when she's around.* Christmas was only ten days away and there was a mass of data to be processed before next week's meeting. Jace looked up, about to bring their discussion to a close, when she was struck by the complete trust in Taryn's eyes. The walls she had rebuilt came tumbling down and for the first time in weeks she smiled openly at the young woman.

Taryn blushed and returned Jace's smile. Trying to sound focused, she said, "I don't want to blow the reports next week. I know the meeting is an important one for the Center."

"It's not as important as the one post Christmas," Jace said. "The students' grades will be in then and we can really see how well we did."

"Why don't they wait and have just one meeting after Christmas? Why have the meeting next week?"

"Good question. Mainly we have to decide whether we're going to do the same programs next semester. If we do, then we only have the week after Christmas to finalize inputting student data, unless you feel like coming in the week of Christmas to plow through it, that is."

Taryn shook her head. "Not on your life, but I'm guessing you won't be able to resist."

Jace smiled. The interplay between them was so natural when they gave it a chance. "Okay, here's the table of results. Let me print them out and then we can go through them."

Taryn leaned closer to the computer as she took some notes, and this time Jace didn't move away. She couldn't deny her body what it yearned for, even if the contact was only brief. Taryn bit her lip to prevent her from asking Jace out to dinner. Things were going well between them and she didn't want to blow their tentative truce. "I'll go and grab the printing."

As Taryn left the room, Jace expelled a sigh of relief. She had been a fool to think she could maintain a frosty distance. If she could only keep their interactions on this friendly but professional level for the rest of the academic year then things would be okay.

"Forty-five pages! There are forty-five freakin' pages!" Taryn repeated as she carried the sheets back into the office.

Jace laughed at the incredulous look on Taryn's face. "Calm down. It looks like a lot, but it isn't. What we're looking for are the significant correlations. The program highlights those with an asterisk. The data that has the best significance has two asterisks, and the other has one. So all you have to do is go through and make a note of those. Then we look to see what these significances mean." She looked up to see whether Taryn had understood what she had said, and smirked when she saw how cute Taryn looked when she was confused.

Taryn grinned sheepishly, "Okay, now if you could just repeat that in English I'll leave your office and get to it!"

Jace patted Taryn's hand, the first physical contact she had initiated since Thanksgiving. "I'll show you."

Taryn listened intently while Jace repeated the process. "Oh, now I see it. I can do that. I'm sure with Cory's input on Monday we'll have the report written by Tuesday. Thanks, Jace." Taryn took the data sheets out of Jace's hands, her fingers brushing lightly against Jace's. The contact sent shivers up her arm and her eyes connected with Jace's bright, cobalt stare. Despite her better judgment, Taryn uttered the words that fell unchecked from her mouth. "Can we talk?"

Jace shook her head. "There's nothing more to say." However, she was completely unprepared for the tears that tracked down Taryn's cheeks.

"Please?"

Unable to resist, Jace settled behind her desk, needing a physical barrier between herself and Taryn. "Okay."

Taryn wiped away the tears that had come all too easily. "I know I was wrong. I wish I could take back my comment. I've been so used to having my mother, my aunt...even lovers take my insults or accusations without consequence. None of them ever shut me out or said anything. They always forgave me. But you were right. I should have trusted you more. I know you have integrity and I should have known you would not just break a confidence."

"Yes, you should," Jace said. The pain in Taryn's eyes cut right to her heart. She knew she had the power to erase the hurt, but she was reluctant to be wounded again. Taryn might mean what she was saying, but what would happen next time? One look at the sorrowful eyes answered her question and the final barrier dissolved. "It wasn't all you, Taryn. I had given you something I don't often give away — my friendship, with that comes my trust. I felt rejected when you thought I had broken your confidence. I thought you knew me better."

"I do." Taryn stood in front of Jace thoroughly ashamed. "And I miss you."

Jace rose and walked around the desk. She leaned against the edge and opened her arms. "I missed you, too. Come here."

Taryn closed the distance between them and stepped into Jace's embrace. Resting her forehead on Taryn's shoulder, Jace told herself not to blow it. She desperately wanted to taste Taryn's lips, but she couldn't. Taryn's reactions were that of friendship, and nothing more.

She smiled gently, and cocked her head to the side, happy to see Taryn's brown eyes twinkling. "Anne will be pleased we're talking again. She was worried about Christmas dinner." She felt the body in her arms tense. "What's wrong?"

Taryn shrugged, and took a small step back, uncomfortably aware of physical sensations she hadn't experienced around Jace before. "I'm not going to be at Anne's for Christmas. I can't go through what happened at Thanksgiving again."

"Oh." Jace said, disappointment running through her. "It's

kind of ironic really. I've spent the last few weeks worrying how I was going to deal with you being there at Christmas and now that I'm looking forward to it, you're not going to be there." She was surprised at how easy it was to admit these feelings. "Where will you be?"

"I don't know. I wanted to give Dylan and Cory some room. It's their first Christmas together so I thought I'd move out for the week. I was thinking I could go stay with my grandparents in Florida." Taryn sighed, only five minutes into their renewed friendship and she was already burdening Jace with her problems. Trying to make light of the whole conversation, she added, "At least it'll be warmer than here."

"True," Jace replied, "but lonely. Do you really want to spend Christmas with pensioners?"

Taryn nodded in agreement. "I don't have any other choice. Marti offered, but I don't want her to think reconciliation is a possibility."

Jace was surprised at Taryn's mention of her ex-lover's name. "You and Marti are talking?"

Taryn nodded. "We've hung out a few times and she calls me occasionally."

Jace felt a knot of jealousy being added to the other emotions she so rarely encountered. "Look, it's getting late and neither of us is going to get any work done. How would you feel about maybe...grabbing some dinner and ...er...maybe a film?" she stammered.

Taryn giggled at Jace. "Wow, you must be a hit with the ladies if that's your usual way of asking them out..." She stopped what she was saying when she saw the wounded look in Jace's eyes. "Dinner and a movie sounds great."

Jace couldn't get upset over Taryn's innocent comment. She had no idea how close to the truth she had come and Jace wasn't about to tell her. She said, "Go get your stuff. I'll see you in five minutes."

TARYN REALLY DIDN'T want the evening to end. She didn't want to go back to the mundane 'hellos' that had been their only conversation over the past few weeks. They had begun to wander back toward the parking lot.

When they reached the Jeep, she said, "Thanks for this. I had fun. Maybe we could do it again some time soon?"

Jace looked down into the unsure eyes of her coworker. "Sure. I was thinking ..."

Taryn's eyebrows furrowed together. "What?"

Jace swallowed the nervous lump in her throat. She hoped she was doing the right thing. It felt like the right thing, but after their tentative evening out, she didn't want to jump the gun. "Maybe you could stay closer to home this Christmas. Would you?"

Taryn leaned against Jace's Jeep, wondering where Jace was going with the conversation. "Sure, but I've run out of ideas. Besides, a hotel is way out of my budget."

"You could stay with me," Jace suggested.

Taryn was stunned into silence. She hadn't even considered asking Jace. But after all she'd done to mess up their friendship, her boss was still offering to help her. "I couldn't put you out. Thanks for asking though."

"You wouldn't be putting me out. It would solve everyone's problem. You'd get to stay near home, Anne and the kids can see you Christmas Day, and... I wouldn't be lonely over the vacation. I mean, if you didn't mind my company."

Taryn played Jace's idea over in her mind. She was very tempted. It would be good to see the kids open their presents on Christmas Day. But she'd vowed not to go to the house if there was a chance Patrick would be home. "Thanks, Jace, but I might as well go to Florida, I won't be with you guys on Christmas. I already ruined Thanksgiving, and I don't want to be the reason the kids have a lousy Christmas."

Jace's mind raced for ways around the situation. She could tell Taryn was not completely committed to Florida. "What if I guarantee you'll see the kids at Christmas, and there won't be any drama? We can have everyone over to my place." *You're practically begging, Jace. Back off! She's said no twice. How many more times does she have to say it?*

Taryn reviewed her options and concluded she had nothing to lose and everything to gain. "Okay, I'll stay with you. I was thinking of moving out Sunday evening or Christmas Eve morning. Is that okay?"

Jace was a little shocked. Overjoyed, but shocked nonetheless. She hadn't expected Taryn to change her mind. *Oh my God! What have I done?* She had no idea how she was going to cope with having the woman she had tried so hard to push out of her mind, in her house. "No problem."

Tentatively, Taryn engulfed Jace in a hug. "Thank you! I think you're my Christmas angel. My mother always said she'd send an angel to look after me."

"You're welcome." Jace breathed in the cool air mingled with Taryn's fragrance. "Maybe both our moms are looking down on us."

Chapter
Fourteen

JACE GLANCED UP from her hot chocolate and caught the contemplative look on Taryn's face. The fire was roaring and its heat was sending a wave of tiredness through Jace's aching body. The two women had finished watching a DVD after saying goodnight to Dylan and Cory. At Jace's insistence, the two friends had promised to attend the Christmas Eve gathering.

"A penny for your thoughts!" Taryn whispered quietly as she saw Jace smile into the fire.

Jace turned her relaxed features to Taryn. "They're not worth a penny, but give me a cookie and I'll tell you all of them!" She grinned at Taryn, and stretched her long legs out in front of her. "I'm just happy to have you here. I don't realize how lonely I am until I have company. Usually, I sit here moping around after guests have gone, but tonight I get to share one last drink with you. It's nice."

"Jace, I really do appreciate this. I was worried about spending my first Christmas alone. You saved me from that and I'll be eternally grateful." Taryn took a sip of her drink before asking what was on her mind. "Can I ask you a personal question?" She visibly saw the tall woman tense. "You don't have to answer it."

Jace tried to relaxed her shoulders and breathe normally. She knew deep down she could trust Taryn to keep anything she said private, but she was still a little raw from their misunderstandings. *You promised to forgive her...now show her you have!* Her conscience admonished her. "Sure. Same deal as before. You can ask and I'll try to answer it as best as I can. Shoot."

Taryn turned ninety degrees in her chair and looked into frightened blue eyes. "I just wanted to ask why you're so lonely? I mean, you're gorgeous..." She blushed as she said the words, "And a catch for any woman. Did someone break your heart or are you not into commitment?"

Jace rolled her neck, the tension inside making her head

begin to ache. It was time to lay her cards on the table, and be honest with Taryn. She had replayed this conversation over and over in her mind. "I've never had my heart broken. I've err...I've never had the opportunity to commit to anyone. I would love to meet someone and settle down."

"So, you've just played the field?" Taryn was a little confused.

Jace shook her head. "Not exactly."

"Okay. So, you've never had your heart broken?" She watched as Jace nodded her head in confirmation, "and you're ready for a commitment?" Again she saw the slight nod of Jace's head. "And you don't play the field?"

Jace shook her head, "I've never played the field."

"So, when was the last time you dated someone?"

Jace's heart beat furiously and she squirmed in her seat. She knew she could lie, but that would surely come back and bite her on the ass. She sucked in another deep breath, "I've...I've...never been on a date."

"Never!" Taryn spluttered, her drink spilling onto her sweater. "I'm sorry, it wasn't meant to sound like that. So..."

Jace nailed Taryn with laser blue eyes, "So... I'm a thirty-five year old virgin." She said acerbically.

Taryn took one of Jace's hands in her own. "Jace, don't say it like that. It doesn't matter. It's kind of sweet."

Jace lowered her eyes. The last thing she wanted was Taryn's pity. She reclaimed her hand. "I just never had time to date. I guess I dealt with my father's rejection in exactly the opposite way as you."

Taryn's pulse rate increased and her breathing deepened. She looked into sad blue eyes and realized that Jace wasn't berating her, but simply comparing their lives. She swallowed the biting comment on the tip of her tongue. "I guess so. I was so afraid of being discarded by lovers and friends that I just used people before they could do it to me. You just hid away from life. It makes sense. So, are you sure it's women you like?"

Jace rearranged her body so she mimicked Taryn's position on the couch. "I think so." *I know so when I'm with you.* "I guess I'll never really know until I pluck up the courage to try it."

Taryn examined Jace's expression and re-assessed her own feelings in the light of what she'd now learned. Taryn didn't want to mess with Jace. They were two people on completely different roads and she wanted Jace to be happy. Jace certainly didn't need someone like her messing things up. "Well, we'll have to rectify that. Maybe, we should go out to the bar again."

"Maybe." Jace faked a yawn, disappointed that her

confession had not prompted a different reaction from Taryn. "I'm going to turn in."

"Goodnight, Jace, and thank you...for everything."

TARYN LEANED AGAINST the doorframe and observed her companion. Jace was wearing a pair of Lycra shorts and a long-sleeved shirt. Sweat was pooled under her armpits and down her back. The usually loose curly hair was gathered into a ponytail, with stray curls plastered to the side of her head. Despite their conversation the previous night, and her resolution, Taryn couldn't help the tiny flutter of desire as she watched Jace move gracefully around her kitchen.

The soft Christmas music, the aroma of freshly baked cookies, and the blinking tree lights all helped to create the perfect Yuletide atmosphere. Jace seemed so contented, Taryn didn't want to distract her so she returned to her tasks in the living room, humming along to the songs. Her 'to-do' list had shrunk dramatically. Another half hour fighting with rolls of wrapping paper and tape and she would be through.

In the kitchen, Jace did a little happy dance. Her holiday was developing into the best she'd ever had. She glanced at the clock. They only had half an hour before the guests would begin to arrive. She placed the pizza dough on one of the baking stones and began rolling it out. No matter how hard she tried, the dough would not stay circular. After a few minutes her frustration level rose and she began to pound the dough.

"Come on! Roll out! Stay there!" She kneaded it back into a ball and tried the whole process again.

Taryn heard the shouts and pounds of aggravation and went to see what was causing the outburst. She watched from the door as Jace pounded the dough and finally threw the large ball onto the counter.

"Don't let it beat you! You have to treat it like a woman!" Taryn hinted tenderly.

Jace turned around. "I didn't hear you come in."

"I'm not surprised between all those insults. Pass it here, let me try."

Jace raised an eyebrow, but silently passed the pizza dough over. She watched Taryn gently roll the dough on the board and sprinkle the corn meal onto the baking stone. "So, what was I doing wrong?"

Taryn scratched her face with a finger, and turned a flour-stained face to Jace. "You were fighting with it. What you need to do is tease it gently. Watch." Taryn took the ends of the dough and carefully shook it downwards, letting gravity aid the process. She turned it in her fingers, teasing and shaking it.

Jace watched in amazement at the deft way Taryn manipulated the pliant material, rotating the dough every few seconds, pulling and shaking until the familiar pizza shape emerged. "Wow. Where did you learn this trick?".

"A semester working at a pub and pizza bar. Okay, now it's big enough, I have to flick it around on my hand. This is the tricky part as I have to make sure my hand doesn't go through the dough."

Taryn placed the pizza base on the stone and began the same process with the second package of dough. Jace pushed off from the counter and reached out. "Can I try with this one?"

"Sure. Here, hold it like this."

Jace diligently copied Taryn's actions. When she felt the dough beginning to tear, she also felt a pair of hands on top of hers. She puckered her brow and tried to concentrate on the job, and not on Taryn's soft hands squeezing hers. Together they managed to produce a second pizza base.

"Well that was an experience." Jace said, as she wiped the flour off her face. Tenderly, she leaned forward and stroked the same markings off Taryn's cheek. "Want to help me with the rest of it?"

"Sure." Taryn smiled. She had enjoyed watching and helping Jace. The woman looked so childlike when she was learning something. The avid blue eyes had not left her hands the whole process. She realized just how innocent Jace was in the real world. At college, she was in control, full of knowledge, and led with experience. But here, in the world of relationships and friendship, Jace was just as naïve as a young child. Taryn was beginning to truly understand what a precious gift Jace was to her.

TARYN SWALLOWED THE last bit of pizza, and picked up a second bottle of beer. The family was scattered throughout the living room. Cory and Dylan had arrived just in time for the pizza. They had brought gifts for the children. Taryn had been touched by this gesture. For once in her life she felt totally secure.

When everyone had finished supper, supervised by Bill, Ricky and Josie began passing the presents out one by one until every person had a few gifts in front of them.

At Dylan and Cory's surprised faces when they read the gift tags on their gifts, Bill said, "You're part of the family now, guys. We wanted to thank you for the support you've given Taryn."

Taryn looked at her presents. One of them was a small package wrapped neatly in gold colored paper, tiny white snowflakes imprinted subtly on the paper. On the tag was the now familiar bold handwriting, expressing a short sentiment that said, *Merry Christmas, Taryn. Love Jace.* She glanced over at cobalt orbs, and she mouthed words of thanks.

Jace was a little nervous. She'd never had to pick out a present for anybody without first checking what they might want. She watched as Taryn nimbly opened the small package. She saw the subtle rise of Taryn's brows as the blonde's interest was piqued when she lifted the envelope out of the box.

Taryn looked questioningly at Jace. "You're a lady full of surprises."

Jace blushed, "I try. Are you just going to stare at it?"

"No. I'm just trying to keep the suspense going a little longer. This is my favorite time. Your mind is trying to work out what the other person knows about you, and has internalized enough to buy a gift reflecting their knowledge. I'm just curious to see what you know about me!"

Jace smiled. Taryn was sometimes just as logical as she was. "So, what do you think I got you?"

Taryn looked down at the envelope and grinned. "I have no idea!" She slipped her finger under the seal of the flap and ripped the edge open. Inside was a folded printed document. She opened the paper and read its contents, the small smile turning into a huge beam. "You've booked me a snowboarding weekend!"

Jace shrugged. "I know you used to ski a lot as a child, Anne told me. I figured maybe you'd like to try something new. It's for two, so I thought you could take a friend." Jace was pleased to see the grin on Taryn's face. The present had gone down well.

"But...I can't accept this...it must have cost a lot."

Jace's exhilaration turned to disappointment. She turned to see everyone else chatting and helping the kids to open their gifts. "Please...ignore the price and accept the gift."

Taryn nodded her head. "Okay! I at least wanted to pretend. I'm psyched! I've always wanted to try snowboarding." There was a small card in the envelope, too. She read the inscription.

Taryn,
    I hope you enjoy this Holiday season, as much as I hope to. Maybe we can reclaim some of our lost childhoods together.
Best wishes and friendship
Jace

Taryn nodded at the sentiment. "Thanks. Are you going to open your gift?"

Jace searched through the packages on her lap and saw the one from Taryn. She shook the little box and pursed her lips trying to play Taryn's guessing game. She tore the wrapping paper off, opened the box lid, and stared at the stylish silver fountain pen. She admired the engravings on the Waterman pen. "It's beautiful, Taryn."

"You like it?"

"Yes." Jace looked closely and saw the initials JX engraved at the end of the shaft. "Thank you, I'm always losing my pens. I'll treasure this one."

"Look at the kids, they're in heaven."

Both women watched as wrapping paper went flying and excited squeals of delight erupted. Jace settled back against the sofa pillows and soaked up the atmosphere. She kept Taryn's profile in her peripheral vision. She just hoped events went smoother this holiday than the last one.

Chapter
Fifteen

"I CAN'T BELIEVE another Christmas is over. All that hype and commercialization, and it's over in the blink of an eye!" Taryn muttered. Her eyes surveyed the littered room of abandoned toys and scattered crayons. "Look at all the stuff the kids got!"

Jace opened one of her eyes and scanned the destruction her living room had sustained. "I know, but it was fun! I don't think I've heard such a scream of surprise as Ricky's this morning."

"Tell me about it. I'm sure I'm still deaf! I can't believe I slept all night with him on the sofa. Why didn't you wake me?"

"I told you why earlier. You looked so cute together. Did you have a good day?"

Taryn nodded lazily. "The best. We should make this a tradition. It was the best Christmas ever. No tension, no worrying about Patrick."

"Did you see the smirk on Anne and Bill's face when they put all the kids in your room for the night? I know what was on their mind."

"Please, Jace. I don't want to imagine what my aunt's up to in there. She mentioned making babies and I switched off."

"Oooh should we disturb them?"

"Lalalalalalala...I'm not listening to you." Taryn covered her ears with her hands and closed her eyes. "When you've finished ruining my tender mind, I'll listen."

Jace gazed at the crackling fire. She had so many questions she wanted to ask about Taryn's past. What little of Taryn she knew had always been told in a very guarded manner. Jace needed to see if Taryn's trust in her was true. She glanced at Taryn not wanting to ruin the peaceful look on her face but feeling that there would be no better time for the truth. "Taryn, what happened to make Patrick so bitter? I know part of the story, but I feel like I'm missing something."

Taryn scowled. Jace's question had come out of the blue and

she hadn't been prepared for it. Automatically, she moved further over on the couch, putting more distance between Jace and herself. "Anne's side of the story is pretty accurate."

Jace dropped her head against the couch, her thoughts whirling inside, teasing and taunting her. *She doesn't trust you! You let her in but she still can't let you in!*

Taryn not only saw, but also felt Jace's withdrawal. Realizing she was the source she tried to push her doubts aside. "I didn't mean to brush you off."

"It's okay. I know the rules. We can ask questions, but the other doesn't have to answer." Her eyes never left the television as she spoke.

You're a complete idiot; she thinks you don't trust her! Taryn had no intention of risking their friendship again. "Please, Jace...I don't want a repeat performance. It's not that I don't want to talk about it. It's just I've shut it so far away in my mind that I'm unsure how to talk about it. That's completely different from not trusting you. I trust you so much."

After a few moments of quiet contemplation, Jace turned smoky, dark eyes in Taryn's direction. "Show me."

Taryn's mind drifted back to a cold, bleak morning in Ireland. The morning she had asked her mother the same question Jace had asked her. "Mom would never tell me why Patrick resented me so. Never. So, as a child I made up all these crazy reasons. I know the official story that Anne and my grandparents still use to explain his behavior. I know about the twin brother he lost, but it just didn't seem real to me. I would have thought that he would have been psyched to have a kid of his own." When Jace didn't interrupt, Taryn continued. "I would ask my mother and she just kept quiet. All those nights I would cry myself to sleep and she never answered my questions. I thought she couldn't answer them."

"I can only imagine how frustrated you were. I knew the answers to my questions, Taryn. But I still hypothesized other reasons. Every child does. What happened in Ireland?"

"Mom's illness got progressively worse physically and mentally. The medications she was on made her very relaxed and uninhibited at times. One morning, after a particularly restless sleep she was muttering about him. So, I gave her the medication, waited for it to kick in, and then I asked her."

Jace reached out and took Taryn's hand in a show of support. "I would have done exactly the same, Taryn. No one should have to live always wondering why." She felt the tremors in Taryn's hand and realized the woman was crying. "Come here." She opened her arms and encircled her fragile package.

Taryn welcomed the comfort. Secrets her mother had wanted to take to the grave were fresh in her mind. Knowing that Jace didn't despise her for her actions soothed her. "My mom told me everything. About when she'd first met Patrick, how he seemed so nice, and then she found out the truth. Patrick was fine when he was sober, but when he'd had a few beers he became violent. He would hit her, but nowhere visible. She put up with it because it didn't happen often, and he was always sorry afterwards. After a while, their sex-life lessened, while his violent behavior increased."

"Did she ever leave him or try and get help?"

Taryn squeezed her eyes shut, welcoming the warmth of Jace's body, as the images spinning through her mind caused shivers down her spine. "Once," She spoke in a monotone voice. "He came home early and saw the packed bags. He beat her really bad and...raped her. Mom wouldn't say too much, but I think he went crazy and brutalized her...he wouldn't let her go. Eventually, he passed out and she fled." Taryn sobbed with relief. It actually felt good to get her secrets out.

Jace gritted her teeth. She wanted to drive around and blow the bastard's balls off with a shotgun. She could feel Taryn's tears soak through her thin pajama top. "What happened next?" She whispered desperate to know the full extent of Taryn's demons.

Taryn wiped her face on Jace's top. Her nose was blocked and her head pounding. "Mom went to the ER. They cleaned her up. Luckily, nothing was broken. She didn't tell them about the rape. Her friends took her in, but then she found out she was pregnant. Mom didn't tell me much about her pregnancy, just that I was born and her friends couldn't house her any more. Mom decided to confront Patrick with what he'd done to her. He accused her of sleeping around, and tried to poison my grandparent's minds. Mom says I was a constant reminder to Patrick of that night. He even admitted in one moment of clarity that he'd gone over the edge. He...never touched mom again...not physically."

Jace ran her fingers through Taryn's hair. She kissed the soft hair and muttered soothing words of acceptance and love. After a few minutes of silence, Jace decided to ask the question that had been on her mind. "Taryn, when Patrick hit you on Thanksgiving, you made a comment that you couldn't believe he'd hit you again. When did he hit you before?"

"When I was a little younger than Ricky, I overheard my grandfather shouting at Patrick and demanding he accept his responsibilities as a father. After that I was so excited. I didn't

understand how it all worked; after all, I was just a child. I had
no idea how you became a daddy or a mommy. I thought Patrick
had been sent to be my daddy. But when I began calling him
daddy, he would yell and scream at my mother, telling her to
make me stop. I didn't get it." Taryn took a deep breath, the pain
of those early years still fresh in her mind.

"You were a kid just trying to make sense of the world."

Taryn turned her head and saw the tears glistening on Jace's
cheeks. "You're crying?" She stated. "I didn't want to make you
cry."

"You didn't make me cry. Hearing your story makes me
realize in a bizarre and fucked up way that my childhood could
have been worse. I guess I'm just feeling your pain, but it's not
your fault. So what happened when you called him daddy?" Jace
grabbed the box of Kleenex, and offered one to Taryn before
taking one herself.

Taryn took a tissue and blew her nose. She wiped her face
and tried to gather some strength in the fact that she wasn't
alone. "One day I came home, and it was only a few days until
Father's Day. We'd made cards in school. I had been so happy
that year because it had been the first time I had a father to make
a card for. I presented him with the card and he tore it to shreds.
I cried, and he told me to stop, but I couldn't. When I didn't stop
crying he slapped me across the face, and then he told me not to
tell anyone or he'd do it again even harder. I never did tell
anyone until now."

Jace rubbed Taryn's back. Words were useless. There was
nothing she could say to take away the hurt. All she could do
was encourage Taryn to talk about the past and maybe then they
could both work on the future.

The soothing circles on her back calmed her and she settled
against the tall woman. "After a few more of his 'lessons', I
learned never to call him daddy or tell anyone who he was." She
stifled a sob, shaking her head as she thought over what she had
said. "All those years of wishing he would accept me as his
daughter...and now, I just want him to disappear. You know,
I've often dreamt that things could be so different, that my
mother lived and he died. Does that make me a bad person?"

Jace wiped a hand over her face, "No. Those thoughts have
gone through my head a few times. Why does God take the good
ones and leave the bad? I like to believe it's because he needs
more angels. I have to believe that...otherwise I'd give up on any
belief in God."

"I hope so." Taryn closed her eyes. She actually felt a little
better. Her mind wasn't as cluttered. In fact, she had a sense of

relief that she'd finally told someone.

Jace massaged the back of Taryn's neck with one hand, and continued to hold the other woman's hand with her own. She could feel the rigidity slowly seep out of Taryn's body, and saw a more peaceful expression appear on Taryn's tear strained face. "Opening up feels good, doesn't it?"

Taryn opened her eyes. "Yes. A little, but it's also exhausting, if we don't go to bed now we're going to regret it tomorrow. The kids get up very early! I wanted to throttle Ricky this morning when I realized it was only five o'clock!" Taryn looked at the sofa. She really didn't want to be alone. She felt safe in Jace's arms and the thought of going to sleep was scaring her. Dreamtime was when the demons chose to taunt her.

Jace released her hold on Taryn, stretched, and then stood up, towering over the smaller woman. "It's becoming a habit of mine leaving you to sleep on the couch." Jace pointed to the blankets and pillows near Taryn. "I made sure you had some proper pillows tonight, and the comforter is down by the side of the sofa if you get cold." She turned away, knowing she would come back later when Taryn was asleep and check to see that she was okay. She'd done it several times before.

Taryn looked up at Jace's retreating form, the dim light of the TV giving her an ethereal shadow. "I...I'm a little scared...would you stay with me? Hold me until I fall asleep."

"Sure but if I'm honest my back is still hurting from last night on the sofa. I think we both need a good night's sleep and we won't get that sleeping on the sofa. Maybe, we should sleep in my bed?"

Taryn nodded, relieved that Jace wasn't turning her away. She didn't need rejection tonight; she needed acceptance. "Sure."

The pair walked into the dark bedroom, Jace switched on her bedside lamp and then pulled down the comforter. Awkwardly, she crawled into her bed, and waited as Taryn took her position on the left side of her. Jace could feel the sudden shift between them. On the sofa, her ministrations had been instinctive and natural, one person supporting another. But here in her bed, her mind was no longer on supporting Taryn. All she could feel was the awkwardness of her body, the uncertainty of what she should do, and the things she knew her body wanted to do, but couldn't.

Taryn had also felt the change in atmosphere. Jace's usually relaxed demeanor was gone and in its place was a certain discomfort. Taryn rolled onto her side. In the glow of the nightlight, she could make out Jace's clenched facial features. "Are you okay?" she asked tentatively. "You seem a little nervous."

"Remember what you said last time about how it wasn't everyday you had your employer sitting on your bed in her pajamas?"

"I remember."

"Well, it's even weirder having my employee lying in my bed."

"I know, but, I'm not your employee at the moment...I'm your friend and I need a hug."

That comment spurred Jace into action. Without thinking, she opened her arms and waited for the Taryn to snuggle up to her and get settled. The smaller body pressed along the length of Jace's left side. Her lips touched the top of Taryn's head. She felt the heat rise in her body. What was supposed to be a comforting moment was turning her mind to mush. Her center throbbed and she wasn't sure she was going to survive the encounter without imploding.

"How's this?" Taryn mumbled lazily into Jace's chest.

"Good." Croaked Jace, unable to relieve the pressure building in her body. The feather light caress of Taryn's breath on her breast only made matters worse. Her body trembled and she struggled to disguise the tremors.

Feeling the shudder, Taryn instinctively moved away. "What's up?"

Jace was thankful that the room was dark as she could feel the blush rising up her neck. *For Christ's sake, you're an adult act like one!* She tried to control her body's reactions and hoped she wasn't going to explode in Taryn's arms. "I've never shared my bed with anyone...I'm a little unsure how I'm feeling."

"I'm sorry, Jace. I didn't mean to invade your space. I can sleep on the couch."

Jace held onto Taryn not wanting her to leave. "I'm okay." She knew she'd get no sleep if Taryn slept wrapped around her, breathing on her body, but she didn't want her to leave completely. "If you roll over, I could hold you and still have my own space, if that's okay?"

"Sure. Goodnight, Jace. Thanks." Taryn kissed the petrified woman's cheek, and turned her impish smile to the wall.

Jace raised her hand and touched her cheek. "Night, Taryn." She pulled Taryn's body to her and tried to clear her mind of anything other than holding onto the sensation.

JACE LOOKED UP as her front door opened and Taryn walked in smiling. She'd spent the afternoon visiting with Dylan and Cory.

"How are they?" Jace asked.

"Good. They have that look of love on their face. My guess is they've been doing it likes rabbits since I've been gone." Catching Jace's blush, she added, "I'm sorry, I didn't mean to embarrass you."

"No apologies needed. Remember you promised to rectify my innocence, so I figured these comments were just the beginning."

"Speaking of innocence, I borrowed some DVDs off Dylan." Taryn looked slightly self-conscious.

Jace gulped. "Should I be worried? What kind of DVDs are you talking about?"

Taryn punched her lightly on the arm. "You'll have to see. What's that I smell?"

"Your dinner. Beef stew."

"Awesome. You're spoiling me.."

"Do you want to eat in here or on the sofa?"

"Sofa. We can watch one of the films. Have you seen Coyote Ugly?"

"No. I heard it was supposed to be good." Jace scooped some stew into a bowl for her guest, and then did the same for herself.

Taryn smirked evilly as she took her food. "You'll see. I thought tonight could be the beginning of your transformation from a lurking lesbian to slightly more aware lesbian."

"Thanks for the warning."

"Relax, I'm not expecting you to run out into the road and announce it to the world! In fact, everything we're going to do can be done on the sofa."

Jace had to grip her bowl tighter as her shaking hands trembled with nervousness. "Why, oh why, do those words not comfort me?"

Taryn tasted the stew. "Wow. I may have to make you cook for me even when I'm not here." She pressed the play button on the DVD.

Twenty-five minutes later, Jace was confused about why Taryn thought she should see the movie, but she was enjoying it all the same. Watching some girls dance in an early morning café, she remarked, "Uh huh. I bet that happens all the time."

Taryn smiled. "Stop being picky. It's setting the scene for what's to come. They have to get that blonde's attention somehow. She's hardly likely to go to the bar they work in, so the producers had them dance in the café while they're having breakfast. Anyway, that's beside the point. The real question is, do any of the girls catch your eye?"

Jace did a double take. "What?"

"Well, you said you're pretty sure you're gay. So, I was interested in what type of girl you would go for."

Jace found her attention riveted to the blonde. She was wearing a very tight tank top. "She's kind of cute."

"Really?" Taryn surveyed the woman on the screen. She was definitely buff, and nice to look at. "Okay, that's a start, why?"

She reminds me of you! "She's pretty, in a natural looking way. I mean, she's got a good build and isn't afraid to dominate. I like women who can stick up for themselves." Jace dared a glance at Taryn. "What about you? What type of girl do you go for?"

"I wouldn't say I have a specific type. I know what I like when I see it. The tall brunette catches my eye, but she's a bit of a bitch. I like most women if I'm honest, but I am partial to any with blue eyes." Taryn dropped the hint to see what reaction she would get.

"Okay. If I had to go for a specific color of eyes I'd have to say brown. I really like Anne's eyes. They're so expressive. Sometimes they swirl around and change colors, especially when she gets emotional." *There you go, a safe answer, but I wonder if she knows her eyes are the spitting image of Anne's.*

"Jace, can I ask a question?"

"Sure. I didn't realize we were still at the stage where you had to ask me first."

"I was just curious about you and Anne. Have you ever had feelings for her?"

Jace's eyes rounded. "No! I mean, she's attractive and a really good friend, and I love her...but no."

"Hey calm down, I was just curious." Taryn looked back at the film, "Does the guy's body do anything for you?"

Jace shook her head. "Nope. Nothing moved on my heart rate monitor. Why do I suddenly feel like a rat in a laboratory experiment? It's still the blonde boss. I guess I'm into the power thing."

They watched the film in comfortable silence for a while, then Taryn asked, "Hey Jace, would you ever get a tattoo?"

Noting the tattoo on the bar owner's arm, Jace answered, "Never thought about it. What do you think about me having one on my bicep like her?" She rolled her T-shirt sleeve up and flexed the muscle. "Do you think it would suit me?"

Taryn tried not to laugh at her usually serious boss pretending to be a tough broad. She pointed to the screen. "Ooh! Look at the ice going down that woman's stomach. Now she's hot! I like them tall and lean."

Jace lifted an eyebrow. "Really?" The ladies were now writhing around wet on the bar top.

"Sure." Taryn gulped down some of her beer. "I think you'd look like that if you wore a leather skirt hitched up to your panties, and a top that flashed your cleavage." She winked at Jace to show she was kidding, well half kidding.

"I'm way too old for that look!"

"Bullshit! You run every morning. Your body doesn't look a day over twenty, and you're only four years older than me!" Taryn blushed as she heard the words leave her lips.

"Thanks." Jace's blush matched her own. "You've got a pretty good body yourself."

Taryn smiled. *She's flirting with me! Oh my God, my boss is flirting with me!* "Well, we should start up a mutual appreciation society."

Jace reclined her chair, smiling inwardly at the knowledge that Taryn found her interesting. As the film rolled on, she realized she wanted to move over to the sofa and sit by Taryn, especially when the film turned serious and began discussing bad childhoods. She listened carefully to the conversation between the characters Lilly and Jersey. "I hope we never have to have that discussion."

Taryn looked over. "She thought Lilly was her friend, but Lilly never said that. She was just her boss."

"I want you to know that you're my friend, Taryn. I just hope I never have to do what Lilly did because you broke a rule."

"Remember the bite mark?"

"Yeah. I felt bad afterwards, especially when you told me about Marti's behavior. However, I still had to do my job."

"I know. It's nice to hear that we're friends. I've really enjoyed staying here with you, Jace."

"Same here." Jace laughed when she heard the bar owner describe herself as a cast iron, heartless bitch. "Oh, I bet that's what you thought I was when you first met me!"

Taryn laughed. "Well, maybe a little. But I think you considered me stubborn and pigheaded at first. Admit it!"

"You are stubborn and a little fiery, but I like you!"

"I think the film would have been much better if Jersey and Lilly had gotten together. Can you imagine the sex scene?" Taryn said with a disingenuous grin.

Jace squirmed in her seat. "Don't tease me! I'm new to all this."

Taryn stood up and stretched her back out as the credits began to roll. "Ah, what a nice film. It makes you all cozy inside!"

"Yeah, it was pretty good. What's next on the agenda?"

"Another beer, and a lesbian classic. It stars Sharon Stone and Ellen DeGeneres. If Walls Could Talk 2."

"Sharon Stone played a lesbian?"

"She sure did. I think you'll appreciate this film. It has lots of blondes in it...and some lesbian sex. Think of it as the next step in your development. You'll get to see what you think of two women getting it on."

Speechless, Jace gazed after Taryn's retreating body then got to her feet. She felt slightly restless and all too aware of the distance between her chair and the sofa. Impulsively, she settled onto the warm seat Taryn had just vacated.

"Geez, would you jump in my grave that quickly?" Taryn protested from the kitchen doorway.

"I just wanted to stretch out a little." Jace lied. "You can share the couch with me if you want."

Taryn passed her a cold beer and sat down in the chair. Vaguely disappointed, Jace tried to keep her attention on the next movie. It was much more serious than the first, three stories in one. "Makes you realize how hard things can be for gay people," she remarked when the older lesbian lost her home after her partner's death. "Even nowadays, there's prejudice in the world. Are you ready for that?"

"Well, I'm not planning on shouting it from the rooftops, but I am sick of being lonely."

"What about work? Would it bother you if people knew you were gay?"

Jace considered the question. "I would hope my partner and I could be discreet, but it wouldn't bother me if the Center staff knew. I've seen how accepting they are of you and Cory. I would hope they'd accept my sexuality, too." Jace stifled a gasp as the two women in the next story began making love.

"Is it making you uncomfortable?" Taryn asked.

Jace blushed. "A little. I've never watched two women make love before. It's interesting."

"Interesting? Now that's a word I wouldn't have used. How does it make you feel?"

Jace buried her head into the nearby cushion. She couldn't admit how she felt, not to Taryn. It was too much, too soon. "Err...next question."

Taryn could sense Jace's embarrassment and wondered if she was pushing her too hard. She contemplated turning the DVD off, but instead tried to shift the focus slightly to herself. "If I told you it turns me on, would that make you feel better?"

Jace turned smoldering blue eyes on her. "It does?"

Taryn nodded. "Yep. It's at times like this I wish I had someone to hold and be with, don't you?"

Jace swallowed a sigh. The only someone she was interested in holding was Taryn, but she was not about to say so. "I guess so," she admitted, trying to sound casual.

"What do you think?" Taryn asked. "Do you think it's hot?"

Jace hesitated. Did the image make her hot? Did looking at a woman's naked body make her tingle? The answer was yes. With a jerky little nod, she said, "Yes, it's hot."

The reluctant answer and the uncertainty in Jace's eyes amazed Taryn and she realized that frank discussion of sexuality was genuinely new to Jace. She was not sexually self-aware at all. Taryn tried to think back to her teenage years. She could barely remember what it was like to discover her awakening sexuality. For Jace to be in her thirties, and yet so innocent must be bewildering, especially when she was so in control and knowledgeable about other things. Deciding that she had pushed the conversation to its limits, Taryn stopped asking questions and settled down to watch the final show in the trilogy. She liked seeing Sharon Stone cavort with Ellen.

As they watched the interplay between the two women, Taryn sensed Jace relax a little more. The evening's conversation had definitely helped Taryn resolve her own mixed feelings about Jace. She doubted very much if she and Jace could have a romantic future; they were so different. Taryn didn't want to give her heart away, especially to someone who was so unsure about her own sexuality, and had no experience at a relationship. A friendship was all she could offer Jace. Anything more would be a huge mistake.

Chapter
Sixteen

"IT'LL BE MIDNIGHT soon," Taryn said, hazily aware that she'd had one drink too many and was having trouble sticking to her resolution to treat Jace as nothing more than a friend. She cast a covert sideways glance at the beautiful woman in the driver's seat and before she could stop herself, she said huskily, "I've been desperate to kiss you all evening."

She heard Jace's small, shocked gasp and smiled to herself. Why shouldn't they have some fun? They were on their way back to Jace's after the traditional New Years Eve outing with Anne and her family. For the past few hours, Taryn had felt Jace's eyes on her constantly. Every time she intercepted that dark blue gaze, she read desire before Jace could look away.

Throwing caution to the wind, she said, "Pull over."

"Here?" Jace sounded disbelieving. "Why?"

"Because I want to make out in your Jeep."

Jace drove a few more yards, her eyes darting sideways to Taryn every few seconds, then she swerved off the road onto a dirt track and turned off the motor.

"Are you sure about this?" Jace asked. "I mean, you've had a little to drink. I — "

"Do you want to kiss me or don't you?" Taryn unfastened her seat belt and turned to face Jace. As Jace seemed lost for words, Taryn leaned forward and brushed her lips against Jace's. She pulled back slightly and watched the pupils of Jace's eyes dilate and contract as they focused in on her.

Jace opened up her arms inviting Taryn into them. "Okay. Be my guest. Kiss away."

Taryn didn't need any further invitation. She crawled onto Jace's lap, knocking her leg on the gear stick as she tried to maneuver her body. She reached down and pressed the lever beside Jace's chair, shooting the chair back, and a surprised Jace, into a more horizontal position. "See, it's not as easy as it looks."

"I'm beginning to realize that. It looks easier in the films."

"Everything looks easy in the films. Now where was I?" She pulled Jace's lips onto her mouth as she straddled Jace's hips.

Jace's breathing hitched when she felt Taryn press down on her lower torso. The stretch of denim pulled against her skin and she could feel the tightening of her groin against the seam of her jeans. She gripped Taryn's hips and used her arms to keep Taryn's weight where she needed it. She tried to concentrate on kissing Taryn's mouth, but wandering hands caught her attention. She tried to forget that nimble fingers were rising dangerously close to her left breast. She couldn't stop the tiny moans escaping from her mouth.

Taryn found her way under Jace's sweatshirt. As if on autopilot, her hand sought out the pert breast and no amount of self-control could prevent Taryn from touching the bra covered skin. She could feel Jace pressing into her and when she pulled away, Taryn dipped her hand inside the bra cup.

Jace's hips bucked upwards the first time Taryn squeezed her nipple. She pulled away from the kiss, opening her eyes to look into Taryn's. "Don't stop." She gasped as she felt Taryn's fingers roll over her tight nipple.

"I won't." She leaned back away from Jace and slipped her second hand under Jace's top. Soon she had a breast in each hand and she began to knead them simultaneously.

Jace could feel the tingling sensations travel southwards and center in her swollen groin. The wet that pooled there intensified the need for release. Her hands rose to Taryn's waist and she began to move them upwards. She could feel the swell of Taryn's breast and mirrored Taryn's actions. "Ca...can I touch them?" She saw the sexy smile and nod of consent.

Taryn could feel the pump of Jace's hips against her own. She released the pressure on the breasts and stroked them gently. She watched as Jace's eyes dropped to the edge of her sweater.

Jace lifted the edge of Taryn's top and tentatively moved her hands up the front of Taryn's torso. The skin felt soft and warm and she could feel a slight hitch in Taryn's breathing as she ran her fingers across the front of Taryn's bra.

Taryn could feel cold fingertips stroke gently up her body. The cold air that followed caused her skin to develop goose bumps and she leaned back further placing her hands on the side of Jace's body to steady herself.

Jace looked up from Taryn's chest area into eyes urging her on. She watched as Taryn's hands reached behind her body, and in seconds, Jace felt the silk material of the bra give way. Jace lifted the edge of the bra over the small mounds and felt the smooth skin and slightly rougher nipple against the palm of her hand.

"Are you okay?" Taryn asked as she watched Jace who seemed mesmerized by the actions of her hands.

"Uh huh!"

Taryn glanced briefly out of the window, desperately hoping they were still alone and cursing that their first sexual exploration could potentially be witnessed by others. The condensation that was gathering on the side windows and windshield helped mask their actions. "I'm not rushing you, am I?"

Jace lifted her eyes to Taryn's. "I'm good. This is good." *Great vocabulary skills! Get your mind back in place, Jace! You sound like a prepubescent school kid!* "I've wanted to do this for ages." She fondled the breasts a little more fervently. "I can see why men are fixated on these, they feel awesome."

"Not just men, Jace. I happen to be very partial to breasts myself."

Jace removed one hand from under Taryn's sweater and placed it gently on the back of Taryn's neck. "Come here!"

Taryn liked the authoritative tone of Jace's command and immediately gave in. They resumed kissing, each exploring the other's torso and breasts.

Jace didn't want to interrupt their make-out session one little bit, but she could feel the slight tugging sensation running down her left leg. She half concentrated on the kissing and at the same time on stretching out her stiff leg muscle. Unable to relieve the pain, she pulled away from Taryn.

"Problem?"

"Cramp in my leg." Jace helped Taryn off her legs. She could feel the blood begin to circulate more freely down her thighs and into her calves.

Taryn laughed. "You never see this in the movies."

Jace stamped her foot on the floor. "I hear you. Not that I'm complaining." She grinned over at Taryn. "I'm *definitely* having fun!"

Taryn wiggled her eyebrows suggestively. "I aim to please!"

"You do that very well." Jace leaned over the center console and kissed Taryn gently. "Thank you for being so patient with me."

Taryn concentrated on returning the kiss before she replied,. "You're welcome. Now where were we?" She placed her free hand under Jace's sweatshirt and tickled her way up the tender skin, climbing back onto her lap. "I think my hand was here."

"Good memory!" Jace murmured as she nibbled lightly on

Taryn's ear lobe. "You have great breasts."

"Thanks." Taryn beamed. She really wanted to taste Jace's skin and suckle on the tight breasts she had now memorized by touch. She kissed Jace's lips a little, pulling gently on her probing tongue and licking along the full lips swollen from their joint passion. She kissed down Jace's neck and felt the strong pulse as she gently nuzzled the major vein that marked out Taryn's pathway. After a few seconds on each part of Jace's neck, Taryn moved her head lower and at the same time slowly lifted Jace's sweatshirt up. As she began to coordinate her final assault over the bunched up sweatshirt, she felt Jace's hand move hers and stop her movements.

"Not here." Jace whispered, disappointed at her own cowardice.

Taryn pulled Jace's sweatshirt down and removed her hand. "Are you okay?"

Jace looked away. She wished she could block out the here-and-now and just go with her feelings. *Great move, idiot! She's going to think you're such a prude!* "I'm fine."

She was lying, but the physical and emotional overload on her senses was close to exploding point. Taryn climbed over the center console and back onto her side of the jeep. When she saw that Taryn was clear of her seat, Jace flicked it back upright, grimacing when she felt the warm wet patch spread against her skin as she moved.

"Are you sure you're okay?"

Jace flashed angry eyes at Taryn. "I'm fine! I just didn't think flashing my goods to the world was a good idea. I'm sorry." She turned the key in the ignition and was relieved to hear the engine growl to life. "We need to go."

One step forward, two steps back! Taryn couldn't stop the hurt that she felt at Jace's abrupt attitude. She blinked back the tears that threatened to fall and tried to reason out Jace's behavior. She dropped her head in defeat. She had let her own needs get ahead of Jace's and she had done exactly what she'd intended not to do. Jace wasn't someone she could have a casual one night stand with, yet she was seducing her as if that's what they would be doing. Worse still, she'd made Jace uncomfortable. *You knew she needed to feel in control and you pushed.*

Taryn glanced at Jace's tight grip on the steering wheel. The knuckles on her hand were a pale contrast to the darkened skin of the back of her hand.

Jace's mind was screaming at her. *You are an idiot! A fucking idiot! Say something before she thinks you're a lost cause!* She knew she'd acted irrationally. The thought of Taryn seeing her naked breasts had scared her. No one had ever touched her so intimately and the feeling of Taryn's caress still burned her skin. But more importantly, she knew that Taryn had done it all before. All of a sudden her confidence had evaporated and she'd been frightened that her body just wouldn't be good enough.

Taryn stared out of the window. *How can one moment of bliss turn out so disastrously?* She glanced back at her silent companion and knew if she stared hard enough Jace would look her way. *One...two...three...* She counted patiently in her head. *Four...five... six...seven...*She saw the turn of Jace's head her way. *Bingo!* "Hey."

Jace smiled sadly. "Hi, I'm an idiot." She shrugged and returned her eyes to the road.

Well that's a start. Taryn was just happy that Jace was communicating. "Want to talk about it?"

Jace shook her head. "I'm fine. I over-reacted. I'm sorry. Can we move on?"

Taryn knew it wasn't the whole story but she wasn't going to pressure Jace any more than she already had. She put her hand on Jace's firm thigh. "I had a great time this evening."

"Really?" Jace took her eyes off the road to smile at her, almost as if seeking reassurance.

"Really. And I'm hurt you couldn't tell." Taryn stuck her bottom lip out as far as it would go and pretended to pout.

For the first time since they started for home, Jace relaxed and released her death grip on the wheel. "I had a good time, too." She hesitated. "Want to come back to my place and watch the ball drop?"

Taryn checked her watch. It was only half an hour until midnight. "Sure, why not?"

JACE PUT SOME champagne on ice and said, "Let's put on our own music." She clicked the remote control, switching the CD player on. The sultry tones of Eva Cassidy wafted into the living room. "Okay," she faced Taryn, "if you could have your dream date, what would you want to be doing at this time on New Year's Eve?"

Taryn thought about the question carefully. "That's a tough one. I don't really want to dwell on it, as it reminds me how lonely I am. But I guess if I had to think about it, I'd be dancing slowly with my date. How about you?"

"Dancing would be nice." Impulsively, Jace extended her hand. "Would you like to dance with me, Taryn?"

Without a word, Taryn stepped into Jace's arms and both

women swayed in time to the music. Taryn enjoyed losing herself in the moment. One song became three, and soon she was nestled in the crook of Jace's neck. The musky, vanilla scent that was Jace seeped into her nostrils and lingered on her clothes. She glanced at the television screen. "Hey there. The countdown has begun. Are you ready?" She felt Jace's head lift from her shoulder.

"Sure. Ten...nine...eight...seven...six..." Jace mumbled watching the numbers flash on the screen.

"Five...four...three...two...one. Happy New Year, Jace."

"Happy New Year, Taryn." Jace bent down and kissed Taryn on the cheek.

Taryn didn't let go of Jace's hand and body. She could still feel the tingle of the kiss on her cheek. She was unsure whether to proceed with what her mind was yelling at her to do. *Kiss her! Just stand up straight and kiss her!* She looked into tumultuous, swirling blue eyes and recognized the uncertainty shining back at her. Hadn't she already decided not to get into a relationship with a woman who had no experience? Hadn't she promised herself she would only be a friend to Jace? Hadn't she escaped complications by quitting while she was still ahead in the Jeep just a half hour earlier?

Jace was in turmoil. She could see straight into Taryn's soul. Her eyes were boring into Jace's confused blue ones. She couldn't work out if Taryn was just lonely and with her for comfort, or whether she was really interested. With every second that passed, their heads came closer together. Jace tried to control her body, but intense desire was so new to her, she felt lost in her senses. A tremble traveled down her spine and into her legs. She took a deep breath and closed her eyes. She needed some control.

Tentatively at first, Taryn took the lead and pulled Jace's head even closer. She looked at Jace's closed eyes, licked her lips, and then closed the final distance between Jace's lips and hers.

Jace's mind exploded. Stars burst in her brain. She tried to make sense of the overwhelming emotions rushing through her body. Her knees shuddered, and she felt Taryn tighten her grip on her body. Taryn's teeth gently grazed across her bottom lip and Jace opened her mouth even more, moving on instinct alone. Taryn's tongue hesitantly explored her mouth. Finally, when she couldn't control the racing of her heart, and had no strength left in her legs, she pulled away from Taryn. Her breathing was labored, and her body was quivering from head to toe.

Taryn smiled shyly. "Happy New Year! That kind of rocked

my socks."

Jace looked into the deep, dark eyes of the woman she was sure she loved. "So, it was okay?"

"Yes! You have no catching up to do there." Taryn studied the innocent and loving face of the woman she was beginning to care for. She took Jace's hand, and led her in the direction of the bedrooms.

Jace panicked when she saw where Taryn was leading her. *Oh crap, I am not ready for this! Shit...tell her!*

Taryn stopped in front of her temporary bedroom. She stood on tiptoes and kissed Jace again, a teasing sweet kiss that made her senses crave much more.

Jace tightened her arms around Taryn and breathed in the jasmine scent of her shampoo mixed with the smell of winter. Her inhibitions were fading as fast as her heart beat and she couldn't believe that this dream was coming true. No matter how much she reasoned with herself that this was not a good idea and she wasn't ready, there was no way she could resist what Taryn was offering.

She lowered her head and kissed Taryn's lips. She could taste the slight hint of wine and deepened the kiss. Her tongue pressed against the barrier of teeth and she groaned when she felt Taryn open her mouth slightly to allow her access.

Taryn tried to quell her emotions and desire. Her nerves were sensitive and every motion of Jace against her body made her want more. She could feel firm hands roam over her back and down her side. She didn't want them to stop and she knew that she'd have to remain conscious of where her hands were going if she wanted Jace to keep kissing her.

Jace felt Taryn's hands lock around her neck. She opened her eyes and through slightly blurred vision saw that Taryn's eyes were shut. She broke the kiss and waited for Taryn's eyes to meet her own. "We could continue this..." she hesitated, "in the bedroom...if you want?"

"I want." Taryn admitted hoarsely.

Jace tried to control her nerves and the trembling quivers that were making their way down her legs. She pushed the bedroom door open and followed Taryn in.

Observing Jace's nervous composure, Taryn stopped short of the bed and drew Jace toward her. "Hey."

Jace looked shyly at Taryn. "Hey yourself."

The two women met each other in a kiss. Each explored the other's face.

Taryn could feel the bed against the back of her legs. She lowered herself slowly onto it never losing contact with Jace, drawing her down beside her. When she felt Jace relax against her, she moved one of her hands to the front of Jace's shirt. "May I?"

Jace had lost the power of speech the moment Taryn's hand moved across the front of her shirt. She had hoped Taryn would take the lead, but now her blood was racing and she felt slightly disorientated from nerves and emotions. "Be…my…guest." she stuttered.

When Taryn's fingers didn't move, Jace looked down at the hand and back to Taryn's questioning eyes. A nod of assent was her answer.

Take it slow! Do not rush her! One button at a time! Taryn tried reigning in her impatient nature and fought the urge to rip the shirt off. Instead, she tentatively undid the first button. She could feel Jace's intense gaze on her and she lifted her eyes to maintain eye contact. She moved forward and resumed their kissing. When she felt Jace's tongue probe her mouth, she slowly pushed the shirt open and felt bare skin against her hand.

Jace tried not to gasp as cold air rushed over her exposed skin. She felt self-conscious as the shirt was tugged gently off her body. She was also very aware of the warm hands that danced across her skin, making a northward journey toward her breasts. Gripping the edge of Taryn's sweater, she slowly moved the material up and stared down at the white skin before her. "You're beautiful!"

Tentatively at first, Jace's fingers moved toward the edge of the black silk bra that stood out in stark contrast against the pale skin. Summoning up all of her courage, she stroked the silk. With each stroke, she became more confident and soon she was fondling the supple breast. Her eyes never left her hand and she watched as the nipple pushed against the material.

She swallowed the saliva that had pooled in her mouth and looked at Taryn. "Can I?" Her fingers were poised to delve into the cup of the bra.

"I have a better idea. How about we take it off and you can have full access." Taryn winked playfully, trying to maintain a light atmosphere. She didn't want to stop what they were doing. To her amazement, the slow agonizing steps that Jace was taking were actually arousing her more and more. When there was no answer from Jace, Taryn took the silence as a yes and swiftly unhooked her bra.

Jace felt all the liquid in her body head south. She captured one of the nipples between her fingers and instinctively squeezed. At Taryn's gasp, she looked up apologetically and withdrew her hand.

"No, no, no. Don't stop. You didn't hurt me." Taryn reached forward and gently stroked the top of Jace's cotton bra. "I'll show you." She could feel the nipple respond to her touch and she increased the pressure until she heard Jace suck in a deep breath. "Feels good?"

"Yes!" Jace gasped.

Taryn's groin pulsed. Every touch was fueling the desire fully ignited within her. When the urge to kiss Jace's breasts got too much, she gently leaned forward and kissed the swell just above Jace's bra. "I want to kiss these, Jace. I need to kiss them."

Jace couldn't deny Taryn anything. The woman had been more than patient with her. "Okay." She felt the material over her breasts give way as Taryn deftly unclipped the bra with one swift motion. "Impressive!" she drawled into her ear, feeling dizzily intoxicated.

Taryn giggled. "A girl's got to have a few tricks up her sleeve."

She lowered her head and gently sucked in the hardened nipple. She could feel Jace's heart beating against her hand as she licked and kissed the soft skin before taking the nipple back into her mouth. She alternated between sucking and gentling biting it.

Jace strained against the seam of her pants as Taryn's sucking increased. She felt Taryn's hand slip inside her pants and strong, firm fingers gently spread the moisture over her swollen clitoris. It didn't take more than a couple of strokes before her body shook and the blood rushed to her head. Small shudders erupted in her groin and traveled to her stomach. Her nipples were suddenly exquisitely sensitive and she placed her hand against Taryn's face. "Who...a," she stammered.

Taryn pulled her close. "I've got you. It feels good, doesn't it?"

Jace let herself be held. She liked feeling Taryn's breasts against her face and she needed time to calm her heart and mind. *Breathe! Just breathe in and out! The last thing she needs is you fainting on her!*

Stroking Jace's bare back, Taryn tried to take her mind off the pulse she still felt between her legs. The deep breathing of her partner against her naked breasts was intensifying her own need. She knew she was becoming frustrated and needed to release the pressure before she literally exploded. She lifted Jace's chin and looked into her eyes. "Are you okay?"

Jace nodded mutely.

"I...err...I need to come, Jace. I thought I could control myself better, but I can't. It hurts."

Disarmed by Taryn's frank statement but uncertain if she could please her, Jace asked, "Would you like me to...touch you?"

Taryn kissed Jace's lips. "I don't think you're ready to touch me, are you?"

Jace lowered her eyes to Taryn's groin and shook her head disappointed in her own cowardice.

Taryn lay on her back and pulled Jace slightly on top of her. She waited until Jace made eye contact with her. "Hey, no big deal that's why I was given my own hands. If it's okay with you I could touch myself while you kiss me." She saw the uncertainty flicker across Jace's eyes. "Or I could go to the bathroom and we forget I mentioned anything."

Jace closed her eyes and lowered her mouth to Taryn's, she hoped her actions would speak louder than her words.

Taryn kept one arm securely wrapped around her torso and with the other hand, she undid her fly and slipped the other hand inside. As she rocked against her own hand, Jace deepened and quickened the pace of their kisses. It didn't take long before Taryn felt the initial stirrings of her orgasm.

A few minutes later, after she'd caught her breath, they lay side by side staring up at the ceiling. As the silence extended, Taryn was gripped by dismay. She had never meant for this to happen, and could sense an unease in Jace. She turned her head slightly and could see the tension on Jace's face.

It was New Year's Eve, she rationalized, and people did things they regretted the next morning but agreed to move on. She and Jace were adults. They could do the same thing. Her eyes met Jace's and she looked quickly away but took her hand, wanting to communicate what she couldn't say. That everything was okay and she wouldn't expect anything to come of this.

JACE PLACED THE coffee pot on the counter and proceeded to get two mugs. She could tell by Taryn's sober mood that the imminent conversation was not going to be all she'd dreamed of. She waited patiently as Taryn placed the bagels on a tray, fussed around the counter tops, and finally took a seat next to her at the counter.

They ate in silence for a few minutes. Out of the corner of her eye, Taryn watched Jace chew more of her bottom lip than the bagel. She put her half-eaten slice of bagel down, and grabbed hold of one of Jace's hands. "Jace, I do like you. I really do."

A little shocked at the sudden outburst, Jace said, "That's

good to know." She took in Taryn's glum face. "However, I sense there's a 'but' coming."

Taryn nodded sadly. "We can't be together." She lifted her hand to wipe a strand of hair off Jace's forehead. "You have made this week so special for me. I'm not going to pretend last night was a spur of the moment thing. I've been wanting to kiss you for a while. But I didn't mean for it to go any further. We'd both had wine and..."

"You don't want to be more than friends?"

"Jace, we're not just two women who've met and like one another. You're my boss and direct supervisor. It could be awkward at work if we got involved. I'm not a person who likes to hide how I feel. You chewed Anne out when you found out she was my aunt. What was the quote, oh yeah, 'a conflict of interest.'" She squeezed Jace's fingers, trying to reassure her that she was just as down about it. "I'm also a student, Jace. I'm sure there must be rules about staff dating students."

Jace nodded, her eyes dull. "There are, but I don't think it really relates to us. It's more a rule to protect undergraduates from faculty and staff. But you're right about me being your supervisor."

"I'm sorry," Taryn said. "I don't regret last night. I just think we need to put it into perspective."

Jace took a moment to swallow a rush of anger. Their intimacy could not possibly mean so little that Taryn thought they could just brush it aside and carry on as before. Wanting to break through the wall of common sense Taryn seemed to be hiding behind, she said, "I understand what you're saying, but Taryn, I really like you. I tried not to, but I couldn't help myself. I'm not good at expressing how I feel...but just for the moment, can you forget that I'm your supervisor, forget that you're a student, and just look at me as a woman? Would you date me?"

Taryn pushed her stool away from the counter and stood up. Slipping between Jace's long legs, she lifted a hand and gently caressed her cheek. "Jace, you're probably the most beautiful person I know, inside and out. I've thought about this all morning, and my answer would still be no."

She could tell Jace was crestfallen and felt terrible . "Hey, let me explain. For starters, I've never stood on my own, Jace. I've always run away. And as tempting as it is to run into your arms, I need to find out who I am." She felt the tiny nod of agreement against her hand. "I'm also just getting over a long-term relationship. It hasn't even been two months since Marti and I split up. I'm not ready to be in another relationship. You don't need my baggage."

"I understand." Jace whispered.

Taryn sucked in a deep breath. "There's more."

"Wow, you really have analyzed this." There was a bitter edge to Jace's voice.

"My final reason is probably the most important. Jace, you're new to all this and you need to investigate how you feel about women a little more. I think you need some time to understand what you're getting into, and if it's really what you want. I'm sorry, I'm probably being very selfish, but I don't think I'd cope very well if we got involved and then you rejected my lifestyle and me.

Jace fought the tears that threatened to fall. She had to be strong. She needed to keep her control. "But I don't need any time. I've thought of nothing but you for the past six months." She saw Taryn's eyes widen in surprise.

"I'm flattered, Jace." Taryn could tell that Jace was beginning to get agitated with the situation. "I'm not rejecting you, I swear. If things were different...if I was in a different time or place, than I'd be jumping your bones right here and now." She saw a little spark ignite the fire in Jace's eyes. "I just need time...and you need to date others." She lightly kissed Jace's lips.

Jace was stunned at Taryn's comment. "I don't want to be with others. Taryn, I want you."

"Jace, I said date. You don't have to sleep with them." Taryn gazed into the deep cerulean eyes and felt a sharp pang at the mix of trust and disappointment she found there. She pulled Jace into her arms and hugged her fiercely. "Friends?"

Jace snuggled into Taryn's chest, enjoying the comfort Taryn's body offered her somewhat battered soul. Part of her felt rejected, but another part of her was unsurprised by Taryn's retreat. As much as Taryn wanted to claim this was all about Jace and her inexperience, Jace suspected there was another side to the story. Taryn wasn't able to trust that they could make something work. *I will win your heart, Taryn Murphy! I've waited thirty-five years; I can wait a few months.*

"Friends?" she echoed, lifting her head so she could meet Taryn's eyes once more. "Yes. Always."

TARYN WALKED INTO the quiet Center. It was weird seeing the normally bustling place so desolate. The usual hum of industriously working students was gone, and in its place was the quiet hush of whispered voices. She checked her watch. Anne had asked that all grad assistants report to work by nine o'clock,

the second day of the New Year. Taryn had come in earlier on
the off chance of seeing Jace before they got caught up in all the
pre-spring semester business. She continued toward her office
area, saying hello or wishing those she met a Happy New Year.
She paused in front of the closed wooden door. Jace's Jeep had
been in its usual parking spot. She listened carefully at the door.
When she heard the shuffling of paper, she tentatively knocked
on the door.

"Come in," Jace's serious tone instructed.

Taryn pushed the door open a nervous smile on her face.
Hoping to disguise the tension she felt, she said cheerfully,
"Hey."

Jace smiled when she saw her. She had missed Taryn's
presence in her life. Twenty-four hours could be a long time
when you missed the very essence of someone. "Hey yourself.
What have you bought me for breakfast?"

Taryn released the breath she'd been holding. She had
expected to find Jace harboring some animosity toward her. But
in front of her, was the usual cheery Jace she had come to know
so well.

"Who says I've brought anything?" Taryn teased, reassured
by the sparkle in Jace's eyes.

"Because you're a creature of habit, and you want to make
sure your boss is a happy woman!" She wiggled her eyebrows in
a suggestive manner.

Taryn placed the bag on Jace's desk. "I got toasted bagels.
Donuts are too unhealthy, and my New Year's resolution is to
eat a much healthier diet. I'm even considering joining a gym!"

Jace laughed and openly appraised Taryn. "There is nothing
wrong with your body, Taryn. So, because you're on a healthy
diet, I have to be? No fair! I run four miles a day. I deserve my
donut!" She pretended to pout.

"Suck it up! You can do breakfast every other day, and we
can have donuts when you're buying!" Taryn handed one of the
bagels and a cup of coffee to Jace.

Jace watched as Taryn smeared her bagel with cream cheese.
She snorted in disbelief, when she saw her cover every available
bit of bagel.

"What?" Taryn asked, taking a huge bite.

Jace lightly creamed her own. "I was just amused at how
much cream cheese you used. You might as well have had the
donut, because there's a ton of fat in it."

Taryn poked out her tongue. "Smarty pants!" She relaxed in
her chair.

"Thank you for breakfast. I was a little worried that my

declaration would have sent you running." Jace said in a hushed manner. She knew work was not the time to be having this discussion.

"Not as pleased as I was to see you smile at me. I was worried you'd hate me. The first time you open your heart to someone, and they hand it back."

Jace nodded glumly. "That's life. But you didn't rip it up or tear it out; maybe it got a little bruised. You actually gave me a little hope." She winked at Taryn, a mischievous smile transforming her mood. "I thought about what you said, and I think I do need to get out there and date. I was wondering if you knew of any places or ways I could go about doing this?"

Taryn had a difficult time hiding her surprise. Even though she had suggested Jace date, the little green-eyed monster reared its head. She hadn't expected Jace to follow her advice. "That's great, Jace," she faked enthusiasm. "We're heading down to watch Dylan play again on Saturday and then we'll head to the bar. Why don't you join us? I think your first outing into the world of dating should be supervised, don't you?" Taryn commented.

Jace pretended to give the suggestion some thought. She had noticed the look of shock in Taryn's eyes, and detected a hint of irritation in the younger woman's tone. *You wanted friendship, Taryn. Suck it up!*

ANNE SURVEYED JACE with a long-suffering expression. "Remind me again why we're doing this?"

"To win Taryn's heart." Jace took clothing from her closet and tossed it on her bed.

"How does openly dating women get you Taryn?"

"She's the one who suggested it, And I want to show her I like women. I figured I'd try and get a few women interested in me. We'd go out a few times, and this will do two things. First, it'll show Taryn that I've dated, and second, the jealousy will force her to admit she likes me."

Anne laughed out loud and assessed the clothing scattered across Jace's bed. She'd had no idea her friend had such sexy garments in her wardrobe. "I'm amazed. A few weeks ago, the mere thought of talking to a woman scared the crap out of you."

Jace pulled a pair of jeans up over her long tanned legs. "Okay, what top should I wear?"

"It depends. What image are you going for?"

"I don't know. I want to appear sexy, but I want to be comfortable. It's damn cold in that rink. I'd usually wear a sweatshirt, but I don't want to become a wallflower. The whole idea is to attract a woman." Jace held several tops up to model.

Anne threw her hands in the air. "When are you going to realize how god damn sexy you are. You'd turn heads if you showed up in a Hessian sack. Personally, I like you casual. How about the blue hooded sweatshirt, over a white T-shirt? At least you'll be warm. Oh...and put your black boots on, too."

Jace followed her instructions and asked, "How's that. Sexy enough?"

Anne nodded enthusiastically. "Okay, time to try out some moves. Give me a 'come on' look."

Jace raised both eyebrows. "A what?"

"Pretend I'm a woman." The arched brows rose a little higher. "I mean, pretend I've caught your eye. How are you going to get my attention?"

"I don't know. I'd probably try to make eye contact, maybe smile." She practiced subtle eye contact and a rakish smile. "How was that?"

Anne laughed impishly, "Pretty good. Okay, you've got my attention. Now what?"

"I don't know."

Anne shook her head. Her friend really was a novice. "You could ask them to dance." She saw Jace's eyes widen. "Just like you did with me. And didn't you say you danced with Taryn on New Year's Eve."

Jace looked uneasy. "I don't want to give anyone the wrong impression. I mean, I want them to be interested, but I have no intention of leading them on. What if they try to kiss me?"

"Calm down. You won't send anyone mixed messages."

"I'm not sure I know how to avoid it," Jace grumbled.

"You'll be fine. Now pay attention. You'll probably end up leading. Your height and strength makes that inevitable, but you have to believe you can do it. If you try it out here, you'll be more confident when you do it for real."

Jace put a compilation CD into the stereo and drew Anne into her arms. After a few songs, and a little coaching, she felt more certain of her own capabilities.

"Okay, stud. I have to get going. I expect a detailed report in the morning. Don't leave anything out, either."

Jace kissed Anne on the cheek. "Okay, boss. You'll get every sordid detail, trust me."

Chapter
Seventeen

TARYN THREW THE Beanie Baby across the room. Her mood was decidedly foul and no amount of sweet-talking was going to lift her spirits.

Dylan picked up the toy and placed it back on the shelf. "If you have to be destructive, then do it to your own property."

"Sorry," mumbled Taryn.

Dylan placed a plate of spaghetti in front of her. "You're not usually in on a Wednesday evening. What happened to your night out with Jace?"

Taryn shrugged. "She has a date."

"What? Another one with that girl she met at the bar?"

Taryn shook her head. "No, Jace said she was too clingy and wanted to move in after their initial date. This new woman actually works across campus in the psychology department. Apparently, she spotted Jace with me at the Country Club and collared her in the parking lot last week."

Dylan swallowed a forkful of pasta. "Why are you so down? I thought you wanted Jace to date?"

Taryn pushed her food around her plate. "I did. I mean, I do. I just didn't think she'd be this enthusiastic about it. This is the fifth woman she's dated, and it's only been a month."

Dylan took a few more mouthfuls, and then checked her watch. She didn't want to be late picking Cory up from class. "I didn't think you were interested in Jace. You were the one who needed space. The woman is only doing what you asked."

Taryn pouted. She knew Dylan was right, but having it pointed out to her wasn't helping her mood. "I know. I just didn't think it would eat into my time with her so much."

"Taryn, as far as I can tell, Jace and you spend plenty of time together. As friendships go, you spend a majority of time with each other. If I'm not mistaken, isn't Jace usually at Anne's on a Monday evening while you tutor Ricky?"

"Yes."

"And, don't you usually go to the movies on Wednesday evenings, and then dine out?"

"Yeah, except for tonight."

Taryn knew she was acting like a child. She couldn't help it. She'd heard all about Jace's last date in great detail, and the emotions that had surged through her body had made her sink to the depths of despair. The thought of another woman touching Jace made her feel sick. Not that Jace had mentioned anything physical, but she'd blushed when Taryn asked. Taryn's mind had filled in the rest. She kept getting images of Jace's pert breasts and smooth, tanned skin whenever she thought of Jace kissing another woman. And, no matter how hard she tried, she couldn't forget Jace's face when she'd come in her arms. She resented the fact that she couldn't erase their night together.

"You even stayed over at her place last weekend when Helen and Jo were here," Dylan continued.

"I know."

"So, what's the problem? It's not like you can't see her at work."

Taryn didn't answer the rhetorical question at first. She knew darn well what the problem was, but didn't want to admit it. "I don't know. I guess I'm just frustrated. It's been nearly four months since Marti and I split up. I guess I'm ready to start dating again. I just wish I didn't have to go through the whole dating process. Why can't I just wake up one morning and find the perfect woman right in front of me?"

She knew the answer to that question, too. The perfect woman was right under her nose, but she had been too pigheaded to admit it. Now, it looked like she'd missed her window of opportunity.

Dylan sized up her melancholy friend and told herself she shouldn't interfere in other people's lives. On the other hand, a little matchmaking couldn't do any harm.

"HEY THERE. HOW'S it going?" Dylan asked as she met Jace in the small corridor that linked the Center to the staff offices.

Jace grinned. "Not bad. Work has calmed down a little. So, what brings you here on a Thursday afternoon?"

Dylan ran her fingers through her hair. "I was coming to ask either you or Anne a favor. It's Cory's birthday this weekend, and I wanted to make it special. I thought I'd surprise her and take her to Vermont for the weekend. I know it's a bit short notice, but could she take tomorrow off?"

Jace chewed on her bottom lip, mentally reviewing the plans for the next day. "Walk with me to my office." She led the way, and then closed the door after Dylan had entered. "It shouldn't be a problem. She'll have to make the hours up. I'll email Patty and let her know. Cory's in her office now, if you want to go and tell her the good news."

"Thanks, I'll let her work a little longer. I wanted to touch base with you. I hear through the grapevine that you've been very busy these past few weeks!"

Jace rubbed her chin. "I've been fairly busy since we last talked."

"I'd say so." Dylan gave a low whistle. "Eight dates with five different women. I have to tell you, Taryn's pretty pissed, but trying not to admit it."

"You don't say." Jace relaxed in her seat. The dates had been good. The women had been pleasant, and Jace always suggested activities that required minimal contact and conversation. Since starting her dating experience, she had been to the cinema three times, bowling twice, had two home cooked meals, and the previous evening she'd ventured into Boston to see a play.

Dylan gave her an old-fashioned look. "You're making her crazy. Don't tell me you haven't noticed."

Jace shrugged. "Taryn made her choice." She hoped that comment would be passed straight back to the person it was intended for. Innocently, she continued, "Can I ask your advice?"

"Fire away."

"Vanessa was interested in going out again this weekend, but I'm having doubts. She's getting a little pushy, and this would be our third date. I don't want to give the impression that I'm interested in anything serious. It's just about...er...having fun."

Jace could have sworn she heard Dylan choke slightly. "Maybe it's time to move on."

"Yes, you're probably right. She's cute, but there are plenty more where she came from."

"Well, if you're not in any hurry to replace her, how about doing Cory and me a favor and spending some time with Taryn this weekend. She misses you, buddy."

"Really?" Jace felt like a ten-year-old who'd just been given a bowl of candy, but she kept her expression nonchalant.

"She's a monster to live with."

"She sounded fine when I called her to cancel, last night. She said she had lots of college work to do."

Dylan threw her hands up in defeat. "Hey, I'm just telling

you what I see. She wanted you to date, and you dated. Maybe it's time for you to see if she still thinks that was a good idea. Just a thought."

Jace nodded slowly, as if giving the idea some room. "Sure. If you think it will make her feel better."

Dylan's eyes flooded with perception and she reached over to shake Jace's hand. "I underestimated you, Jace. I can see you don't need me telling you how to get under her skin. Cory and I will be back Sunday evening. Would you like to come over for a piece of birthday cake?"

"Sounds good. Just text me with a time." Jace handed a business card to Dylan, and once she'd sauntered out of the office, flipped open her cell phone and pressed the speed dial button. She waited for it to connect. "Hey."

Taryn checked the Caller-ID. "What's wrong?" she asked, surprised that Jace had called her during the workday.

"Is that any way to greet a caller? We're going to have to work on your people skills. Nothing's wrong. I just wanted to see if you would like to hang out later."

"No date?" Taryn snapped sarcastically.

Jace smiled at the tension in Taryn's voice. *Ooh, someone's in a bad mood.* "Nope. No date. My night off, and I wanted to spend it with a friend. If you're busy, I can see if Anne wants to play."

Taryn's mood lifted when she realized Jace had chosen to call her over Anne. "No, I'm sorry. I was in the middle of a tough section of my research project. I didn't mean to snap."

"Do you need any help?"

"If you're offering, I'll take anything."

Jace grinned. "I'll take that as a compliment. How about I get a couple of subs and come over after work?"

"Steak and cheese?" Taryn asked meekly.

"With mushrooms. I sense we need to go for the big guys. You sound really down."

"I am." Taryn admitted. "Give me a call when you're here. I'll check what Cory and Dylan are doing."

"Didn't Dylan tell you? She's whisking Cory away for the weekend. That reminds me, you'll be running the groups solo. If you need additional help, I'm around."

"Thanks, Jace." A long pause followed. Taryn's soft breathing was audible. She started to speak again, but broke off.

"Did you say something?" Jace prompted.

"No." Another pause. "It's not important."

Resisting the urge to press her a little harder, Jace said pleasantly, "Okay, then I'll catch you later."

JACE JUGGLED THE bottles of beer and food, while flicking the phone open. "Hey, I'm outside the back door."

"I'll be right down." Taryn placed her laptop on the table and headed down the single flight of stairs. She opened the door, a little perturbed when her heart fluttered at the sight of Jace. "You're a sight for sore eyes."

"Thanks, I think. Come on, I'm starving." Jace headed for the stairs. "You get the plates and I'll grab the napkins."

Taryn placed the subs on the floor. The sofas were covered with her notes, books, and old research papers. "I can clear some room if you'd prefer to sit up there."

Jace looked at the scattered work. A grimace curled her face when she remembered her time as a student. Research papers were no fun. She looked back at Taryn and saw the dark circles under her eyes. She refrained from rubbing Taryn's back. "When is it due?"

Taryn pulled at the meat in her sub. "Chapters one to three are due on Monday." She saw the raised eyebrows and concerned look coming from Jace. "Don't worry, I'm not that silly. It's basically an expansion of the proposal." She explained what she had written so far, painfully aware that Jace was sitting so close. She found it distracting and several times she lost track of what she was explaining to Jace. Finally, she cut to the chase. "My main problem is the literature review. I need eighteen pages, and I can only stretch it to fifteen."

Jace opened two beers and passed a bottle to Taryn. "Would you like me to read it?"

"You've worked all day on reports. Do you really want to spend the night looking at mine?"

"Answer me honestly, Taryn. Would you really be able to relax tonight knowing that you have to hand it in Monday?" She saw Taryn shake her head. "So, how about you stop being so pigheaded and let me look at it."

Taryn passed the paper to Jace, painfully aware of the brush of Jace's fingers against her own. *I could have had her here all the time if I'd given it a chance! But, what do I have to offer her?* Taryn tried to focus on anything but the regrets pounding in her head and the physical reminder of Jace seated so close to her. "I can print you a neat copy if this is too messy."

Jace shook her head. "No, this is fine." Ten minutes later, she removed her reading glasses and said, "I'm impressed. This is really good. My only advice would be to extend your literature review to look more in the area of learning communities. I think that could be your missing link." She noted down some useful websites and journals before passing the paper back to Taryn.

"Now, I am demanding you take a short break. Too much work is bad for you. Doctor's orders!" *And I need to know how you feel about me!*

Taryn dropped the papers. "That's not fair, you're not a medical doctor."

Jace poked out her tongue. "Well, I am a doctor and I'm demanding you give me some quality Taryn time." She pouted and nudged Taryn.

Taryn cracked her knuckles. "Okay, I'm all yours." *I wish it were true.* "I can work on this thing over the weekend, especially with Dylan and Cory away."

Jace waited for Taryn to clear the sofa, and then stretched her body out over the three seats leaving no room for Taryn to sit next to her. *Keep your distance and your mind clear.* "How are things going here?"

Taryn shrugged. "Same old, same old. I feel like I'm in the way a lot of the time. I know Dylan's recently been promoted, so I doubt they need my money like they used to. I was thinking about maybe getting my own apartment."

"Seriously?" Jace asked in surprise.

Taryn relaxed on the other sofa. "Sometimes I am, and then I think about how stir crazy I get when left to my own devices. How do you do it?"

"I used to enjoy it but since the vacation I've been lonely. I miss having you around. I miss being able to touch you..."

"Jace, I thought we'd moved on from this."

Jace hid the disappointment well. She'd hoped her admission would be an opening for Taryn to admit her feelings. "I know. I just wanted you to know that it was a good experience for me, us sleeping together. It's helped me realize what I want."

Taryn's interest was piqued, but she didn't want to revisit their lovemaking. Jace's words reloaded images of their bodies touching and the intimate caress of Jace's soft skin against her own. "Well, you've had plenty of company recently."

Jace closed her eyes. She was tired of playing games, but she wasn't sure how much to disclose to Taryn. "It's been interesting."

Taryn saw the tired expression on Jace's face. She controlled the urge to reach across and run her finger along the lines under Jace's eyes. *Tell her how you feel. Tell her you can't bear to think of her in the arms of other women.* But like a sadist, she was desperate to know more.

"I was surprised you didn't date Jenny more. You two seemed to get on really well at the bar." Jenny had been the first person that Jace had shown any interest in.

Jace opened her eyes. "She was nice, but she had an irritating laugh and not much conversation. I need to be mentally stimulated."

Taryn probed, "What about the new woman?"

"Vanessa?"

"If that's her name. What's she like?"

Jace took a moment to think about the question. She was trying to assess what Taryn wanted to hear. *Enough of the games.* "Vanessa's a psychologist. Last night, we went into Boston. The show was good and she asked me to go out Saturday. I'm not sure whether to go."

Taryn sat up straighter, trying to work out how Jace felt about this new woman. *Why are you torturing yourself? Just tell her you made a mistake. Tell her how you feel!* "How old is she?"

"My age."

"What does she look like?"

Jace rolled onto her side. "What is this, twenty questions?" she snapped.

Taryn bristled. "I was just trying to take an interest."

"No, it's me. I'm just tired of dating different women every other week. I don't know how you did this dating thing. I've only done it for a month, and I'm tired of the same old acts and routines."

Taryn fiddled with her hands. Anger swelled beneath the surface as she thought of other women touching Jace. "Well, I didn't exactly participate in the art of dating. I went for the even older ritual of just plain old screwing." The bitterness in her voice was clear. "At least you know your date's name in the morning!"

Jace shook her head and stood up. "I wasn't referring anything by my comment. I should go we're both tired."

"No, please stay for a few more minutes." Taryn implored, frustrated and unsure why the mood had changed so quickly.

Jace paused, "Is there something you want to tell me? You've been edgy all evening."

Taryn shrugged in frustration. "It's just I've been thinking about what I want and it hurts not being able to get it."

"Get what?" *Let it be me! Let her want me!*

"Love, security...a future." Taryn declared, all the time looking into blue eyes that sent shivers down her spine.

Jace took a few steps toward Taryn. "You could have all that with me, Taryn. You just have to say the words."

Taryn struggled "Until the next Jenny or Vanessa comes along and I'm dropped like a hot potato."

Jace gasped. Failing to control her temper, she grabbed her keys off the table and paused at the door. "I'm tired of defending myself all the time. I've tried to be a good friend. I've tried to follow the rules you set out. Now I know how you really feel about me. You're un-fucking-believable. Thanks for the trust!"

She let the door slam behind her and headed into the night.

Chapter
Eighteen

TARYN WAS GRATEFUL when the last study group finished. It was all she could do to concentrate for ten seconds, let alone several hours. She reclined in her seat, and tapped her pencil absently on the table, stopping only when she realized how loud and rapid the taps were becoming. Forcing her mind to her tasks, she completed the attendance sheet for the support groups, pulled out the planning sheets for the following week, and filled in the dates at the top. As soon as she wrote 14th February, she groaned and sank down onto the desk, her head on her arms. *St. Valentine's Day! Great – just another reminder of my crappy life!*

Her morose contemplations were interrupted by her aunt, who tapped on the door frame and marched up to her desk. "Taryn. I need to talk to you."

"Can't it wait?" Taryn said crossly.

"No. I need to tell you something...about Patrick."

Taryn's heart lurched. The bastard's name always had that effect on her. "What's he done now?"

"He crashed his car the other night on route 18."

"Pity he didn't kill himself."

Anne controlled her temper. Taryn had every right to despise her father. "His car swerved off the road and hit a tree. He broke his arm. The police tested his alcohol level because his speech was slurred, but he was under the limit."

"Amazing," Taryn remarked.

"He was the only one involved."

"Well, that's something," Taryn said bitterly. "He's already destroyed enough lives."

Anne took a deep breath. No matter what Patrick had done in his fifty odd years, he was still her brother and she cared for him. "The doctors did some scans, and they think he had a mild stroke or blacked out. The results came in this morning."

Taryn shrugged. She didn't really care what his state of

health was, but she could see Anne needed to get the news off her chest. "And?"

"His liver isn't working properly. He has cirrhosis...they've given him a few months."

Taryn opened her mouth to speak, but no words came out. She had dreamed of this day so many times in her life, the day when her tormentor would no longer be around. Now that it was suddenly imminent, the news shook her somehow. There were no words to describe what was running through her mind or body.

"I...don't know what to say."

"I know. It doesn't seem real," Anne said, her face full of compassion.

Taryn wasn't sure whether she was sensing sympathy or grief from her aunt and she had no idea what her own numbness meant. She realized she should say something to comfort Anne, but she couldn't.

"I can't deal with this now," she said. "I need to leave...I'm sorry."

Dismayed, Anne extended a hand to Taryn's arm, wanting to detain her and talk a little more, but Taryn avoided her touch and hurried from the room.

Anne stared after her, distressed by the calm eeriness with which she had taken the news. She had hoped Taryn might have shown some grief, or anger. Or asked some more questions. Instead she had shut Anne out yet again.

Gazing helplessly around the office, Anne concluded there was no urgent work to be done and if everyone else was going to take the day off, then she was going to do likewise. She needed the comfort of her husband's arms.

JACE'S STOMACH PLUMMETED when she saw Taryn's Camry parked out front her house. Surprised by the late evening visit, she pulled the Jeep onto her drive and turned nervously to her date.

"Vanessa, I have to apologize. It seems I have a guest — my graduate assistant. I asked her to drop by if she needed any help on her report. I didn't realize she'd be so eager." Jace winced at the lame excuse. "Let me open the door for you and I'll go talk to her."

Vanessa stroked the side of Jace's face. "Anything, sweetie." Her voice dripped honey. "I'm just pleased you decided to call and take our relationship further."

Jace's stomach instantly turned into a mass of jelly. She

walked the eager psychologist to the front door and let her in, then turned back toward Taryn's car, trying to frame what she was going to say.

"Shit! This is all I need." Taryn was stunned by the bizarre scene unfolding before her. Jace had brought a woman back to her house. Taryn felt stupid. She had spent half the evening thinking about her father and how life could change, just like that, and how much she regretted the mistakes she'd made. And now, here she was, on the brink of asking Jace to forgive her and for them to have a relationship, and Jace was about to have sex with another woman.

Angry and despondent, she started the engine and was about to drive away when Jace tapped on the driver's window and demanded, "What are you doing here?"

Taryn took in Jace's tight top and cleavage. She had never seen her dressed so provocatively. Consumed with jealousy, she spewed out, "I just came around to see how you are, but it looks like you're doing fine!"

Jace could feel the tension rolling off Taryn, but she was in no mood to revisit their last conversation. "As you can see I have a guest."

Taryn finally managed to look at Jace's face. When she did, she saw a stranger. Gone was the woman she had opened her heart to. In her place was a cold, stone-faced outsider, eyes narrowed with anger. Taryn bit her lip to prevent the tears from falling. "Why are you being this way?"

Jace shook her head. "I can't do this now. Vanessa's waiting."

"Vanessa? But...I mean...I thought you weren't that interested in dating anymore."

"So, I changed my mind. I'm not getting any younger, and there are women out there who actually know what they want and it seems like they want *me*." She forced an impersonal smile, avoiding Taryn's stormy eyes. "Look, this isn't the time. I need to go."

"When is the time?" Taryn begged, trying to connect to the old Jace. When she got no response, she said, "I came here so we could talk."

"I think we've done enough talking. You made your opinions very clear the other night and I am just getting on with my life."

"You don't understand how hard this is for me," Taryn burst out.

"Guess what?" Jace said angrily. "Everything is not about you. We all have issues. But most of us take some responsibility

for our own and try to deal with them. Let me know when you're
ready to grow up and we'll talk."

Taryn gasped. "I have no idea what I've done to deserve this
treatment."

"I rest my case." Jace turned away and started walking.
Glancing back over her shoulder, she said, "I'll see you Monday.
If you see Anne, can you tell her I won't be around this weekend.
I have other plans."

Taryn shook with rage and sucked in the cool night air,
trying to calm herself. "I am not your lackey," she hurled after
Jace. "When you can find some time to think about others before
yourself, you might want to call Anne." Jealousy and anger
mixed inside her, and she decided to swing the lowest blow
possible. "She just found out her brother is dying, and could
have done with her best friend today."

Shock made Jace stand up straight. She headed straight
back toward the car, but Taryn took that opportunity to gun the
engine and drive away. Jace pulled her fingers through her hair.
When was life going to return to normal? She headed back to the
door, her heart bleeding and her spirits deflated.

JACE KNOCKED ON the deck door and walked in on the
family breakfast. "Good morning."

Anne turned tired eyes to her. "Hey, yourself."

"Hey, kids." Jace took a seat at the table and buttered some
toast. Joining the Weston family for weekend breakfasts had
been a common event over the years. Anne always made more
than necessary, just in case she stopped by. This morning, Jace
waited patiently for the children to finish their breakfast and
leave the table, before she raised the topic that had kept her
awake most of the night. "I heard about Patrick."

Bill nodded sadly. "It was on the cards. He's been drinking
heavily for over thirty years." He stood up from the table. "I'll
go check on the kids."

"So, Taryn caught up with you?" Anne asked.

"Briefly. She didn't say much. What's happening with
Patrick?"

Anne took a few minutes to tell Jace about the accident and
the tests. "We went last night and he's not in a good state of
mind. The doctors say he's going through some kind of
withdrawal. He hasn't had any alcohol since Tuesday, and that's
a long time for an alcoholic. The medications help, but they can't
give him too much until they know how damaged his liver is.
The accident may have accelerated his liver disease. Basically,

he's a mess, both physically and emotionally."

Jace took Anne's hand. "I'm sorry.

"Speaking of Taryn, did she say whether she was coming over?" Anne asked distractedly. " I tried to call her cell and home number last night, but she never picked up. I didn't think to call yours. I should have known she'd be with you."

Jace didn't want to upset Anne any more than she already was. "She wasn't at my place for long. I'm not sure what she was planning for the weekend."

"How did she seem?"

Jace thought about the question. "Out-of-sorts." *Okay, now you're bending the truth. She was a lot out-of-sorts.* "How did she take the news when you told her?"

Anne swallowed the nervous lump. "I think it was a shock to her. She seemed stressed before I even mentioned it, and what happened in your office yesterday? It looked trashed."

Jace felt a tidal wave of red flush over her face. In her anger, she had kicked wildly at anything in her path. "Would you believe my own style of anger management?"

Anne nodded. "What's going on with the two of you?"

"Nothing. Hormone overload...who knows! I just couldn't concentrate. Taryn kept creeping into my system, and I needed to vent my frustrations. I went home, changed into my own clothes, and then I went for a drive." It was the truth, except she left out her phone call to Vanessa, and the trip to pick up the psychologist for their date.

Bill's presence interrupted the conversation. "I'm going to visit Patrick. Then you can do the honors this afternoon. Good to see you, Jace." He bent down to kiss his wife. "Don't fret too much, okay?"

"I'll try not to." Anne stroked his cheek. "Thanks, sweetheart," She turned sad eyes Jace's way. "It's good to see you this morning. One less person to worry about."

Anne looked worn out. The usually perky woman was washed out and the fire in her eyes had smoldered to nothing. Jace felt guilty for causing her extra stress. "I wish you'd called me as soon as you knew about it. I could have taken care of the kids if you needed to be at the hospital."

Anne shrugged. "You're not a mind reader. I tried to tell you yesterday, but from what I saw, you had your own problems."

Jace poured some coffee and she stretched her sore and tired legs out in front of her. "We don't need to discuss my situation. Tell me about Patrick. How long will he be in the hospital?"

Anne shook her head. "I don't know. He may be released this weekend, or in a week or two. He's lucky in a way. Bill said

that he was close to being fired, and if that had happened he'd be
without insurance. Mom's distraught. I think Dad realized
something was going to happen. Patrick's been on a path of self-
destruction all his life."

Jace got out of her chair and stood behind Anne. She
massaged her friend's shoulders. "Why don't you go and have a
hot bath? I'll look after the kids. You deserve a few moments of
indulgence, and you look exhausted."

Anne stood up. "What would I do without you?"

"My troubles pale in comparison to yours, and frankly, I'm
sick of thinking about them. Let me look after you a little.
Okay?"

TARYN PULLED INTO Anne's street and swore aloud when
she saw the navy Jeep parked in the driveway. "Fuck!"

She drove past the house and turned back onto the main
road. She had drunk herself to sleep the previous night. Demons
floating through her mind had been suppressed by the numbing
of the warm alcohol. The pounding hangover hadn't helped
quell her depression. She had finally managed to clear her mind
and body of the alcohol enough to drive safely to Anne's, only to
find the enemy already camped out in the house.

She drove around the neighborhood for a bit and then
pulled into a small parking area and drummed her fingers on the
steering wheel. Finally, when she couldn't resist the temptation
anymore, she flipped the glove compartment open and took out
her emergency cigarettes. Amazingly her old Zippo lighter
produced a flame on the first attempt. She sucked in a lungful of
smoke and spluttered slightly as her body rebelled from the
shock of a long gone habit. But she continued to drag from the
Marlboro Light all the same. Silent tears tracked down her face
and she leaned back against the headrest and closed her eyes.

Loneliness invaded the safety of the car, and Taryn couldn't
control her emotions. She kept smoking and crying until three
cigarettes later, and with a very sick stomach, she put the car
into drive and headed back to her aunt's. She had things on her
mind that wouldn't or couldn't wait for Monday.

JACE HEARD THE car pull onto the drive. She went to the
window expecting to see Bill's truck. Her gut twisted when she
saw the gold Camry outside. She couldn't hide. Taryn wouldn't
have missed seeing the Jeep; it was right in front of her. She
looked at the bodies of her sleeping friend and tiny son. Sucking

up all the strength she had, she opened the front door and put a finger to her lips.

Taryn was slightly thrown off by Jace's actions as she was led non-too-gently to the kitchen. She shrugged her arm from Jace's grasp, but continued to follow the intimidating woman. She watched Jace close the kitchen door, and then erupted. "Who the hell do you think you are? I came here to visit my family, not to be ordered around, and shepherded into the kitchen."

Jace gritted her teeth. *What's happening to you?* Taryn reeked of alcohol and cigarettes. "Anne's sleeping. She's close to the edge. Patrick's illness is eating away at her and she's worried about both of us. So, I lied. I told her we were fine." Jace nailed Taryn with an icy glare, "And if you care about her, you *will* play along!"

Taryn walked over to the kitchen counter. She wanted to put some distance between herself and a livid Jace. She ground her teeth as she thought of a quick retort to Jace's demands. "Fine. Where are the kids?"

Jace backed up to the door. She hated seeing the animosity in Taryn's eyes. *How can things be so different between us?* "Josie and Ricky are upstairs. Tom is sleeping with Anne."

"Where's Bill?" Taryn took some steadying breaths and glared at Jace. *What went wrong between us?*

Jace closed her eyes and pinched the bridge of her nose. "He went to see your father..." The slam of a hand on the countertop drew her attention to what she had said.

"Don't you ever use those words around me!" Taryn seethed. "You pretend that you understand, but you know nothing." She rushed to the door, but a tall, menacing form prevented her escape.

"Where are you going?" Jace continued to block her getaway.

"I'm not staying here with you. I'll come back later. Move!"

Jace gripped Taryn's wrist. "Stop being so childish! Your aunt needs you, and you *will* be here when she wakes up. Grow up, Taryn! Stop running, and start thinking of others before yourself."

Taryn's eyes darted to Jace. "Give me a break. I'm not running! Don't think so highly about yourself and take your hands off me!"

Jace contained her fury. She turned steel eyes on Taryn. "Where are you going?"

"I'll be upstairs with the kids." Taryn grabbed hold of the door handle.

Jace turned her eyes away. "Well, I suggest you go to your

bedroom first. You reek of smoke, and I can smell alcohol on you. The kids don't need to see you turning into Patrick!" She dropped her hold on Taryn and moved away from the door. She didn't need to look at Taryn to feel the glare piercing her chest. Her heart crumbled into a million pieces.

Chapter
Nineteen

"I DON'T KNOW what you're even doing here?" Taryn said without looking at Jace.

She had chosen to sit as far away from Jace as possible and was pretending to watch the television. Jace watched the subtle tapping of her foot on the rug, a definite sign that she was pissed.

"I'm here because Anne asked me to be here."

For some reason the calm reply infuriated Taryn. Before she could think twice about what she was about to say, the words spilled out. "In case you've forgotten, this is my family, not yours. I can be trusted to take care of the kids on my own."

Jace counted to three so she would not reply in kind. That one of them was being immature and irrational was enough. Taryn had averted her head again and was biting her nails. Jace had watched her do the same thing days earlier when they'd been trying to fix her research paper. *Her paper! She should be home working on her paper. It's due on Monday!*

"Don't you have a paper to finish?" she demanded.

Taryn kept her gaze pointedly on the screen. "No."

"I thought it was due Monday."

"It is."

"When did you finish it?"

Taryn couldn't believe the woman had the audacity to question her. One minute Jace didn't want her around, and the next she was acting like she had a right to know everything about her. She turned and stared angrily at her.

"Not that it's any of your business, but I did it last night. I tend to turn to work when I'm stressed, and I'd been trying to track down a good friend. But it turns out I had nothing to worry about...my *friend* was doing fine without me!"

Neither woman blinked, nor could they tear their eyes away from the other. Jace kept a stoic mask of calm and control on her face. She sensed Taryn was pushing her, trying to drive her away, and she wondered why she didn't just take the hint and let go. Even if Taryn was just acting out and would one day figure out what she really wanted and needed, why should Jace wait around? Especially when it meant putting up with this.

In a matter of fact tone, she said, "Taryn, this is one of those times when a family member thinks about someone, other than herself. Anne and Bill will be back from the hospital soon and the least we can do is help them get though this."

"I am helping," Taryn protested. "Why do you think I'm here?"

"You tell me."

Taryn hesitated. "Because I love them."

"And so do I," Jace said. "Listen, can we agree to put our personal differences aside and work together...for Anne's sake and the kids'."

Taryn's head swung her way. "Don't use the kids as emotional blackmail."

Jace sighed. It was impossible to keep up with Taryn's logic. And she had news Taryn wasn't going to want to hear — that was the main reason she was here, trying to talk with the woman who had hurt her feelings.

"Actually, I need to talk to you about the kids," she said. "Patrick is getting out of the hospital soon, and Anne is planning to take him down to Florida."

Taryn frowned. "Why?"

"I gather your grandmother wants him near her so she can make her peace with him."

"She can't take care of him," Taryn looked alarmed. "She's not well herself."

"There's a nursing home near you grandparent's condo. They're going to check Patrick in there."

"It's amazing," Taryn said, almost to herself. "He spends his whole life not giving a damn about anyone but himself, and now everyone is taking care of him."

"Your aunt and uncle are good people," Jace said. "Why would they be anything less than who they are just because Patrick has been a fool? Does he deserve to be given that much power?"

Taryn was silent for a long while. It struck her that she had fallen into that trap herself. She gave Patrick so much power in her own life, it corrupted the way she looked at everything. How could she change that? Quietly, she said, "I see what you mean."

"I've told Anne she can take next week off, so she can do this. The thing is, Bill's new project is in New Jersey and he can't be here to look after the kids. They called his parents, but they're going on that cruise they've been talking about all year." She met Taryn's eyes. "I said we'd move in here temporarily and look after them between us."

Taryn's jaw dropped. "Both of us?"

"Well neither of us can do it all alone. I have work to consider and I'll be covering for Anne. You have commitments, too." Jace had been running all kinds of scenarios and schedules through her head ever since Anne spoke to her about the trip. She knew it would take a team effort to manage the situation well, but a team effort required good communication and mutual trust. She met Taryn's unhappy stare and said, "I don't like it any more than you do. But it's only for a week."

Great, I'm going to be living with the enemy! The one time I want and need my space, we're going to be stuck playing happy families together. "I suppose so, and we probably won't even see each other most of the time," Taryn said, miserably conscious that Jace was still angry with her.

"So that's a yes?" Jace asked.

"It's my place to be here," Taryn said, trying for a dignified tone. Jace was treating her like she had no idea of responsibility and Taryn was suddenly determined to prove her wrong. "Anne and Bill and the kids are my family, Jace. My *only* family."

A WEEK LATER, several days after Anne and Bill had left, Taryn finished putting the kids to bed and went into the family office to study. The room was quite large with a desktop computer and workstation as the center feature. Two large desks stood on either side of the room. The shelves were filled with books from counseling to architecture and building.

Taryn remembered back to her childhood, a time long before computers. She remembered her grandfather sitting at the oak desk. The man always seemed to be writing or doing his accounts. Her grandfather's business deals had afforded the family a comfortable legacy, and she was sure it was that money that was paying for Patrick's nursing needs now. She glanced at the other desk. There were pendants over the top, depicting the Boston Red Sox and New England Patriots. She looked at a picture of Patrick and his very first car. She remembered her Gram telling her stories of how proud he was when he bought it. Taryn smiled sadly. It was a shame the guy hadn't had the same feelings about his daughter. She looked at the desk drawers and wondered what secrets lay waiting to be discovered.

After she finished her assignment, she glanced back at Patrick's desk. What harm would it do? The guy was going to be dead soon, and all the contents would be poured into a brown box and placed in the attic. She had a right to know what her so-called father considered important. She felt like a thief as she slowly turned the key, hearing the click as the old-fashioned lock snapped open. She pulled the drawer toward her, and stared at the contents. Inside was worthless trash and memorabilia. Old racing tickets, Red Sox ticket stubs, and lottery slips. Taryn moved some of the debris, and pulled out a little black book. Inside were names of women, written alphabetically. The guy's life had been a sad cliché. She wondered how many other women he'd treated like her mother. How many other children out there were his unclaimed kin?

She continued to move the sparse contents of the drawer around, her hand stopped on a small, brown padded wallet. She looked at the tiny photo holder. She opened the top cover, expecting to find old cards and business numbers. What she found shocked her to the core. Each section was filled with photos of her. She flicked the pages. It was a chronological diary of her formative years. Inside were all her school photos, up to the age of about twelve. She flicked through the dog-eared photos of her smiling face.

She turned over the one of a toddler sitting on Santa's lap, and read the inscription: 'Taryn Meghan Murphy Clary – aged 2 years and 1 month, 1973'. She recognized her mother's handwriting, and the name she had lived with until she was old enough to realize Patrick was never going to accept her. When she had turned eighteen, much to the disappointment of her grandparents, she had dropped the Clary part of her surname. She flicked through the photos one more time, and then placed them in her sweatshirt pocket. She wiped her itchy eyes, refusing to allow any tears to drop. She soon heard the familiar beep of her watch timer, and collected her belongings. She felt the photos that had been locked away burn a hole in her side.

All those years she'd believed she was nothing to the man, and now this. Why had he kept them? Why had she looked? Tears came to Taryn's eyes, and she couldn't stop them falling.

Seeking comfort, she crept into her little cousin's bedroom and lay down next to him, slipping an arm beneath him. She spent a long time holding Tom and watching him sleep. She wondered how often her mother had done the same for her. She was so glad that Tom would never know rejection like she had felt. He had a house full of love and, in Jace, a godmother who would go to the ends of the world to protect him.

The previous evening, Taryn had watched the two at play. Jace's love for the boy had shone in her eyes, and Taryn had recognized the expression as one she had seen many times aimed at her own face. She remembered the sweet taste of Jace's mouth and the tiny tremors that had shaken her as they made love. Taryn thought back to the previous Thursday, those same eyes had shone with love for her.

How could those feelings have turned against her so completely? Taryn knew she had behaved badly but being rejected by a woman she had trusted more than any other lover made her so miserable she could hardly bear it. Knowing she could not contain her sorrow, Taryn eased away from Tom and hurried down the hall to her own room. There she sat on her window seat and lit a cigarette.

She felt like a sneaky teenager, secretly smoking out of her bedroom window. She blew the smoke out and watched the gray fumes swirl on the wind of the cold winter's night. She leaned her head against the wall. She spotted Orion's Belt and moved her eyes a little to the left. One star in particular twinkled more than the others. She smiled.

"Hi, Mom. What a mess I've made of my life. I miss you." A lonely tear tracked down her cheek.

She threw the cigarette butt out of the window and took the bulging photo holder from her pocket. She took out each photo and read the back. The first picture in the pack was of a tiny fair-haired baby under a Christmas tree. The inscription on the back made the tears flow faster. 'To my daddy, Merry Christmas, Taryn Meghan, 2 months, Christmas, 1971.' She flicked through the inscriptions, noting the changing handwriting and sentiments, until it was only Taryn's first name and the year scribbled on the back of each one.

She was surprised to see a small photo of her graduation from high school. The photo had been taken at a distance, but Taryn could make out her features. She checked the date on the back of the picture just to be sure. Printed neatly on the back was the date 05/89. She saw the faint pencil markings TM HS graduation.

She closed her eyes. Why had the bastard pretended all those years that he didn't care? She had the evidence in her hands. He had gone to her graduation. He had cared. Why hadn't he ever told her? The pain she felt tore at her guts. It was worse knowing the truth. She wished she'd never looked. She'd never get a chance to ask him, and she didn't even know if she cared. The tears fell; there were no more barriers to hold them in.

She dropped the photos on the floor and stared up at the star. *Why you? Why not him? I need you, Mom! I can't handle this alone,* she silently pleaded to the bright star.

JACE PEERED INTO each bedroom. The little nightlights helped her see that every child was where they should be. Content that everything was locked up, Jace continued to her bedroom. She glanced at Taryn's door as she passed by. There was no light coming from under it. She hadn't seen Taryn since an altercation earlier in the evening.

On entering her temporary bedroom, Jace pulled off her sweatshirt and pants. Earlier that evening, she had learned a valuable lesson that work clothes were to be removed before playing with the children. Her body was exhausted. She missed her down time after work. She wasn't used to the constant activity. She opened the bathroom door and noticed the adjoining door was ajar. She knew she shouldn't, but she couldn't resist looking in on Taryn. Tentatively, she pushed the door a little until she could peek into the dimly lit room. All she could make out was a huddled mass in the middle of the bed. She closed the door quietly.

Jace glanced around the bathroom. She picked up Taryn's shower gel and smelled the fragrance. Memories of their night together flooded her mind. She finished her bedtime ritual but before leaving the bathroom she slightly opened the door leading to Taryn's room. She needed the closeness however minor it was.

Once she was back in her bed, Jace lay staring at the ceiling. She couldn't relax. She couldn't erase the images of Taryn lying in her arms. She couldn't comprehend how distant they had become. As she lay there, she heard a muffled whimpering. She turned her head to the baby monitor. She moved closer and listened to the light sounds of Tom sleeping. Her heart slowed down, and she lay back against her pillow. She checked the clock; it was nearly two in the morning. She nestled deeper into the pillow and tried some breathing exercises.

Again she was disturbed from her dozing to the sounds of crying. Unnerved, Jace got out of bed and went to the hallway. She listened in the dark corridor. Nothing. She walked back into the room and heard the noise again. This time she knew exactly where it was coming from. She crossed the bathroom and pushed the adjoining door. She peered around. The room was darker than before. Without the aid of the bathroom light, Jace struggled to make out Taryn's shape. After a few moments, she heard a throaty sob and saw the thrashing of the bed covers. Instantly, she moved across the room, nearly injuring herself as she slipped on several small pieces of paper scattered on the floor.

Jace gently nudged Taryn, but, there was no response. She climbed onto the bed and pulled Taryn into her arms. She could feel labored breaths against her chest. She knew Taryn was still asleep. Taryn wouldn't have let her near if she'd been awake. She rocked Taryn slowly. She was pleased when she felt Taryn's body relax against her, and the sobs quiet down. Jace wondered what demons were torturing her while she slept.

JACE PILED THE dirty plates into the dishwasher as Taryn walked into the kitchen. "I can do that, Jace. You did all the work this morning."

She took in the stress lines at the corners of Jace's eyes. She had to fight her own emotions and not stretch out her fingers to trace the lines.

"I'm doing fine," Jace said.

Taryn's heart clenched. The stranger she saw hurt her. She wanted to block out all that had gone wrong between them and start again, without the confusion and misunderstandings. "Why didn't you wake me? I could have helped out!"

"It's okay. I've nearly finished." Jace wiped the counter top, not able to meet Taryn's eyes. "I thought you might appreciate a lie in. You looked tired last night and you did a tough breakfast duty yesterday. I was trying to help."

Reminding herself that Jace was dating other women, Taryn said, "I don't need your pity, Jace. I am capable of looking after my cousins. Yesterday was an off day. Tom wasn't used to me, and he never will be if you don't give me some of the control. Tomorrow, I'll get breakfast and you can leave for work at your usual time. Now, I need a cigarette."

As Taryn stalked out of the kitchen Jace threw the sponge across the room. Nothing she did seemed good enough. She flipped open her cell phone, and scanned down the saved numbers. She looked at the name flashing in front of her. Her inner psyche screamed: *You're running again! She needs you, Jace, even if she doesn't show it well, and you need her. It's time one of you stepped up to the mark and said the scary words!* Her thumb hovered over Vanessa's name then she flicked the phone cover shut, and lifted her head to the ceiling. *What the hell do I do now?*

Impulsively, she followed Taryn out to the deck and propped herself against the doorjamb. The cold, frosty February air made her shiver. Taryn leaned against the deck rail, gazing out at the early morning. She looked cold. Jace watched as Taryn's hand lifted to her mouth. She tried to ignore the cigarette; it was none of her business.

"You should put your coat on," she said. "You'll catch a chill."

Taryn turned stormy eyes Jace's way. "I'm fine. Stop fussing over me." She choked back the tears of confusion. She missed her friend. She wanted the closeness they'd had so many days ago.

Jace couldn't see the expression on Taryn's face. Her head was averted again and her shoulders stiff. Resigned, she said, "I'll be going then. Do you want a ride?"

"No, thanks." Taryn's voice sounded husky. "I'll see you at work."

Chapter
Twenty

CORY HELPED TARYN pack away the files. "You still look tired. Are you sleeping okay?"

Taryn shrugged. "I think so. I even went to bed early last night. I have a lot on my mind." She kept her voice low, aware of the fact that the room they were in was linked to many others and had no enclosed ceiling.

With Anne's absence, she had revealed that she was her niece to the Center staff, and explained her reasons for hiding it, so they were all asking her about the kids now and were fascinated that Jace was staying at Anne's with her.

"I just wish I knew where I stood with Jace," she told Cory. "One minute she's all concerned, and the next she's snapping." She thought about her comment and then added. "It's not all her, though. I had a chance last night to talk to her, but my pride got the better of me, and I bit her head off instead."

Cory continued to tidy up. She saw the dejected look on Taryn's face. "Have you heard from Anne or Bill? Dylan said she spoke to Anne briefly yesterday, but the children had grabbed the phone before she was able to ask how things were."

Taryn nodded. "Bill called last night, and Jace spoke to him. I think Anne called back, but Jace answered yet again. I was hiding upstairs. I really should swallow my pride and talk to her."

"I saw her before group started. She looked like hell. If I didn't know better, I'd say she was out on the town all night."

Taryn looked at Cory. "She looks that bad?" *She looked okay this morning. A little tired, maybe. Who am I kidding? Murphy, you're so self-absorbed you can't see past your own ass!*

Cory nodded. "Go and see for yourself, if she's still there."

Taryn checked her watch. "I should check in with her."

Reluctantly, she made her way down the bustling corridor. She reached Jace's office. The door was open, and Taryn spent a few seconds looking at her boss. Cory was right; Jace looked awful. Taryn tapped the open door, and for a fleeting moment she saw the real Jace. In front of her was a worried and scared woman. As quick as the emotions had appeared, they were gone, and in their place was the cold, calm expression of Jace the Ice Maiden. Heavy bags made Jace's usually striking eyes seem lackluster. Her face was paler than normal, and her sharp wits seemed dulled. "Hey."

Jace assessed Taryn's features, unaware that Taryn was scrutinizing her own sleep deprived system. "Hey, yourself." The younger woman still looked tired, but nothing like what Jace had expected. Taryn's sleep had been restless and every time Jace had risen to go, Taryn had cried out and held her in place. In the end, Jace had watched the dawn rise over the house. She had finally managed to escape Taryn's embrace and return to her room unnoticed by the younger woman. On the journey back to her room, Jace had seen the discarded photos. She had wanted to stay and look at them, but she hadn't wanted to be caught. She was already in Taryn's bad books. She didn't need to give her any more ammunition.

"I...err...I wanted to catch you before you left." She saw Jace squeeze the bridge of her nose. She knew that was a sign that Jace was tired and overstressed. "Any news from Anne?"

Jace rubbed her palms over her forehead, scratching the edge of her hairline as she did so. Taryn was an enigma. She ran hot and cold. Jace didn't have the patience or the will to deal with any more tantrums. Her nerves were frayed, and her sleep-deprived body desperately needed some calm. She forced a smile onto her face. "She called last night. Patrick's a little more settled. He's reacting well to the drugs, but has lost a lot of weight since the weekend. Your Gram isn't doing so good." She saw the flash of panic streak across Taryn's face. "I told Anne you'd call her tonight." She saw Taryn open her mouth and expecting a biting comment, she interrupted her before she could speak her mind. "I know I had no right to plan when and who you call. I didn't know what to do and your aunt was upset."

Taryn closed her mouth as she listened to Jace explain her actions. When she felt Jace had said her piece, she continued with her original thought. "I was going to say thank you. I'll call Gram tonight, I promise. Did Anne say when she was coming home?"

Jace shook her head. "Close the door, Taryn." She watched as Taryn closed the door and took a seat opposite her. "No. I don't think it'll be this weekend. I got the impression that she's staying there until he passes. I spoke to Bill, and he's pretty worried about her. She's had a lot to deal with over the past few months, and I know she's more concerned about her parents. Bill said the doctors have given Patrick a month, at the most. He apparently has had some warning symptoms, but ignored them. He went to the doctor earlier this year and they did a few tests. He was given advice, but chose not to take it." She saw Taryn's eyes widen in disbelief. "I know. That was my reaction last night. Bill is in a quandary. He wants to come home and see the kids, but he also wants to support his wife. His manager has given him Friday off, and Monday is President's Day. I suggested that he catch a plane to Florida. He's going to call and see what you think. He feels like he's putting us out by asking us to take the kids over the weekend."

Taryn looked at Jace's forlorn expression. "He should be with Anne. I'll talk to him. Jace, you look worn out. I can pick Tom up if you need a break."

Jace sat up straight and stretched out her muscles. The confident, straight-faced woman in front of her was nothing like the frightened child she had held through the night. She wondered if Taryn even knew she had been there. She doubted it from the innocent statement. "I'm okay. I may even take an afternoon nap with Tom. I'll see you later. Forward any emails you think need my urgent attention."

Taryn took those words as an instant dismissal. She reluctantly left the office. At least they had managed to have one civil conversation. It was a start.

"IS UNCLE PATRICK going to die?" Josie asked.

Jace looked at the young girl. She was always so forthright. No messing around, or talking around a point. She always wanted to know the facts. Jace nodded her response.

"Are we going to go to Florida to see him? Why isn't Taryn looking after him? He's her daddy." The young girl turned to Taryn. "When your mommy was sick, you looked after her. Mommy said you went to live in Ireland. Why don't you go and look after Uncle Patrick, and then mommy can come home."

Taryn flinched at the comment, but didn't react. Josie was just using childhood logic. It was true. If circumstances were different, she would be the one caring for her father. "It's not the same, Josie. You know Uncle Patrick and I don't get on."

"How am I going to send mommy her Valentine's card?" Ricky asked again.

Jace sighed. "We can send it tomorrow. If you give it to me, we can same day Fed Ex it. Your mom will get her card. Just to be sure, we can send her an e-card as well. Your mom said there were Internet computers in the hospital. How does that sound?"

"Okay. I'll go and find it."

Jace looked at the sad expression on Taryn's face. She knew Josie's comment had upset her. Jace had been impressed with Taryn's handling of it. She had half expected Taryn to explode at Josie, and run out of the room. Instead, Taryn had kept her calm and given a decent explanation. "Are you okay with what we've said, Josie?" She tried to use the girl's advancing maturity to their advantage. "We're going to need you to help us look after Ricky and Tom. You're nearly ten, and we know how grown up you are. What do think your dad should do?"

Josie chewed thoughtfully on her afternoon snack. She liked being treated as an adult. She really did miss her mom, but she knew how much her dad loved her mom, too. "I miss him, but I think he should go and be with mom. He always makes her smile, and you and Taryn are cool." She paused feeling a little uncomfortable with both women's eyes on her. "Can I leave the table? I need to do my homework." Uncharacteristically, she hugged both Jace and Taryn before she left the room.

Jace wiped Tom's mouth and let him out of his seat. "Do you think we did the right thing telling them?"

Taryn peeled the skin off her last grape. She had been thinking the same thing. "Yeah. At least they know what's going on. They may not like it, but it may help them to be more cooperative. And I think they'll both tell Bill to go down to Florida. Do you mind tidying up while I go and help Ricky find his card and homework?"

Jace nodded. "I'll be fine. I'm going to read Tom some stories."

"I thought I'd go pick up dinner in a while," Taryn said.

"That would be great," Jace gave her a smile that almost made her knees buckle. "I'm too tired to cook tonight."

TARYN TUCKED THE Kentucky Fried Chicken bucket under her arm, and just as quietly tiptoed through to the kitchen. After putting the bucket in the fridge, she went in search of Jace. Her previous suspicions were confirmed, when she caught sight of Jace's slumbering form. She was cuddled up to Tom. The little boy had his thumb tucked into his mouth, and was nestled in the crook of Jace's neck. Her dark hair framed his face. They both looked so angelic, and Taryn wished she had a camera. It was rare that she saw this side of Jace. She had only seen Jace asleep a few times. Usually, it was Taryn that fell asleep on Jace, or woke up too late to observe her friend asleep. *Friend. Is she still a friend?* Taryn asked herself silently. She knew the answer was yes. No matter what happened, her life was interwoven with Jace's, even if it was just the connection through her family.

Taryn looked at the loose hair hanging over Jace's forehead. She liked the way the curls bounced, and couldn't resist moving one of them off Jace's eyes. She was halfway done when pale blue eyes connected with hers. Embarrassed at being caught, Taryn froze. She smiled weakly, and indicated her hand to Jace. "I...I was just ..." *What the hell was I doing? I'm sorry, Jace. I was just feeling your hair because I couldn't resist you! Wake up, Taryn and just move your hand!* She dropped the curl and sat back on her haunches.

Jace lifted her head slightly, and tried to subtly wipe the drool that had pooled at the edge of her mouth. "I can't believe I fell asleep." She rubbed her eyes and tried to move without waking Tom.

Taryn shook her head. "I don't know how Anne gets dinner and the kids' homework done. I..." She paused, suddenly filled with uncertainty. She sucked in a deep breath. They needed to talk and try to at least clear the air. She didn't want to spend the whole weekend hiding upstairs. "I was hoping we'd get a few minutes to talk...about us."

Jace looked over surprised that she'd heard those words coming from Taryn's mouth. She had had similar thoughts herself, but hadn't been brave enough to voice them. "Sure. But I need to wake Tom. If he sleeps too long, we'll never get him off later."

She saw uncertainty flutter in Taryn's eyes. "I'm not saying we shouldn't talk. We should. It's been hell sharing a house with you, and not really communicating. I'm just trying to be practical. Can we do this later?" Realizing that Taryn might take her words as a rebuttal, she leaned over and grabbed Taryn's hand. This action forced Taryn to look at her. "Thank you for being brave enough to make the first move."

Taryn forced a small smile onto her face. If Jace was willing to be nice, then she could try. "You're right. Let me wake him up and change him. It'll give you a chance to wake up properly. You look a little better."

TWO HOURS LATER, and three children sleeping in bed, both women were back downstairs.

"Here, you look like you could use this." Jace passed Taryn a glass of wine. She had picked up a few adult goodies earlier while she'd been to the shops.

"Thanks. How was Josie?"

"Her usual practical self. What about Ricky?"

Taryn shrugged. "It's hard to say. He seems okay and quite excited, but I think he internalizes a lot of his problems." She saw Jace's eyebrows rise. "Don't say it...I know it runs in the family."

Jace leaned back against the sofa cushion and closed her sore eyes. She was way too tired, but she knew she'd promised Taryn a chat. She just hoped it didn't get out of hand. Her emotions were raw, and she didn't think she could cope with any more of Taryn's anger.

Taryn caught Jace's furtive glances from the corner of her eye. She really wanted to talk to Jace, but also knew the woman was running on empty. She took a few more gulps of wine, trying to pluck up the courage to talk to Jace. Finally, she turned in her seat.

Jace saw the motion to her left and steeled herself for the conversation. She turned her head and caught Taryn's questioning gaze.

"You look bushed. Are you sleeping?"

Jace bit her bottom lip. Taryn had no idea that she was the reason for her tiredness. Jace rubbed her face and smiled at Taryn. "I didn't get much sleep last night." She saw Taryn's forehead burrow into a frown, and knew she could either wait for the question or expand on the reasons. "I worked late on those reports. When I came to bed, I was too wired to sleep, and then I heard you."

"Me?" Taryn squeaked.

"You." Jace smiled, trying to lighten the mood. "I heard crying. The bathroom doors were open, and when I peeked in I saw you thrashing around the bed and crying out. I tried to wake you, but you didn't respond. In the end, I climbed onto the bed and held you. Every time I tried to leave, you cried out." Jace fiddled with her glass. She hadn't looked at Taryn the whole conversation.

Taryn squirmed in her seat. She had no recollection of Jace's visit and it frightened her. "I'm sorry." She mumbled. "Did you get any sleep?"

Jace nodded. "Little catnaps. I'll be okay. I think this week's been unsettling for everyone. I know my routine's been shot to shit."

Taryn smiled. She knew Jace was trying to make her feel better. "Thanks, Jace. For being there...for looking after me."

Jace turned in her seat, and took in her friend's somber face. "I promised you I would. That hasn't changed, Taryn."

Taryn licked her lips. Her eyes flickered around the room as she digested the information. Finally, she sucked in a lungful of air and let it out slowly. She needed to know the answer to her unspoken question. "I'm sorry, Jace? Last week, I didn't think before I spoke. I guess I got scared with what you were offering me."

Jace grimaced. "I know that. It was my fault really. I ran. I got scared and I ran."

"Scared of what?" Taryn thought she knew most of the answers, but she needed to hear Jace say the words.

Jace's eyes remained fixed on her lap. She chewed the inside of her lip for a few seconds, and then began to speak. "I was scared that you would begin to see I was vulnerable. I was scared of how you make me feel. And, I was scared that these feelings will make me fuck up, and I'll lose all I've worked for."

Taryn's heart lurched when she heard the honest words. She restrained herself from reaching over and pulling the woman into a hug. They needed to get everything out, and find out exactly where they stood. No more games. She knew with Jace that it would be all or nothing. "How do you feel about me?"

Jace's eyes lifted to Taryn's. The question had caught her by surprise. She could see no malice in Taryn's dark, probing eyes. "I can't get you out of my head. I can't work because you're all I see. I can't sleep because your body is in the next room. I can't smile because seeing you hurt and knowing I did it, kills me." She tried to swallow, but a lump had settled in her throat and caused her voice to break. At that moment she knew there was no going back. "I think ...I'm...in love with you." She felt her eyes tingle and itch, and she knew that tears were on their way. She breathed in deeply and closed her eyes, trying valiantly to keep some control over her crashing emotions.

"What about Vanessa?"

Jace fidgeted in her seat. "Vanessa's not important. She knows that."

"Things didn't look like that the other Friday. Did you sleep with her?" The thought had been burning in Taryn's mind all week. She had never felt jealousy like she had that Friday.

Jace turned fiery eyes Taryn's way. "No."

"Did you want to?"

Jace shrugged dejectedly. "I thought I did. I just wanted to be normal. I went on the date purposely to try and rid my mind of you. You'd made it perfectly clear New Year's Day that we couldn't be together. As callous as it sounds, I wanted to get more sexual experience, so you'd see me as an equal. Anne's only slept with one man and no one thinks anything different about her. I hadn't slept with anybody, before you, and suddenly I'm different. I'm tired of being different."

"That's not true, Jace!" Taryn stated.

"It is."

"What happened with Vanessa?" Taryn knew she needed to deflect the conversation off an argument. She wanted to know what Jace did and thought.

"I'd spent the evening flirting and she responded to all my suggestions. It wasn't difficult. I knew Vanessa wanted to make our relationship more physical. All the others, Taryn, were just to make you think I was dating." She admitted sheepishly.

Taryn gasped. "It worked!"

"I know," Jace replied guiltily.

"So, what made Vanessa different?"

Jace shrugged. "She was very persistent. She took the lead a lot of the times, and pushed my personal boundaries. I'd finally gotten my head into a place where I could consider being physical, and then you were there right in front of me. I never meant to push you out, Taryn." She glanced at the puppy-dog eyes. Her heart was melting and her guilt rising. "But, I couldn't get you out of my damn head. I thought that if I distanced myself from you, I'd do better at work and on my dates. It didn't work. After you told me about Patrick and Anne, I realized how stupid I'd been. I felt guilty that I'd been so self-obsessed that I hadn't bothered to ask Anne how she was doing."

Taryn touched Jace's leg, initiating the first contact between them. "You weren't the only one."

"The rest you know. I meant to apologize. But after my attitude, I couldn't blame your actions or thoughts toward me. I promised not to hurt you...and I did. I did it intentionally, Taryn. I promised that I wouldn't hurt you and I did." Jace couldn't stop repeating the same sentence.

Taryn's resolve broke and she moved over to hold the crying woman. "Shh. You didn't mean to. It was self-defense. I'm still here and I'm still your friend. Nothing's broken, Jace."

Jace tentatively placed her hand over Taryn's heart. "This is. Ricky told me. He said you were crying."

Taryn smirked. "Wow. I'm going to have to watch what I say or do around him. I see we have a little spy in our midst!"

Jace flashed a smile at Taryn. Her eyes were blurred with tears and her head hurt, but it felt good to finally have her friend back. She wiped her nose on the back of her hand, and tried to breathe through it.

Taryn passed Jace a tissue. "Here. I think you and Tom are spending way too much time together. You're picking up his habits. Wipe your eyes and blow your nose. My problems were my own doing. I snooped where I shouldn't have."

Jace stopped mid blow when she heard Taryn's remark. "What happened?"

Taryn shook her finger at Jace. "That's another story." She saw Jace frown. "And I will tell you. I just think we should concentrate on one thing at a time. I'm tired of us playing emotional tennis. I ask you something, and you respond with a question. Then I reply with a question, and we end up going back and forth. We need to sort out what's going on between us."

Jace's eyes brightened. "What do you mean?" She asked coyly, trying to get a rise out of Taryn.

"See you're doing it again!" She saw the mischievous grin and playfully swatted the smiling woman. "It's good to see you smile, Jace. I've missed that."

"I missed seeing you happy, as well. How have you been this week? I mean, how do you feel about the past few weeks?" Jace mumbled.

Taryn knew Jace had spoken from her heart, and she also knew the rule still stood between them. If a question was asked, they either answered honestly or not at all. "I was so happy to spend time with you."

"Me, too." Jace added. "Sorry, go on."

"My jealousy just kept eating away at me. I hated knowing other women were spending time with you and it was all my doing. Then you acted so distant toward me, I felt like I'd lost you."

Jace's eyes widened. She gulped back her question. Her body stiffened, and she could feel the blood pounding in her ears. "I blew it big time, huh?"

"We both did." Taryn muttered.

Jace took Taryn's hand, and also a very deep breath. "So, how do you feel about me?"

"Jace, when I gave you those reasons last month, I omitted one big thing. I didn't tell you how scared I was to take that step into a relationship with someone who wasn't safe."

Jace pouted and frowned simultaneously. "Explain what you mean by 'safe'."

Taryn brushed her fingers against Jace's cheek. "I mean, going into a relationship with someone who could break my heart. I've come to rely on you so much for friendship and support. I've finally found someone who I can be open and honest with. You don't take any shit from me, Jace, and you give as good as you get. That's exciting, but also scary. There's a passion between us that I've never felt before. I was too scared to tell you this. The reasons I gave were real. Anne was afraid that I made them up because I was running. But I really did want you to be sure, and I did need time to sort myself out. And I learned a lot these past six weeks."

Jace took Taryn's fingers in her own and stroked them gently. She looked into frightened eyes. "What did you learn?"

"I just told you. I was so jealous it drove me crazy. I couldn't stop hating the fact that other people got to be intimate with you."

Jace pulled Taryn's hand to her lips. She lightly brushed her lips over the skin. "They meant nothing, and we did nothing."

"You kissed them." Taryn pouted.

"Some of them, but they were nothing like our kisses at New Year's. I was only doing it because I thought it would get your back up."

Taryn almost smiled at Jace's panicked expression. It was hard to stay mad when she seemed almost as dismayed by her dating as Taryn was. "So, did you learn anything from the dates?"

Jace nodded. "I definitely know that I like women. I like going to gay bars, and I definitely like holding you and dancing. This whole experience has made me realize that I am gay, Taryn, and proud of it."

"I'm pleased."

"So, I've dated, and I know what I want. You just said you cleared your head, and I think after all these weeks being on your own, you can't possibly need any more time to figure out what you want.." She saw Taryn open her mouth.

"That brings us back to the workplace issue." Taryn rebuked.

"It's no big deal. You're not some innocent undergrad, and I'm not marking your assignments or quizzes. It wouldn't look too good, but it's not our biggest problem."

Taryn nodded. "I know. But I'm still your employee, Jace. If people found out, you could lose your job."

"I doubt it." Jace mumbled.

"But you'd know, Jace. Could you handle breaking that rule? Even if they didn't fire you, your reputation would be screwed."

Jace almost felt she was falling into Taryn's dark eyes as a thought hit her. "You're talking as if you're thinking really seriously about this. Do you want this?"

Taryn could not resist Jace's azure, bright eyes. She hadn't seen her so happy in a long time. "The other things I learned were that I miss you when you're not around. And I like being held in your arms...and that I've never been kissed and had such sensations run through my body before. I hate it when we don't talk, and I struggle to keep my hands to myself when you're around."

"So, what does that mean?" Jace knew she was entering territory that she'd sworn she'd never go into, but life was too short and she was sure they could work something out. She wasn't going to risk losing Taryn. Not when she'd finally found someone to share her life with.

"It means, Jace Xanthos, that I think I've fallen in love with you, too. It means that I can't bear to be away from you. And if you don't kiss me, I'll be forced to throw myself at you."

Jace gulped. She took Taryn's face between her hands and held it steady. Her body shook and the nerves made her arms tremble. She leaned forward, never taking her eyes off Taryn's face. Taryn tentatively licked her lips, and then her eyes were shut. Jace could feel Taryn's breath on her face. As Taryn's lips connected with hers electricity shot through her body, and she felt the warmth spread all over. Her heart raced and she slipped her hands around Taryn's neck and back, instinctively pulling her closer. Her breasts arched into the smaller body and her groin throbbed. Seconds turned into minutes, and Jace's body shuddered with unexpected sensations. Finally she broke away, gasping for air and needing an anchor for her swirling emotions.

Taryn drew Jace into a hug. She needed to keep the connection alive. She had a feeling if she gave Jace too much time to think, they'd be back to square one. She tilted her head back a little to look at Jace's tired features. "I think it's time for bed!" she stated quietly.

"Alone?" Jace asked even quieter.

"No. Together. To sleep...together."

"To sleep." Jace smiled, holding on for all she was worth to the woman who anchored her as nothing and no one ever had.

JACE WRIGGLED AROUND in the bed. "Hey," she muttered shyly as Taryn exited the bathroom and climbed onto the bed.

"Hi, yourself. Don't go all shy on me. I promise to behave myself and not have my wicked way with you." She saw the flush rush over Jace's face. "You are so cute when you blush." Jace lowered her head under the covers. "Hey, come back. I was teasing. May I?" Taryn lifted the edge of the covers. She wanted to make sure everything was on Jace's terms.

"Taryn, it's your bed. Come on, get in." Jace lifted the covers sending a silent hint to Taryn that she wanted her close. She watched as Taryn turned off the main light. She opened her arms, guiding Taryn's body into them, and smiled when she felt Taryn's body meld against her own. "Comfortable?"

"Mmm, very." Taryn rested her head on Jace's shoulder and wrapped her arm around the trim waist. She could feel the deep and erratic breaths coming from her partner. "Are you sure this is okay?"

Jace felt Taryn's hot breath whispering over her neck and upper chest.

Taryn snuggled closer to Jace. "Are you tired?"

"My body's exhausted," Jace said, wearily. "But my mind won't rest."

"I know what you mean," Taryn paused. "Jace, when did you decide to stop running from this?"

Jace moved her chin down and looked at the spikes of hair. Even in the dark, she could picture the various shades of blonde. She kissed Taryn lightly on the head. "I guess I began to wonder what I was doing when I saw you fall apart on Saturday. I didn't like the way you were dealing with your anger and grief." She felt Taryn hold her closer. "It also hurt when you said those things to me in the kitchen. When you pointed out that I was the one running. It got me thinking. I decided I would either tell you how I felt and to try and work something out, or I would have to let you leave my life completely."

Taryn's hand slipped under Jace's tank top and she gently rubbed the taut stomach muscles. "That would never happen, Jace."

"You say that now." She paused for a second. "But things were shaky between us. If fate hadn't caused Patrick to have that car crash and his health wasn't deteriorating, we might never have been forced to talk. You may not have come over to my house and I could have slept with Vanessa."

Taryn lifted up and turned onto her side, resting her head on her hand. "You said downstairs you wouldn't have slept with her."

"I'll never know for sure. Seeing you outside my house blew me away, and made me see reason." Thinking aloud. she added, "We said some mean things to each other. I hate that."

Taryn leaned forward and kissed Jace tentatively on the lips. She went slow and made sure Jace understood that it was a chaste kiss. She didn't want to get either of them overexcited. "I guess the old saying is true. You really do hurt the one you love."

Jace stroked Taryn's face. She placed her other arm under her head and gave a gentle sigh. "So, when did you start to have feelings for me?"

"Umm that's a hard one. I think I really began to notice you after Thanksgiving. Your pajamas didn't leave much to the imagination. Don't get me wrong. I'd noticed your looks and body before, but never in a romantic way, more as an appreciation of the female body. It kind of crept up on me. The more time we spent together, the closer we got. The week I stayed at your house made me see how compatible we are and I saw a different side of you." She stifled a yawn. "I really missed you when I moved out. Then you became the 'catch of the week' in Massachusetts and I was jealous."

Jace pulled Taryn back against her body. "I'm all yours."

"Did you check the alarm? I don't want three pairs of eyes staring at us tomorrow morning!"

Jace opened one eye. "I checked it three times. Night, Taryn."

"Night, Jace." Taryn kissed Jace's lips and lingered when she felt Jace respond. She turned toward Jace's body, feeling the insistent push of Jace's tongue against her teeth. Unable to deny Jace access, she opened her mouth slightly.

Jace took the opportunity and deepened the kiss. She used her tongue to caress Taryn's teeth and mouth. She couldn't quell the groan that escaped her lips when she felt warm hands roam across her stomach. She broke the kiss and pulled Taryn into a hug. "Have I told you how much I love being you?"

Taryn stroked the side of Jace's face. "The feelings mutual."

"I hate to say this, but, I don't think I have the energy to stay awake." Jace lazily traced a finger down Taryn's back as she spoke.

Taryn yawned, "I know. Hopefully, we'll have plenty of time *very* soon to continue this... and we will!" She kissed Jace gently on a cheek and settled down for what she hoped would be a restful night.

Chapter
Twenty-one

JACE WOKE UP lying flat on her stomach. She felt a heavy weight on her back. *What is it about this woman? She thinks I'm the bed!* Jace smiled. It was nice knowing that even in her sleep Taryn needed to be close to her. She managed to maneuver her body out from under the sleeping woman. She placed a light kiss on Taryn's cheek, and quietly tiptoed out of the room.

An hour later, Jace ran back up the stairs. She carefully reached inside the carrier bag and quietly placed a surprise on each of the children's pillows, kissing every child while they slept. She reentered Taryn's room and left the door ajar. She placed the bag next to the bed and climbed back in, wrapping her arms around her cute sleeping partner.

Taryn felt the mattress move and cold arms circle her stomach. "Where did you go?" She mumbled into the pillow, her brain still far off in la-la land.

"You'll find out soon enough." Jace snuggled her head into Taryn's hair. "Good morning, sweetheart."

Taryn rolled over. "Is it time to get up? I never heard the alarm."

Jace pulled Taryn as close as she could. She wanted to bottle this feeling. She closed her eyes and tried to memorize this perfect moment. "I shut the alarm off. I would say that in about three minutes we're going to have our own little human alarms in the room."

This comment made Taryn open her eyes slightly and give Jace a puzzled look. "Why?"

"Surprise!" Jace kissed Taryn lightly on the lips. "Happy Valentine's Day."

"Happy Valentine's Day." Taryn deepened the kiss.

Jace pulled away from Taryn. "Close your eyes!" She ordered, pleased to see Taryn obey her command. She climbed out of the bed and picked the gift out of the bag. She knelt on the floor, very aware that tiny humans could interrupt them at any time. "Open your eyes."

Taryn opened her eyes and blinked a few times. They focused in on a red teddy bear with the number one written on its chest. Around the teddy was clear wrapping with hearts printed over it. Inside the bear's arms was a bag of Hershey Kisses. "Jace...that's so cute. When did you get it?"

"This morning, you've got to love 24 hour shops!" They both turned their heads when they heard excited whooping and squeals coming from Ricky's room.

Taryn raised an eyebrow. "Did the Valentine Fairy visit the kids, too?"

Josie was at the door with Ricky behind her, a big white bear in his arms. "I got a Valentine's bear and a bag of Jelly Beans." He looked at Taryn. "You got one, too?"

Taryn nodded. "Yep. What else did you get?"

"A card." He handed it to Taryn.

She read the short sentiment: *Happy Valentine's Day, Ricky. We love you. Aunty Jace and Ryn.* She looked over at Jace and mouthed, "Thank you." Just as the baby monitor erupted with happy sounds.

They strolled along the hall and found Tom ecstatic over his new toy, pressing the tummy to set off screeching sounds that echoed in the quiet of the room.

Oh, boy. Next time pick a silent one. Jace cuddled Tom to her then shooed the other children out of the room, telling them to get dressed.

"You're really good with them, Jace." Taryn linked her fingers with Jace's and they snuggled for a few moments.

"Anne really wanted me to be a hands-on godmother. If anything happens to Bill and her, I become their legal guardian." She fell quiet. It was a difficult conversation to have with Taryn. She knew that if circumstances had been different that Taryn would have been in her shoes. "I didn't know you existed in their lives," she said, with a pang of sorrow for all Taryn's estrangement had cost both her and Anne's children. "I wasn't trying to replace you."

Taryn pushed back old hurts. "Hey, I know that. Bill and Anne had to look past family ties and to the person best equipped for the job. You have a large home, and you're financially stable to take on three kids." She met Jace's eyes, her expression open as seldom before. "What about kids of your own?"

"Never given it much thought. I need to run soon. Would you mind doing breakfast?"

"For a price!" Taryn smirked impishly.

"Can I afford it?"

"A proper good morning kiss." Taryn replied.

"I can deliver that one." Jace closed her eyes and lowered her lips to Taryn's, tasting the sweet chocolate of the candy kisses. When they finally paused for breath, she said, "I was wondering what you were doing later?"

Taryn fluttered her eyelashes coyly. "It depends what you were thinking about."

Jace blushed. "I was going to ask you for a date." She swallowed her nerves and then continued with her question. "Taryn, will you go out with me?"

Taryn's brow furrowed. "We have the kids. Where would we go?"

"It's in-house entertainment. I was wondering if you'd just pretend. It's Valentine's Day, and I've never been out on a Valentine's date. If circumstances were different, I'd have asked you out. I tried to think of a child minder but no one I know would be willing to give up a night with their significant other."

"I can do make-believe. So, when are you picking me up for our date?"

"After the children are in bed, about eight-thirty. Oh, the dress code in this establishment is casual." Jace smiled coyly at Taryn and then continued with her meal. The day was just getting better and better.

TARYN WALKED NERVOUSLY down the stairs. She had offered to read to the children as Jace had 'things' she needed to do for their date. She could hear the quiet music coming from behind the living room door. She stood for a moment outside the door trying to collect her thoughts. She had no idea why she was feeling so nervous. They'd already been intimate with each other. She contemplated that fact for a while and knew in her mind it was for that exact reason she was a little anxious.

A light tapping on the front door interrupted her thoughts. *Who the hell is calling this late at night?* She cautiously looked through the frosted glass and beamed at what she saw.

Jace jiggled anxiously on the front door step. The idea of knocking on the front door had seemed good at the time, but now she wasn't so sure. As she heard the tiny squeak of the door handle, she held the flowers up to her chest. "Hi." She said bashfully.

"Thank you." Taryn took the flowers. She had no idea what to do next. "I wanted to get you a gift, but I wasn't sure what you'd like. You don't seem to be a flowers or a stuffed toy kind of person. I...er...I..." A pair of lips brushed across her own cutting off her words.

"You are my gift," Jace said. Taking Taryn's hand, she led her to the living room.

Taryn gasped as she took in the soft lighting and candles. There were snacks on the table and a bottle of wine in an ice bucket. On the floor, Jace had placed a fleece blanket and plenty of sofa cushions. "Jace, it's beautiful."

Jace poured two glasses of wine and handed one to Taryn. "To new beginnings," she toasted and they tapped glasses. "I was hoping we could really relax." She indicated the blanket as she spoke. "I got us a DVD."

Taryn settled on the blanket and rested her head against the edge of the couch. "Sounds good. Would it be okay if I just soaked up the atmosphere and your company for a few minutes?"

Jace lay next to Taryn. "Anything." She fiddled with a piece of fluff on the blanket.

Sensing her anxiety, Taryn reached over and tugged the sleeve of her sweater. "A cuddle would be good. I know this is our first 'date', but I think we've crossed the initial intimacy borders."

Jace rolled closer to Taryn and wrapped her arms around her waist. She rested her head on Taryn's lap. She felt gentle fingers massage her scalp, and a low moan of delight escaped her lips. "This feels great. I hope you weren't expecting to do something exciting."

Taryn lowered her head and looked into deep blue eyes. "This is more than great. It's just nice to be able to relax after being with the kids. It's good just spending time with you...like this."

Jace closed her eyes and reveled in the moment. "It's excellent. I'm looking forward to the weekend." She kept her eyes shut as she pondered whether to talk about her thoughts. She decided the timing couldn't get any more perfect and she rolled over and leaned up on an elbow. "We're going to have to either pretend to just be friends or tell our friends about us. What do you want to do?"

Taryn fought the temptation to just lean forward and kiss the full lips that moved temptingly close to her own. "I've always been very open. I kind of go on the theory of take me as I am or leave me. I consider Cory and Dylan to be my closest friends, and I like Jo and Helen. I don't have a problem telling them we're girlfriends, but I don't want you to feel pressured. What do you want to do?"

Jace shrugged. "I think, I would rather the four know about us and we can be natural together. Wow, I have a girlfriend!" She uttered, and then immediately felt embarrassed when she realized she'd actually verbalized the comment.

Taryn hugged Jace to her. "You are so cute."

Jace pulled back and arched one dark brow. "Are you making fun of me?"

"No! I swear, Jace. Your innocence in all of this is so refreshing. It's ironic, really. To begin with, it was what scared me so much, and now it's kind of alluring. You're so different in work than out of work. It's like our roles kind of switch from you being the leader in work, to me being the more experienced out." She caught the crestfallen look on Jace's face. "But that won't always be the way. As my mother would say, I'm making a real pig's ear of this, aren't I?"

Jace shook her head. "No. I think sometimes we over-analyze our thoughts and then other times we internalize too much." Deciding she didn't want to lose the mood, she held out her hand. "Would you like to dance with me?"

Taryn let Jace set the pace. Her body seemed to fit into every niche of Jace's. Where Jace was curved and hard, Taryn's own body seemed to naturally fit like a piece of a puzzle. Her head was level with Jace's shoulder and she rested it there. She felt the warmth of Jace's body immediately and closed her eyes, breathing in the scent that invaded her senses.

Jace moved them around the tiny living room. As the minutes ticked away, she slowly forgot to move her feet and ended up just swaying slightly to the slow rhythm. She gently brushed her lips over the soft spikes of blond hair. When she felt Taryn squeeze her a little harder in response, she purposely kissed the top of Taryn's head and then moved her head slightly so she could kiss the edge of Taryn's forehead. She pulled Taryn even closer and kissed the lips that had turned her way. She ran her tongue over Taryn's bottom lip and gently pushed against the smooth teeth, which were blocking her entrance to the warm mouth.

Taryn could feel Jace's tongue pressing on her teeth. She opened her mouth wider and felt the warm tongue enter her. At first she sucked gently on it and then the passion overtook her and she couldn't get enough of Jace. She wanted to taste more and more. She could feel the slight trembling of Jace's arms and legs against her own shaky limbs, and without breaking the kiss she steered them back to the blanket. Taryn pulled Jace down never breaking the contact. Finally, needing to breathe properly she broke the kiss. "I think I've found a new hobby. I love kissing you." She gasped before she reclaimed the moist lips that hovered above hers.

Jace savored the kisses. Her need to get closer to Taryn was driving her insane. No matter how deep she plunged or sucked, she never seemed to get enough. The veins at the side of her head were pulsing with life and energy and she didn't want the moment to end. She could feel Taryn's hands sliding down the side of her sweater and she remembered how quickly she had lost control before. She felt Taryn's hands rise back up her torso, touching her skin. Her nerve endings were very sensitive and she felt an involuntarily shiver follow in the pathway of the hands. She broke from the kiss.

Taryn felt the tremor pass through Jace's body. She knew her hands were hovering very close to the edge of Jace's bra and she slowly lowered them to the outside of Jace's sweater. "Sorry. I got a little carried away."

Jace rolled over onto her side, still caressing the side of Taryn's cheek, not wanting to lose contact. "No. I don't want you to stop."

Taryn sighed in response. "We're not really in a position to lose control in here. The kids could interrupt us at any moment."

Jace stroked Taryn's cheek and then down to her neck. She continued the trail until her fingers stopped short of Taryn's breasts. She swallowed a gulp of saliva that had suddenly pooled in her mouth. She kept eye contact with Taryn and willed her fingers to move the half an inch that would have them fondling what she desperately craved. "I want to touch you so much. It's all I've thought about this week." Her hand brushed Taryn's hardened nipple.

Taryn looked nervously at the door. "The kids?"

Jace moved her hand and pulled Taryn into her body. She relished the feelings of contentment she felt within herself. "I know. It would be our luck to be in the middle of something and have Josie come in and ask for a glass of water."

Taryn giggled. "Could you imagine her reaction? Oh my god, Anne would kill us."

Jace relaxed against Taryn and kissed her forehead lightly. "Oh boy! I can just picture the scene. How about we just settle for a little cuddling and watch the film I rented? Unless you want to talk or have other ideas?"

Taryn shook her head and rearranged her body so she was at least comfortable. "Let's watch the film. We'd better have some alone time this weekend or I'll explode!"

Chapter
Twenty-two

A COUPLE OF very long days later, after they'd all been out for dinner, Jace pulled the SUV onto the Weston's driveway and turned confused eyes to Taryn. "Bill's truck is here."

Taryn was having the same thoughts as she took in the red pickup truck. "He didn't say he was coming back here. You spoke to Anne yesterday. Did she mention anything to you?"

Jace shook her head. "We talked about the kids and how we were going to cover the vacation, but she never said anything. Maybe, Bill got the week off?" She shrugged her shoulders.

Ricky leaned forward in his seat, catching sight of his father's truck. "Daddy's home!" He squealed.

"Daddy! Daddy!" cried Tom, even louder than his brother.

Jace opened the passenger door and Josie didn't waste any time as she ran toward the house. The front door opened and everyone turned upon hearing Josie scream her mother's name at the top of her lungs.

Taryn watched the sweet reunion of mother and child. Ricky scrambled out of his seatbelt and shot past her.

"Mommy!" The oldest son charged up the steps and tried to climb over his sister to get to his mother.

Jace helped Tom to the floor. There were tears in his eyes when he saw his mother. "Mommy. Go to Mommy." The small boy wobbled on his legs as he tried to run faster than they could carry him.

Anne untangled herself from her older children who turned to hug their father. "Tom. You've grown!" She met her son half way and swung him into the air. "I've missed you."

"Tom miss mommy." The youngster planted wet kisses on his mother's lips.

Jace watched the reunion from the side of the car. She felt Taryn's presence beside her. She looked down into frightened eyes. "Are you okay?"

"A little shocked. Anne said she wouldn't be home until..."

"Until Patrick died." Jace finished the sentence for Taryn. She placed her arm around her girlfriend; unsure of what Taryn was feeling. "He was holding his own last night. I don't think she'd have left so soon. How about we go and find out what's changed, rather than guess?"

Anne handed a reluctant Tom over to his father and opened her arms as her friends walked toward her. "My heroes." She hugged them. "The kids look great."

"We're a little in shock. We weren't expecting you." Jace said, as she kissed Bill.

Taryn placed her hand in Jace's needing the reassuring touch. "I mean, we're glad to see you, but why didn't you call us?"

"It wasn't planned," Anne patted Jace's arm. "Patrick's doctors have managed to stabilize his condition. He's not out of the woods, but when Bill spoke to them on Saturday, the initial prognosis has changed and they now aren't sure what his chances are." She saw Taryn frown.

"So he's not dying?" Taryn asked incredulously.

"His illness is still terminal, they just can't give us a time and day." She shrugged her shoulders. "I did what I could this week and my presence helped Mom and Dad out. Patrick's mood swings were a little too much to bear. Anyway, Bill talked to him on Saturday. There are things Patrick wants with him from the house, so, we decided it was better if we came home for a while."

"We didn't want to get the kids' hopes up if we couldn't get on the flight today." Bill added.

"Well, it's good to see you." Jace replied.

Anne turned her attention to the children playing in their yard. "I missed the children so much this week and didn't realize the pressure I'd put you two under."

Jace turned quizzically to Taryn. She observed Taryn's mirrored facial expression. Confused she looked back at Anne. "What pressure?"

Anne laughed. "Josie told me last night that you have a lot of work to do this week and I should come home."

Jace sat on the doorstep and propping her head in her hands. "We'd have managed."

Taryn settled on the step below Jace's. "We had a plan, Anne. Josie really shouldn't have said anything to you." Taryn cursed herself for leaving her young cousin alone with the phone.

"Don't blame Josie. She just answered my questions when I asked her. I don't even think she knew what she was saying. She told me how busy Jace is next week and that she needed you to help at work, too. I talked with Dad and Bill, and we decided that I should be with the kids." She could still see the downcast looks on her friends' faces. "She did me a favor. I'm actually relieved. It was time to come home and be where I'm needed the most."

"Well in that case, you're a sight for sore eyes." Jace chuckled.

Anne opened her arms and let Tom climb on to her lap. "Were you good for Auntie Jace and Taryn?"

"Tom good." He smiled up at his mother.

Jace waited for Tom to run back to his father and siblings who were playing on the swing set. "How's your mother holding up?"

"Now that the shock has worn off, she has set her mind to making peace with Patrick. She's of the mind that no one should die without penance."

Jace nodded. "It's got to be hard burying a second son. No parent should have to bury a child." She patted Anne's shoulder. "I'm going to unload the trunk and then you can have your car back."

Taryn's eyes followed Jace down the pathway. "I should go and help her." She felt her Aunt's hand on her knee.

"Taryn, we need to talk about Patrick."

"There's nothing to say." Taryn stood up.

Anne caught hold of her niece's sweater, causing Taryn to stop in her tracks. "Taryn, just listen to me before you storm off. What I have to say isn't what I personally think. I'm not sure I even like what I'm about to say." She could sense from Taryn's body language that she had her attention. "This message is from your Gram. I told her you wouldn't want to hear what I have to say, but she made me promise I'd tell you." She looked into storm filled eyes and shrugged apologetically, "You know how persistent she is."

"Go on."

"She wants you and Patrick to bury your differences. She wants you to forgive him so that he can die in peace." She felt the muscles in Taryn's arm go stiff. "It's not my opinion, Taryn. She said if I didn't talk to you, she would and she's not a well woman. I'm scared if she does try to convince you that she'll die trying, literally."

Taryn returned to her seat on the step. "How bad is she?"

"Her blood pressure's high. Her doctor's worried about her heart palpitations. Dad had to give Patrick an ultimatum about dying alone or making sure he didn't upset his mother. Dad said he wouldn't let Mom visit Patrick if she was going to get upset. Even Patrick couldn't bear the thought of losing his mother. They actually talked quite a bit this week. She wants you to visit him over Spring Break."

Taryn felt crushed. Her grandparents were very important to her and she knew she owed them a lot. Their faith in her mother had assured that Taryn had everything she had ever wanted as a child. Her mother had told her how thankful she had been for the Clary's love. "I'm not sure I could ever look at him again."

"I know. I tried to talk her out of it. She said your forgiveness was the only chance Patrick has of going to Heaven. She's hoping your Mom can forgive him when he gets there, but she wants you to at least try and show him remorse."

Taryn blinked back tears. "I have wanted to see that man in hell for so many years. I've wished it for so long and my one chance of sending him there is being blocked by a person who saved me."

Anne brushed her fingers across Taryn's cheek. "I know. Taryn, I would never put you in this position if I didn't think it would make Mom happy. You don't need to make any decision today, just think about it. Maybe talk it over with Jace."

At the mention of Jace's name, Taryn's mood brightened. "No promises. Tell Gram I'll think about it."

"Thank you. You've made me very proud, Taryn."

Taryn winked at her aunt. "I try. I was actually going to ask you if you still want me to move back here?"

"Seriously?"

"Seriously. I talked it through with Dylan and Cory and they were very supportive. My moving in with them was temporary and I think it's time I let them have their house back."

"What about Jace?"

Taryn looked blankly at her aunt. "What about her?"

"How does she feel about you moving in here?"

Taryn shrugged. "She said it was a good move, if I could get rid of the memories. I was thinking I'd move into my old room first. Then maybe after Patrick's death, I could redecorate the annex and make it my own."

"Taryn, we'd welcome you back with open arms. When were you thinking of coming home?"

Taryn smiled. "I think I've begun to move things in already. I have most of my clothing here and I rearranged the bureau the other day. I thought the weekend would be good. Since I'm on vacation, I'd have time to really move things around. Is that okay?"

"Sure. It's going to be so good having you home."
"I hope so. I better go and see what Jace is up to."

TARYN WALKED DOWN the stone steps and pulled her jacket around her body. The fresh air felt good against her face, if not a little chilly. She pulled the packet of cigarettes out of her jacket and stared at them. *You don't need them any more. Just throw them away. One more won't hurt. No, a clean slate is what you need!* She shook her head as her internal psyche debated the consequences of one more cigarette. She heard the door shut and looked up to see Jace tentatively walking her way. "Hey."

"Hi." Jace's eyes were fixed on the cigarette in Taryn's hand. "I...I didn't realize you were still smoking."

"I'm not. Well, I haven't had one today if that aids my defense."

Jace rubbed Taryn's back and wrapped her arm around the smaller woman's waist. "I wasn't accusing you of anything. I just never realized you were a smoker."

"I'm not! I mean I wasn't. What I'm trying to say is, I used to when mom was ill, but I stopped. Now it seems to be a therapy thing for me. A bad kind of therapy, I'll admit. I'm not proud of myself. My old therapy was women. Last week I didn't want women. Well, I wanted one particular woman, but the alcohol and smoking were easier to get." She felt the arm around her tighten. "I actually came out here to throw them away, but my internal demons were battling over me having one more. I'm sorry if I let you down or made you think I was less than perfect."

Jace kept her hold on Taryn, but turned her body so they were face-to-face. "Taryn, I don't hold any illusions about you. I am disappointed to see you smoke because it's a quicker way to the grave and you're too precious to lose. You're an adult and you know the risks. I came out here to be with you. I know there's things on your mind. We promised to talk about them, I just want you to know I'm here for you." She paused to kiss Taryn lightly on the lips, before adding, "No matter what."

Taryn twirled the cigarette around in the fingers of her left hand. With her right, she flicked the lid of her lighter. Her head was listening to what Jace was saying, but the craving she felt was overpowering. In the short time, the addictive nature of the cigarettes had taken a grip on her body. "I'm trying to stop. It took me a long time after mom's death to break the habit, but only a week to become hooked again."

Jace took the cigarette out of Taryn's hand and placed it in

Taryn's mouth. "So, today we go with you having one and then maybe tomorrow none. See how it goes. Did you ever have a problem with alcohol?"

Taryn lit the cigarette and took a few steps away from Jace. "Not really. I did learn *something* from Patrick. I don't drink a lot. You've seen me when we're out. I know my limits. There are times when I will drink to forget, but the repercussions the next morning are enough to make me steer clear for a while. I'm very aware that I could develop Patrick's addictive personality." She sucked in the smoke, enjoying the sensation of the nicotine in her system. "What about you? Ever smoked?"

Jace shook her head. "No. I never really saw the appeal. It's the smell that I find repulsive. It irritates me when I smell it on others, but even more so when I leave a bar or restaurant and wake up smelling the smoke in the house."

"I bet I've been driving you crazy this week then?"

Jace shook her head. "No. To be honest, I thought you'd stopped after the weekend. I hadn't seen you smoking or smelled any on you."

"I learned a long time ago that smoking outside helps and having body spray." They spent a few minutes just star watching, taking comfort in the presence of each other.

Taryn sucked one last time on the cigarette and tapped the end on the gravel floor. "I've missed holding you."

Jace made a small sound of affirmation. "I wanted to kiss you this morning at work. I had to resist the urge to pull you into the copying room and kiss you senseless." She pecked Taryn on the tip of her nose. "I wish I could sleep with you tonight, but it might look kind of obvious if we rush away to my place the minute Anne and Bill are home."

Taryn rubbed Jace's stomach. "Well, I could maybe offer you a kiss and a cuddle on the porch if you're that desperate."

"No. I think I can manage. See you've spoiled me. Thirty-five years of sleeping on my own and a few nights with you and I'm addicted."

Jace released her hold on Taryn. "I have some wine in the fridge, if you're interested?" She walked indoors and headed to the kitchen with Taryn's hand firmly in her own.

Taryn took a seat at the counter and watched as Jace nimbly pulled the cork out in one swift movement. "It's just been a bitch of a week, but also amazing."

Jace poured their wine and clinked her glass to Taryn's. "Here's to spending more quality time together."

"I'll toast to that." Taryn took a few minutes to relax. Sipping her wine and enjoying the comfortable silence. She gently stroked Jace's hand. *She knows how you feel. She's been there. Share your pain. She's there for you. She promised.* Quietly, she asked, "If your father was ill, would you visit him?"

Jace thought about the question. Her brows furrowed as she weighed up her options. She could feel Taryn's eyes assess her face. "Tough question."

"I know. Would you go?"

Jace shrugged her shoulders slightly. "It depends. If he asked me to visit, then I think I would go." She saw Taryn's questioning expression. "In my book, if he personally asked me to visit then in a way I'd know I was kind of welcome."

Taryn nodded. "That makes sense. What if he didn't ask?"

"It would still depend on how ill he was. If he needed a blood transfusion or a donor from one of his children, then I'd go if I were compatible. It would be kind of ironic justice that the child he's denied for so long was actually his and saving his life. It wouldn't take the pain away, but then he'd owe me in a crazy way. Does that sound bitter and twisted?"

"No. You'd do that for him?" Taryn asked a little awe in her voice. "Even after all he put your mother and you through?"

"Yes." Jace whispered. "I've always dreamed that one day he would accept me."

"What if he was dying?"

Jace stared into pained eyes. "Taryn, this isn't about what I'd do. Our situations are so different. I escaped my father's grasp years ago and haven't had to endure years of abuse from him. I didn't think you ever wanted to see Patrick again?"

"I didn't.... but I found something the other day that made me think things could have been different." Taryn stood up and took the photo wallet out of her coat pocket. She sat down again, passing the wallet to Jace. "I found these last week."

Jace flicked through the album, recognizing the contents as those that had been scattered on Taryn's bedroom floor days before.

"They belonged to Patrick. I found them in his desk drawer." She looked guiltily at Jace. "I snooped."

Jace went through the pack, her mind churning over the events of the past week. She could see why Taryn had been rattled. Stopping at one photo, she said, "You were a beautiful baby."

"Thank you."

"Was this why you were upset last week?"

Taryn nodded. "Partly. It was a mixture of this and our fight. I was confused."

Jace rubbed Taryn's fingers between her own. "I can see

why. I would be, too. Have you talked to Anne about it?"

"No. I'm a little embarrassed that I stooped so low as to snoop around his things. I just don't know what it means. He has never shown any interest in me, yet these photos go up in age until I started college." She flicked to her graduation picture. "This one is the one that is most significant. Mom or Gram probably gave the other photos to him, but this one had to have been taken by Patrick. My Mom and grandparents were with me in the audience. This shot was taken from a distance. He was at my graduation." A lonely tear tracked down Taryn's cheek.

Jace tenderly wiped the tear away. "How do you feel about him?"

"I still despise him."

"Do you want to see him?"

Taryn shook her head vehemently. "No."

Jace stroked her hand over Taryn's back, slowly massaging the tight muscles. "Well, there's your answer."

"I wish it was." She closed her eyes. She could feel Jace's touch on her back and it helped to ground her thoughts. "I just want the truth. Part of me never wants to see the guy again. Another part of me wants to ask him why. This could be my last chance to get any answers." She tried to calm the nerves fluttering around in her stomach. "I'm scared."

"It's okay to be scared." Jace moved her hand to the base of Taryn's neck. She gripped the skin firmly and worked out the kink that she felt there.

"God, that feels so good." Taryn felt the hand still. "Don't stop! Please." She dropped her head further forward and tried to stifle a groan as Jace loosened a particularly tight spot. "Gram wants me to forgive Patrick." Taryn continued.

"Did Anne tell you that?"

Taryn moved her head from side-to-side. The muscles were definitely more relaxed. "Thanks." She picked up her wineglass and turned to face her girlfriend.

"Yeah. She's said that Gram thinks if I forgive Patrick, then he'll stand a better chance of going to Heaven."

"Or he could confess his sins to a priest and ask for forgiveness." Jace added, bitterly.

"True." Taryn took Jace's hand and looked closely at the various patterns that swirled over her palm and down into the fingers. She traced over the top of the fingers and back down the hand. Jace's fingers looked delicate, but Taryn had just experienced the hidden strength in them. "While I may hate Patrick and owe him nothing, I love my grandparents and if there is something I can do to relieve their pain, I feel like I should do it. I owe them so much."

"That's not really fair, Taryn. You have to make the decision for your own peace of mind." She empathized with Taryn and knew there was no answer that would make everyone happy.

"I know. When Anne first told me, I wasn't happy, but the more I think about it, the more confused I become. I wanted to see what you thought."

Jace shook her head. "I can't tell you what to do." She watched Taryn drop her head. Immediately, she placed her hand under Taryn's chin and lifted her head so she could look into eyes brimming with tears. "But I can support you and be there for you. If you decide to go to Florida and need someone to lean on, then I'm your woman. We'll make the trip together."

Taryn's emotions did a somersault at the words. Her nerves disappeared and were replaced with a tickling, giddy sensation. She smiled appreciatively at Jace. "I think that's what I wanted to hear all along. Thanks." She wiped her eyes as the tears flowed.

"Hey. I made you cry!"

"Happy tears. Happy tears are good, Jace. It's just nice to hear that someone is there for me and I'm not alone anymore."

Jace wrapped her arms around Taryn. "I hope you'll never be alone again. I...I love you." She hadn't said the words to Taryn since their initial declaration and she enjoyed hearing them roll off her tongue.

"Good because I am hopelessly head-over-heels in love with you, too."

Chapter
Twenty-three

TARYN PUSHED THE door open and hesitantly stepped over the threshold. She had to try really hard to stifle the gasp that threatened to spill out of her mouth. The man who lay propped up in the bed bore no resemblance to the man she had grown to hate. Patrick's eyes were closed and Taryn took a few more moments to assess the changes in his physical features. She could tell from his bony arms, and what appeared to be stick-thin legs under the covers, that he had lost a lot of weight. She looked to the side and saw the urine bag that held some of his waste product. He didn't scare her anymore; he looked pathetic and weak.

Taryn mustered up all her strength and uttered his name. "Patrick."

One eyelid opened. "Pops said I had a visitor, he neglected to tell me it was you. I suppose you've come to gloat before I'm gone?" The phlegm in his chest rattled with his every word.

"Don't think so highly of yourself. I'm only here because Gram asked me to come down and see you." The whole family had made the trip, preparing for the inevitable.

Patrick tried to sit up further in his bed, but his upper body strength was obviously drained and he fell slightly to the side.

Taryn automatically took a few steps toward him.

"Stop!" Patrick demanded, wheezing as the effort to halt Taryn's movements hurt his chest. "I don't need your help and I never have." He placed his hands on either side of his body and managed to pull himself back into a sitting position. "Go home. I don't need your pity."

Taryn took a few moments before she replied, half tempted to do just what Patrick had said. She could leave the room right now and run into the arms of Jace, but she had come to deliver a message, and deliver it she would.

"Don't fool yourself. To pity you would mean that I actually cared about what happens to you... and I don't." The words she had come to say were coming out all wrong. When she had practiced, Patrick had been a willing listener. In reality, the man she despised was living up to all the reasons she hated him.

"So go!" he said.

Taryn almost did but the need for some answers to her questions made her stop short. She took the wallet of photos from her pocket and tossed it onto Patrick's legs. "Just tell me why? You owe me that!"

"I owe you nothing," Patrick said in a slow, scratchy voice. "Why the hell do you care what I think? You just told me you didn't give a fuck what happens to me."

Taryn choked back the tears. *Just leave! He's not worth the pain. Turn around and leave the room, you'll never have to see him again! The past is the past, look to the future.* No matter how much her common sense yelled at her, she needed to ask the one question that had haunted her for years and that she would never get the chance to ask again.

"Why don't you love me?"

Patrick picked up the wallet and with one hand he flicked slowly through the photos. "I couldn't," he whispered.

"Why?" Taryn cried freely.

Patrick's weakness and her distance from him made her feel safe. No matter what, he couldn't physically hurt her anymore. Only his words could wound her, but no deeper than they already had. She could finally say the things she'd wanted to and he couldn't stop her. He couldn't hit her or threaten her. Before her was a miserable man and she was determined to at least tell him what she thought.

"Why did you keep those photos if I meant nothing to you?"

"Your Gram gave them to me. She never gave up, so I just put them in here to keep her quiet."

"But the graduation one wasn't taken by Gram or Gramps. You were there, weren't you?" Her question met a stony silence. Unable to hold her tongue, she lashed out with all the venom she'd been holding back. "For Christ's sake, you're fucking dying and you still can't be honest. Would it kill you to tell me the truth? I know what you did to my mother, you bastard. I know how I was conceived."

Various emotions flickered across his frail features, and urged on by his shock and bewilderment, she said, "I wanted to make you suffer! And, from the looks of things, someone is finally making you pay for your sins. So, for once in your sad, sorry life be a man and take some responsibility. What did I ever do to make you hate me like you do?"

"Why does it matter? You hate me and I certainly don't want

to own up to having a pervert for a daughter." Patrick's lungs heaved for oxygen. He held his hand to his chest and Taryn saw him pick up the button that would call a nurse to his room.

"Still running after all these years? You're just a weak, pathetic man. Nobody knew I was gay until I was in my twenties so don't use my sexuality as an excuse. You hated me all my life. Just tell me why, honestly if you can, and I'll leave."

"I never asked to be a father and I never wanted to be. It's as simple as that. Now go!" he rasped at her.

Taryn knew her question was futile. She had lived a dream all her life. Somewhere in her mind, she had dreamed that Patrick would break down and admit his feelings for her. Now, she knew that it was never going to happen. The man before her had never been her father and never would be. Even on his deathbed, he didn't see her as his daughter and he was never going to.

"Okay, I'm going. I just have one thing to say to you and only because I promised Gram that I would. I forgive you, Patrick. I forgive you for being the *worst* father on this earth. I forgive you for being the *biggest* bigot I've ever known."

She walked to the door and, holding it open slightly, turned to take one last look at the decrepit man.

"And, my mother sent a message that is long overdue. On *her* deathbed, she actually forgave you for raping her and making her life miserable because you gave her the one thing she treasured. You gave her me. She wanted you to know that. You're the loser, Patrick. You always have been and you always will be. I swear on my life, if you don't play along and tell Gram that we made up, I will tell her and Gramps what you did to my mother and then you will die alone!"

She slammed the door shut behind her, falling into the arms of forever.

Jace held Taryn to her. She had just watched Taryn's grandfather turn deathly pale and storm down the corridor. "I've got you. It's over, babe." Jace rocked Taryn's shaking body. "Come on, let's get out of here."

Taryn let Jace lead her out of the building. They stopped when they reached a bench.

"I should go back and say goodbye to Gramps."

"He's not in there. Babe, he left the building after he heard what you said to Patrick."

"He heard? Fuck!"

Taryn dropped her head into her hands and closed her eyes. Her stomach churned as she thought about her grandfather's feelings. A secret that should have died with her mother was now out to someone else in the family. "Do you think I was too hard?"

Jace rubbed her lover's back. "No. To be honest, I couldn't hear Patrick's side of the conversation or the beginning of yours until you got angry. How are you feeling now?"

"Part of me feels numb, but there's a side of me that is actually relieved that I finally got things off my chest. Now, I'd better go and find Gramps."

Jace scanned the area. She could see the Avalon that Taryn's grandfather owned. "He hasn't left the hospital grounds. I don't want you to have to go back into Patrick's room. How about I go and check with the nurses to see if he's back there and you check the grounds? Call me if you find him. We'll meet up here, okay?"

"Okay."

TARYN WANDERED AROUND the perimeter of the hospital building until she came across a small flower garden. Taking a chance, she followed the pathway to a pond area. There she found her grandfather feeding the ducks. With tears in her eyes, she walked to the edge of the pond. "Hey, Gramps."

"Hi, Squirt."

Unable to keep the words in her mouth, Taryn sobbed, "I'm sorry. Mom didn't want anyone to know, not even me."

Her Grandfather threw a piece of bread into the pond with more force than was necessary. "If I'd known, I would have thrown him out. I would have protected you and your mom with my life."

Taryn placed her hand on her grandfather's back. "You did, Gramps. Mom said we wouldn't have survived without you and Gram." She watched the ducks fight over the last crumbs of bread. "I made a mess of the whole thing."

"You tried. Things are beginning to fall into place. I never did understand him. He's my boy, my flesh and blood, but something isn't right with him. I couldn't understand why he acted like he did, but now I see things a little more clearly."

"What do you mean?" Taryn lowered herself to the ground and looked up at her grandfather who towered above her.

Pat Clary shook his head. "I was just thinking out loud. No sense in raking up the past."

"Please tell me. I have so many questions and no answers. I know I was kidding myself earlier when I thought he'd answer my questions."

Her grandfather sat down next to her, and placed his much larger, rougher hand over hers. "He never said much about you or Penny. I tried to get him to take an interest in you, but there was always so much disgust. I know where that disgust came from now. It was guilt and seeing you only kept the guilt alive. He could never love or accept you because he couldn't accept what he had done."

"Maybe." Taryn stared at the ripples on the water. "Are you going to tell Gram?"

"No. It would hurt her to know what a monster her son really is. As far as I'm concerned, you came and you forgave him. I heard you say the words and so did he. As for me, I'll support my wife, daughter and granddaughter and we'll move on, as a family." He tore up another piece of bread and asked, "How are you holding up?"

"I don't know how I should be feeling. I guess I expected him to break down and accept me. Isn't that what people do on their deathbeds?"

"In films and books. Unfortunately, Patrick only had one person on his mind his entire life. If it's any consolation, I've told him exactly what I think of him."

Taryn wiped at her itchy eyes. *You will not shed a tear for that bastard! He made your life hell!* But deep in her heart, she knew the tears were not for Patrick. They were for her grandfather who was about to lose his son. "I never meant to cause you any pain."

"I have to take some blame for how he turned out, Ryn. One day, you're going to be a parent and it's the hardest job there is. I look at our Anne and I know your Gram and I did a good job, but with Patrick something went wrong. He always felt like life owed him something. Over the years, I bailed him out of certain problems. I gave him money when he needed it." He looked gravely at Taryn. "I'm going to tell you something, but it's between you and me. Is that understood?"

At his stern tone, Taryn reverted automatically to the stock reply of her childhood. "Yes, sir."

"Your Gram took a long time to recover from Sean's death. I know you've heard bits and pieces over the years, but we never really told anybody the extent of her breakdown. She was very ill. She felt God was punishing her and Patrick became a casualty of her grief. She couldn't nurse him and wouldn't hold him."

"It must have been terrible for her."

He nodded. "She pushed everyone away, me included. Eventually she recovered but she was always telling Patrick about Sean and how unfair life was. I think he felt second best."

"Children blame themselves." Taryn felt strange knowing she had something in common with Patrick—they'd both been rejected by a parent and both harbored a deep well of anger over it.

Like her, Patrick must have wondered what he'd ever done to lose the love of his parent. Knowing this made her vow all over again that she was not going to become her father; she would not destroy other people's lives. She was going to deal with this and move on.

Puzzled by something, she said, "Gram always seemed to defend him and make excuses. I thought they were close."

"They became that way for a while after Patrick knocked himself out in a swimming pool and almost drowned. We thought we were going to lose him and your Gram was beside herself. After that she doted on him for a few years and I think Patrick finally felt she loved him, after all. Then Anne came along."

Fascinated, Taryn watched her Gramps stare out over the pond. He hadn't made eye contact with her since the start of his story. "Gram always said Anne was a present from God," she murmured.

"It sure seemed that way—we never even considered your Gram was pregnant. She was over the moon and she spent every waking hour with Anne. She was so paranoid that Anne would be taken away like Sean was, she didn't allow Patrick near her in case he passed something on or there was some accident."

Gram needed a good therapist. Taryn sighed. She'd never thought much about Patrick's past, but his insecurities were making more sense now. "He must have resented Anne."

"He did. He'd always doubted his mother's love and I guess in his mind, Anne proved him right. I tried to make him feel part of the family, but he was a boy and I wanted him to become a strong man so maybe I didn't do enough to show him he was loved." He shrugged dejectedly. "He told me he could always see how much I loved Anne and your mom, and you, by my words and actions. But it wasn't the case with him."

Taryn squeezed the rough hand. "Times were different then, Gramps. Anyway, most people don't have a perfect childhood. They find ways to move beyond it."

"He never did. He never accepted responsibility for anything. He just got in the habit of blaming everyone but himself for everything that happened in his life."

Thinking aloud, Taryn said, "He never moved beyond his anger. It ruled him all his life and it still does." She found herself deeply disturbed by this insight, conscious of her own anger-driven choices and what they had cost her so far.

"Well, it ruined his life," her grandfather concluded. "He's not a happy man. He did care for you, Ryn, in his own way. He couldn't show you his love, because he didn't know how to."

"I'd like to believe that, but you know what I think ... I think adults have more choices than children. He knew about being hurt as a child and he could have chosen to do things differently with me. He owed me that much. But the truth is, he's just a very self-centered man and he didn't love me enough to make the effort."

Taryn met her grandfather's eyes and smiled, suddenly feeling more confident in herself. She had the opportunity to have the life she wanted and no one to blame but herself if she screwed things up. That was the big difference between her and Patrick. She was willing to lay her past to rest and take responsibility for her future. Just knowing that made her feel good.

She kissed her grandfather's bristly cheek. "Thank you for telling me."

They both stood up and he glanced back toward the hospital. "Where's Jace?"

"Looking for you."

"She's a good one, Squirt. Hold on to her."

"I intend to." She tucked her arm into her grandfather's and said, "Want to walk back with me."

"No. I'm going to feed these fat ducks some more. I'll see you later, at the hotel."

They hugged warmly, and as Taryn wandered off the way she'd come, she looked back over her shoulder occasionally to the lonely figure of the only man she'd really loved.

Chapter
Twenty-four

THE SOUND OF knocking woke the sleeping pair, and Jace untangled herself from Taryn, grabbed a robe, and sleepily walked to the door. Through the peephole, she saw Anne. Her expression told Jace all she needed to know. She opened the door and her arms to her friend.

"He's gone." Anne whispered into Jace's chest.

Taryn wrapped the sheet around her body and crawled to the edge of the bed, taking in the scene. She knew from her aunt's stance and the forlorn look on Jace's face what had happened. *Shit! It's happened. He's dead.* She had prayed for this day for so long, but now that it had happened she felt dull inside. She put on her robe and went over to the two women. Jace's arm circled her waist.

"When did it happen?"

Anne wiped her eyes. " About an hour ago. The hospice called Dad late last night, so he took mom over to be with him. "

Taryn wrapped her arms around her aunt. "Are the kids awake?"

Anne shook her head. "Josie stirred when the phone rang, but she didn't wake up fully. I should get back to them."

"No. I'll stay with them," Jace said. "Your mom and dad are going to need you at the hospice." To Taryn, she added, "I think your Gram might need her granddaughter, too"

Wanly, Anne said, "Mom was so excited when she heard that you and Patrick had sorted out your differences."

Taryn winced. She just hoped that she could keep up the charade for her Gram's sake. "I'm glad I could do something for her," she said carefully.

JACE PACED BACK and forth across the room. The children were still sleeping and she hadn't heard from Taryn or Anne. She hadn't asked Anne whether she should tell the children what had happened. As she stared at her cell phone, she heard the rustling of bed sheets and the snuffling sounds of a child awakening. She looked down into the wide, startled eyes of the oldest child.

"Hey, Josie." She tried to sound cheerful.

Josie sat up while looking around the room. She rubbed her eyes. "Where's Mommy?"

Jace sat down on the edge of the sofa bed. Deciding that the truth was probably the best answer, she clasped her hands together and looked at the questioning child. "She had to go to the hospital."

"Why?"

Jace took a deep breath and released it slowly. "Your Uncle Patrick died this morning, sweetheart, and your Mommy and Ryn went to take care of your Gram."

Tears filled the young girl's eyes. "Did it hurt?"

Jace placed her hand on Josie's back and began to rub in a circular motion. "No, it didn't hurt. The doctors gave him lots of medicine to take the pain away."

"Did he go to heaven?"

Jace turned her head and saw Ricky's sad eyes looking her way. *I hope not! He should go to Hades for what he put his child through!* She rubbed her forehead and tried to dampen down the bad feelings she felt for Patrick. *No thinking ill of the dead! It is not up to you to judge another person's worth in this life!*

She looked at the open, honest faces of the two children. What did she say to their questions? "I don't know, Ricky."

"Will he be with Ryn's mommy?"

If he is, I hope she's kicking his ass! Jace shook her head. "I don't know." She looked into Josie's sad brown eyes and asked, "Are you okay, sweetheart?"

"He was funny. I liked his jokes. Mommy was going to take us to see him. I made him a card."

The comment rang a bell in Jace's memories. It was true; Patrick had always made them laugh and had seemed a real charmer. But that was before Jace saw him with Taryn. Her views of Patrick had since been tainted by the truth of who he really was. She looked over at Ricky. The boy had gone very quiet and seemed to have hidden further under the covers. "How are you feeling? It's okay to cry."

He lifted confused blue eyes to her. "I'm okay."

Jace opened her arms to invite the two children for a hug. She was disappointed when Ricky stayed on his side of the bed.

TARYN STROKED HER Gram's hand. The older woman had been given a sedative to help calm her down and allow her to catch a few hours of restful sleep at home in her apartment.

Taryn glanced up when her Gramps walked into the bedroom. "She seems peaceful."

His hands came to rest on her shoulders. "Even though we knew it was coming, nothing prepares you for the moment."

Taryn didn't know what to say. She wasn't sure what she felt beyond an odd sense of relief, like a door had swung closed and she would never again need to fear what it concealed. A phase of her life had ended with his departure. She could look back on it and wish some things had been different, but she could accept that they never would, and let go. She met her grandfather's eyes and asked, "How are you doing?"

"Hard to say. I have a lot to think about."

Taryn took that to mean he needed space and privacy to deal with his feelings. "I'm sorry," she said, for his loss.

Her grandfather was silent for a moment, and Taryn sensed he was composing himself. "There were some last words he wanted your Gram to pass on. He said he wished you two could have gotten past your differences and that you made him proud when you became a teacher." He lifted his eyes to hers. "I know this comes too late, but he said he was sorry."

A lump rose in Taryn's throat and she looked away, determined not to cry. "Is there anything you need me to do?"

Gramps shook his head. "No. The funeral directors are collecting his body. Patrick and your Gram organized the funeral arrangements. It was just a matter of waiting for the inevitable to happen."

The coldness in his voice unnerved Taryn. She'd never heard him speak so matter-of-factly about death before. It was as if he was speaking about the passing of a stranger. There was no emotion in his face, either. He spoke like a family death was an everyday occurrence.

ANNE HELD A towel out for her son as he waddled his way toward her, water dripping everywhere.

"Mom!" Josie yelled from the other side of the hotel pool.

Anne waved at her daughter, treasuring the young life that she held in her arms. The past few hours had taken its toll on her fragile emotions. She had seen Patrick's hollow shell before the funeral directors had taken away his body. Although they had had their differences, she would miss her brother's presence in her life and home.

Jace climbed out of the pool and grabbed her towel. She looked around the pool area and up to the balcony that was her room. "Where's Taryn?"

Anne stared at her, eyes narrowing as she took in Jace's concern. "I thought she was in your room."

"No. I thought she was with you."

Anne ran her fingers through Tom's wet hair and kissed his head. "Well, she went over to see Mom with Dad a few hours ago. Maybe she's still there."

"She isn't. I phoned them to convey my condolences and your father asked me how she was doing."

Anne shrugged. "She'll be back."

"Why would she go off somewhere without saying anything? Was she upset?"

Anne could tell Jace was becoming agitated, but she didn't have the energy to deal with it. A little impatiently, she said, "I have no idea. She and dad talked, but I didn't have the impression she was upset."

"What did they talk about?" Jace persisted.

"Jace, I don't know! Try asking her." Anne waved to her oldest son and her daughter as they got out of the pool and hurried over to welcome her back. "How were my little monsters?"

Jace glanced down at the three children all huddled into their mother for love and comfort. "They've been fine. I told them about Patrick."

"Thank you." Anne sighed. "Look, I didn't mean to snap at you earlier. It's been a long morning."

"It's okay." Jace patted Anne's shoulder, feeling bad to have pressured her best friend at a time when Anne needed support. "I'm going to go and check if Taryn's back."

She hurried into the hotel, knowing in her heart that Taryn wasn't there. She had thought they were past hide and seek games and childish sulks. *Where are you, babe? What's going on in that pretty head of yours?*

The room was empty and she strode out onto the balcony where she could see the entranceway to the hotel. Her eyes flicked from the glass revolving doors to the pool and back again as she waited for Taryn's familiar form to come into view.

Eventually, she heard the runners of Anne's balcony door slide open and Anne asked, "Any sign of her?"

"No."

Anne leaned on the balcony fencing that separated hers from Jace's. "She'll turn up. I don't know exactly what happened today but I do know she wouldn't do anything stupid."

"It's been five hours." Jace tried to ignore all the nasty scenarios that passed through her mind when she thought about everything that had happened since they'd arrived in Florida. What if she'd gone somewhere to get drunk and forget her problems and something had happened? "Are you sure she had her phone with her?"

Anne scratched her head with both hands. "It wasn't in the car and you said it wasn't in the room, so I'm assuming she has it. Jace, she'll call if she needs us. She's not a child."

Jace trained her attention back on the hotel entrance. She was glad her sunglasses covered her eyes so that Anne wouldn't see the sadness she knew she couldn't hide. *That's just it, Anne. She should need me! I'm not much of an expert in relationships, but I know that if I were hurting I'd want Taryn to soothe my pain. She's shutting me out, like she has shut everyone else out of her life. One step forward, three steps back...*

Jace dropped her head back against the chair and closed her eyes, reluctant to believe that the changes she had seen in Taryn recently were just her own wishful thinking. *Don't give up on her. She needs you,* whispered a voice from deep within.

TARYN SAT ON the beach looking out onto the Gulf of Mexico. The late afternoon sun beat down on her and she cursed as she felt her fair skin burn slightly in the strong midday rays. After leaving Gram and Gramps, she'd had every intention of going back to her room but she needed some time alone. She felt emotionally disoriented and too raw to talk to Jace yet.

On an impulse, she went downstairs and took one of the cabs lined up outside the hotel. As soon as she saw signs for the pier, she paid the driver off and got out, setting off on a walk along the waterfront.

The tears had long since dried up. She hadn't grieved for Patrick's death. Instead she had cried for the lost years, slowly working through all the 'what ifs' that plagued her. Overall, she regretted the fact that her grandfather's faith in Patrick had been dented by her own careless disregard for other people's feelings. She had never given Patrick's childhood any thought; never wondered what had turned him into the monster that she had always pictured him as.

She now knew that Patrick had been stuck in a self-fulfilling prophecy and one that she too had been in before Jace's presence in her life. The apple certainly didn't fall far from the tree. Try as she might, she had her father's genes in her and it was time to stop denying it.

She watched the pelicans playing in the sea near the pier. Fishermen lined the edge of the pier wall and the pelicans were waiting for any tidbit to be thrown their way. Farther out to sea, Taryn saw the dorsal fins of the dolphins that visited the area looking for the very fish that the men were hauling out of the water.

The serenity of the moment overwhelmed Taryn and, for the first time in her life, she felt truly at peace with herself and others. She knew she should probably return to the hotel, but she was not ready to let go of the rare contentment she felt sitting, watching, as day slowly advanced toward night. The beauty of the sky was breathtaking, red stripes painting the horizon. Taryn was sure she heard the hiss of the bright, red sun as it appeared to touch the ocean. The magnificence of the sunset drew crowds upon crowds who eventually left the pier as darkness overtook.

Her stomach grumbled, reminding her that she had yet to eat. Guiltily she took out her cell phone and pressed the on button, only to get the flickering picture of a battery with an X through it.

"Goddamn, stupid, piece of crap!" She shivered as a cool evening breeze tingled over her sunburned arms. It was time to get home; she knew Jace would be worried by now and felt bad that she hadn't called her sooner.

The lack of food and too much sun made Taryn's body rebel when she stood up, and dizziness swept through her. A wave of nausea quickly followed and she sank to her knees again. *Oh, God! Stop the world from spinning.* She waited a few minutes and tried again. Her arms and face hurt from the sunburn and she desperately needed some water.

From the pier, it was only a ten minute cab drive back to her grandparent's apartment, so Taryn waited until her head stopped spinning then very slowly got to her feet and set off. Almost twenty minutes later, she tapped on the door and it swung open instantly, as if she was expected.

"What happened to you?" her grandfather asked, looking her up and down in consternation.

Taryn leaned against the door, her legs trembling slightly. "I forgot how brutal the Florida sun can be, even in March." She kissed her grandfather's cheek, as she entered the house.

"Well, I'm pleased to see you. Anne and Jace are going crazy with worry. I thought we brought you up better, young lady."

Taryn hung her head. "I'm sorry." Her body shivered. "Can I get a drink of water?"

"I'll fetch that for you. Go into the living room and say hello to your Gram. Then I think you'd better make a phone call."

MUCH LATER, BACK in the hotel room, Taryn's head was pounding but the soothing, cool facecloth that was being tenderly stroked across her forehead felt wonderful. She tried to focus her eyes on the angel of mercy in front of her. Her mouth was parched and she tried unsuccessfully to lick her lips.

Jace placed a straw against her lips. "Take it slow."

The water felt refreshing as it slipped down her throat. "Thanks." She looked into her lover's concerned eyes. "I needed time to think."

She knew she owed Jace more of an explanation, but it was a start.

Jace lowered her lips to Taryn's. "It's okay. You're safe and that's all that matters.

"I love you, Jace." Taryn shook her head slightly and tried to focus her eyes on Jace's beautiful smile. "I don't think I've ever been in a relationship where I've been able to be myself. You know more about me than anyone and you still love me. You've been so patient with me this whole time and you didn't demand I give up smoking. You didn't lecture me. That means a lot to me."

"It means a lot to me that you're letting me in," Jace said. "I couldn't care for you the way I do if you didn't."

Taryn touched her hand. "I was just thinking about that earlier ... about self-fulfilling prophecies. I don't want to live my life that way, and you give me the room to choose something different." She broke off, stifling a yawn.

With an indulgent smile, Jace asked, "Want to sleep?"

"Maybe. Maybe not." A teasing smile lifted Taryn's mouth and her expression changed from weary bemusement to mischief. "How about you?"

"I'm not sure sleep is at the top of my agenda, right now, but I could definitely do with getting out of these clothes."

Taryn grinned. "Can I watch?"

"You're not well," Jace reminded her, an evil glint in her eyes. "I don't want you getting over-excited."

Taryn giggled. "My, my, someone definitely is getting a little cocky!"

"I've been told I'm a fast learner." Jace's smirk changed into a shy smile. "I like feeling your breasts against mine. Is that okay?"

Taryn kissed her gently. "That's fine by me."

Jace noticed that Taryn's eyes had dropped down to take in the sight of her breasts. "Anything you fancy?" she asked in soft challenge.

Taryn flicked one of Jace's nipples with her fingertip and

winked at her blushing lover. "Everything."

Jace's stomach dropped at the hunger in Taryn's eyes. "Why do I feel like you're a predator and I'm on the menu?"

"Because you are!" Taryn's eyes glinted mischievously. "Afraid?"

Jace's face grew serious. "Only of losing you."

"That isn't going to happen," Taryn said. "I don't know how to explain it, but something has changed. I feel different about everything." Intentionally lightening up, she said, "And now, I'm off to the bathroom. You can join me, if you want?"

Jace flopped back onto the bed with an inane grin plastered on her face and watched as Taryn wiggled her cute ass. She moved onto her side as she waited for Taryn to return, lifting the sheets so her lover could slip in beside her.

Taryn didn't waste any time. She dived into Jace's arms and snuggled against her body with a sigh of contentment. "I'll be glad to get home," she said sleepily. "I want to start our life together properly."

Jace kissed Taryn's forehead, her cheeks and her lips. "I can't wait. We have all the time in the world, but I'm still impatient."

Chapter
Twenty-five

TARYN TURNED DOWN Marti's offer of dinner. She checked her watch and wished she'd agreed to meet her ex somewhere else. Having decided to move back home to Anne's, Taryn had wanted to collect the rest of her belongings from Marti's. The redhead had stored her bike, books, and a few furnishings that Taryn hadn't been able to take to Cory and Dylan's small apartment.

"I appreciate you looking after my things, Marti."

"You're welcome. I kind of kept them because I always hoped you'd change your mind about us, but I guess I was wrong."

Taryn nodded. No matter what had happened in the past, Taryn owed Marti the truth and she knew it. "Patrick's dead. I've been down in Florida with my grandparents."

"I'm sorry. How are you feeling? How have you been?"

Taryn took a deep breath. *Here goes nothing! At least she can't ruin your stuff; it's all packed away in Dylan's truck.* "I'm doing okay. I've taken a little time to look at my life. You were right about one thing, Marti, Jace does like me."

"I knew it! Did I not tell you that?"

"Yes, you did. What I didn't know was how much I like her."

Coffee spilled from the mug in Marti's hand. "But you said she was your boss and you'd never fall for her."

Taryn chewed on her lip as she waited for the eruption to come. When Marti paused, Taryn stepped in. "I was wrong."

Marti mopped up the mess she had made with the spilt coffee. She didn't want Taryn to see how upset the news had made her. "When did this happen? Is this why we ended?"

Taryn shook her head vehemently. "No! I promise you, I had no idea how she felt or how I felt. New Year's Eve was when she told me. We decided to try dating each other not long ago."

Marti threw the wet paper towels into the trashcan and

turned furiously to Taryn. "You lied to me."

Taryn threw her hands in the air. "I did not. I never lied to you. God, I came around to apologize to you. I now understand what it's like to date someone like me. I must have infuriated the hell out of you."

Marti calmed down. "So, you're finally getting a spoonful of your own medicine?"

Taryn smiled and rolled her eyes. "You could say that. It's hard sometimes to know what she's thinking and I know I have a similar problem. I really want things to work out between Jace and me, but I also want to keep my friendship with you. I should go." She turned and hurried out of the kitchen, eager to get out of the awkward atmosphere.

Marti walked Taryn to the door. She couldn't get the image of Jace and Taryn hugging each other at the Country Club out of her mind. "Look me in the eyes, Taryn, and tell me the truth. Did you finish with me because of Jace?"

Taryn reached for the door handle. She was angry that Marti couldn't see her part in their separation. She could tell that Marti's mind was only on one thing. She looked into Marti's eyes and without blinking delivered her statement.

"Marti, we ended because I didn't feel comfortable opening up to you. I didn't trust you and you used our love making to hurt me physically." She watched as Marti blanched. "We had a destructive relationship which fuelled my need for control and the more you pushed the faster I ran. I did not end our relationship because of Jace. I ended it because I didn't love you anymore." When Marti didn't respond, Taryn took the opportunity and walked out of the house. As the door shut behind her, she knew another part of her past was a closed book.

THE TELEVISION DRONED on in the background, but neither woman was watching it. Their minds were focused on other things. After a while, Jace lifted her head off the arm of the couch.

"I should get going, Dylan. I'm wiped."

"You're more than welcome to stay."

Jace shook her head. "Thanks for the offer, though. And, thank you for entertaining me. I'm sorry I wasn't much company...I miss Taryn. I really toyed with the idea of going away with her rather than fix up the apartment."

"I know how you feel. But our girls get to have fun up in the mountains and you know she's going to love her graduation surprise. It'll be all worth it."

"I feel really selfish that you're missing out on being there with them."

"Don't beat yourself up. I'm on-call. I couldn't go anyway."

"Well, at least Taryn got to use the snowboarding trip tickets I gave her for Christmas. Although when I got them, I had hoped in my heart that I would be the one with her."

"That sucks, but there'll be other times," Dylan replied supportively.

"I know. I still can't believe that May is just a few weeks away. In a month, Taryn will graduate and one stress will be lifted from her life." Jace stood up and stretched her tall frame enjoying the feeling of cramped muscles being released. "So, are we all set for tomorrow?"

"I'm pretty sure we have everything. All the gear is in the truck. I'll meet you at Anne's for breakfast." Dylan walked Jace to the door. "Okay, this is my last time asking, I promise, but are you sure you want to do this?"

Jace grinned. "Positive. Anne and I talked about it and the sooner, the better." She saw the raised eyebrow. "Trust me, I'm a doctor!"

Dylan shook her head and laughed at the words. "Sometimes those words scare me! Drive safe, my friend, and I'll see you tomorrow."

JACE WOKE EARLY the next day and felt like she was still half-asleep as she showered and drove to Anne's. She rapped on the patio doors before entering.

"Good morning." She glanced around the unusually quiet kitchen. "No kids?"

"Bill's parents volunteered to look after the rascals for the whole weekend. You look tired, are you okay?"

Jace snagged a piece of toast off a plate and took a seat opposite her friend. "I'm okay. I'm having a few problems sleeping. It's no big deal!"

Anne smiled smugly. "I remember not so long ago that someone was having worries about sharing a bed with another person. Look at you now, three months later and you can't sleep without her!"

Jace rolled her eyes to the ceiling. She couldn't deny Anne's statement because it was true. She missed Taryn, especially her presence at night. Since returning from Florida, they hadn't spent a night apart.

"How's Taryn? Is she having fun?"

After taking a sip of coffee, Jace responded, "She called last night. Unfortunately, there's not a lot of snow around, but, the hiking trails are pretty decent and they're going to try one of those today."

"Does she have any idea what you're doing?"

"No. We've talked briefly about the future, but whenever I've mention the apartment annex she changes the subject."

Anne fiddled with her silverware, debating whether to ask the question on her mind. "I never thought you'd be asking to remodel the annex. By doing this... aren't you lessening the chances of Taryn moving in with you?"

Jace hesitated slightly before answering. "Maybe, but Taryn and I living together doesn't have to be at my place."

"You'd live here?" Anne gasped slightly.

"If Taryn wanted me to, I would."

"What about your place?"

"I'd rent it out. It's a good investment. "

Anne's brow furrowed. "You'd give up a spacious, private ranch house to move into a two bedroom cramped annex. Why?"

Jace didn't hesitate. "For Taryn. I think she needs the security of her family at the moment. I know she's hurting inside and whatever was said between your father and Taryn is haunting her. She won't talk about it and I haven't pushed. I think she needs to be here and maybe deal with a few more of those ghosts she has floating around in her head."

"It's a selfless choice, Jace."

"Not really. In a few weeks, Taryn's going to have to look for a new job and start a whole new chapter of her life. I want to be here supporting her, not making her choose options she doesn't want because it'll make me happier. Does that make sense?"

Anne nodded in agreement, "I hope she appreciates what you give her."

"I hope so, too! But, this is all theory. I'm not going to make the decision for her." Jace turned her head toward the door when she heard other voices. "Our relaxation time is over. Let the building begin."

THE ANNEX CONSISTED of two moderately sized bedrooms, a bathroom, living room and small kitchen area. Anne and Bill had built it years earlier for Patrick, and after returning from his funeral they'd emptied it of all his belongings, donating all of his furniture to Goodwill.

Jace was relieved that they'd done so. She wanted this to be a new start for Taryn, with no memories of Patrick's presence there.

The renovation plans for the annex were simple enough. Patrick had always used the front door to the main house as his entrance. However, Jace wanted Taryn to be able to come and go, as she liked. Bill had knocked a hole in one of the outer walls and was currently attaching a door frame. Dylan was busy screwing in the last boards of the deck section that led to the doorway. Inside the apartment, Anne, Jo, Helen and Jace were cleaning, painting and rearranging the inside.

By the end of the first day, six sweaty, grimy people were drinking cold beers on the new deck.

"It looks phenomenal, guys!" Jace exclaimed as she surveyed the small deck area and sturdy steps leading down to the driveway.

"We try!" Bill answered modestly. "So, you really like it?"

"It's awesome! Taryn's not going to recognize the place when she comes home."

"That's the idea!" Dylan butted in.

"So, do you think we'll have all this finished by Monday?" Jace asked, nervously.

Bill checked his list, crossing off items as he read. "I think so. Dylan and I will collect the furniture tomorrow. You guys still have a lot of painting to do but I think it can be completed by tomorrow evening. Then on Monday we'll put the finishing touches together."

"I appreciate this, guys." Jace said.

Anne gave her a quick hug. "She's our family. And to be honest, we always hounded Patrick to get this place remodeled. You never know, in the future this could be a potential home for one of our kids or yours!"

Chapter
Twenty-six

TARYN STARED AT the four vehicles parked on the drive. There was no room for her to fit on the driveway, so she parked on the edge of the front yard and honked the horn a couple of times. As she popped the trunk of the Camry, she said, "Thanks for coming with me, Cory. I had fun."

"Same here, pal."

The pair took their bags from the trunk. Cory placed hers in the back of Dylan's truck and walked with Taryn to Anne's front door.

"Where is everyone? You'd have thought they'd come out to greet us." Taryn grumbled. She tried to open the door, but to her consternation it was locked. She fumbled through the pockets of her backpack, trying unsuccessfully to locate her keys. "Shit! Remind me to put my house keys on the same chain as my car keys!"Cory caught sight of the large group of people hiding at the edge of the house and winked.

"Surprise!" The group yelled, coming out from their hiding place.

Taryn glanced around, unsure who the surprise was for. "What surprise?"

Jace pushed her way gently through the kids and enveloped her girlfriend in a hug. "I've missed you," she whispered in Taryn's ear.

Taryn stayed in Jace's embrace for a second or two before pulling back. "What is this about a surprise? What did you do?" She felt a small, sweaty hand make its way into her own and looked down into bright blue eyes.

"It's awesome, Ryn," Ricky exclaimed excitedly. "I helped, too."

Taryn turned her attention to Cory who was happily hugging Dylan and exchanging little chaste kisses. "Do you know what they're talking about?"

"I might," winced Cory as she saw the look of fire flash across Taryn's face. "What's going on, Jace?"

Butterflies swirled inside Jace's stomach. "I wanted to surprise you. Well, actually, we all wanted to surprise you..." She saw confusion flit across Taryn's eyes, "An early graduation present. Come with me." Jace to led Taryn around the corner of the house.

Taryn caught her first glimpse of the decking. "Wow! What is this? When did...wow..."Jace squeezed Taryn's hand, "Hold onto those thoughts until you've seen it all." She escorted her girlfriend up the steps. On the deck was a small table laden with glasses and drinks. To the side was a small grill and chairs that matched the table. "Do you like it?"

"Yeah, it's great. Whoa... there's a door! I don't understand. Why is it numbered 214A?"

Anne stepped forward. "Honey, the main house is 214 Heartfield Road; therefore, the attached apartment should really have it's own address."

"Apartment?"

Jace tightened her hold on Taryn's hand as she felt the limb begin to tense. "Come with me." She opened the door and led Taryn through it. She could feel Taryn resist her motions to go any further.

"But..." Taryn's protests stopped as she took in the airy living room. Gone was the dark, foreboding wood. In its place was a pine entertainment cabinet, with a matching coffee table and picture table. The navy blue couch and chair took the place of the tattered, tartan three-piece couch that used to take up half the room. She glanced around at the walls. They were painted in a light cream and edged with blue. She could see a large photo of her mother framed on the main wall. "It's beautiful."

"There's more." Jace turned to see Anne and Bill holding the kids back and retreating to the deck. She showed Taryn around the fitted kitchen and they peeked into the bathroom that was decorated with bright greens and blues. The shower curtain had a variety of tropical fish printed on it and seashells were stenciled along the edge of the bath and ceiling.

"You did all this in one weekend?" Taryn struggled to take in the complete transformation. The rooms looked nothing like before. Even Patrick's scent had left the air to be replaced by the fresh aroma of paint and polish. She could smell a hint of vanilla and followed her nose to where the smell was coming from. She paused at the threshold of Patrick's old bedroom.

Jace felt Taryn's muscles stiffen as she reached for the doorknob. "I'm right behind you, babe. I did this for us." She reached over Taryn's shoulder and pushed the door open.

Taryn stood at the threshold and took in the room with a small gasp of surprise. A new cream rug matched the walls and cranberry curtains echoed the shade of a tall bureau and two bedside tables. A king size bed was covered with a beige comforter and matching sham. The huge pillows were covered in a cranberry and beige plaid, and large back pillows matched the comforter. Small reading lamps stood on the night tables and Taryn's eyes were drawn to a framed photo also on one of them. It was of Jace and herself, taken in Florida.

Tears rolled down Taryn's cheeks. "I'm a little overwhelmed. It's such a transformation." She sat on the edge of the bed. "It must have taken a lot of work and planning."

Jace let out a sigh of relief. "I had lots of help." She bent down and opened one of the night table drawers, extracting a small pink envelope, which she handed to Taryn. "This is for you."

Taryn took the envelope and gazed down at the familiar handwriting on the front. Tentatively, she slipped a finger under the flap and slowly pulled the seal apart. She took out the card and read the front sentiment: '*You are one in a million...*' She looked up into loving eyes and opened the card.

To Our Squirt,

Your Gram and I are very proud of all of your accomplishments. We both wanted to thank you for your help and support over the past few weeks. You have made us very happy and were a welcome surprise to the family all those years ago. You continue to surprise us every day and have grown into a remarkable woman.

Please accept our graduation present — we will be up on graduation for a proper celebration and expect a cookout on that new grill of yours.

All our love,

Gramps and Gram xx

Taryn couldn't speak as she allowed the sentiments to sink in. Her grandfather's words helped to heal her last open wound. She felt Jace's hand on her back, and took a few moments to collect herself, before looking into the eyes of the woman she loved beyond words. "I don't know what I did to get such a wonderful woman, but whatever I did I hope I keep doing it forever."

Jace sat down on the bed next to her lover. "I hope so, too. I really did miss you while you were away and I think I poured my heart into making this as special as I could." She kissed Taryn gently. "The bedroom furniture is a gift from your grandparents. If you'd like to follow me, I'll show you what Anne, Bill and the kids supplied."

Intrigued, Taryn took Jace's hand. "Lead on."

Jace walked them out of the bedroom and into the guest room. The light green paint made the room seem very bright. There was a double bed against one of the walls and a computer desk on the opposite side. "Anne and Bill took Patrick's old desk for the kids. I thought this would be good for your computer when you get one. The room has a lot of natural light and I put a little sofa over here for afternoon naps."

"It's wonderful. I'm a little lost for words, which for me is a first. I can't believe you did all this."

"Anne and I have been planning it for a while. Whenever you went to class or the library I would come over here and get to work."

Taryn felt her heart pound a little harder. Knowing that Jace had been working so hard for no reason to her than to give her something made her feel incredibly lucky. Jace loved her enough to do something like this just to make her happy — the realization almost made her feel giddy.

"I should go and thank everyone," she said, touching her lover's cheek.

Jace felt a rush of pleasure that Taryn had been so quick to accept the gift she'd been given and was so willing to show others what it meant to her. They both stood and walked outside.

"I can't believe the difference the deck makes to the side of the house," Taryn said, pausing at the door. "Was that your idea?"

"A little bit of us all combined. It was my present to you — that, and the living room furniture."

They walked out onto the deck and stood in front of a quiet family. Taryn tried to keep the stern look on her face, but after one look at Ricky's tense face she opened her arms to thank everyone who loved her.

TARYN LEANED AGAINST the deck railing much later that day, when they were finally alone. "Jace, I don't think I can handle anymore surprises. Can I open my eyes yet?"

"No," Jace insisted. "Two more minutes, I promise. No peeking."

"You do know you're killing me, don't you? I was never any good at surprises or waiting. I'm not known for my patience..."

Jace's lips covering her own cut off her words. "Shush! Come with me, but keep those eyes shut." Taryn held onto Jace's arm tightly, trusting her lover not to walk her over the edge of the deck or dump her on her ass. She felt Jace sit down and tried to follow. The seat wobbled against her weight and she instinctively opened her eyes.

"A hammock!" She exclaimed.

"Our very own." Jace made herself comfortable and then pulled Taryn against her body. "I like the privacy of the deck. The hammock in the garden can be seen from every window in the house, so I never got a chance to do this." She lowered her head to Taryn's and gave her the first passionate kiss of the evening.

Several minutes passed and their desire began to burst into flames of passion. "Whoa..." Taryn gasped as she broke for a much needed breather. "I'm still trying to get my head around all the changes you guys have made to this place. It looks so different...I never thought I'd ever find myself thinking of this section of the house as my home."

"Is that what you're thinking?" Jace looked up at the stars, her heart hammering as she thought of the next step in their relationship.

"I'm not sure...I guess that would depend on what you thought."

"Well, I wouldn't have done all this if I hadn't hoped you'd live here."

Shit! How could I have read her so wrong? There I was thinking she wanted me to move in with her. I couldn't have been more wrong if I'd tried! But where does that leave us? Taryn searched out her mother's star and looked at the twinkling object for a while. Finally in a very quiet voice, she whispered her thoughts. "I guess I thought that maybe...well, maybe you might ...well, that you and I ...we could maybe have moved into your place together...as a couple."

Jace shifted quickly on the hammock, nearly tipping them both onto the decking below.

"Too soon, I guess?"

"No...I've been thinking something similar." She saw uncertainty in Taryn's eyes. "Wait here a minute. I have one last surprise." She saw Taryn's brow lift. "I swear, only one more surprise."

Taryn heard a car door slam and a minute later, the silhouette of Jace appeared carrying a large object.

Jace tried unsuccessfully to hide the surprise behind her back as she climbed the steps. She placed the object beside the hammock and nervously sat next to Taryn. "It was like a dream come true when you agreed to date me and I've enjoyed every minute of our time together. So much so, that I dread evening times because I hate to be apart from you."

"I know. It hurts me, too. But we've managed to spend every night together since spring break." Taryn took Jace's shaky hands in hers.

"I know. It's been awesome but I know in the future we're both going to be busy with work and I don't want to spend any more time than I have to away from you." Jace looked into dark eyes and struggled not to kiss the beautiful woman beside her. "It would have been easy to ask you to move into my place with me, but you've done that before and I wanted it to be a first for both of us."

Taryn tried hard to keep up with the conversation, "Okay. I feel the same way, so where does that leave us?"

Jace bent down, picked up the mailbox, and handed it to Taryn.

Taryn took the decorated box. On one side there was a small Star Spangled Banner with the number 214A stamped in the middle, beside that were the names Murphy & Xanthos. Taryn traced the names with her index finger, unsure of the true meaning behind the gesture. She looked into anxious eyes; the answer to her next question clearly written on Jace's expectant appearance.

"I've never moved into a girlfriend's house before and you've never had anyone move into your house. If it's not too soon, I'd like us to live together. Is that something you'd like to do?"

"You want us to live together?" Taryn turned her eyes to the new front door, "Here?"

"Yes. I'd live anywhere with you, Taryn."

"But, what about your place?"

Jace tried to settle the nervous feeling in her stomach. *She hasn't said no to you yet. Relax! But she hasn't said yes either. Okay, it is now or never to make the statement of your life, Xanthos.* "My place has never felt like a home to me. I think we both missed out on the traditional childhood and siblings. When I'm here, I feel like I'm part of a family and I think you do, too. So, I think for a while it would be fun to be part of a family, but have a place where we can be a couple. Maybe in the future we'll want to move back into my place or buy a place together. I want you to feel equal in our relationship, Taryn, and I think me moving in here will do that. You need to be with your family and deal with what's happened recently. It's time to leave the past behind and that means we both deal with our pasts in order to make a future together. What do you think?"

Taryn wiped the tears off Jace's cheeks with her thumb and then did the same to her own. "You are so wonderful. I thought about you so much this weekend and realized my life has changed so much since you came along. In fact, I can't think back to a time in my life when I have been happier. It's been nearly a year since we met and I can't think of a better way to say goodbye to my past and greet my future."

"So, is that a yes? You're killing me here!" Jace feigned her heart stopping as she waited impatiently for Taryn's answer.

"That's a yes. I love you more than I can express. And, I can see from what you've accomplished this weekend and the gift you just offered me, that I have your complete love and trust."

Jace hugged Taryn. "I can't wait to tell the whole world that you're my girlfriend, partner and live-in lover."

Taryn pulled slightly away from Jace, "Isn't having the same address going to cause problems at work?"

"Well, technically I'll still have my place and hadn't planned on renting it out right away. I wasn't a hundred percent sure you'd want to even take the next step. Would it be okay if I didn't change my address on the records until after your grad assistantship ended?"

"Jace, I never want to be the one to put any pressure on you. How about we have a great coming out/celebration party when I leave the Achievement Center? Then we can shout it from the rooftops."

"Deal. So, if I said my bags were packed and in the Jeep, would you think me presumptuous?"

Her answer was a loving kiss, each woman dreaming of the future that lay before them.

THE SOFT GLOW of the bedside lamps illuminated Jace's way to the bed. She glanced down at Taryn's wide-eyed, open-mouthed expression. "Hi."

"Hey...yourself..." Taryn's thoughts were definitely not focused on conversation. Jace was naked and her skin seemed to go on forever. Taryn could see where the sun had darkened her limbs and she couldn't prevent her eyes from focusing on the dark patch of pubic hair that was just as black as the hair on Jace's head.

Jace looked down at her naked skin and fought the

temptation to cover herself with her arms. She looked coyly at Taryn. "I don't know why, but getting naked seemed a good thing to do while I was in the bathroom." When Taryn didn't say anything, Jace picked up the edge of the blanket and tried to slide into the bed.

Taryn watched as the image she loved slipped out of view. "Whoa! Get back out!" She winked at Jace. "I was enjoying the show."

Jace lowered the cover. "You like what you see?"

Taryn nodded enthusiastically. "Can't you tell? I'm practically drooling." She patted the bed. "Want to join me on the covers?"

Jace lay down and propped her head up with her arm. She traced a finger down Taryn's cheek and neck until she reached the edge of the covers. When Taryn didn't stop her movements, she continued to pull the covers off Taryn's bare torso. She lifted her own body to allow the smooth motion of the cover down the bed. Jace's eyes lowered to the boxer shorts. Her fingers lightly traced the edge of the waistband. Her confidence was growing and she was desperate to see Taryn's whole body naked.

"Can I take these off?" she asked.

Taryn tried to act like having her underwear removed was the most normal thing on earth. Yet inside, her mind was racing. *She's naked! She's taking the lead! My God, she's beautiful. I think I'm going to explode.* "Be my guest." She managed to get out without stammering.

Jace took her time lowering Taryn's boxers down the shorter body. Her eyes followed her hands and she paused slightly when she caught sight of the golden hair before her. She crawled back up the bed and lay down beside Taryn, her hands stroking the side of Taryn's body. "You have an awesome body."

Taryn kissed Jace on the cheek. "That makes two of us."

Jace looked into eyes swirling with desire. "Taryn, will you make love to me?"

Taryn's brilliant smile was her answer. "Yes, and I can do one better. I can make love *with* you."

Jace felt Taryn's light touch as it teased its way down her body. Taryn's fingertips burned a path down her body. When Taryn's fingers reached the apex between her legs, Jace opened them wanting her lover's hands there; needing her lover's hands there. The tingling intensified as Taryn's competent fingers stroked the lips of her sex. She felt Taryn's fingers pause at the entrance to her vagina and her eyes opened automatically. She met brown eyes that held a questioning gaze. "Please." She gasped as she felt Taryn's finger enter her.

As she heard Jace's plea, Taryn slowly slipped one finger into her. She felt no resistance as Jace's body opened up to her. She increased her rhythm and slipped in another finger when she felt Jace's body respond to her. With skilful fingers, she moved in time with Jace, kissing her lover's neck and whispering her love as they moved as one.

Jace could feel Taryn's fingers move in and out. The instinctive need to move with Taryn drove Jace's hips up and down. The tingling sensation she had come to associate with a developing orgasm swept through her body.

Taryn relaxed her rhythm as she felt Jace's breathing hitch and her hips began bucking. She wanted to prolong their first time lovemaking in their new home. "Open your eyes, Jace. Look at me."

Jace could feel herself poised on the edge of ecstasy. She heard Taryn's plea and opened her eyes, taking in all that Taryn had to offer her. "I love you."

"I love you, too. Come for me, babe. I know you want too."

"I do!" With one last thrust, Jace felt the shudders travel up her body and the stars explode behind her eyelids. She collapsed limply against Taryn.

Taryn held Jace in her arms. She felt the racing pulse of Jace's heartbeat under her hand that rested behind Jace's neck. The other hand felt the pulsing aftershocks of Jace's orgasm. She could feel the walls twitch against her fingers. She waited a couple of minutes and then removed her hand from between Jace's thighs. She licked the moisture off her fingers and reached under Jace's chin to lift her girlfriend's head up to her. She kissed the swollen lips lightly and met teary blue eyes. "Hey."

"Hi."

"How are you feeling?"

Jace beamed at Taryn. "Like I just lost my virginity. Again!" She leaned forward and captured Taryn's lips. "I'm sorry I couldn't resist saying that." She nibbled gently around Taryn's lips. "I feel great. My head feels like it's off in space somewhere."

She could feel Taryn's own desire as her partner shifted against her. Hesitantly, she lowered her hand and felt Taryn turn toward her. Worried that she was doing it wrong, she opened her eyes to look at Taryn's face. What she saw was complete happiness and desire. Fuelled on by this, Jace followed her instincts and went to places she knew she herself liked. She found the tiny ball of nerves and stroked it up and down. This action caused a slight growl to leave Taryn's mouth.

The feel of Jace's fingers stroking her was bringing Taryn

closer and closer to the ultimate pleasure. Long fingers slipped in and out of her and seemed to be playing her like a musical instrument. With every stroke, Taryn felt herself edging nearer and nearer to the precipice. When she could no longer keep her orgasm at bay, Taryn jumped headily over the edge and sank down into Jace's welcoming embrace.

"Fast learner." Taryn muttered into her lover's ear as she toppled over the edge time and time again.

Much later, as they lay in one another's arms, Jace said. "Let's do that again soon."

Taryn laughed just knowing they could do anything they wanted, whenver they wanted. It was their future, to create in any way they chose. "I love you," she said.

Jace sighed. It suddenly felt so easy, because it was so right. She kissed Taryn's damp check and said playfully, "In case you hadn't noticed, I love you, too. Now where were we..."

Postscript

ANNE PASSED THE drinks around the deck area. It felt good to have people from work at her home and she particularly enjoyed hearing her kids laugh with their grandparents. She hoped that the atmosphere wouldn't change when the guests heard what Jace had to say.

Near her, Patty nudged Brenda as they saw the two familiar figures come 'round the corner. "Don't they look cute together?"

"Yeah. It's too funny that they think we don't know about them."

Patty laughed, "I know. I wasn't really sure until I saw their names on the mailbox. It's kind of cute and Jace has sure been different since the blonde bombshell arrived. I'm going to miss the little spitfire."

Brenda nodded, "I am too, but at least we'll know that she'll visit. She definitely has ties to the Center."

Anne interrupted their talk. "What are you two sniggering about?"

Patty nodded in the direction of their boss. "The cute couple."

Anne's mouth dropped. "Who told you? I made the kids promise to keep quiet until Jace's announcement."

Brenda placed her hand on Anne's arm. "No one told us. But you should give the boss a little message, if you're trying to keep something secret, then don't place your name with your girlfriend's on a mailbox and then invite your employees over for a cookout."

Anne gave a big belly laugh, "I forgot about that and from the looks of things so did they. I should go over there and tell them to quit the charade and hold each other's hand." She watched as Taryn greeted some of Bill's family and Jace hugged the Clarys.

"Don't you dare! I want to hear it from the horse's mouth. We can keep up a charade of our own and watch her squirm for a little longer." Patty exclaimed.

Anne's eyes flicked from her colleagues to her boss and back again. "Okay. But if she kills me when she finds out then I'm sending her your way."

Jace finished her beer and placed her empty plate and bottle into the separate trashcans. *Okay, Anne's bringing the cake out. It's now or never. You take the cake from Anne and then announce to the world how special Taryn is to you. How hard can it be?* She jumped when she felt Anne's hand on her back.

"Jace, you don't have to do this. Taryn already knows how committed you are to this relationship."

Jace shrugged and took the cake out of Anne's hand. "I've thought about it a lot. To be honest, I'm not doing this totally for Taryn. I know how much she loves me and we've spent a lot of time talking about a future together. I'm doing this for me. It's time I began to trust more in people and that includes those I care about. Isn't that what families do?"

Anne kissed her on the cheek. "I'm behind you all the way. Go get 'em, Tiger."

Jace carried the cake onto the deck and tapped Taryn on the shoulder. Her actions caught the eye of all the guests and a hush descended on the small gathering. She cleared her throat and took a deep breath. With trembling hands, she passed the cake to Taryn and turned to address the quiet audience.

"I just want to say thank you to all of you for coming to celebrate Taryn's graduation at our home." As Taryn put the cake on the side table, Jace took her hand for support. "It's been a gruelling year for a lot of us at the Center and I know Taryn has had many challenges in her personal and school life. One of her biggest challenges was taking me on as a girlfriend and I just wanted to tell the world that I love this woman more than I could ever express in words."

She turned to Taryn and kissed her soundly on the lips, then blushed profusely as she caught Brenda's eye. "I'd like you to raise a glass and congratulate Taryn on gaining her master's degree."

"Congratulations," yelled the guests.

Taryn took the knife from Anne and held it on the cake. "I want to add my thanks for you all coming today. I've made some very special friends at the Center..." She held Cory's gaze for a few moments before continuing, "and if circumstances were different I'd be fighting tooth and nail for a job there. However, I wouldn't change the reasons for my leaving even if you paid me a million dollars. This year has been a year of growth for me. I've learned a great deal in such a short time and I hope to take what

I've learned to my new job and show them how good my training was at the Center. I'm going to miss you guys tremendously, but I'll be back. I have a vested interest in the Center."

She cut the cake and offered the first piece to her partner. "I love you, Jace."

Jace took a bite of the creamy frosting covered cake and licked her lips. She chewed a few times and then leaned over and kissed Taryn's cheek. "Here's to the future."

Taryn passed the knife to her aunt and wrapped her arms around Jace. "It's definitely goodbye to the past, hello to the present and eagerly awaiting our future together."

She opened her mouth to the piece of cake Jace was holding to it, then raised her frosting covered lips to Jace's and sealed the promise with a kiss.

Borderline
by Linda Crist

Set on the Texas-Mexico border, against the backdrop of Big Bend National Park, this story picks up where *The Bluest Eyes in Texas* left off.

Longing for a bit of peace and quiet, Kennedy takes Carson home to meet her family. But you never really completely shake your childhood, and Kennedy's past collides with the present, threatening to tear her family apart and, and placing her life and Carson's in the very balance.

Meanwhile, Carson must come to terms with her feelings for Kennedy. Will she settle for what has become comfortable for her in a very short time, or is she ready to take things to the next level, reaching for something infinitely more satisfying?

There are mysteries to solve, and decisions to be made, while walking the borderline.

Coming November 2006

Sweetwater
by Mickey Minner

Sweetwater is the story of two young women who meet in the Montana Territory of the 1870's. Jennifer Kensington wants more from life than the arranged marriage and future her father has planned for her. Jesse Branson expecting to inherit the family ranch is left, seemingly, without a future when she suddenly discovers the ranch has been sold.

Jesse and Jennifer's paths cross on the dusty street of Sweetwater and it is love at first sight. They face threats from rustlers and bandits as they struggle with their feelings for each other and start to make a life together. Along the way, they enjoy the natural wonder of the wild country they call home. But with so many challenges ahead can they look forward to a long future together?

Coming November 2006

DIVING INTO THE TURN
by Carrie Carr

Diving Into the Turn is set in the fast-paced Texas rodeo world. Riding bulls in the rodeo is the only life Shelby Fisher has ever known. She thinks she's happy drifting from place to place in her tiny trailer, engaging in one night stands, and living from one rodeo paycheck to another – until the day she meets barrel racer Rebecca Starrett. Rebecca comes from a solid, middle-class background and owns her horse. She's had money and support that Shelby has never had. Shelby and Rebecca take an instant dislike to each other, but there's something about Rebecca that draws the silent and angry bull rider to her. Suddenly, Shelby's life feels emptier, and she can't figure out why. Gradually, Rebecca attempts to win Shelby over, and a shaky friendship starts to grow into something more.

Against a backdrop of mysterious accidents that happen at the rodeo grounds, their attraction to one another is tested. When Shelby is implicated as the culprit to what's been happening will Rebecca stand by her side?

ISBN 978- 1-932300-54-3

THE BLUEST EYES IN TEXAS
by Linda Crist

Kennedy Nocona is an out, liberal, driven attorney, living in Austin, the heart of the Texas hill country. Dallasite Carson Garret is a young paralegal overcoming the loss of her parents, and coming to terms with her own sexual orientation.

A chance encounter finds them inexplicably drawn to one another, and they quickly find themselves in a long-distance romance that leaves them both wanting more. Circumstances at Carson's job escalate into a series of mysteries and blackmail that leaves her with more excitement than she ever bargained for. Confused, afraid, and alone, she turns to Kennedy, the one person she knows can help her. As they work together to solve a puzzle, they confront growing feelings that neither woman can deny. Can they overcome the outside forces that threaten to crush them both?

ISBN 978-1-932300-48-2

Other YELLOW ROSE Publications

About the author:

J Y Morgan, known online as Jules Matthews, is English but currently residing in beautiful New England, with her partner and cats. She enjoys reading lesbian works of fiction, watching movies, pottering around in the garden and generally hanging out with friends; online and real life.

VISIT US ONLINE AT

www.regalcrest.biz

At the Regal Crest Website You'll Find

- The latest news about forthcoming titles and new releases

- Our complete backlist of romance, mystery, thriller and adventure titles

- Information about your favorite authors

- Current bestsellers

- Media tearsheets to print and take with you when you shop

Regal Crest titles are available from all progressive booksellers and online at StarCrossed Productions, (www.scp-inc.biz), or at www.amazon.com, www.bamm.com, www.barnesandnoble.com, and many others.

Printed in the United States
70080LV00003B/282